REIYALINDIS

REIYALINDIS

✕ ✕ ✕ ✳ ✕ ✳ ✕ ✳ ✕ ✳ ✕ ✕ ✕ ✕

CORY POULSON

Sweetwater Books
Springville, Utah

The views expressed within this work are the sole responsibility of the author and do not necessarily reflect the position of Cedar Fort, Inc., or any other entity.

This is a work of fiction. The characters, names, incidents, places, and dialogue are products of the author's imagination, and are not to be construed as real.

ISBN 13: 978-1-59955-288-0

Published by Sweetwater Books, an imprint of Cedar Fort, Inc., 2373 W. 700 S., Springville, UT 84663
Distributed by Cedar Fort, Inc., www.cedarfort.com

LIBRARY OF CONGRESS CATALOGING-IN-PUBLICATION DATA

Poulson, Cory, 1980-
  Reiyalindis / Cory Poulson.
    p. cm.
  Summary: An Elven girl named Reiyalindis goes on a quest to save her
kingdom. Along the way she recruits some colorful characters to help her in
her pursuit. A strong bond is formed between them, but Reiyalindis harbors a
secret and refuses to speak of her past to anyone.
  ISBN 978-1-59955-288-0
  1. Fantasy fiction, American. I. Title.
  PS3616.O857R45 2009
  813'.6--dc22
                            2009010145

Cover design by Angela D. Olsen
Cover design © 2009 by Lyle Mortimer
Edited and typeset by Heidi Doxey

Printed in the United States of America

10 9 8 7 6 5 4 3 2 1

Printed on acid-free paper

To my wife, Calie Mae,
my greatest support and inspiration.

ONE

Vaelon Sahani groaned a little as he sat down; it had been a long day. He'd spent most of it fixing and cleaning up his house, which had fallen into disrepair since he had left for his third tour of duty with the Elven military. His third, and his last, for even though he was barely twenty-four, he was now retired from the military. He had been seriously injured during his last tour and had spent the better part of the last year recovering. Though he had been tended by the best Elven healers available, the injury was still not fully healed—no amount of magic could do that.

Briefly his mind slipped back to that fateful moment—the sudden searing pain, the horror of the dark magic ripping through his flesh . . .

Vaelon quickly tore his mind from the memory, lightly touching the suddenly aching spot on the right side of his chest. He had barely survived and had been honorably discharged from any future military service. Though the injury no longer caused constant suffering, there were still times when he could barely move for the pain. Pain not even High Elven magic could assuage.

It was growing dark outside, and Vaelon, after a short rest, rose to shutter his windows and bar the door. Moving stiffly to his kitchen, he began preparing a small meal, noticing with little surprise the light patter of rain beginning to fall on his roof. Clouds had been threatening rain all day, and he was lucky it had not begun earlier.

By the time he finished preparing his meal and sat down to eat, the rain had turned from a light patter to a steady downpour. A flash of lightning shone briefly through the window shutters, followed almost immediately by a shocking peal of thunder. Vaelon paused to listen, his fork poised over his plate. Finally he skewered a bean and began to raise it to his mouth.

At that moment there came a knock at his door. Vaelon frowned, setting the fork down on the plate as he pushed back his chair and rose. "Now who in the world could that be?" he wondered aloud. His mother, perhaps? Though he had been back in his own house only a few days, having spent the bulk of his recovery period with his parents, she had come to visit him at least twice a day—usually trying to convince him to come back and live with her and his father for a while longer. Perhaps she had been caught in the storm on her way.

When Vaelon opened the door, however, he did not find his mother standing there. Instead he found himself looking down at a young Elven girl—no older than nine or ten. She was soaked to the bone and shivering violently, staring up at him with wide, dark green eyes. Her reddish black hair was disheveled, strands of it crossing her face in wild patterns that made her look almost like a drowned cat—and yet utterly failed to hide the striking, almost surreal grace of her features, an innocent beauty that was somehow both childlike and beyond her years. He was so startled that he didn't speak, and then the girl spoke instead.

"My name is Reiyalindis Amarainein," she said, her young voice broken, "and I am alone."

TWO

Striking a flint with a blunt knife hanging next to the fireplace, Vaelon lit a bundle of crushed bark on fire. He had not intended to build a fire that night, but circumstances had changed. He looked over at his couch, where the strange girl was sitting, staring at the fireplace longingly. "Come sit over here," he said, indicating a wooden chair near the fireplace. "I'll have you warmed up in no time."

"Thank you," she said softly, rising and walking over to the chair. Her movements had that same beautiful grace as her features, and Vaelon shook his head, wondering what such a girl was doing here. She was clearly High Elven. No Common Elf, like he was, could ever possess that almost unnatural elegance. Why was she here? There were houses all around his, grouped on both sides of the road in both directions. She would have walked past all those houses to get to his.

Within a few minutes the fire was crackling cheerfully, and Reiyalindis huddled close to it. Vaelon rose and fetched a wool blanket, laying it over her shoulders as she sat there.

"Thank you," she said again.

"Would you like something to eat?" he asked, picking up his untouched supper and offering it to her.

"Oh, thank you, sir," she said. "I'm sorry to impose, but . . . but I am very hungry."

"It's no problem. Here." He handed her the plate, and she began eating hungrily. He watched her for a moment and then sat in another chair facing her. "So . . . Reiyalindis, what brings you here?"

She paused for a moment, glancing furtively at the door. Then she whispered, "They attacked us. We were on our way here when they appeared. I fear that Koän is dead." Her voice became choked when she said that, and a tear trickled from her eye. "I am alone now. I . . . I wish it were not true, not yet. It was wonderful to not be alone."

Vaelon leaned forward. "They? You mean the Ghost People?"

She nodded mutely.

"Good heavens! Are you all right? Did they hurt you?"

"I am not harmed," she said quietly. "Koän made me run while he held them back."

"Who is Koän?"

"My friend. He took care of me. I want to hope he is all right, but I'm afraid to."

Vaelon blinked, not sure what to think. "I wasn't aware the Ghost People had appeared today."

"It was earlier, before dark," Reiyalindis said. "They never appear at night. Only when the sun is up."

"Yes, I know. So you ran all the way here?"

"Yes," she said quietly. "We had been traveling a long time to get here."

"Get here?" Vaelon asked. "To this city?"

She looked up at him, her eyes deep and impenetrable. "To you."

"Me?" he asked, surprised. "You passed all those other houses because you were looking for me?"

"Of course."

"But why? I don't even know you!"

"I don't know you, either. Except that your name is Vaelon Sahani, and you are a great warrior."

"Great warrior?" he asked. "Who told you that?"

"No one. I just know."

"Uh . . . right. Well, I hate to disappoint you, but I'm no great warrior. A broken warrior is more like it."

Her eyes turned questioning. "What do you mean?"

"I mean I'm not exactly whole. I was injured in a battle over a year ago, and I still haven't fully recovered. I may never recover."

"The Sanretsu," she said. "I know."

Again he was startled. "How did you know that?"

She slowly reached toward him, tracing with her finger the spot on his chest where he had been injured. "I can feel the dark magic of Daaku Chikara in your body," she said in a quiet voice. "It haunts your every moment, doesn't it? I am sorry, Vaelon. It must have been awful."

Vaelon nodded shortly. "It was. So you see, I'm not your great warrior. And you still haven't told me why you came here."

"I came because I need you," she said. "You are still a great warrior, Vaelon, though you carry a terrible wound. I need your help."

Vaelon stared at her, not sure what to think. "You can't be more than ten years old."

She shrugged uncertainly. "Somewhere around there."

"And you're running around seeking a so-called great warrior because you need his help? Would you mind telling me what's going on?"

"I wish I knew," she said softly, sadly.

He stared for another moment and then said, "Uh . . . well, finish your supper and get dried off. You'd better get some sleep; we'll talk this over in the morning."

She nodded. "All right. And thank you again."

Three hours later, Reiyalindis was fast asleep, but Vaelon remained awake. He sat by the fire, keeping it going so the house would stay warm for the girl. He ran over the unusual events of the night in his mind. There was something strange about Reiyalindis—she spoke as though she were some kind of seeress. Very few Common Elves had any magical abilities, but many High Elves did. The abilities she seemed to possess were very rare but not unheard of. She had, after all, been able to sense the origin of his wound.

He sighed, absently rubbing at the injury. She had sensed the evil magic in his wound, all right—unless she had already known about it. It was not as if his injury was a secret; anyone who knew him could have told her about it . . .

His thoughts were interrupted by another knock at the door, this one a much heavier knock than the girl's had been. Reiyalindis awoke with a start, sitting bolt upright on the couch. Vaelon stood, and not wanting to take any chances on such a bizarre night, grasped the sword he kept above the mantel before moving toward the door.

He hesitated at the door for a moment but finally raised the bar and let it swing open, keeping his sword firmly in his hand. The rain had stopped, but clouds still obscured the moon and stars, so it was very dark outside.

At first Vaelon could barely make out the tall figure outlined in the doorway, standing a few feet away from the door. "Who are you?" he asked.

The figure did not answer but stepped forward. Vaelon still couldn't see any features, but the glow from the fire was reflecting from the figure's eyes—blank white eyes. Vaelon raised the sword a little, uneasy at those unnatural eyes. He said firmly, "I say again, who are you?"

But still the dark figure said nothing.

Suddenly, Reiyalindis slipped from the couch. "Koän?" she asked hesitantly. "Is that you?"

The dark figure moved again, coming fully into the firelight, and Vaelon gasped. The man was an Elf, but not a Common or a High Elf—his gray skin and white hair marked him clearly as a Dark Elf, a race of Elves that were generally distrusted by the other races of Rimurea. The Dark Elves practiced magics that were controversial at best and evil at worst; their alliances were not firm, and their motives were obscure and questionable. To find one standing on his doorstep in the middle of this dark and strange night was decidedly unnerving. "Stay back, I warn you!" he snapped, pointing his sword directly at the Dark Elf's chest.

"Koän, Koän, it's you!" Reiyalindis cried, running past Vaelon and throwing herself into the Dark Elf's arms. She began sobbing and was barely able to speak at all. "Oh, Koän, I was so afraid! I'm so glad you're all right and that you found me!"

Vaelon stepped back, thinking that he'd had about as many surprises as he could take in one night. This High Elven girl's companion was a Dark Elf? Common Elves were wary enough of Dark Elves, but the High Elves held a particular distrust of them. This whole thing was getting very strange indeed! "Um . . . sorry, I didn't know who you were," he said, lowering the sword. "Come in."

The Dark Elf picked Reiyalindis up, as the little girl refused to let go of him, and walked into the house. He was a little taller than Vaelon and was quite a formidable-looking fellow; aside from his obvious Dark Elven features, he carried a long broadsword at his waist and a pair of shorter swords across his back. Now that they were closer to the fire, Vaelon could see that the Dark Elf's eyes weren't truly white; they were covered with a strange white film that made him look like a blind man. Yet it was obvious he wasn't blind, for he found his way to the couch and sat down on it with no trouble at all. He was still wet from the storm, but Reiyalindis didn't seem to care. She continued to hold onto him tightly, sitting in his lap.

Vaelon sat down by the fire again. "What a night," he muttered to himself. "So . . . Koän, is it? Are you hungry?"

The Dark Elf shook his head but said nothing.

Reiyalindis twisted a little so she could see Vaelon and said, "He doesn't talk much. I hope you won't let that bother you."

"Uh . . . of course not, I suppose. So this is your friend, then. I wouldn't have expected to see a High Elf running around with a Dark Elf."

She sighed. "It is a bit strange, I know, but I promise you that you can trust Koän completely. He is a good and honorable man, and has been my guardian for nearly two years now."

"Your guardian?"

"Yes. Before I met him I was alone. His real name is Shomérosh Erallioch, but he prefers to just be called Koän."

Vaelon stared at his guests thoughtfully and then said, "You keep saying things about being alone, Reiyalindis. What exactly are you talking about?"

The girl's expression immediately turned downcast. "It is my destiny to be alone," she said in a sad little voice. "I was always alone until I found Koän. But even he will leave me someday, and I will be alone again."

Koän's face turned grim at that and he stared darkly at the floor. Reiyalindis gently touched his face and said, "You know it is true, Koän. I would rather you leave of your own will than be taken from me. I was so afraid that had happened today."

Vaelon shook his head. "Wait, wait," he said, "just what is this all about? Who took care of you when you were a baby? Who took care of you before Koän?"

Reiyalindis shook her head sadly. "No one."

"Babies can't fend for themselves, Reiyalindis."

"I know. I am as confused as you. Somehow I was cared for, but I have no memories before I was five—well, I think I was five, I kind of had to guess about that—and I was alone from that time until I found Koän."

"But . . . even then, how did you survive on your own?"

"I have a little magic," she said quietly. "The forest was my home. It watched over me. But the forest is not a person, as much as I love it. I hate being alone; I am afraid of it. I wish things did not have to be this way."

Vaelon rubbed at his temples, feeling very tired. "If you were sent here to befuddle my mind, you've done a grand job," he said. "What do you want from me, Reiyalindis? What help could I give you that you couldn't get from someone else, someone whole?"

"No one else will do," she said. "Only you. I need you to help me stop the Ghost People."

Vaelon froze, slowly lowering his hands as he stared at her. "The Ghost People?"

She nodded. "They are strange people, of a race no one recognizes; no one knows what they are or where they come from. They appear out of thin air, sometimes merely passing by but sometimes attacking anything near them. They linger for only a little while before fading back into nothing—sometimes only a few seconds, sometimes as long as an hour. When visible, they can be fought and killed, but their bodies, blood, and weapons vanish when their time expires."

"I know about the Ghost People, Reiyalindis. But what do they have to do with me?"

"Their appearances are becoming more and more frequent since they first came five years ago," she said. "Soon they may come so often that we will not be able to withstand them. Soon they may come in such strength as to destroy us all. They must be stopped."

"But what does that have to do with me?" he repeated.

She sighed. "I don't know, Vaelon. I wish I did. All I know is that I need your help."

Vaelon leaned back in his chair. "Are you telling me you're a seeress?"

"Sometimes I see a little of the future," she replied. "But most of the time I just know things. Your name came to me some weeks ago, as did the names of a few others we must also find. I don't know why or how, only that it did. Please, Vaelon. You must believe me. Please."

Vaelon thought for a while and finally stood. "We'll discuss this in the morning. I need to get some sleep."

The girl nodded. "As you wish. Good night, Vaelon."

✘ ✳ ✘

The following morning Vaelon didn't feel very rested. He rose wearily, ignoring a dull throb from his chest. He dressed quickly and went back into his front room where Reiyalindis was still asleep on the couch. Koän was sitting in a chair by the fire, his milky eyes open and alert. Vaelon went into the kitchen and put together a little food. He brought it back out into the front room and offered some to Koän, who accepted it with a silent nod.

Reiyalindis woke up not much later, sitting up and stretching with a yawn. "I like your couch," she said to Vaelon. "It's so soft!"

Vaelon raised an eyebrow. "That's not what most people tell me. My mother always complains about how hard and lumpy the pillows are."

"Really? Well, it's much softer than the ground." She glanced at the food but then looked away, placing her hands in her lap and pretending not to have seen it.

Vaelon couldn't help but smile a little. "Hungry?"

She looked back at him. "Me? Oh. A little."

"Help yourself."

"Oh, thank you!" She came to the table. She was obviously trying very hard not to appear hungry, but though she ate slowly and deliberately Vaelon could plainly sense that she was starving. The plate he had given her the night before obviously hadn't even touched her hunger.

"Reiyalindis," he said finally, "there's no need to stand on ceremony here. Why didn't you tell me you were still hungry last night?"

She lowered her eyes, looking embarrassed. "I didn't want to seem rude," she said in her soft voice. "I'm not used to being around people, but I thought it wouldn't seem very proper to ask for more from a complete stranger."

"Well, don't worry about it. Eat as much as you want, and there's more in the kitchen if that's not enough. My mother insists on keeping my cupboards well stocked. She seems to think I eat as much as an army."

The look of gratitude in Reiyalindis's eyes made Vaelon feel a strange warmth in his soul.

"Thank you, Vaelon," she said. "You are very kind."

He shrugged awkwardly. "Don't mention it."

Vaelon waited until Reiyalindis had eaten her fill before speaking again. "All right," he said, "I need to know exactly what it is you want me to do before I agree to anything."

Reiyalindis sighed. "Well, all I really know is that I need to find some others to help us."

"What others?"

"First we need to go to Cim's Hill. Do you know how to get there?"

Vaelon nodded. "It's just a few hours' journey from here."

"Really? Oh, good. We need to go there to find Ciroy Xagalliack and his wife, Safaya Elithinæn Xagalliack."

"And just who are they?"

"I'm not sure. I only know that they work together as hired guards."

Vaelon let out a long sigh. "Look, Reiyalindis . . . I'm not sure what to think about all this. I mean, you have to admit that it's very strange. How do I know you're being honest?"

She was quiet for a moment and then said, "I can prove to you that I sometimes know things no one else knows. Would that be enough?"

"Well . . . we'll see. Go on."

"I know something about you. Something you have never told anyone."

Vaelon hesitated for a moment and then said, "All right. What is it?"

She looked sad as she spoke. "You were wounded in battle because of the cowardice of one of your friends. He intentionally placed you in danger to protect himself. He was killed anyway, and you never told anyone what happened because you did not want his parents to know what their son had done. You did not want that dishonor to haunt them along with their son's death."

Vaelon felt his gut tightening almost painfully as he looked at her. He stood abruptly, walking over to a window and staring out of it. Finally he turned back around. When he spoke, his voice was carefully controlled. "How did you know that? No one else was there—at least, no one who survived the fight. How could you possibly know what happened?"

"Is that proof enough for you?"

Vaelon forced himself to let the tenseness in his body slip away. "All right. I believe you."

"Oh, thank you!" she exclaimed, running to him and hugging him tightly.

Startled, Vaelon awkwardly patted her head. "Um . . . sure. I suppose we ought to head for Cim's Hill, then?"

"As soon as possible," she said, finally letting go of him.

"Fine. Just let me get a few things together."

Within only a few minutes they were on their way. Vaelon lived near the edge of the city, so before long they were out in the countryside, walking along the well-worn road that led to Cim's Hill. As they walked, Vaelon wondered if he was getting himself into something he'd regret later.

They hadn't gone far when they passed a Halfbreed on the road. He was a man, though apart from his general body shape he looked nothing like the Human race his kind had formerly belonged to. He had the long snout, floppy ears, and tail of a bloodhound, and every inch of his skin was covered with short brown fur. He crossed to the other side of the road as he passed them, watching them warily from the corner of his eye. Koän alone would probably not have concerned the Halfbreed, as their kind had good relations with Dark Elves, but Vaelon, and especially Reiyalindis, were a different story.

The Halfbreeds were a race of part Human, part animal creatures. They had been created long ago by dark magic. Evil sorcerers had captured hundreds of Humans and performed experiments on them, attempting to create an army that could destroy their enemies. The experiments had gone awry, however, and most of their captives had escaped. Those poor souls had gone into the deep forests of southeastern Rimurea, shunning contact with other races. Only in the past twenty years had the Halfbreeds begun to emerge from their long hiding.

High Elves avoided them, knowing them to be spawned of dark magic and therefore believing they could not be trusted. The Common Elves shared this view for the most part and regarded Halfbreeds with trepidation or even fear. The fact that Halfbreeds got along well with Dark Elves only served to make High and Common Elves even more wary of them. Even Humans were uncomfortable around them, and Halfbreeds were equally uncomfortable around their original race. They had little to do with each other, preferring to remain apart.

Reiyalindis watched the Halfbreed go and then said, "Have you ever met a Halfbreed, Vaelon?"

"A few," he replied. "But just in passing. They're not very common this far north."

"Why not?"

"Well, most of them live in the deep forests in the southeast. They don't venture this far very often. Most of their trade is with the Dark Elven communities in the east."

"I've never met one," she said. "That man didn't look like he wanted to talk, though."

"No, he didn't."

"Do they all look like that?"

"What, like dogs?"

"Well, no, I know they take after all sorts of different creatures. But do they all look that much like animals?"

"No, not all of them. Some have hardly any animal characteristics at all. Others, though, look so much like animals that you'd think they really were animals. It's all a little random, from what I understand; the characteristics of the parents don't seem to have any bearing on those of the children."

"I've never met a Human, either. Are they very different from us?"

Vaelon shrugged. "Well, they have funny rounded ears, for one. And they tend to be a little bigger and stronger than we are; they make excellent fighters, for the most part. Any Elven garrison is happy to accept Human volunteers."

"Where do they live?"

"Lots of places. They're only a very small portion of the population and they live mostly in scattered groups around the kingdom. They don't have a territory of their own."

"I don't know much about my own kingdom, do I? I know it's called Rimurea, but that's about it. Would you teach me? I haven't been around people very much."

"Why haven't you?"

She looked up at him. "The forest is my home. I was afraid to leave it."

"I don't understand, Reiyalindis. If you're so afraid of being alone, why did you stay in the forest? Why didn't you come find other people?"

"I can't really tell you, Vaelon."

Vaelon took a deep breath and let it out slowly. "I don't understand this, Reiyalindis."

"I know, and I'm sorry. Really, I am."

"So how did Koän become your guardian, anyway?"

Looking down at the ground, she said, "I'm sorry, but that's another of those things I can't tell you, Vaelon. He wouldn't want me to."

"Why not?"

"Please, just trust me."

Vaelon shook his head. "You're full of mysteries, aren't you, little one? I wish I at least knew *why* you won't tell me these things."

Sudden emotion made her voice tremble. "Please, Vaelon," she whispered, "I don't want to talk about it any more. Not now. Please."

Vaelon nodded slowly. "All right," he said. "All right. But if you do ever feel like telling me, I wouldn't mind knowing."

She nodded and then took Koän's hand. She walked for a long time with her head resting against his arm, a distant and sorrowful look in her big eyes.

The rest of the trip was very quiet, but by the time they reached the little town of Cim's Hill, Reiyalindis seemed to have returned to her normal cheerfulness.

"I've been in this town a lot," Vaelon said as they entered Cim's Hill. "Not a bad little place, but some of the inns are pretty rough. We'll want to stay there, at Gumber's place." He pointed to a large inn just down the road. "He's a friend of mine. Good man."

"All right," agreed Reiyalindis.

When they walked into the inn's common room, a large, cheerful Common Elf wearing an apron spotted them. "Vaelon!" he boomed over the low babble of conversation in the room. "Good to see you again, lad!" He approached them and shook Vaelon's hand warmly. "How's the ol' war wound?"

"Same as always, Gumber," Vaelon replied.

"Not improving, eh? Sorry to hear that. What brings you to Cim's Hill?"

"Just passing through," Vaelon replied. "These are my friends, Reiyalindis and Koän."

Gumber didn't bat an eye at the appearance of the Dark Elf. "Welcome!" he said to Koän. Looking down at Reiyalindis, he said, "Well, aren't you a pretty little thing! High Elven too! A High Elf, a Common Elf, and a Dark Elf all in one little party? Now that's a sight a fellow doesn't see too often. How many rooms?"

"Two," Reiyalindis replied. "Koän never sleeps in buildings. He'll probably guard my door all night."

Gumber blinked uncertainly.

"Don't worry about it," Vaelon said. "Koän's her guardian, and he takes his job very seriously."

Gumber evidently decided not to question the strangeness of a Dark Elf being the guardian of a High Elf, for he simply nodded and said, "Right then, two rooms. I'll show you to them."

✖ ✳ ✖

Once settled, the trio sat in the common room for a bit of late lunch. "So where do we find these two hired guards?" Vaelon asked Reiyalindis as they ate.

"They'll be at an inn called the Blue Sow in about an hour," she replied.

"That soon?"

"Yes. We should go wait for them as soon as we're done eating."

They finished their meal and then left the inn, walking through town to the Blue Sow. It wasn't a bad inn, but Vaelon hesitated to bring Koän to it. The innkeeper was known to look upon Dark Elves with little tolerance.

When they entered the Blue Sow, the innkeeper was not present, and they sat in a corner table to wait. A serving maid came to them, and, just to avoid curiosity, Vaelon bought them each a glass of spiced cider. Reiyalindis sniffed curiously at hers. "What is this?" she asked.

"Cider," Vaelon replied. "Just apple juice with some spices in it. Haven't you ever had it before?"

"No." She took a sip, and her eyes brightened. "My goodness! It's very good."

As they sat sipping their drinks, the innkeeper appeared from the kitchen. He spotted them immediately, and his eyes darkened when he saw Koän. Vaelon prepared himself for a confrontation, but after a few moments the innkeeper just turned and walked away again. Evidently he had decided it wasn't worth the trouble to try to throw out a customer who had already bought a drink—or he was afraid to offend Reiyalindis.

Vaelon nursed his drink slowly and was barely half finished when Reiyalindis suddenly perked up.

"Here they are!" she said excitedly.

Vaelon turned to look toward the doorway. When he saw the pair coming inside, he couldn't help but stare. The man was a Human, but Vaelon hardly noticed him, for his attention was arrested by the woman—she was a Halfbreed.

She was tall, with a slender, graceful figure. Her hair was snowy white, as was her luxuriant, surprisingly fetching, fox tail. The only other features that defined her as a Halfbreed were her pair of white fox ears and plainly nonhuman eyes. She was dressed in snug-fitting leather and was armed with a longbow and a light sword.

She was certainly a beauty, and that surprised Vaelon a little; he hadn't seen many Halfbreeds in his life, but those he had seen had been anything but attractive. But this Halfbreed wore her animal characteristics proudly, with all the confidence of a woman who knew exactly how good-looking she was.

But no matter how attractive this woman was, she was still a Halfbreed, and Vaelon wasn't sure she could really be trusted. The Halfbreed race had, after all, been created by dark magic. "Are you sure that's them?" he asked Reiyalindis. "I really don't think a Human would ever marry a Halfbreed."

"It's them," she said confidently.

Vaelon, still not convinced, turned his attention to the Human man. He was the same height as the woman, with short-cropped blond hair and light gray eyes. He was strongly built and moved with the sure manner of an experienced fighter. Besides the saber at his waist, he had a long knife strapped to each leg and a heavy machete on the other side of his belt. He wore a loose-fitting white shirt and a leather vest, leather trousers, and calf-length boots. "Innkeeper!" he called. "Do you have a room to spare?"

The surly innkeeper glared at them. "We don't serve Halfbreeds here," he growled, "or those who run around with them."

Oh, great, Vaelon thought. He had a feeling this was going to get ugly.

The woman rolled her eyes, and the man said, "Really. Any particular reason? Besides mindless bigotry, I mean."

The innkeeper scowled even deeper. "Just get you and your sorry mongrel out of here!"

The woman put a hand on her hip, and the man let out a sigh. He took a step toward the innkeeper, laying a hand on his shoulder. The innkeeper flinched a little, but the Human didn't strike. "Look," he said, "this is your establishment, so I suppose you have the right to decide who you'll let use it and who you won't—but nothing gives you the right to insult my wife."

The innkeeper nearly choked. "Your wife?" he demanded, letting out a hoot. "You actually married one of those monsters?"

"I need you to take back the things you said about her," the man told the innkeeper, still calm and reasonable. "Now."

"Why should I?" the innkeeper demanded.

"Because," he said patiently, "I love her, and I don't like it when people call her names. Although it may not be very charitable, I might have to hurt you. So let's avoid all that unpleasantness, shall we? Just apologize."

"No," the innkeeper said insolently, brushing the man's hand from his shoulder. "And don't think you can threaten me, because I've got three lads in the back who'll whip you good if you so much as touch me! Now get out!"

The Human sighed. "Fine." In a swift move he punched the innkeeper in the stomach. The innkeeper doubled over with a pained grunt and dropped to his knees. The man then patted the innkeeper's head and said,

"Sorry. I'm sure you understand." Turning, he took his wife by the hand. "Let's get out of this dump."

Reiyalindis rose. "Come on." Koän and Vaelon followed her as she went after the couple, who were out in the street by that time.

No sooner had Vaelon, Koän, and Reiyalindis left the inn than three burly Common Elven men burst out the door behind them, apparently following through on the innkeeper's threat. One of them nearly knocked Vaelon down as he barreled past. The three men ran after the couple, brandishing stout clubs.

The Human and Halfbreed heard them coming and turned. The man's hand went for the hilt of his sword, but Koän shot forward with astonishing speed, coming to a quick halt between the three men and their targets. His sword was out, and he faced the innkeeper's thugs with a grim expression that was unmistakably hostile. The three men ground to a halt at the appearance of the strange Dark Elf, suddenly not so sure of themselves.

Finally one of them spoke. "Hey, now, get out of the way!" he said. "Our quarrel is with that thickheaded Human!"

Koän didn't move, and the three Elves started fidgeting. Finally their natural fear of Dark Elves won out, and they turned and walked back to the inn, muttering curses as they passed Vaelon and Reiyalindis.

"Uh . . . hey there," the Human said to Koän. "Thanks."

Koän turned to face him but, as usual, said nothing. Vaelon and Reiyalindis came up beside him. "Hello," Reiyalindis said the man. "I am Reiyalindis Amarainein. I hope we aren't intruding."

"Intruding?" the woman asked with a slight smile. "I'm sure we could have handled those bouncers, but all the same the help is appreciated." She looked at Koän, nodding her head slightly, and he nodded in return.

The Human stuck out his hand. "Hi there. Name's—"

"Ciroy Xagalliack," Reiyalindis said as Vaelon shook the man's hand. "And your wife is Safaya Elithinæn Xagalliack."

Ciroy nodded. "I see you've heard of us."

"Yes—well, in a way," Reiyalindis replied. "As a matter of fact, we need your help."

"Oh!" Ciroy's eyes brightened. "So you need a job done? Now, there's a few things we need to clear up right now—first off, we don't do anything illegal, and that includes guarding a load of illegal goods. Second—"

"No," Reiyalindis said, "I don't think you understand. We aren't trying to hire you."

Ciroy blinked. "Uh . . . so what do you need, exactly?"

"Your help, as I said. We've been looking for you."

"You'll have to excuse her," Vaelon said. "She has a habit of saying odd things and expecting people to know what she means."

Reiyalindis blushed a little. "Oh, dear. I do, don't I? I'm sorry."

Safaya smiled, obviously taken with the Elven girl. "Don't worry about it, little one. Why don't we find someplace to sit down and we'll talk?"

"Yeah," Ciroy agreed. "Good idea. This sounds like it might take some explaining."

Vaelon rolled his eyes. "Yes. It might."

"Thought so. Um . . . we don't usually operate this far north. Know any good places to stay that won't have a problem with Safaya?"

"Oh, yes," Reiyalindis said. "Come, I'll show you to the inn where we're staying. The innkeeper is a very nice man." She took Safaya's hand and began leading her down the street, and Safaya, a little bemused, went along.

"Well!" Ciroy said, watching them go. "She's not shy, is she?"

"Not really," Vaelon replied.

As they walked, Reiyalindis looked up at Safaya. "You're very beautiful," she said.

"Thank you," replied Safaya. "So are you."

Reiyalindis blushed. "Oh, I don't know about that. So what kind of animal do you take after? You look like a fox, but I've never seen a white fox before."

"Neither have I, to be honest." Safaya smiled. "You're such a nice little thing, Reiyalindis. Most Elves don't like to even be around Halfbreeds, especially High Elves."

"Oh, that's silly, if you ask me," said Reiyalindis. "We're not all like that. I love your tail, by the way. It's very pretty."

"Thank you." She winked. "Ciroy likes it too." Behind her, Ciroy let out a whistle, and Safaya laughed.

Reiyalindis giggled. "I like you two," she said. "I'm glad you'll be along; it will be much more fun." Then she lowered her voice. "Not that Vaelon isn't nice, but he's very reserved."

Safaya's eyes turned questioning. "Along? Along on what, little one?"

"I'll explain everything when we get to the inn. I'm sorry, I sometimes get ahead of myself."

"Boys, I'm in trouble," Ciroy announced quietly. "Those two are already best friends, I can tell. Whatever it is you want us to do, I have a bad feeling I'm stuck with it whether I like it or not."

"Reiyalindis has a way of doing that," Vaelon said ruefully.

Ciroy glanced at him. "What, she roped you into whatever this is?"

"I'm afraid so."

"Well! I'm really curious now."

Once they arrived at the inn, Ciroy and Safaya paid for a room. Gumber hardly seemed to notice Safaya's race, not acting any differently than he did with other customers. Once that was settled, they joined the others at a table in the common room. "All right," said Ciroy, "let's hear it."

"I should introduce my friends first," said Reiyalindis. "This is Koän. He has been my guardian and friend for the past two years. He doesn't talk much, so please don't think he's rude if he doesn't answer when you talk to him. And this is Vaelon Sahani. He's retired from the military."

"Retired?" Ciroy asked with a raised eyebrow. "You look mighty young to be retired."

"Medical discharge," Vaelon said. "I was injured during my last tour of duty."

"Oh." He looked back at Reiyalindis. "Well, we know your name, but we still don't know who you are."

"I am Reiyalindis," she said. "My name is all I know."

Looking at her with an expression of puzzlement, Safaya asked, "What do you mean by that?"

"I'm as much a mystery to myself as I am to others," she said a little sadly. "I know nothing about my life before I was about five, and since that time I have been alone, until I met Koän."

"Alone?" Safaya asked.

"Yes. But I don't really want to explain all that right now. What I need to explain is why I need your help."

"Okay," said Ciroy, folding his arms across his chest. "Spit it out."

"I need you to help us stop the Ghost People."

Ciroy jumped a little. "The Ghost People! What the blazes—!"

"It sounds strange, I know," she hurried on, "but please, you must believe me."

Ciroy stared hard at her. "Just what makes you think we can do anything against the Ghost People?"

"I don't know," she said in a small voice. "Sometimes I just know things. I . . . I had a feeling. It led me to Vaelon, and it has led me to you."

"You have some kind of magic?"

"Yes. A little."

Ciroy and Safaya glanced at each other and then back at Reiyalindis. "How can we trust you?" he asked. "We don't even know you."

She hesitated and then said, "I know something about you. Something you have never told anyone."

"About me?" he asked.

"About both of you."

"All right, then, what is it?"

She looked embarrassed. "It's . . . uh, not really something you probably want anyone else to hear."

"Really. Then whisper it to me."

The little girl rose from her seat and went around to Ciroy, cupping her hands up to his ear and whispering something. Ciroy turned a little red, and then straightened, absently tugging at his collar. "Uh . . . yeah. Hum."

"What did she say?" Safaya asked curiously. Ciroy leaned over and whispered into her ear, and she immediately blushed. "How did she know *that*?"

"I don't know," Reiyalindis said. "It just came to me. Perhaps so I could convince you that I'm telling the truth."

Ciroy drummed his fingertips on the table. "All right, so you do have some magic. But even so, I still can't see what you could possibly expect us to do against the Ghost People. Do you know where to go?"

With a helpless shrug the girl said, "No."

"I'm confused."

"There is one more person we need to find," Reiyalindis said. "I'm hoping that perhaps he knows something about this."

"Who is he?" asked Ciroy.

"I don't know much about him, only that he is very learned and that his name is Baden Solignis."

"Wait," said Ciroy, "I've heard of him. He's an Elf. Common Elf. Lives in Coebane, down around where we usually work."

Reiyalindis looked excited. "You know where he lives? Oh, good! He's the only one I didn't know how to find."

"We know where he lives, all right," said Safaya with an amused chuckle. "He has a fortress on the outskirts of Coebane, and lives there in that huge building all by himself—he's filthy rich and crazy to boot."

"Crazy?" asked Vaelon.

"Yeah," said Ciroy. "Completely nuts, according to the people of Coebane. We've never actually met him, but we've heard some pretty weird stories."

"Such as?"

"Mostly odd noises and bright flashes coming from his fortress at night. Sometimes explosions. People have seen him running around on top of his walls staring up into the sky through strange metal tubes and such. I've heard he fancies himself some kind of scientist, but beyond that all I know is that most people in Coebane think he should be locked away. And even though he's got more money than the rest of the city put together, no thieves ever try to rob him—they say he's got that fortress booby-trapped."

"Sounds like a winner," murmured Vaelon.

"I'll tell you what," said Ciroy. "We'll go with you at least long enough to see what Baden has to say about all this. Then we'll see how things look after that. Fair enough?"

Reiyalindis nodded. "You've got a deal."

THREE

After spending the night in Cim's Hill, the group headed south toward Coebane. Ciroy and Safaya walked in front, holding hands most of the time. They were cheerful, easygoing people, and it wasn't hard to like them. Vaelon found himself losing a lot of the preconceptions he'd always held about Halfbreeds. Safaya was a warm and friendly person, not reclusive and secretive in nature as he'd always pictured Halfbreeds.

He waited for a long time for Reiyalindis to ask the odd couple how they had ended up getting married because he was sure the little girl would. She didn't, though, and finally his curiosity got the best of him. "I don't mean any offense," he said, "but I have to admit I'm curious about how you two got together. I was under the impression Humans and Halfbreeds don't like one another much."

Safaya laughed lightly. "Oh, they don't, usually," she said. "But despite my better judgement I couldn't resist Ciroy's charms."

"My charms?" Ciroy said with mock surprise. "It was me who couldn't resist your feminine wiles, remember?"

"Oh, was that how it went? I seem to remember otherwise." She looked back at Vaelon. "We met in the forest near where my people live. Ciroy had been hired to track down a thief, and he'd just cornered the fellow when I chanced upon them."

"Only it turned out that I'd followed the thief right back to his hideout," Ciroy said, "where all of his buddies were waiting for him. By the time I realized what I'd stumbled into, all eight of them were charging me. I, being the bold adventurer I am, of course, defeated them single-handedly.

Except for the five Safaya killed for me."

"Five?" Vaelon asked, surprised.

"Yeah, it was crazy," Ciroy replied. "There I was watching them running at me, and I'm saying to myself, 'Self, this might get nasty,' when suddenly these arrows start flying past my head. Bam, bam, bam, three in a row just like that. The rest kind of slowed down, y'know—thought they'd been ambushed or something, and while they were standing there looking stupid, I charged them. Got me three, and the last two ran, but they didn't get far before two more arrows got them. So I turned around, and there she was. Just about lost my jaw when I saw her."

Safaya sighed dreamily. "It was all downhill from there. I knew he was Human, but he was just so gorgeous! What was a poor girl to do? We started talking, and the more we talked the more I liked him."

"It was the tail," Ciroy said. "Had me right from the start. And the way she walked—you know, with her hips going back and forth like that . . . And everything else about her too. We hit it off so bad we started seeing stars."

Safaya nodded. "Well, I knew my family would never want me to get involved with a Human, so I told him I had to go and started running back home. But the strangest thing happened—somehow I got turned around, and before you know it, there I was right in front of him again."

"Imagine that," Reiyalindis teased.

"Yeah, go figure, huh?" said Ciroy. "I didn't want her to leave but I guessed she didn't want to hang around a Human, so I started heading back home too. But I'll be buggered if the same thing didn't happen to me. So there we were again."

Safaya giggled. "And then he said to me, 'Say, uh, you want to, I don't know, take a walk or something?' And I said sure, and off we went. Within an hour I knew I was hopelessly in love with him. So we made a deal. We said we'd both go home and wait two weeks to see if maybe it was just a stupid little fling of puppy love. If either of us still wanted to see the other one by the end of the two weeks, we'd go back to that spot where we met and wait for one day. If the other one didn't show up, we'd know it was off and go home. But if we both went—then we'd court."

"Yeah," said Ciroy. "Couldn't get her out of my mind for a second the whole two weeks. I went back three days early and camped out just to make sure I didn't miss the deadline. And she showed up two days early." He grinned. "When she saw me there she let out this cute girlish squeal, grabbed me around the neck, and dang near choked me to death."

"So you courted," said Reiyalindis.

"Yes," said Safaya. "For a whole day. Then we went to find someone to marry us."

"Took three weeks to find someone willing to join a Human and a Halfbreed," said Ciroy. "Longest three weeks of my life." He hooked his arm around his wife's waist and pulled her close. "But let me tell you, she was worth the wait."

"Sounds like a fairy tale," Vaelon said.

"It felt like it too," said Safaya. "Sometimes I still find myself expecting to wake up from a dream, even though we've been married five years now."

"That's so romantic," Reiyalindis said. "I wish something like that could happen to me someday."

Safaya winked at her. "Who knows? It might."

Reiyalindis smiled, but Vaelon could tell it was forced. He knew that she was thinking that Safaya was wrong, that such a thing could never happen to her, and he again wished Reiyalindis would tell him why she was convinced it was her destiny to be alone. What a strange little girl she was.

"No children?" Reiyalindis asked, changing the subject.

Safaya's face fell a little, and she looked ahead. Reiyalindis sensed that she'd struck a sore spot, and she quickly started to apologize.

Ciroy interrupted her. "Hey, kid, don't worry about it," he said, patting the little Elf on the shoulder. "We knew before we got married that it might not work out that way. Seems our species aren't compatible, or something. Just like how Humans and Elves can't have children together, either. It's just the way it is."

"I'm very sorry," said Reiyalindis.

After that an awkward silence settled, but it didn't take long to wear off. As the day progressed Ciroy, Safaya, and Reiyalindis chatted amiably amongst themselves. Vaelon joined in occasionally. Koän, of course, said nothing. Reiyalindis had told them he didn't talk much, but Vaelon was beginning to wonder if he talked at all.

When night fell, they made camp in a small cluster of trees near the main road. After a small meal they all went to sleep, except Koän, who sat watchfully near the edge of the camp. Vaelon, as he lay there, wondered if the Dark Elf ever slept. He didn't have much time to ponder the question, though, for sleep overtook him quickly.

Three hours past midnight, Vaelon awoke to excruciating pain.

The sudden fire in his chest was so intense that it completely clouded his senses. The pain filled every inch of his body, and he convulsed uncontrollably as it ripped him into tiny, burning pieces over and over again.

How long it went on, he didn't know, but it felt like an eternity. Finally, though, the pain began to abate slightly, and the convulsions lessened to spasmodic twitching. He was vaguely aware of voices but couldn't understand them, and he couldn't see anything.

Gradually he became aware of someone gently stroking his hair, and the striking contrast between the soothing sensation and the pain seemed to jolt him out of his shock. He blinked a few times, trying to clear the fuzzy image in his eyes. A few seconds passed, and then his vision fully returned.

He found himself looking at the worried face of Ciroy Xagalliack. The adventurer smiled when he saw Vaelon's eyes focus, and he said, "Hey, kid. You had us worried. You okay?"

Vaelon rolled his eyes upward, and saw that Safaya was kneeling near him. She was the one who was stroking his hair. Reiyalindis was sitting on his other side, her small face streaked with tears and her hand resting lightly on his chest. He tried to speak, but couldn't quite form any words, and it came out as a strangled grunt.

"Shhh, just rest," Safaya said soothingly. "Don't try to talk."

Ciroy let out a great breath. "Dang," he said, "what the blazes happened to him?"

"It's his wound," Reiyalindis said in a strained voice.

"Wow. Must've been pretty bad."

"He was injured by a Sanretsu warlock."

Both Ciroy and Safaya gasped. "Sanretsu!" Safaya exclaimed.

"Yes. His company was attacked by Sanretsu during a regular patrol near their border. Not even the queen herself can fully heal the poison of Daaku Chikara."

Ciroy spat on the ground. "Danged demon-worshippers," he muttered. "Can't see how any people who were once Elves could ever sink that low. Is he gonna be okay?"

"It will take a little while to wear off," she said. "It's happened to him before, more than he'd like to admit."

"Well, we'd best just let him rest, then," said Safaya as she stood up. Ciroy sat against a tree, and Safaya snuggled against him, both of them still watching Vaelon.

Reiyalindis stayed with Vaelon, softly tracing the outline of his wound with her finger. Oddly, it seemed to Vaelon that the touch made him feel better. He wondered how she could possibly know the outline of the wound so perfectly; even if he hadn't been wearing a shirt, the wound itself was invisible. The strange magical sphere the Sanretsu had struck him with had left not the slightest mark on him, even though it had nearly killed him and had left him infected for perhaps the rest of his life.

At length, Ciroy and Safaya fell asleep again, and then Reiyalindis also grew too drowsy to sit up any longer. She lay on her side next to Vaelon, resting her head on his arm, and fell asleep. Vaelon, though, could not sleep, and it seemed to him like a very long time before the sun finally rose.

Ciroy was the first one awake—not counting Koän, who had never gone to sleep—and he carefully extricated himself from Safaya and came over to Vaelon. "How are you doing?"

Vaelon shrugged. "Better. Help me sit up, will you?" He gently slipped Reiyalindis's head off of his arm, and though she stirred a little, she didn't wake up.

Ciroy chuckled as he helped Vaelon ease up into a sitting position. "You scared the living daylights out of me. I thought the Ghost People had decided to start showing up at night."

"Sorry about that."

"No worries. So you got mixed up with a Sanretsu warlock, huh? Bad business. Why'd they attack you?"

"Who knows? That's why we patrol the border. No one ever knows what those fanatics will do. I think we just stumbled across one of their foraging parties."

"Foraging?"

"That's what we call them. They send groups out every now and then to gather sacrifices. Animals, mostly, but they'll snatch unprotected travelers too."

"Dang. I don't see why we don't just storm in there and wipe them out."

Vaelon shook his head. "Because we don't know enough about them. We have no idea how many there are, how well armed they are, how fortified their positions are. No scout or spy we sent into their territory ever came back. The military brass won't risk a battle without that kind of information, not without more reason than a few scattered incidents."

Ciroy looked thoughtful. "No scouts ever came back, huh?"

"No. We don't have the kind of magic we'd need to protect ourselves in there."

"Haven't any High Elves tried?"

Vaelon let out a sigh. "We sent in a High Elf once. When he didn't come back, the High Commander decided it wasn't worth the lives to keep trying, and they stopped sending spies entirely. Honestly, the only people who'd have a decent chance of spying out the Sanretsu territory are the Dark Elves. But they won't get mixed up in what they call 'our business.' "

"Ours?" Ciroy looked amused. "I'd say it's more their business than anybody's. The Sanretsu used to be Dark Elves themselves, anyway, even if they are enemies now."

"The Sanretsu are the enemies of everyone. Human, Elf, Halfbreed, everyone." He grimaced as a stab of pain shot down his torso.

"Are you going to be able to travel today?" asked Ciroy.

"Yeah, I'll be fine. Just give me a while. I need to walk it off."

"If you say so. Just don't try to be a hero and make it worse."

"I've done this before. I'll be fine."

Just then Safaya woke up. She rose, brushing some dirt from her hip. "Hey, there, Vaelon," she said. "How are you?"

"Not so bad," Vaelon replied.

The Halfbreed chuckled a little. "Right. Do you feel like eating?"

"I could use a bite."

"Well, you just sit tight, then, and I'll scare something up for you."

"Thank you," he said. "That's nice of you."

"Oh, think nothing of it. We're a team now."

"We are?" Ciroy asked mildly. "I was under the impression that we weren't going to settle on that until we talked to Baden Solignis."

"Well, we may as well be a team until then." She knelt near the fire, stirring it a little, but after only a moment she stopped. She glanced at Reiyalindis and then quietly stood up and walked over to kneel beside Vaelon and Ciroy. "Vaelon," she said in a very quiet voice, "I need to ask you something."

Vaelon nodded. "Sure."

"Yesterday, when we were talking with Reiyalindis about how Ciroy and I met, she got really sad when I said that thing about her maybe meeting someone too. You know what I mean? She smiled, but she didn't mean it."

Vaelon nodded slowly. "Yes. I know what you mean."

"You know something about it. I could tell that you knew she was sad too, but you didn't seem surprised."

"You're really good at reading people."

Ciroy winked. "Always has been. I can never surprise her with anything; she can always tell exactly what I'm thinking, somehow."

"Call it animal instinct, if you want," said Safaya. "But tell me, Vaelon—what's going on?"

With a sigh Vaelon said, "She's got this strange notion that it's her destiny to always be alone."

"What?" Safaya looked startled, as did Ciroy. "Why?"

"I don't know. But she really, truly believes it. She's completely scared to death of it too. I tried to get her to tell me about it, but she got all choked up, and started crying, and wouldn't talk about it any more."

Safaya's face softened. "Oh, the poor little thing. I wonder—"

She stopped abruptly as Reiyalindis stirred, blinking a few times. Reiyalindis seemed a little disoriented at first but then she sat up with a start. "Vaelon!" she exclaimed. At the same moment she saw him sitting right next to her, and she briefly closed her eyes with a sigh of relief. "Oh, you're here. Are you all right? How do you feel?"

"I'll be fine," he replied. "I wish everyone would stop fretting over me."

"Do you!" Safaya exclaimed. "You wake up in the middle of the night screaming and shaking like your insides were trying to get out and you expect me not to fret? Men! Always trying to be tough."

"Oh, come on, honey," said Ciroy. "We could never be as pretty as you womenfolk, so we have to act tough, or we'd be ugly *and* feeble."

"Mister, you couldn't be ugly if you tried." She pinched his cheek. "Aww, isn't he cute, Reiyalindis?" The little Elven girl just giggled.

"All right, that's enough of that!" declared Ciroy. "Where's that food you promised Vaelon?"

"Oh!" Safaya exclaimed. "I forgot. Hold on, Vaelon, I'll get it ready."

"I'm not an invalid," he said, trying to convince himself more than her.

Safaya stood up, putting her hands on her hips. "No? All right, then, stand up and show me how tough you are."

"Ah . . . maybe later."

She sniffed. "Thought so. You just sit tight and stop trying to not be a bother."

Within another hour, Vaelon was up and walking, and though the pain was fierce at first, it wore off quickly once he was able to move around. Coebane was normally a week's journey from Cim's Hill, but they traveled quickly and were able to make it to the large coastal city in five days. "The fortress is on the east side of the city," said Ciroy, "about a mile out of town. Should we stop in town first, or just head straight for Baden's place?"

"What would we do in town?" asked Vaelon.

"I don't know, grab a hot meal or something, maybe. I'm getting a little tired of trail rations," Ciroy said.

"Let's just head for the fortress," said Safaya. "There's no point in wasting time."

Ciroy sighed. "All right. Here we go."

Baden Solignis's fortress was a large, forbidding structure—square and high, with a squat tower on each corner. The gates were massive, made of solid oak, and bound with thick straps of iron. "Wow," said Reiyalindis. "It's big. He lives there alone?"

"He must be rich," said Vaelon, "to live in a place like that."

"Oh, he's rich, all right," said Ciroy. "That fortress is his ancestral home. One of the richest Common Elf families in the kingdom. I'm actually quite interested to meet him and see what he has to say about all this."

When they reached the gates, Vaelon stared up at them. "How will he know we're here? Unless he's standing right on the other side, he'll never hear a knock."

"What about this?" Safaya said, touching a chain that hung down from a small hole in the gates. An engraved metal sign beside the chain said, *Pull.*

Ciroy shrugged. "Give it a yank."

Safaya gave the chain a good pull, and a loud, booming gong reverberated through the fortress.

"Wow," said Reiyalindis. "That's loud."

They waited for several minutes before a creaking sound announced that the gates were beginning to open. They opened only a few feet, and a voice from inside called, "Well, come on in then, I suppose."

Koän entered first, followed by Vaelon. Safaya took Reiyalindis's hand and followed Vaelon, and Ciroy brought up the rear. Once inside, the gates creaked shut again, seemingly of their own accord.

"What kind of magic is this?" Ciroy muttered.

"Oh, it's not magic," said the voice that had called to them. A Common Elf appeared from a small shack just inside the gates. He looked to be around the same age as Vaelon, and was strongly built for an Elf. His black hair was cut very short, and he was wearing a thick leather apron that was stained and burned. "Just a complex system of pulleys and gears. Well, well, but this is an interesting group. One of each Elven race, one Human, and one Halfbreed. Very interesting indeed! What do you want?"

"Please," said Reiyalindis, "we need to speak with you about something very important."

"Well, if you're here looking for money or magic, you can forget it. I don't give handouts to strangers, and I don't have any magic. And don't think that using a pretty little High Elven girl will melt my heart."

"We're not here for either," said Reiyalindis, "and I'm not trying to melt your heart. We're here for you."

"Why?"

"Because we need your help."

"Help?" He shed the apron, tossing it back into the shack. "What kind of help?"

"It's a long story," she said. "And a strange one. Please hear me out before you make any decisions."

His eyes narrowed as he looked at her. "What's your name?"

"Reiyalindis Amarainein. And these are my friends—Koän, Vaelon Sahani, and Ciroy and Safaya Xagalliack."

"And you're Baden Solignis, I presume?" said Vaelon.

"That's right," said Baden. Upon hearing their names, his demeanor changed considerably; his suspicion seemed to vanish, and he smiled cheerfully. "Well, I'm flattered to have such prestigious company! Come this way." He turned and began walking.

Reiyalindis was confused, and as they began following him, she said, "Baden . . . I'm sorry, but do you know some of us?"

"Oh, not personally," replied Baden. "Ciroy and Safaya I've heard of—reliable hands, from what I hear. But I was actually referring to him." He jerked his thumb over his shoulder at Vaelon.

Ciroy glanced curiously at Vaelon but didn't say anything. Vaelon, though, began to feel distinctly uncomfortable and coughed to cover it.

Baden did not offer anything further, and soon they were across the fortress courtyard and into the main building itself. Finally, Ciroy said, "Well, what exactly did you mean by 'prestigious'?"

Baden came to a sudden stop, turning quickly. "You mean you don't know?" he asked incredulously.

"Uh . . . know what?"

"Never mind," Vaelon said. "It's nothing."

Baden barked a short laugh. "Nothing? Don't be modest." Looking back at Ciroy, he said, "Have you ever heard of the Crimson Star?"

Ciroy blinked. "Well, sure, it's a medal the Elven military gives to wounded soldiers."

"Not just any wounded soldiers, my dear man. Only those who received their wounds through the greatest of valor. And have you heard of the Golden Star?"

"That's the highest honor that can be given to any soldier," Safaya said. "Only nine have ever been awarded in the Elven military's history."

"Wrong. There have been ten," said Baden. He pointed at Vaelon. "The tenth—and a Crimson Star as well—belongs to him."

Safaya and Ciroy stared at Vaelon with shock. "You have a Golden Star?" Ciroy demanded.

Vaelon shrugged. "Yeah, I guess."

"You guess!" Baden hooted. "Amusing. Yes, Ciroy, my good man, you're in the company of one of the most highly decorated Elven soldiers in the world—a young lieutenant, retired at twenty-three with higher honors than any general alive today! The queen herself presented his medals to him after personally attending his wounds—though at his insistence the ceremony was kept very private instead of proclaimed throughout the kingdom as is usually done. Still, though, I can't believe you didn't know about him."

Ciroy folded his arms across his chest and frowned at Vaelon. "Well, he didn't exactly tell us any of this."

"It's not a big deal," said Vaelon.

"Single-handedly killing four Sanretsu warlocks and saving your entire company from obliteration isn't a big deal?" Baden asked mildly.

Safaya gasped. "Four warlocks! Oh my goodness, I heard about that!" She stared at Vaelon. "That was you? That's how you were injured? Vaelon, why didn't you say something?"

"Because I knew everyone would make a fuss about it," he grumbled.

Reiyalindis threw her arms around Vaelon, hugging him tightly. "I knew it!" she cried. "I knew you were a great warrior! And you told me you weren't!"

"I'm not!" he snapped, a bit more impatiently than he'd meant to. "Not anymore."

She drew back, a little surprised at his tone. "Vaelon," she said softly, "I wish you wouldn't say things like that. You give yourself far too little credit."

He sighed. "Reiyalindis, you saw what happened to me. What if that happens again when you need me the most? I'll let everyone down. I'm more a danger to this company than a help."

"Vaelon," she said firmly, "I will not have you speaking of yourself like that any longer. You were chosen to lead this mission because you were the best choice."

Vaelon blinked. "Lead? You never said anything about me leading anything!"

"Well, now you know. Come on, we need to explain things to Baden."

"I'll say," said Baden with an amused look in his eyes. "This is all getting very interesting."

There wasn't much more talk as they followed Baden to a small chamber that contained a haphazard collection of stuffed chairs. "Have a seat," he said, waving at the chairs. He dropped down into one himself.

Vaelon stared around the room. It was filled with strange devices he had never seen the like of. There were several long, thin tubes that looked like they had glass stuck in the ends; a strange-looking crossbow with a lever attached to a steel box on the underside; and a great variety of other devices he could hardly begin to describe. He took a seat, still looking around as the others sat too.

"So," said Baden, "from what I've gathered already, you five are on some sort of mission. Apparently the young girl here is in charge of the whole thing, though she seems to have designated Vaelon to be the leader." He looked at Koän. "So, you call yourself Koän, do you? What's your real name?"

Reiyalindis was startled. "Baden, how did you know that isn't his real name?"

"Simple, my dear girl. Koän is an Old Elvish term, and that tongue died over a thousand years ago. It's not the sort of name a parent would give a child—it's the sort of name someone would give himself." He watched Koän as he spoke, his eyes probing. "You see, it means 'one who is marked for death.' It originated during the rule of King Ulfendil the Cruel, who was known to have peasants tortured to death for entertainment; it was a term used for someone who was chosen to become one of his victims. In later centuries, it broadened to denote people who were condemned to die by the powers that be for any reason at all."

Ciroy looked curious. "How do you know all that?"

Baden shrugged. "Books. I find your choice of names interesting, Koän. I assume you knew the meaning of the word when you chose it."

Koän, as usual, said nothing; he simply looked at Baden with an unblinking stare.

"Not a very talkative fellow, are you?" said Baden.

"He . . . he doesn't talk much," Reiyalindis said quietly. "Please forgive him. His real name is Shomérosh Erallioch."

"I see. Just how is it a Dark Elf became the protector of a High Elf?"

Again Reiyalindis was startled. "You knew he was my guardian?"

"It's obvious. He watches you like a hawk. He was the first to enter the fortress, ready for danger, but he walked beside you as I led you to this room. And he chose the seat right beside yours when we got here. Not only that, he is clearly tied to you, as you're the one who has been speaking for him."

Vaelon was impressed. "You're very observant, Baden."

The Elf shrugged. "I just pay attention to things people normally overlook, that's all. But you didn't answer my question, Reiyalindis. It's very strange for a High Elf to have a Dark Elven protector."

Reiyalindis glanced at Koän and then looked down at the floor. "It's a matter I really don't wish to talk about. I'm sorry."

"I see. Well, I suppose I shouldn't be surprised; after all, you're in the company of a Human married to a Halfbreed. So, down to business— what do you want from me? I could use an answer a little more specific than 'your help,' if you don't mind."

"All right," said Reiyalindis. She took a deep breath. "We need your help to find a way to stop the Ghost People."

Baden's reaction was entirely unlike those of Vaelon, Ciroy, and Safaya. He leaned forward intently, his eyes alight, and exclaimed, "Aha! Excellent! I have been waiting for a seer to finally be told to do something about those pests!" He jumped to his feet, going to a nearby bookshelf and pulling a thick tome from it.

Vaelon was astounded. "Now hold on!" he exclaimed. "How in the world did you know she was a seeress?"

"As I said, my good fellow, I simply pay attention. She knew you were a great warrior, but didn't know why; she told you that you were chosen to lead this company—her exact words being 'You were chosen' rather than 'I chose you,' which naturally implies that the decision was not hers, but that of a higher source. And any halfwit could have deduced that she was a seeress by the simple fact that she sought me out." He dropped the book on the table with a thud. "I have been studying the Ghost People for years—but I have never told anyone of my studies. Were she not a seeress, she would have had no reason to come here."

Ciroy glanced at Safaya. "Well," he said, "I guess that sort of settles the matter, doesn't it?"

Safaya nodded. "I told you we'd end up helping her."

"I know, dear."

Baden opened the book. "So, do you know much about the Ghost People beyond what is already common knowledge?"

"No," said Reiyalindis. "I was hoping you did."

"I might, as a matter of fact." He tapped the page. "You all know that the Ghost People never attack at night. You are probably also aware that various attacks across the kingdom on any given day happen simultaneously—every day in which there is an attack, there are always multiple attacks across the kingdom that happen at the exact same time and for the exact same length of time. As far as we've been able to determine, anyway."

"Yes," Vaelon said. "We know that."

"Good. With this and some other information, I have come to the conclusion that the Ghost People attacks are somehow linked to the sun."

"The sun?" Ciroy questioned. "What evidence is there of that? Maybe they just don't like the dark."

"And buildings?" Baden asked. "There has never been an incident of an attack inside a building unless that building had windows or other open places that allowed direct sunlight."

Vaelon's brow creased. "Are you certain of that?"

"Absolutely. I had the good fortune of being attacked myself not too long ago. A Ghost Person appeared standing in the sunlight coming through one of my windows. He saw me and started to charge, but the instant before he left the direct sunlight of the window, he stopped. He just stood there, staring at me." Baden looked around at all of them. "I have personally witnessed six Ghost People attacks out in the open, and always the Ghost People avoided shady areas. They attacked only those they could reach in direct sunlight."

Vaelon blinked, thinking back to the Ghost People attacks he had seen himself. "You know," he said, "I was always too busy trying to stay alive to notice that before, but I think you're right."

"But why sunlight?" wondered Safaya. "I thought ghosts were supposed to come around at night, not in broad daylight."

"They aren't really ghosts," said Baden. "We just call them that for lack of a better word. I shot the Ghost Man who appeared in my home, and in the time before he vanished again I examined his body quite thoroughly. Their anatomy is very similar to ours; were it not for their unusually shaped skulls and lack of reproductive apparatus, they are almost exactly like Humans."

"Lack of what?" Reiyalindis asked, confused.

Baden hesitated. "Um . . . you know, the parts used to reproduce."

Reiyalindis blushed. "Oh. Oh, yes. I see."

Ciroy looked confused. "They don't have . . . But why not?"

"Think about it. No one has ever seen a female Ghost Person—they are always male. Most believe that this is because, like us, Ghost People do not bring their women into battle. But I believe otherwise. I believe we see no females because there *are* no females. These are not actual people, in the strictest sense. I tend to think they're something more along the lines of supernatural manifestations."

"You mean someone's creating them?" asked Vaelon.

"Not necessarily someone—but almost certainly something. And I can make a fair guess as to what."

Safaya snapped her fingers. "The sun?" she guessed.

"Exactly," said Baden.

Ciroy looked flabbergasted. "That's nuts! Why would the sun be creating those bloodthirsty freaks?"

"I'm not sure if the sun is directly creating them itself, but I'm certain that sunlight is a necessary factor in their creation."

Reiyalindis looked excited. "Do you know what we can do to stop them?"

Baden shook his head. "No, I'm afraid not. I would like to study the sun more, but I fear my equipment isn't adequate for the kind of study I need to do. I can't see it well enough with the limited magnification my current telescopes provide."

"Tele-whats?" asked Ciroy.

Picking up one of the metal tubes with glass on each end, Baden tossed it to Ciroy. "Telescope. Invented it myself. Look through the narrow end and point it across the room—toward that bookstand there. Push it together or pull it farther apart to adjust the focus."

Ciroy dubiously raised the telescope to his eye, looking across the room at the bookstand, which had an open book lying on it. The distance was a good twenty feet, but after a moment Ciroy exclaimed, "Dang! I can read that book from here!" He lowered the telescope, examining it. "Wow. How does it work?"

"I'll explain that some other time," Baden replied. "That telescope was one of my early models, and has very, very weak magnification. With some of my more powerful ones I could read that book from a hundred yards away."

"Serious?" Ciroy asked. "Dang, you could see people coming from miles away with one of these!"

"Yes," said Baden with a sigh, "but I can't use them to study the sun without being blinded. I've tried holding a piece of paper behind the telescope, letting the image of the sun hit the paper instead of my eyes, but it's a very imprecise method. And there's not even a way to know if the telescope is powerful enough to study the sun the way I would like—it all depends on how far away the sun is."

"How far away do you think it is?" asked Safaya curiously.

Baden laughed. "I wouldn't dare pretend to know that. To estimate that distance we'd have to have some idea of how big it is, which of course we don't."

"It doesn't look that big," mused Safaya, "but I suppose it would have to be pretty big if it was, say, a hundred miles up in the sky. Do you think it could be that far?"

"My guess would be farther," replied Baden. "Much farther. But it is only a guess."

"So . . . what can we do, then?" asked Vaelon. "We know we're supposed to do something, but I don't have even the vaguest idea what."

"A good place to start, I think," said Baden, "would be to capture one of the Ghost People."

"Capture?" asked Ciroy. "Why?"

"I mean to interrogate him," replied Baden. "The Ghost People, so far as we know, have never spoken, but that doesn't mean they can't. I also want to try another experiment—I want to drag one, dead or alive, out of direct sunlight and see what happens to him. I did not dare do it to the one I killed here, because I wanted to examine him and didn't want to risk having him vanish."

"So do we just go find some sunny field and wait around for them to attack?" asked Ciroy.

"Do you have a better plan?"

As the others continued talking, Vaelon noticed Reiyalindis quietly slipping from her chair and wandering to one of Baden's bookshelves. She gently ran her fingers over a few of the well-worn books. Abruptly, interrupting another of Baden's long explanations, she said, "Baden, what do you need to get more information about the sun?"

Baden hesitated and then said, "Well, a bigger telescope, for one—the bigger, the better. I have plans for one drawn up, but I lack the necessary equipment—it calls for a glass lens that's twenty feet across, plus other smaller ones as well."

"Twenty feet?" Ciroy exclaimed.

"Or larger. As I said, the bigger, the better. And it can't be just any sheet of glass, either; it has to have a very precise shape. As I said, making one would be next to impossible."

"Supposing you can't get that telescope," said Reiyalindis, "is there any other way to get the information you need?"

Baden shrugged helplessly. "I have a lot of ideas, but again, we don't have the kind of technology such instruments would require, if they are even possible."

Reiyalindis turned to face him. "Anything is possible with magic," she said quietly. "If we can find someone powerful enough, he could help you build your instruments."

Baden thought that over. "Do you know of such a person?" he asked skeptically. "They would have to be able to manipulate existing materials, and create completely new materials as well. That kind of power is rare."

"I do know of such a person," she said. "Alhalon Cui Kahathilor, one of the most powerful sorcerers to ever live."

Vaelon almost choked. "What?!" he demanded. "Alhalon the Black? Reiyalindis, that man died two hundred years ago!"

"No, he didn't," said Reiyalindis, a strange, faraway look in her eyes. "He still lives."

For a moment everyone was silent, and then Baden cleared his throat uncomfortably. "According to history he was destroyed by the High Elves," he said. "He was one of the most powerful Dark Elves in the world, but his magic drove him to evil, and he became an enemy to all. It took fourteen High Elven sorcerers to defeat him, and only three of them survived."

"Two survived," she said. "The third was Alhalon."

Baden's eyes widened. "He . . . he took the place of one of the sorcerers who tried to kill him?!"

"Yes. The others destroyed their own friend without knowing it. If you read the histories very carefully, one of those three survivors supposedly killed himself before reaching home."

"Yes, yes, of course," Baden breathed. "According to the other two he could not cope with the horrors he had seen during the battle, and he simply willed himself out of existence. But he didn't really, did he?—it was Alhalon, simply making a convenient escape that would leave no one wondering! But Reiyalindis—how do you know all this? Oh, of course, why should I ask? Amazing! That clever old rascal!"

Most of them were looking at Baden as the eccentric Elf began pacing rapidly, but Vaelon, watching Reiyalindis, saw a deep, strange pain briefly cross the young girl's features. It was gone in a moment, but Vaelon saw that he wasn't the only one who'd noticed it—Safaya was also watching Reiyalindis, looking worried.

"Even if Alhalon is alive," Ciroy said, "what help could we expect from him? He's reputed to be thoroughly evil! Why do you think the High Elves tried to kill him in the first place?"

Reiyalindis shook her head. "The Ghost People might intrigue him enough to help us. And I do not believe he will kill us, so long as we don't threaten him."

"Are you sure about that?" asked Vaelon.

Reiyalindis nodded, her face somber. "I am. You'll have to trust me."

"This is crazy," Baden said with a grin. "I might even like it."

Ciroy sighed. "Man, this is getting to be a lot more than I bargained for."

"I'm sorry," whispered Reiyalindis, tears beginning to brim in her eyes. "I didn't want to drag all of you into this, I really didn't. I don't want to endanger you—I just wanted to stay home, but I had to do it, I had to . . . I'm sorry . . ."

"Oh, oh, darling, don't say such things," Safaya said gently, going to the little Elven girl and taking her face in her hands. "We know you're only doing what you have to, and that's what we'll do too. Don't you fret."

"I'm afraid," said Reiyalindis. "What if . . . what if you die, Safaya?

How could I ever forgive myself? How could I face Ciroy? And if he dies, what will you think of me then?"

"Now, let's not have any talk of dying!" Ciroy said firmly. "You think too much, little one. We're responsible adults, and we're helping you because we chose to, not because we were forced to."

Baden coughed. "Um ... If I may say so, I believe we've had enough talk for one day. Would any of you care for a bite to eat?"

Reiyalindis wiped at her eyes. "Yes, I'd like that. Thank you."

Safaya affectionately stroked the little girl's hair. "You're such a dear. Come on, let's see if we can cheer you up."

Baden's dining options were somewhat less than luxurious, but were much better than trail fare any day. By the time they were finished eating, evening was beginning to fall. Vaelon, Ciroy, and Baden settled in Baden's study again, but Reiyalindis excused herself to go to bed.

Safaya stayed in the study for a few minutes but then left and went to Reiyalindis's room. Koän was there, standing guard outside her door, and Safaya approached him. "Can I see her for a minute?" she asked. Koän just nodded, so Safaya knocked on the door.

"Yes?" Reiyalindis called from inside.

"Can I come in, dear?" asked Safaya. "I want to talk to you."

"Oh ... of course. Come in."

Safaya entered the room, closing the door again behind her. Reiyalindis had changed into a white nightgown and was sitting on her bed. Her eyes were a little red, Safaya noticed. "That's a pretty gown," she said. "I haven't seen you wear it before."

"Oh ... I don't wear it while I'm traveling," said Reiyalindis. "Only when I can sleep indoors."

"Where did you get it?"

Reiyalindis looked a little guilty. "Well ... Koän got it for me. I never asked him where he got it, but I ... I suspect he may have stolen it. Like my dress. I used to make my own clothes before I found him, but he wanted me to have nicer things than what I could scrounge up in the forest. He tries so hard to take good care of me ... I didn't have the heart to scold him."

"He sounds like a true friend," said Safaya.

"Oh, he is. He's very protective of me."

Safaya nodded, sitting on the bed next to Reiyalindis. "Do you mind if I ask you something?"

"No, of course not."

"Earlier today, when you told us about Alhalon, I saw that even the thought of him brought you pain. Why?"

Reiyalindis shook her head quickly. "Please, Safaya," she said, "don't make me tell you. I . . . I can't."

"You've met him before, haven't you?"

Reiyalindis let out a long sigh. "No, Safaya. I haven't. I didn't even know he was alive until earlier today, right before I told you about him."

"But then why . . . Did you see something else about him?"

"It's just . . . he has done some awful things, and . . . and I'm just so afraid of what he might do to us."

Safaya knew immediately there was more to it than that, but she could also see that even just talking about it was causing the little girl a great deal of pain. She put her arm around Reiyalindis comfortingly. "Have you been crying, dear one?"

Reiyalindis looked mortified. "You can tell?"

"Of course I can. And there's nothing wrong with it. I can tell you're scared out of your wits, and I don't blame you."

Reiyalindis's lip began to tremble. "I wish I was strong like you," she whispered.

"Oh, I'm not so strong," Safaya said with a chuckle. "There have been many times I've cried myself to sleep on poor Ciroy's shoulder."

"It must be very nice to have him," she whispered. "I wish I could have someone like that—oh, when I'm older, of course."

"Why can't you?"

"I . . . I don't . . ."

"Vaelon already told me that you said it's your destiny to always be alone."

A great tear trickled down Reiyalindis's cheek. "I don't want to be alone," she said in a hoarse whisper.

"Well, you aren't," said Safaya, gathering the little Elf into her arms. "You just go ahead and cry all you want, dear one. You don't have to tell me anything you don't want to. I just want to be your friend."

Reiyalindis burst into tears. "Oh, thank you!" she sobbed, throwing her arms around Safaya. She wept uncontrollably, and Safaya rocked her gently back and forth, humming softly and stroking the Elven girl's hair.

Eventually Reiyalindis fell asleep in Safaya's arms. Moving slowly to avoid waking her, Safaya laid Reiyalindis down, tucked her into bed, and then quietly left. Koän was still outside the door, of course, and he nodded briefly to her as she left.

The others were just leaving the study as she approached them. Ciroy took her hand. "Where've you been?" he asked.

"With Reiyalindis," replied Safaya.

"Ah. Well, let's get some shut-eye, eh?"

Once they were in their room, Safaya sat on the bed with a sigh. "Ciroy, there's something wrong with Reiyalindis."

"What do you mean?" he asked as he removed his sword belt.

"Remember what Vaelon told us about her?"

"What? About her thinking she's going to end up all alone?"

"Yes. It's worse than I thought, though. I mean, at first I thought that she was just afraid of it—you know, because of how she grew up."

Ciroy paused. "But it's not?"

"No. Ciroy, I think she's seen it—her own future. It's not just a little girl's fears, it's real."

"Did she actually talk to you about it?"

She shook her head. "No. She cried herself to sleep, though."

"Really? Poor kid must be pretty scared."

"It must be hard for such a young girl to see something like that. There has to be a way to change it, though. I can't bear the thought of her ending up all alone."

Ciroy sat down beside her. "You've really taken a shine to her, haven't you?"

Safaya nodded. "Haven't you? She's such a sweet little thing."

"Yeah," he admitted. "One of these days she's got to open up, though. I wonder why she's so secretive."

"She's afraid to tell us," said Safaya. "That much I've been able to sense in her. What I can't figure out is why."

"Maybe once she gets a little more comfortable with us she'll tell us more. I mean, after all, she's not used to being around people much, except Koän. Another secretive one. Those two are like riddles." He swung his legs up and stretched out on the bed. "Makes my head hurt, to be honest. Man, I'm tired."

Safaya began pulling her boots off. "Let's get some sleep, then."

FOUR

The following morning they all gathered in Baden's kitchen for some breakfast. Baden was already there when the others came, sitting at the table and tinkering with the strange crossbow they had seen in his study the day before. "Say," said Ciroy, pointing at the weapon, "what kind of crossbow is that, anyway?"

"Dangerous," Baden replied simply, applying a drop of brownish oil onto a set of gears near the steel lever that ran underneath the crossbow.

"Really," said Ciroy. "Thanks for enlightening me."

Baden offered it to him. "Here. Pull that lever on the underside."

Ciroy took the crossbow and did as he was instructed. The lever smoothly cocked the crossbow, and Ciroy said, "Neat, but it can't really be all that strong if it's so easy to cock."

"Ah, not so!" said Baden. He took it back and loaded it with a small steel bolt with a chisel-shaped tip. "Watch this." He pointed it at a wooden beam that ran across the ceiling, upon which were hung various cooking utensils. When he fired, the bolt struck a thick cast-iron cooking pot, and it went straight through, shattering the pot and continuing on to completely bury itself in the beam.

Ciroy stared, his mouth hanging open. "Wow. Hey—now hold on, that just isn't possible! Not with a crossbow that easy to cock!"

Baden tapped his head. "Brains, Ciroy." Holding up the crossbow, he said, "I designed this myself. The lever here doesn't directly cock the string; it actually engages a complex set of gears inside here where you can't see. Those gears wind the string back, and it requires relatively little effort to

41

pull a large weight. Here, try to cock it the usual way."

Ciroy took the crossbow again and tried to cock it by pulling the string back himself, but strain as he might, he couldn't so much as budge it. "Dang!" he said finally, giving up. "That's incredible!"

"But it's not the only thing," said Baden. He held up another of the bolts. "I also designed these. They have a super-hard tip precisely shaped to pierce softer metals. One of these in even an ordinary crossbow will punch straight through the heaviest body armor with no trouble at all, even at a fair distance."

Ciroy whistled. "That's pretty crazy stuff."

Baden was grinning. "You think this is wild? Wait until you see my next trick."

Ciroy braced himself. "Okay, what is it?"

Reaching into a small bag on the table, Baden produced another of his telescopes—only this one had an odd bracket on it. Baden slid the telescope into a complimentary bracket on the crossbow, tightening it down with a bolt. "Presto!" he said, holding it up proudly. "A specially designed telescope mounted on the crossbow. The lens has a fine cross drawn on it, enabling me to accurately aim this crossbow at great distances. With this telescope I can reliably hit a man-sized target a thousand yards away."

Ciroy was speechless, and Vaelon was equally impressed. "That's amazing, Baden," he said. "How do you make all these things?"

Baden made a face. "Well, it isn't easy, I'll tell you that. Most of the small parts I make myself in my forge, but I've had to invent a few new ways of working metal to get some of it done too. And glass. Glass is the worst. These lenses are a real headache to make."

"So you make your own glass and your own metal parts? What *don't* you do?"

Baden thought for a while and then said, "Um . . . I don't really cook well. Just enough to get by."

"Well," said Safaya, "suddenly my bow doesn't seem quite so dangerous anymore."

"On the contrary!" said Baden. "Most crossbows have very few advantages over longbows. The crossbow may have a heavier pull, true, but bows have longer arms, so the arrow is able to gain more power before leaving the string. Crossbows often have greater power at point-blank range, but over any kind of distance the shorter arms will counterbalance the heavier draw. Not only that, bows can be fired much more quickly than crossbows, and they tend to have greater accuracy in the hands of a trained marksman. Of course, I've been working on this particular crossbow for quite some time, and it's basically as accurate as you can get." He patted the crossbow.

Vaelon, who was starting to get used to Baden's rambling explanations, nodded vaguely. "I see. So . . . speaking of cooking, mind if I put something on for breakfast?"

Baden waved at the stove. "Be my guest."

Reiyalindis was curiously examining several strange contraptions that lay scattered around the kitchen, but as Vaelon set about building a fire, she wandered over to Baden. "What will happen to your home when you come with us?" she asked solemnly. "Vaelon had little in his home worth stealing, and Ciroy and Safaya don't have a home—but you have a great deal to lose here. All of these things you've made, your life's work, your entire family fortune . . . you have no one to take care of it while you're gone."

Baden smiled, playfully ruffling her hair a little. "Oh, don't you worry about that, Ray. This place is well protected, believe me."

She blinked, her brow wrinkling. "What did you call me?"

"Uh . . . Ray. Just short for Reiyalindis, you know?"

She frowned a little, looking slightly worried. "That's not my name," she said finally.

Baden looked a little taken aback. "Uh . . . I know. It's like . . . a nickname, you know? But hey, I won't call you that if you don't like it."

She nodded. "Thank you, Baden. I like my name, and don't really need another one."

"Sure thing."

"You're sure your home will be all right?"

"Positive. Most everything valuable I keep locked away in the vault, and nothing short of a powerful sorcerer could break into that. Trust me. I invented it myself."

"You're sure no one could just pick the lock?" Ciroy asked. "How did you manage that?"

Baden winked. "Ah, but it doesn't have a lock. At least, not in the traditional sense. It's operated by a series of a hundred small levers—only by pressing twenty of them in the correct order will the lock open. Press the wrong one, and you have to reset the main switch and start all over again." Then he grinned. "Anyway, they'd have to find the vault in order to even try to open it, and that in itself would be quite a feat."

Ciroy shook his head. "Where do you come up with all this stuff? How do you even get these ideas?"

Baden sighed. "It's a curse. The oddest random things pop into my head now and then, and I have to do them or my brain explodes. There are so many things I want to do but just can't figure out how! It's annoying. Take lightning, for instance—all that sheer power! There has to be a way to harness it!"

Ciroy laughed. "Yeah. Good luck with that one."

"You laugh, but someday I will. Oh—Vaelon, don't bother with that flint." He stood up, walking over to his stove where Vaelon had been attempting to light a fire. Baden pulled a small lever at its side, there was a slight popping noise, and then a jet of flame sprayed into the oven, instantly lighting the wood on fire.

Vaelon jumped back. "What on earth—?!" he exclaimed.

Baden tapped the lever. "This releases a highly flammable liquid onto the wood, and at the same time triggers a flint that ignites the liquid."

"What kind of liquid?" Ciroy asked curiously.

"Nothing you'd recognize. I—"

"—invented it yourself, yeah," said Ciroy.

"Yes."

"Have you got a pot about so big?" asked Vaelon, holding his hands about a foot apart.

Baden glanced up at the beam with the pots and pans hanging on it. "Well . . . I used to," he said with a shrug. "Will a different size do?"

✗ ✳ ✗

Once breakfast was completed, they gathered their gear and prepared to leave. Baden met the others in the courtyard, carrying a sword in his hands. "I want to show you something," he said, pulling the sword free of its sheath. It was long and narrow, single-edged, and had a slight curve and an oddly shaped tip that was reminiscent of the armor-piercing points on Baden's crossbow bolts.

"A sword?" asked Vaelon.

"Not just any sword," said Baden with an obvious sense of pride. "This, my friends, is my masterpiece."

Ciroy blinked uncertainly. "How so? It's kind of funny-looking, but other than that it's just a sword."

"That's where you're wrong. This sword was made using a particular

44

technique that I—yes, you guessed it—invented myself. It took me seven years to make this weapon."

Vaelon was surprised at that. "Seven years? How could it possibly have taken that long?"

"I began work on it when I was a teenager," said Baden, "and finished it not very long ago. I won't get into the gritty details, but I'll tell you this much—this is the strongest, sharpest sword you'll ever come across." Then he sighed. "As a matter of fact, it's much too fine a weapon for a novice like me. That's why I want you to have it, Vaelon."

Startled, Vaelon said, "Me? Why?"

"Because it suits you. You're reputed to be one of the finest swordsmen alive—don't deny it—and this is the finest sword ever made. Here, try it out." He handed the sword to Vaelon.

Stepping away from the others, Vaelon gave it a few practice swings, and as he did he had the sudden, strange sense that he'd just met a lifelong friend. The sword was amazingly light and exceptionally well balanced; it felt as though it were part of him, not simply a lifeless metal instrument.

Baden was grinning at Vaelon's expression. "You like it, huh?"

Vaelon swung the sword over his head, amazed and pleased at how easy it was to change it from one hand to the other as he passed it behind his back and up into the air in a lightning-quick slice. "It feels incredible," he said. "But surely it's too light to be much use!"

"Too light to be much use, he says," smirked Baden. "Here. Think fast." He plucked an inch-thick iron bar from where it had been leaning against a nearby wall, tossing it toward Vaelon.

Quickly sidestepping, Vaelon brought the sword around and struck the bar squarely in the center as it passed by where he had been standing. Baden's sword sliced cleanly through the iron, and the two pieces of the bar tumbled to the ground.

Ciroy's jaw dropped. "Holy smokes!" he blurted. "No way!"

Vaelon stared down at the sword, and he couldn't stop grinning. There was not so much as a nick in the blade where he'd hit the bar. He got a sudden understanding of the seemingly endless hours spent perfecting every tiny aspect of the weapon, the intense and often frustrating experimentation that ultimately led to just the right formula for the remarkable metal. "Baden, you are amazing," he said. "I don't know if I can accept a gift like this. This sword must be the most valuable thing you own."

"It's my greatest accomplishment to date, if I may be so arrogant as to say so," Baden said. "But I feel that it will be much more valuable in your hands than in mine."

"Thank you."

"Think nothing of it. Shall we away, then?"

As he walked Vaelon belted on his new sword, leaving his old one in the shed next to Baden's gates. At first he wasn't sure he wanted to leave it behind, but something told him he would not have need of it again.

"So where does this Alhalon character live, anyway?" asked Ciroy as they left the fortress.

Reiyalindis pointed east. "That way. In the deep part of the Gray Forest."

"Really!" said Safaya brightly. "We'll pass close to my home, then. That's the forest where Ciroy and I met."

"We're going to have to go much deeper than that, I'm afraid," said Reiyalindis. "Alhalon lives near the border of Ruzai."

Vaelon froze in his tracks. "Reiyalindis, that's Sanretsu territory."

She stopped, turning to face him. "I know," she said, her big eyes sad. "But that is where he lives."

Ciroy glanced eastward with a worried frown. "The Gray Forest is big," he said. "The northern half does go into Ruzai, but no one ever goes to that part. Why . . . that's practically at the foot of the Great Shield."

"The forest extends into the mountains," said Reiyalindis. "It is there we will find Alhalon's fortress."

They resumed walking, but soon Ciroy frowned and said, "You know, I've been thinking. If Alhalon really is so powerful, why is he still in hiding? It's not as if there are very many sorcerers around any more, and none as powerful as in the old days. The High Elven magic has been failing; everyone knows that."

Reiyalindis shook her head. "I don't know."

"Maybe he doesn't know the magic is failing," offered Safaya. "Or maybe he's afraid of the Dark Elves—their magic is still as strong as in the old days."

"I doubt he's afraid of them," said Vaelon. "The Dark Elves might have the power to confront Alhalon, but they never would unless he threatened them. I doubt they'd so much as bat an eye if he emerged."

"If he started killing High Elves they might do something, though," said Ciroy. "Dark Elves may not be on exactly friendly terms with High Elves, but they'd surely oppose a slaughter like that. They know the High

Elves are important to the stability of the kingdom."

"Debate is pointless, really," said Baden. "I suppose we'll find out when we reach him. And speaking of reaching him, Reiyalindis, I'm assuming you know the way?"

The little girl nodded. "Mostly. I'm not familiar with the forest, I'm afraid, but I can keep us in the general direction."

"Well, I'll be able to guide us for quite a ways," said Safaya. "I grew up in the Gray Forest, and I'm familiar with a fair piece of it. If we move steadily we can reach the forest within a few days; it's not far from here."

"I suppose," said Baden, "that this is the part where someone makes some kind of mission-starting remark—like, 'So it begins,' or something. Right?"

Vaelon gave him a strange look. "What are you talking about?"

"That's what they always do in those melodramatic adventure stories I used to read." He made a fist, jabbing it into the air in the direction of the forest. "Onward, my stalwart companions! The fate of the world rests with our small but highly skilled and unusually lucky company!"

One of Reiyalindis's eyebrows rose. "You're kind of goofy," she said.

Baden rolled his eyes. "Well, that's never what they say to the people in the stories. Fine. Let's just go, then."

✕ ✳ ✕

The Gray Forest was four days' journey from Coebane. The land between was dotted with a few small villages surrounded by farmlands, most of them strung along the main road that connected Coebane and Valsana, the largest city in the southern half of Rimurea. Valsana lay a day's journey from the great forest and was a central hub for trade in the south; in the whole kingdom it was second in size only to the Ruling City, where the queen lived. There was a significant Human population there, and there was also a substantial presence of Halfbreeds and Dark Elves.

Vaelon had never been to Valsana, and as they spotted it in the distance he said, "I've heard a lot about that city. I've been told it's kind of a dangerous place."

Ciroy shrugged. "Oh, it's not so bad—well, most of it. There are some pretty disreputable places, true, but they're small and easy to avoid."

"The size of the city, and its location, makes it a popular spot for criminals," said Baden. "Smugglers, mostly, bringing in illegal goods from the far south."

"Illegal goods?" asked Reiyalindis. "Like what?"

"Poisons, mostly. The far southern end of Rimurea is a desert—not many people live there, but it is home to all sorts of nasty reptiles and strange plants that produce deadly poisons. They're popular with assassins and disgruntled wives."

Reiyalindis blinked, as if not comprehending what he was saying. "Disgruntled wives?"

"Of course. Usually those whose husbands beat them or chase other women, or both."

"Oh, Baden, that's horrible!"

"I think she's had enough education for today," said Safaya firmly, taking Reiyalindis's hand and pulling her closer protectively.

Looking faintly puzzled, Baden said, "Sorry."

Silence settled, until finally Ciroy said, "So are we going to go through the city, or would it be easier to just bypass it?"

"Actually," said Baden, "there are a couple of things I'd like to pick up while we're here. They may come in handy."

"What things?" asked Vaelon.

"I've got a friend here; he's very good at getting rare materials that I occasionally need for certain projects. At the moment I'm actually in the market for a little poison myself."

"What?" exclaimed Safaya. "I thought it was illegal!"

"Actually, no," replied Baden. "Trade in certain poisons is perfectly legitimate as long as you are properly authorized, which my friend and I both are."

"Well, what's the point of making them illegal if people can just go get authorized to have them?"

"Oh, not just anyone can get such an authorization," replied Baden. "In order to get a certificate of authorization, you have to present your case before the queen herself, providing adequate proof that you have some actual purpose for which you need the poisons—legitimate and useful purposes of course. And if she and her advisors decide your proposed use of the poisons is acceptable, they send out all sorts of snoops everywhere in the kingdom to question you, everyone you know, and all of those people's relations, friends, acquaintances, and dogs to determine if you're trustworthy enough to hold such a certification. It was a very long and annoying process."

"Really!" said Ciroy. "Why have I never heard of this certification?"

"Because it's not really very common," replied Baden. "I only know about it because I went to see the queen to ask her for special permission to import one particular poison for an experiment."

"Just what is this experiment and this poison you're after?" asked Vaelon.

"Well, it's extracted from the liver of a strange lizard found in the southern desert," Baden explained. "We found it curious because it kills Elves very quickly, but it has absolutely no effect on Humans, Halfbreeds, or any animals we've been able to experiment on."

Reiyalindis looked profoundly shocked. "Baden—you didn't kill anyone, did you?"

Baden laughed. "Oh, goodness, of course not! What kind of man do you think I am? No, we gathered that information from the authorities— known cases where this poison was used. Despite its relative obscurity and the difficulty of procuring it, nearly a hundred assassinations have been carried out using it."

Reiyalindis looked relieved. "Oh."

"So why do you want it?" asked Vaelon.

"Because," said Baden, "in the event we're able to capture a Ghost Person, I want to see what this poison does to him. If it kills him, it means that the Ghost People have some kind of similarity with Elves that is not shared with other living creatures. If it doesn't kill him, well, that won't prove anything conclusively. I'm also going to pick up a poison that will kill anything—so far as we know, anyway—and see what that does."

Safaya shook her head. "You know, sometimes you're a little frightening, Baden—casually talking about experimenting on people with deadly poisons and such."

Baden shrugged. "Sorry. But it could yield some useful information."

"If you say so."

✘ ✳ ✘

Valsana was a crowded, noisy city. The streets were lined with merchants hawking their wares, and many of the streets were so filled with people that it was impossible to walk anywhere without bumping into someone.

The strange group of companions was making quite the impression on the crowds. The sight of a Dark Elf holding a High Elven girl's hand earned them a great many curious stares. Safaya and Ciroy, who were, as usual, also holding hands, got a few strange looks as well, though many of the people in the city seemed to know them—by reputation at least, if not personally.

One pair of watching eyes, however, was decidedly unfriendly. After one last glance, its owner quickly made his way to a nearby alley, running down it as fast as he could. He took every shortcut he knew to reach his destination, but even then, he knew time would be short.

Slipping into the back door of an opulent mansion, the man ran through the deserted kitchens and servants' quarters. Reaching a long staircase, he bounded upward, bursting into a large bedroom where a slightly portly Common Elf man was bound to a chair. A Human man was standing near the Elf, slowly sharpening a long, ugly knife.

"Did you get the peppers, Luso?" the Human asked. "Our friend here is getting anxious to find out what their juices feels like in open wounds."

"Barc, we've got trouble!" Luso exclaimed, ignoring the question.

The man with the knife turned to look at him. "What sort of trouble?" he asked calmly, still sharpening the knife.

"Baden Solignis is in town. He's headed this way."

The sharpening halted abruptly. There was silence for a moment, and then Barc said, "Maybe we could use him to help convince our friend here to give in, eh? Let him in, Luso."

Luso shook his head vehemently. "No, he's not alone! The Xagalliacks are with him, and another Common Elven warrior, and a Dark Elf too."

Barc frowned deeply. "The Xagalliacks? And a Dark Elf?"

"Yeah—real mean looking, with funny white eyes and armed to the teeth. I don't know if he's a sorcerer or just a warrior, but he looked dangerous!"

Barc swore under his breath and then said, "If he's a sorcerer, they could ruin everything. Get rid of them, Luso. Dress up as the butler and tell them that our fat friend isn't home and to come back tomorrow."

"But his butler was an Elf, not a Human!" protested Luso. "What if Solignis remembers?"

"Tell him the old butler died or something, and you're the replacement. Get going!"

Luso nodded and scurried toward the door. As he was leaving, he heard Barc say, "Now, Raeif, you understand that if Solignis gives us trouble I might have to kill you. So you'd better start talking."

"Here we are," said Baden, opening the front gate of a wrought-iron fence enclosing the well-kept lawn of a large, luxurious mansion. "His name's Raeif, and if you couldn't tell he makes a fairly decent living."

"Yeah, I figured that," said Ciroy, staring up at the mansion.

Baden led them to the front door, but before he could knock, the door opened to reveal a swarthy Human man in a butler's suit. "Yes?" the Human asked.

Baden blinked. "Uh . . . hey, where's Garlin?"

"I'm afraid Garlin met with an unfortunate accident not long ago and was killed," the man replied. "I am the new butler. Can I help you?"

"Garlin's dead? Wow, that's a shame. What happened?"

"He fell from a ladder and broke his neck. Now, please, how can I help you?"

"Well, I'm Baden Solignis. I'm here to see Raeif."

"I'm sorry, but Master Raeif is not at home. He will return tomorrow; you can come back then."

Baden blinked and then said, "Oh. Uh . . . sure. Okay. See you then."

The butler nodded. "Of course, sir." And with that he closed the door.

Baden, lost in thought, began heading back toward the outer gate. The others followed.

"Well, we ought to find a place to stay the night, I guess," said Ciroy. "I know a nice inn not far from here."

Baden closed the gate after they were all outside Raeif's property and began walking down the street. "Raeif's in trouble," he said quietly.

Vaelon glanced at him curiously. "What do you mean?"

"I mean that man wasn't really his butler. He was pretending."

Safaya gasped. "Are you sure? How do you know?"

"For one, that suit was Garlin's. That Human didn't fit it quite right, and there's no way on earth Raeif would allow his butler to wear a suit that didn't fit. Besides, Garlin always had an emerald pin in his collar—said it brought him good luck. The pin was gone, but there was a small hole in the collar right where he always had it."

"What do you think is going on?"

"I think that Raeif is being held hostage. Probably by several men, at least. They're trying to rob his vault, but they can't open it because it's one I built for him."

"All right, so how do you know that?" asked Safaya.

"If you noticed the man's hair, there was a little bit of a fine white powder in it. The only place in that house he could have gotten that powder in his hair is right outside the vault—it's the rock the vault is dug into. He must have put his hand against the wall and then ran it through his hair."

Ciroy looked grim. "They'll be keeping him alive, then. Torturing him, most likely. And once they get what they want they'll kill him."

"We may not have much time," said Baden. "I've got a plan. Come with me."

✕ ✳ ✕

Ten minutes later, Ciroy watched as Koän climbed to an open window on the second floor on the side of the house and crept stealthily through it. Then Ciroy deftly picked the lock on the back door and he and Safaya slipped inside. There was no one in the back quarters, so they silently moved farther into the house.

Just past the kitchens was a long, dimly lit hallway lined with doors. One of those doors was guarded by a Human man who was slouched in a chair, trying to keep himself awake by carving a small block of wood. Ciroy cautiously peered around the corner and studied the situation for a moment before drawing his head back. He motioned to Safaya to wait there, and she nodded, turning her head to keep an eye out in the other direction.

Ciroy slowly drew one of his long daggers, readied himself, and then darted around the corner. He was upon the startled guard so quickly that the man had no chance to react. Ciroy grabbed him around the head, covered the man's mouth with the crook of his elbow, and gave him a solid thump on the head with the pommel of the dagger. The guard went limp, and Ciroy quietly laid him on the floor.

Safaya came around the corner to keep watch as Ciroy rifled through the guard's clothing, looking for a key to the storage room door.

"What do you suppose is in there?" Safaya asked in a whisper.

Ciroy just shrugged.

Presently he found the key and opened the door. Inside were at least a dozen people, all Common Elves and all securely bound and gagged. They were the household staff, Ciroy realized.

Safaya took a lamp from the wall and brought it into the room. Then she and Ciroy quickly went about freeing the servants.

"Just sit tight, now," Ciroy said quietly. "If you go running out, it'll blow our plan, so you're going to have to stay here."

One of them, an older gentleman, said, "You're the Xagalliacks, aren't you? I am Garlin, the butler. What are you doing here?"

"We're here with Baden Solignis," replied Ciroy. "Now tell me—what's going on?"

The old man shook his head. "I hardly know. Just this morning these men stormed in from every entrance, at least twenty of them. They took us all prisoners and locked us up in here, but I fear they may have darker plans for Master Raeif."

Safaya dragged the unconscious guard into the room, and she and Ciroy bound him hand and foot, gagged him, and laid him in the corner.

"All right," said Ciroy, "I need all of you to stay in here. That door can lock from both sides, so take this key and keep it locked until this is over. Nobody leaves—the safest place for you right now is here. Use that guard's weapons if any enemies should happen to come. Got it?"

Garlin nodded. "Understood."

"Good. We've got to go now. Stay calm and keep quiet!"

Leaving the servants in the storage room, Ciroy and Safaya headed back into the kitchens and up another hallway. They scoured the whole first floor, as well as the stairwell and hall that led to the underground vault, finding and eliminating four more guards.

Ciroy was worried. They had found only five men, which meant the bulk of their enemies were on the upper floors—the ones Koän was currently exploring alone. He hoped the Dark Elf was as good a warrior as Reiyalindis had assured them he was.

Evidently thinking the same thing, Safaya whispered, "We weren't expecting so many men. Should we help Koän?"

Ciroy shook his head. "Can't risk it. We've got to be down here in case they try to take Raeif to the vault—that was the plan. Koän seemed confident he could handle it."

"Plan or no plan, if he doesn't signal us in ten minutes I'm going up there."

Ciroy nodded. "Right."

They settled down to wait in the washing room, where they needed to be in order to get Koän's signal. Safaya sat down in one corner while Ciroy stood at the door to keep watch.

Ciroy was just beginning to think that Koän had met with too much trouble when he heard a light tapping coming down the laundry chute at the back of the room—two taps, then silence, then ten, followed shortly by three more.

With a relieved sigh, Safaya rose and tapped the chute five times. "There were ten men on the second floor," she said, "but Raeif wasn't there. He has to be on the third."

Ciroy nodded. "Along with at least five more men, possibly more. All right—let's go signal Vaelon."

They made their way to the front sitting room, which had a large window facing the street. Ciroy parted the drapes and gave three long waves.

He knew two people would see the signal: Vaelon, who was watching through a window in a library across the street, and Baden, who was watching through his telescope from the library roof. Reiyalindis was with Baden, as his position was the safest.

Once Ciroy saw Vaelon crossing the street he and Safaya quickly went to positions farther inside the house. A few seconds later, they heard Vaelon knock loudly.

✕ ✳ ✕

Upstairs, Barc halted, his dagger a hair's breadth from Raeif's finger. He scowled. "Now what? Go see who it is, Luso."

Luso nodded and hurried to the window, parting the drapes slightly and looking down toward the front door. "Barc, it's that Common Elf who was with Solignis."

His frown deepening, Barc said, "Now what could he want? He's alone?"

"Yeah."

Barc sheathed his dagger and went to the window to peer down. "Go get rid of him," he growled. "And be careful. If he suspects you're up to something, he'll get his friends and come back."

"Right." Luso said as he hurried out of the room.

Barc stayed at the window, peering through the drapes, to see what happened. When the door opened, Luso and the Common Elf spoke for a moment—and then the Elf lunged into the house.

With a loud oath, Barc turned to go alert his men, but he froze when he saw Raeif's chair. The pudgy merchant was no longer there, and the ropes that had bound him were lying on the floor. "What the . . . !"

Abruptly a white-eyed Dark Elf appeared in the doorway, a bloody sword in his hand. Barc took a step back as the Dark Elf grimly advanced, his eyes darting frantically around for a way to escape. The two other doors in the room were dead ends, one leading into a closet and the other to a bath. The only other way out was the window, which was a three-story drop to the ground.

Deciding the window was worth the risk, Barc whirled and leaped through it. He felt a sickening lurch in his stomach as he fell, but fortunately for him, his fall was broken by the tall shrubs growing around the house. Pain shot through his body as he felt his arm snap. Blood was running into his eyes from cuts made by the broken glass, but despite all that, he scrambled from the shrubs with surprising speed.

✘ ✴ ✘

Through his telescope, Baden observed the man's leap through the third-story window. Baden had anticipated such an attempt, and even as the man pulled free of the shrubs, a crossbow bolt passed completely through his head.

"Whoops," said Baden.

"What?" asked Reiyalindis.

"Uh . . . well, I meant to hit his leg. He was moving too much for an accurate shot."

"What did you hit?"

"Well . . . let's just say he won't be holding anyone hostage again."

She gasped. "You killed him?"

"Well, it's not like he didn't have it coming," Baden said defensively. "Besides, it's not my fault he slipped like that right after I pulled the trigger! These bolts move fast, but that's quite a distance, you know." He looked down at the street below. Some of the people there were running in panic while others were crowding closer to the mansion's fence, trying to get a look at the body. "Morons," he muttered.

Reiyalindis stood up. "Let's go. I want to make sure Koän's all right."

The next thing Baden heard was a small squeak of fright from Reiyalindis. Baden raised his head from his crossbow and turned sharply toward her. A man was gripping the little girl's neck with one hand, his other hand held over her mouth to keep her quiet. "Drop the crossbow," he grated.

Baden slowly put the crossbow on the roof and then raised his hands. "All right," he said. "Fine. What do you want?"

"Thanks to you and your friends," the man growled, "I'm going to have to take more drastic measures. Leave all of Raeif's erythin poison in a crate in the alley behind his house by sundown, or you'll never see this girl again—not alive, anyway."

"Erythin?" Baden asked, trying to get the man to reveal more about himself. "Is that what your men were after?" As he spoke Baden was taking in every detail he could. He judged from the way he was holding Reiyalindis that the man was left-handed, and he was unusually tall for a Common Elf. There was also a large burn scar on the side of his neck.

"Sundown," growled the man. "If we get the poison, we'll let her go. Don't follow me down from this roof, either, or I'll kill her." His eyes were cold and hard, and Baden knew he meant it. The next moment the man was gone, dragging a terrified Reiyalindis with him.

FIVE

$\mathbf{B}$aden waited for a couple of minutes and then hurried back down into the library and ran across to Raeif's mansion. He met Vaelon in front of the house. "I thought you wanted to question him," Vaelon said, indicating the dead man on the lawn.

"Vaelon, we've got trouble," said Baden.

Vaelon looked at him sharply. "Where's Reiyalindis?"

"That's the trouble. She's been taken."

"What!"

"I'll explain later. Right now we've got to find out who took her."

The two men hurried inside. In the front room they met Raeif, who was grinning broadly. "Baden, old friend, when I heard you were coming here, I knew I was either as good as free or as good as dead. I knew you wouldn't buy that butler story for a moment."

Baden skipped the pleasantries. "They were working for someone else. Do you know who?"

"No—they only referred to him as 'the boss.'"

"Well, let's talk to your new butler about that." Baden looked past Raeif, where the terrified captive was tied to a chair.

Raeif nodded. "His name's Luso."

Moving into the room, Baden pulled up another chair facing Luso. "I'm not going to tell you anything," Luso blurted. "He'll kill me if I talk!"

Baden's expression was cold. "Who will?"

"Don't try to trick me!"

"I'm not trying to trick you. I'm just going to give you fair warning that not talking could be far worse than dying. Your buddy has taken Reiyalindis, and I'll make you wish you were dead if you don't help me get her back!"

"Don't bother with threats, either! I know you honest types—you wouldn't really torture anyone."

Baden sat back, staring at him. After a moment he said, "You're right, I wouldn't—but unfortunately for you, I can't say the same for Koän. Vaelon, would you mind getting him for me?"

Vaelon nodded. "My pleasure." He disappeared up the stairs.

"Koän is a Dark Elf," said Baden. "Kind of a grumpy one too. He's the one who killed all ten men on the second floor."

Luso's eyes bulged a little at that, but he remained silent. Presently Vaelon returned with Koän.

"Koän," said Baden, "I'm afraid I have bad news. Reiyalindis has been kidnapped."

Koän's white eyes narrowed, and his face immediately became murderously angry. Baden went on. "We need this fellow to tell me who he's working for, so we can get her back—but he's being stubborn. Would you mind loosening his tongue?"

Koän slowly approached Luso, fixing him with a hard, unblinking stare. Luso fidgeted apprehensively. Koän drew a long dagger and grabbed Luso by the hair, bending his head backwards. Then he placed the tip of the dagger against the hollow of Luso's throat and began slowly pressing it downward.

"I assure you, friend," Baden said in a hard voice, "Koän would be only too happy to kill you, and we left a couple of your buddies alive for questioning in case you proved too stubborn. We have absolutely no need to keep you alive. Think about that—but not too long."

By then the dagger was drawing blood, and Luso cried, "All right, all right! I'll tell you!"

Koän eased up the pressure and lifted the man's head a little, but did not release him. "Good," said Baden. "Who are you working for?"

"My boss is Barc," said Luso.

"Barc is dead. We want to know who his boss is."

"Look, I . . . I don't know!"

"Yes, you do," said Baden. "I know you do."

"I don't, I swear!"

Koän jerked Luso's head back again and began pressing harder.

Luso screamed, "All right! We were hired by a nobleman—Earl Gawourab!"

"Gawourab!" gasped Raeif.

Baden leaned closer to Luso. "Reiyalindis was taken by a man with a scar on his neck—he was left-handed and was tall and lean. I've seen Gawourab, and it wasn't him."

"That was probably Roagin, Gawourab's bodyguard," stammered Luso. He licked his lips nervously. "Look . . . don't turn me over to the law, okay? If I end up in jail, I'm a dead man—Roagin's a killer to the bone!"

"Well, you should have chosen a better profession," said Baden.

"Speaking of the law," said Raeif, looking out the front window, "here come some city peacekeepers."

Baden nodded, rising from his chair. "Well, Luso, your new landlords are here."

While the peacekeepers were hauling away the would-be robbers, both dead and alive, Baden and the others gathered in Raeif's study. "We need to find Reiyalindis," growled Vaelon. The thought of Reiyalindis being kidnapped and held captive was obviously making his blood boil. Baden was also beside himself, though he was trying to keep a cool head, and Safaya seemed practically frantic with worry. It was hard to tell what Ciroy was thinking; he kept a calm front, but an occasional twitching in his jaw and the tightness of his grip on the hilt of his sword betrayed his anxiousness.

"I know," Baden said. "I know. But we can't just rush over to Gawourab's house and break down the door—they'll kill Reiyalindis if we show our faces anywhere near that place. Raeif, can you think of any reason Gawourab would be so desperate to get his hands on erythin?"

Raeif thought for a minute and then said, "Well, he doesn't strike me as an honest man, but I really never thought he'd murder anyone. And why so particular about erythin? Arsenic kills too, and it's a lot easier to get your hands on."

"There's got to be a reason he'd want a poison that kills Elves but nothing else!"

Raeif and Baden sat down at the study table, thinking hard.

Safaya, though, was obviously not in the mood for thought. "We've got to do something *now*!" she exclaimed. "We don't have time to sit around!"

"Safaya, we can't do anything until we have a plan," said Baden.

"I already have a plan," said a voice that none of them had ever heard before.

All of them stared at Koän, so surprised that they were momentarily speechless. Koän leaned over the table, staring hard at Raeif. "Tell me where to find this man."

Raeif hesitated, and Baden, finding his voice, said, "Uh . . . look, Koän, we can't just run in and kill him, you know."

Koän ignored Baden and continued to stare at Raeif. The pudgy merchant fidgeted a bit, and then said, "He has a big mansion near the center of the city. Just follow the street out front, and when you reach the grand square, look for the mansion with two giant lion statues on either side of the main gate. It's on the south side of the square."

Koän nodded, straightening. "Stay here. All of you." With that he turned and started to leave.

"Koän, wait!" Safaya exclaimed. "It would be better if we all helped! What if you fail?"

He paused but did not turn around. "I won't," he said. Then he was out the door and gone.

They all stared after him, and after a long moment Ciroy said, "So . . . he really can talk."

"What is he doing?" Vaelon muttered. "He shouldn't do this alone!"

"We should tell the peacekeepers before they leave!" said Raeif.

Baden hesitated and then said, "No. It may be best this way. Peacekeepers—and all of us—would probably just get in his way and foul things up."

"I'm not going to just sit here while Reiyalindis is in danger!" Safaya said hotly.

"Neither am I," said Baden. "What we're going to do is come up with another plan in case Koän doesn't succeed. Now let's get to work."

They had a plan in place soon. Raeif and Baden prepared a harmless mixture that looked like erythin, and they were ready to place it outside the house. Most likely their enemies were watching the house, so they did not dare try to get into positions to follow whoever took the poison. Baden was planning to watch from a concealed spot on the roof with his telescope when the time came.

Now they were simply waiting. They were gathered in Raeif's study, all but Safaya sitting around the table. The Halfbreed could not sit still, but was pacing worriedly up and down the room. Silence had settled, unbroken for the most part. Time crawled as they all imagined what could be happening to Reiyalindis and what Koän could be doing.

Then, suddenly, the study door opened, and a short, bald Elf stumbled into the room, followed immediately by Koän. And then, to a chorus of relieved cries from everyone else in the room, Reiyalindis also entered.

Safaya ran to her, kneeling and catching the little girl in a tight embrace. "Oh, Reiyalindis, I'm so glad you're safe!" she said, her voice choked with emotion. A few tears escaped from her eyes.

Reiyalindis hugged her back, nestling her face against the Halfbreed's rich white hair. She didn't say anything, but simply smiled, closing her eyes and letting out a long, happy sigh.

Finally Safaya let go of the little Elf. Then she stood up and went to Koän, hugging him for a moment, as well. "Thank you, Koän," Safaya said. "I should never have doubted you."

Koän looked faintly surprised but just nodded.

"Well, well, look what the cat dragged in," Baden drawled, walking toward Koän's captive. "Good day to you, Earl."

"Can I hit him?" asked Ciroy, his tone perfectly calm.

Baden frowned and said, "Well . . . as long as it's not in the jaw. I kind of need him to be able to talk."

"Fine." Ciroy slammed his fist into Gawourab's stomach, and the earl dropped to the floor with a cry.

"Ciroy!" exclaimed Reiyalindis.

Baden also looked surprised. "Hey—I thought you were kidding!"

Ciroy shrugged. "Sorry." He helped the gasping Gawourab back to his feet and then patted him on the shoulder. "I just wanted to impress upon him the stupidity of kidnapping people."

"I think Koän probably did a good enough job of that. Well, let's see what he has to say for himself."

"Wait—wait a moment, I'm sorry," Reiyalindis said, "but we need to send someone back to his house, if that's possible."

"Why?" asked Baden.

"Well," said Reiyalindis, "Koän had to tie up that man's daughter while he was looking for me, and I imagine the poor girl is terrified and probably not very comfortable. It would be nice if we could make sure she's untied; I'd hate to leave her like that for any longer than necessary."

Raeif nodded. "I'll send a servant to the city peacekeepers. They'll take care of it."

"Good. There are also a dozen or so guards tied up, and some of them are hidden pretty well—oh, and some servants too—and there are six more in barrels in the wine cellar. That's where they were holding me."

Ciroy stared at her. "Koän did all that by himself?"

She nodded. "Yes, but don't worry, he only killed one person—the man who kidnapped me."

"I see," said Raeif. "I'll send someone immediately."

"In the meantime," said Baden, roughly pushing Gawourab into a chair, "I'd like to ask you a few questions."

✗ ✳ ✗

As Raeif left and Baden began his questioning, Vaelon knelt in front of Reiyalindis, examining some ugly red abrasions on her wrists. "They tied you up pretty tight, huh? We should get some salve for these—do they hurt?"

She nodded. "A little. But I'll be all right."

"Come on. We'll see if we can find something for you."

"Thank you," she said, and as he rose she took his hand. He was a little surprised at that, but didn't say anything as he led her from the room.

He had asked where Raeif kept some medical supplies. As he started tending her, he asked, "So what happened? How did Koän get you out of there?"

Reiyalindis hesitated a bit. "Well . . . Koän is not one to trifle with."

"You can say that again." He applied some healing salve to the abrasions and then gently wrapped her wrists with light bandages.

As he worked, Reiyalindis remained quiet, just watching him. But when he finished, she said, "Vaelon, why was everyone so worried about me?"

He raised an eyebrow. "Are you kidding? You were kidnapped, Reiyalindis. Did you expect us not to worry?"

"Well, it's just . . ." She hesitated and then said, "I knew Koän would, because he is my friend, and we've known each other a long time. But you and the others . . . you don't know me all that well."

"We know you well enough, Reiyalindis. You're our friend."

She smiled a little. "Am I really?"

"Of course you are. You should know that."

"I . . . had hoped. But it's nice to hear you say it." She looked away, a slight trembling of her lip betraying some deep inner emotion that she was trying desperately to control.

"Reiyalindis," he said, concerned, "is something wrong?"

A tear escaped from her eye. "You shouldn't be my friend," she whispered. "It's selfish of me to want it, but . . . but I couldn't help it. I'm sorry."

He frowned. "What are you talking about? Why is it selfish? Why shouldn't I be your friend?"

She let out a half-choked little sob, and her shoulders began shaking. "I . . . I don't want you to die," she finally managed to whisper.

Vaelon froze. "What?"

She threw her arms around him, and in a distraught voice she cried, "You've all been so kind to me—I don't want any of you to die!"

Vaelon felt himself going a little cold, and he said, "Reiyalindis . . . do you know something you're not telling us? Have you seen . . . our deaths?"

She took a deep breath to calm herself and then said, "No. No, it's nothing like that. If I saw something like that I don't know what I'd do. I'd go mad. No, it's just . . . Vaelon, I'm so worried. I'm endangering all of you; I dragged all of you into this . . . If any of you die, I will hate myself forever!"

"Stop saying that; we've been over it before. And don't worry. We can take care of ourselves."

She drew back, forcing a smile. "I know. I'm sorry I'm such a worry-wart." She softly kissed him on the cheek. "Thank you for being my friend, in spite of . . . everything."

Vaelon was not normally given to showing affection, but he felt he should do something to give her some kind of reassurance, so he awkwardly patted her head. "Well . . . let's get back to the others, okay?"

She smiled. "Okay. Thank you for taking care of me."

"Of course."

When they got back to the study, Raeif had returned, and Baden was still questioning Gawourab, who was too frightened to make any attempt at withholding information. "So the City Council was planning to strip your rank?" Baden was saying.

Gawourab nodded weakly. "They hadn't announced anything publicly, but they were planning to put it in writing and make the appeal to the queen next week. I didn't know what to do! If I lost my rank, I'd . . . I'd be a commoner! My home is Crown property granted to me by right of my title—the mansion would revert to the queen, and she would bestow it upon someone else or turn it into a public building!"

"You were planning to murder the whole City Council just to keep your home? You'd still have your money—you could have just bought another home!"

Gawourab shook his head. "That's just the thing," he said. "I could never afford a home like that. I've lost most of my fortune from gambling the past few years—I barely have enough coming in from my businesses to feed my family and pay the mansion staff."

"You could have bought a smaller house," said Ciroy.

"And live like a peasant? I couldn't bear the thought."

"All motives aside," said Baden, "why did you need erythin so badly? Any number of poisons that are much easier to get would have done the job!"

"I got the idea from one of Roagin's shadier friends," Gawourab said dully. "A brilliant idea. He'd discovered that erythin, if fed to animals, did them no harm—but made that animal's meat lethal to Elves if that animal was butchered within a certain time after consuming the poison."

"You were planning to feed the poison to animals?" Baden exclaimed.

Gawourab nodded. "Specifically some pigs that the City Council were purchasing for a banquet they plan to hold soon. Erythin in its pure form kills almost instantly, but when diluted in animal meat it can take quite some time for the symptoms to appear. Enough time to practically guarantee that all of the members of the Council would have already eaten some of it before they began dying."

Baden gasped. "Them and practically every other Elf at the banquet! You could have killed hundreds of people, Gawourab!"

The nobleman nodded despondently. "I was desperate. I wasn't thinking clearly. Roagin wanted to just sneak into their homes and kill them himself, but I thought that would be too risky—there would be too much chance of discovery. This way, their deaths would be practically untraceable. It just turned out to be harder to get the poison than I'd anticipated."

"Can I hit him again?" asked Ciroy mildly.

"No!" growled Baden. "It's my turn!" He raised his fist, and Gawourab flinched back, wincing in anticipation of the blow.

"Baden, no!" said Reiyalindis.

Baden paused, breathing heavily, and finally lowered his fist.

"You're going to be executed for this," said Raeif. "I hope you understand that, Gawourab."

The earl hung his head. "I only have one request."

"What?"

He looked back up at them, his eyes pleading. "Don't let them publish the trial publicly. I . . . I don't want my wife and daughter to find out what I was planning. At least not until after I'm dead."

Raeif shook his head. "You can ask the peacekeepers about that, but I wouldn't hold my breath if I were you." He turned to Ciroy and Koän. "They should be back soon. Let's get this piece of garbage out of my home."

The peacekeepers returned only minutes later, and they took Gawourab into custody.

One officer remained at the house to speak with them. He said, "Raeif, I'm going to need you and your friends to stay put for a while. You'll need to speak against Gawourab at his trial."

"I'll be happy to," said Raeif, "but we really shouldn't detain my friends. They have business elsewhere."

The officer glanced around at all of them and then said, "Well, as long as you'll be available, I'm sure there won't be a problem."

"Good. Thank you, sir."

"Sure."

The officer looked at Koän and said, "Did you really do all that by yourself?"

"He sure did," said Baden with a grin.

"And all in broad daylight! That's just amazing! Well, I'll be in touch with you, Raeif."

"Of course." After the officer left, Raeif sighed. "What a day! Good thing for me you happened along, Baden. I haven't had time to ask, but what brings you here?"

"Well," Baden said, "we're on a sort of . . . errand. Not something we want to get spread around, you know, just in case."

Raeif nodded. "Of course."

"Actually, we stopped by here because I need a bit of that erythin."

"Really! That's a popular item today! What do you need it for? More experiments, I assume?"

Baden nodded. "Yes. Oh, and I also need a little arsenic."

"Arsenic?" Raeif looked curious, but he didn't pry. "Certainly. I'll go fetch them both for you."

That evening Raeif fed them a sumptuous dinner, which was followed by an equally sumptuous dessert. Vaelon sat next to Reiyalindis, who had obviously never seen so much food in one place in her life. She seemed overwhelmed by the variety, and though she tried to taste a little of everything she didn't manage to try even half the dishes offered to her before she was too full to continue. The food made her drowsy, so after dinner she asked if she could go to sleep. Raeif sent a servant girl to show her to a room where she could stay, and Ciroy and Safaya went along with her.

SIX

The following day they took their leave, and Vaelon was happy to leave the city behind.

Evidently Ciroy felt the same way, for he let out a sigh of relief. "Man, it's good to be out of there," he said. "I don't really like cities to begin with, and this one's just too crowded for my taste."

"Amen to that," agreed Safaya. "But don't you worry, dear. It'll probably be a long time before we're in a city again."

"Fine by me."

"Me too," said Reiyalindis. "I've never been around so many people. It was kind of overwhelming—especially being kidnapped."

Baden glanced down at her. "Do you mind if I ask you a personal question, Reiyalindis?"

"No," she replied. "What is it?"

"If you grew up all alone in the forest, how did you learn to speak so well? And you seem to know a lot about the world, and you're polite, well mannered . . . not exactly a raised-by-wolves kind of girl, you know?"

She shrugged. "Well . . . I don't really know. I'm sure I learned to speak during the time I can't remember. And a lot of things I just . . . know. My gift teaches me a lot."

"Interesting. And you still have no idea why you ended up in the forest?"

She shook her head. "No. The forest cared for me until I found Koän. The trees gave me shelter and the animals brought me food—nuts, berries, roots . . . Bears would bring me honey sometimes, and that was always a treat. And the wolves and wildcats gave me meat."

"How did you cook it?" asked Safaya.

"I didn't."

Ciroy gagged a little. "You ate raw meat?!"

She nodded. "I didn't know any other way, until I had cooked meat at the queen's palace—" She halted abruptly, as though she realized she'd let something slip.

Baden looked at her sharply. "You've been to the queen's palace?" he asked. "When? And why?"

"I . . . I shouldn't have said that. Please don't ask about it."

Baden looked shrewd, as he always did when trying to sort something out in his mind. "It would have to have been before you met Koän; he knows how to build fires, and I don't imagine he would have let you keep eating raw meat. But I also have a hard time picturing the queen turning you back out into the forest alone."

"Baden, please," Reiyalindis said. "I know that you hate not knowing things, and I know that you're already coming up with all sorts of theories—but please, just stop. I'm sorry I said anything."

"But why?" Baden asked in an exasperated tone. "Why are you keeping these secrets from us?"

Reiyalindis closed her eyes and shook her head. "I'm sorry, Baden, but I have to. I know you don't understand, but you just have to trust me."

He sighed. "Fine. But I just want you to know that it's driving me absolutely crazy."

"I know. I'm sorry." She sighed too and stared despondently at the road as she walked.

They reached the forest as evening was beginning to fall and set up camp among the trees. The Gray Forest was aptly named; most of it was dominated by tall gray pines, and it was also filled with rough protrusions of gray stone.

To Vaelon, Reiyalindis seemed happier than she had in a long while. When they settled down, she went to a nearby tree, rested her cheek against it, and sighed contentedly. "I've missed my forest," she murmured. "It's good to be back."

"This is the forest you grew up in?" asked Safaya.

"Yes, except much farther north—almost as far north as the Ruling City."

"Really? Not many people live in the forest that far north—it's a little too close to Sanretsu territory than most folk are comfortable with."

"I know."

"Didn't it make you nervous?" asked Vaelon. "That's the part of the forest my company patrolled—the Sanretsu send out foraging parties regularly to gather sacrifices."

She shrugged a little. "I never met any."

"Lucky for you."

She nodded absently but didn't say anything else. Ciroy went to gather some wood, humming a little tune to himself as he went. He left as Safaya started clearing a space for a fire and Vaelon and Baden went to get a few rocks to make a fire pit.

On their way back to camp, Vaelon suddenly let out a loud gasp, dropping the rocks he was carrying and falling to one knee.

Baden, right behind him, quickly dropped his own rocks and went to him. "Hey, what's wrong?" he asked. "Are you okay?"

Vaelon gasped a few breaths, squeezing his eyes shut as pain shot through his chest. Safaya and Reiyalindis ran to him, and he waved them off. "I'm fine," he said in a strained voice. "I'm fine. Don't worry."

Reiyalindis gently touched his shoulder. "Is it bad?" she asked.

He shook his head, taking a deep breath as the pain began to subside. "No. It's passing—just a little jolt, that's all. I'm okay."

Baden grimaced. "Sanretsu magic is like poison. Nasty business. Why don't you go rest a bit?"

Shaking his head, Vaelon began picking his rocks back up. "No, I'll be fine. It's almost gone now."

"Are you sure?" Safaya asked him.

"Sure. Come on, let's get back to work." He felt uncomfortable when people fussed over him, and, wanting to avoid any more of it, he stood up and walked quickly toward the fire pit. The others followed him, obviously still worried.

Ciroy was singing to himself when he returned carrying a load of wood. He had a clear, surprisingly skilled voice, but when he noticed everyone watching him, he stopped.

"Oh—don't stop," said Reiyalindis. "I was enjoying your song. What was it?"

Ciroy shrugged. "Just a little song I picked up somewhere."

"Not just a little song," Baden disagreed. "That was a ballad written by the great bard Uchdorn Iazo four centuries ago. It's the story of a man who fell in love with a woman who was already promised—against her will—to a rich baron."

"Oh, that sounds exciting," said Reiyalindis.

"Exciting, maybe, but I doubt you'll like the ending," said Baden.

"Oh, don't spoil it for her," chided Safaya. "It's a terribly romantic song."

"The key word in that phrase being 'terribly,' " Baden said with a roll of his eyes. "I don't know why they were so fond of depressing love stories back then. I mean, what's the point of having this whole song when they just end up—"

"Stop it!" Safaya commanded. Turning to Ciroy, she said, "Why don't you sing it for us, darling?"

Ciroy shrugged. "Sure. But I only know the condensed version. The original is something like four hundred verses long."

"Four hundred sixty-seven, to be exact," Baden said. "Most modern minstrels cut it down to fifty or so."

Safaya frowned. "But how could they possibly leave out that many verses?"

"Honestly, most of them are completely peripheral."

Reiyalindis's brow wrinkled. "Completely what?"

"Sorry. It means that they're not really important. Most are just boring background stuff that doesn't really impact the story—for instance, there's one part where he took thirty stanzas to describe a meal the rich baron ate before . . . uh . . . a certain incident that Safaya wouldn't want me to give away. They really went for that stuff back then—they'd sit for hours just for one song."

"Well, I'd love to hear the short version," she said.

Ciroy nodded. "No problem. But let's eat first. I'm hungry."

After eating, Ciroy began the song. He was a very good singer, possessing an impressive range and precise control. The song was a long one, and, in Vaelon's opinion, quite boring—but Reiyalindis seemed to be entranced by it, and Safaya was staring at Ciroy with a dreamy look in her eyes that made her look like a teenage girl with an incurable infatuation.

Baden was right about the ending, though—the young man ended up being executed by the rich baron, and the young lady was so heartbroken that she quite melodramatically threw herself from the tallest tower in the baron's keep. Vaelon and Baden both had to stifle chuckles, but Safaya actually had tears shining in her eyes by the time the song ended.

Reiyalindis looked very sad, so much so that Vaelon quickly lost his humor when he looked at her. "That's terrible," the little girl said softly. "Those poor people—it must have been awful."

Ciroy blinked. "Uh . . . Reiyalindis, it wasn't real."

Her brow wrinkling, she said, "What?"

"It was just a story that the bard made up. It didn't really happen."

Reiyalindis looked thoroughly taken aback. "It . . . it was just a story? But . . . if he was making it up, why did he give it such an awful ending? Why couldn't he just let them be happy?"

"Good question," Baden said. "I've wondered that myself. It seems that most of the so-called 'classic' stories have depressing endings; if it ends happily, the people who decide what is and is not 'good' literature don't like it."

Reiyalindis's eyes were wide and full of pain. "But . . . why? Why would they want stories to end like that? It's so cruel!"

"Well, it was romantic, though," said Safaya. "I mean, he chose to die rather than give up his love for her."

"Romantic? Would you think it was romantic if Ciroy had died trying to win you? Wouldn't it be so much more romantic if they had been able to be together and live happily?"

"Um . . . Reiyalindis," said Ciroy, "don't you think you're taking this a little too seriously? It's just a story."

Her cheeks began to turn red, and she looked down at the ground. "I'm sorry. I just can't understand why such misery would be considered superior to a happy story. There's so much sadness in the world already, so why add more? I still have a lot to learn, I guess."

"Well," declared Baden, "I, for one, agree with you. I hate unhappy endings. Iazo was rather fond of them, though. He wrote nearly two hundred songs and plays, and all but twelve were tragedies."

Vaelon tossed a stick into the fire. "Did he really take thirty stanzas to describe one meal?"

Baden nodded. "Oh, yes. And another eight describing the girl's agony of soul as she climbed to the top of the tower—which is mercifully omitted from most modern tellings."

"How is it you know so much about this particular song?" asked Safaya. "If you hate it so much, why spend so much time studying it and counting up how many stanzas he took to write whatever?"

Baden grimaced. "I didn't study it. I made the mistake of reading it once."

"You read it once and remember all that?"

"More than that, I'm afraid. It's a curse at times, this memory of mine."

Safaya's eyes narrowed. "Just how much do you remember?"

With a sigh he said, "Would you like me to recite all four hundred sixty-seven stanzas for you? I doubt you'll like it as much as Ciroy's version."

"You have it memorized? From reading it once?"

"I'm afraid so. Actually, I could recite every book I've ever read from memory; I never forget anything I read. I remember other stuff pretty well, but not like things I read. It's almost like the words are burned permanently into my memory when I see them written."

Ciroy was staring incredulously. "How do you fit all that in your head?" he demanded. "That's impossible! Is it some kind of magic you have?"

He shrugged. "Could be. I don't know."

"You're just . . . unnatural."

"I'll take that as a compliment."

Vaelon looked over at Reiyalindis as she let out a long sigh, only halfway paying attention to what was going on around her.

Ciroy noticed too and said, "Hey, kid, if that song got you down, would you like to hear another one? I know a few funny songs."

Reiyalindis brightened. "Oh, yes, thank you. That would be wonderful."

Vaelon watched Reiyalindis as Ciroy launched into a bizarre ditty about a talking cow. He was surprised at how sad the first song had made her. Even though it was just a story, it had seemed to hit her as though it had been real, personal. She was remarkably sensitive in many respects. It was sad to think of such a young person burdened with so many worries. She should be out playing games with other children, not organizing quests against the Ghost People.

Ciroy's silly tune seemed to cheer her up, though, and soon she was smiling and giggling, her momentary sadness forgotten. Afterward, as things quieted down, Reiyalindis curled up on the ground, staring at the fire. Koän carefully laid a blanket over her, and she murmured a quiet thanks to him and pulled it tightly around her shoulders. She was asleep in a few moments, and the others soon followed suit, except for Ciroy, who took the first watch.

When it came time for Vaelon's turn at watch, Ciroy shook him

71

awake. Vaelon, yawned, stood up, and moved to the edge of camp while Ciroy carefully slid under Safaya's blanket. Still asleep, she automatically snuggled close to him, laying her arm across his chest and nestling her head on his shoulder.

The camp was quiet. Even Koän was asleep. As Vaelon stared around at the darkness, just thinking, a brief throb in his chest turned his thoughts again to his battle with the Sanretsu. He grimaced, trying not to think about it, but the memories ran through his head like some macabre parade.

He remembered the cowardly betrayal of his friend and the bloody fight that followed. In his mind, Vaelon could still hear the pain-ridden scream as his friend was caught by a snakelike tendril of some dark power, could still picture with perfect clarity how the man had been torn limb from limb. Vaelon wasn't sure how he had managed to survive the battle himself; he had been surrounded by four Sanretsu warlocks, a death sentence for even a skilled High Elven sorcerer. Yet somehow he had managed to kill all four, despite the blood loss, the broken bones, the torn flesh—but those injuries had been nothing next to the terrible pain of that final burst of dark power from the last warlock, cast even as Vaelon had run him through. He could not remember anything after that except for the pain, which had tortured him even in unconsciousness. He had awakened in the queen's palace a week later. Somehow the other men of his company had managed to keep him alive for two days until they had found a town with a healer, who had mended his battered body before declaring that the last injury was beyond his ability to heal. He had then been taken to the queen herself, the most skilled healer in the kingdom—but even she could not fully erase the effects of Daaku Chikara.

And now they were heading straight toward Sanretsu territory. They would not be entering it, but they would have to go close enough to it to run the risk of being discovered by their foraging parties. Vaelon took a deep breath, trying to clear the smell of blood his mind was conjuring up in his nostrils.

✗ ✳ ✗

When morning finally came, they headed deeper into the forest. They were very close to the part of the forest claimed by the Halfbreeds, and Safaya was excited to be back home again. "I wish we had time to pop in and say hello to my folks," she said as they walked. "Their village is probably too far out of the way, though."

"So . . . are your parents okay with Ciroy?" asked Baden.

Safaya laughed. "Oh, yes, they love him to death. At first they were furious, but once they got to know him, they really started to like him. Now he and my father sit around the fire swapping outrageous stories like a couple of senile old codgers."

"What about your parents, Ciroy?" asked Reiyalindis. "What do they think of Safaya?"

Ciroy shrugged easily. "Oh, they don't exactly take a huge interest in my life. Fact is, they couldn't care less whether I live or die. I haven't seen or spoken to them since before I ever met Safaya."

"Oh. I'm sorry, I didn't mean to . . . Sorry."

"Don't worry about it." He looked at her with a slight smile. "You want to know about it, don't you?"

She flushed a deep red. "Oh—I don't want to pry, Ciroy."

"It's okay, I don't mind." He shook his head. "I just never got along with them, that's all. They poured everything they had into my older brother—proud as can be of him, they always were. He went into business, like my dad, and turned out to be a well off, respectable pillar of the community.

"Me, I was always just a big disappointment to them. I didn't want to spend my life running a business, didn't want to go to some big university and get all smart . . . Yeah, if they found out I married a Halfbreed, their spleens would burst on the spot. Anyway, me and my brother are still good pals, and he lets me know how the folks are doing. He doesn't tell them anything about me, though. He says it always just starts big arguments when he even mentions my name to them."

"Surely they've heard about you, though," Baden said. "I mean, you and Safaya are pretty well known."

"Not in that part of the country," he said with a slight grin. "They live way up north in a tiny village, about two day's travel from the Ruling City, where my brother lives. They never get news about anything up there; that's part of the reason I decided to come down here. Dad always said he'd hunt me down and lock me up in an asylum if I ever became a fighting man."

"Wow," said Reiyalindis. "I thought it was hard to never know my parents, but I imagine it must be worse to know that they're alive but want nothing to do with you."

Ciroy nodded. "It wasn't easy at first, but I've sort of gotten used to it."

Safaya knew by his tone, however, that he had deeper feelings about it than he was letting on.

Baden had a chance to carry out his experiments sooner than they were expecting. Three days into the forest, just as they had started crossing a narrow meadow, they were attacked. Ghost People appeared with such startling suddenness that Vaelon barely had time to realize what was happening before he saw an ugly sword heading straight for his head. Pure reflexes kicked in, and Vaelon whirled aside, his sword flashing from its sheath and shearing the Ghost Man in front of him completely in half.

Instantly the meadow became a battlefield. Safaya, acting quickly, grabbed Reiyalindis and threw the little girl into the protective shadows of the trees, narrowly avoiding the swing of a Ghost Man's axe. Koän immediately slammed into the Ghost People nearest him, a sword in each hand, and within seconds three of them were down. Ciroy didn't quite have time to draw his sword, so he simply sidestepped a blow directed at him and then knocked his attacker flat on his back with a vicious punch.

Baden was also a little slow drawing his sword and he fell back as two Ghost People charged him. But Vaelon intercepted them and killed both within a split second before running back to face the others. He was amazed at the deadly efficiency of the sword Baden had given him; it sliced through armor and bone with ease, despite its being light as a feather. Battle instinct took over, and Vaelon whirled and dodged among the Ghost People, leaving a trail of bodies behind him.

"Leave some of them alive!" he heard Baden shouting behind him. He didn't like taking the risk of capturing them alive while his friends were in danger, but he also knew that Baden's experiments could be very important.

Fortunately there weren't many of the Ghost People left, and soon they were all dead—all but three, who were being held tightly by Ciroy, Vaelon, and Koän.

Baden dropped his pack and rifled through it, producing the two bottles of poison. "Quickly, we may not have much time," he said, handing one bottle to Safaya. "This is the arsenic. Hurry, and be careful with it!"

Safaya quickly took the bottle to the Ghost Man that Vaelon was holding and forced the poisonous solution down his throat. At the same time, Baden forced the second Ghost Man to drink the erythin. "Ciroy, drag that one into the shadows, I want to see what happens!" he said.

Ciroy obeyed, and Baden tried to watch all three Ghost People at the same time. The one who drank the arsenic was dead within a few moments, but the one who drank the erythin showed no signs of being affected. Whatever they were, Ghost People did not share the Elven susceptibility to that poison.

When Ciroy dragged his Ghost Man into the shadows, a most peculiar thing happened—nothing. The Ghost Man became visibly angry, but nothing that Vaelon had been expecting occurred. The Ghost Man didn't vanish, didn't die, didn't do anything but struggle harder. Baden stared, nonplussed, and finally said, "Keep him there for a while, and we'll see what happens."

Not long afterward, however, the captive Ghost Man vanished, along with all traces of the dead ones. Baden let out a frustrated growl, and for a moment they all just stood there, staring at where the Ghost People had been. "Well," said Baden finally, "there goes the direct sunlight theory."

"At least we know that erythin doesn't kill them, but arsenic does," said Ciroy. "Though I'm not sure what that means."

"Well, it doesn't mean much of anything." Baden tapped his chin thoughtfully. "But the one you dragged into the shadows—I just don't get it! If it doesn't harm them, why do they avoid shade so adamantly? And did you notice how angry he got?"

"Maybe they just don't like being in shadow," said Safaya. "Maybe the sun does provide them some kind of boost, even if it's not necessary to keep them alive. I mean, if the sun is what gives them life, why would they ever disappear at all?"

Ciroy nodded thoughtfully. "Yes, I've asked myself that before, as well. Why not just stay as long as the sun is up? And the other question is, if their energy does come from sunlight, shouldn't it still reach them even if they're in shadow? There's still light in shadow."

"Yes," said Baden, "but there should still be some sort of detrimental effect, don't you think? Perhaps it's not sunlight that's giving them power at all—maybe there's something else, something in the sunlight. Something that isn't always there—something that can pass through things light itself can't, or simply fills the entire area without having to have a direct path to it."

"Like what?" asked Ciroy.

Baden frowned. "I don't know," he said. "But it must be something we can't see. Blast, this didn't turn out the way I had hoped." With a sigh he said, "Oh, well. Experiments rarely bear fruit at first—we just have to keep trying."

✘ ✳ ✘

Torches ringed the large room and their orange flames glinted in a pair of equally orange eyes as they slowly opened, staring toward a grotesque mural but not seeing it. "So," said a low, hissing voice, "he still lives."

"My lord?" asked the heavily robed attendant standing nearby.

Slowly rising from his kneeling position before the mural, the orange-eyed man turned to face him, his pupils flattening into narrow horizontal slits as they always did when he was angry. "He was supposed to be dead. How is it he is still alive?"

"Who, my lord?" the attendant asked diffidently.

"He who is prophesied to challenge me. The one called the Paladin in the arcane writings. Why does he still live?"

The attendant took a hasty step backward. "My lord, it is not possible—you saw through your servant's own eyes the final blow he struck to the Paladin, even as he died! A blow no one could survive—you saw him fall, you saw the dark magic poison his body!"

"I did. But he still lives. This man is a threat to me so long as he lives—the very fact he is still alive is testament to his power!"

"But, my lord, the prophecy only says he will challenge you—it does not say who will win."

"I would prefer not to find that out," he said flatly. "Send forth the seven Dokujin."

The attendant bowed. "Yes, dread lord. Where shall I send them?"

"Everywhere. I cannot determine his location—there is some force with him, some kind of magic that does not allow me to discover his whereabouts. I only know that he is drawing near to our lands, and he is not alone. I want every Thræll in the kingdom searching the Gray Forest from top to bottom!"

"Yes, Daaku Shukun."

SEVEN

Squinting up at the light beginning to show on the horizon, Baden stretched and turned from where he had been keeping watch. "Up and at 'em," he said loudly. "It's almost dawn."

Reiyalindis sat up, pulling her blanket more tightly around her shoulders and shivering a little. "It's kind of cold this morning," she said.

"A little," Baden agreed. Two days had passed since the Ghost People's attack, and the weather had taken a gloomy turn.

As Ciroy stirred the fire back to life, he said, "We're starting to get into unfamiliar territory now. Safaya and I haven't been this far into the forest before."

"Things ought to get interesting from here on out, then," said Baden lightly. He prodded Vaelon with his foot. "Come on, sleepyhead."

Vaelon stirred faintly and then his eyes flickered open. Baden noticed he was shivering a little, and his skin was pale and beaded with sweat. Vaelon gritted his teeth as he sat up, and immediately Reiyalindis asked, "Vaelon, are you all right?"

"Fine," he replied, gingerly easing back to sit against a tree.

"You don't look fine," said Safaya.

"Look," he said, "this kind of thing happens to me now and then, okay? I appreciate the concern, but honestly I'd prefer that it just be accepted as a matter of course."

Ciroy grinned. "Fine. Next time you wake up screaming, I'll just roll over and go back to sleep."

"I've only done that once."

Reiyalindis softly touched the tip of her finger to his injury. "I'm sorry," she said quietly. "I can't help but worry. I'll try to be a little less obvious about it, though."

"So does anyone know how much farther we've got to go?" asked Baden.

"Quite a ways," replied Reiyalindis, "but I'm afraid I don't know exactly."

"Neither do I," said Safaya. "From what I know it'll take a good two weeks or longer to reach the foothills of the Great Shield, and from there, who knows?"

✖ ✷ ✖

By the time the sun was up, they were on their way again. They were entering a much more dense part of the forest. The pines were giving way to close-growing aspens, and much of the ground was choked with brush and deadwood. Gnarled scrub oak lay in thick tangles throughout the trees, sometimes barely allowing the path to wind through.

The morning chill subsided quickly, and to Reiyalindis's relief the sky soon cleared as well, letting plenty of sunshine filter down through the trees. All in all, it was a more cheerful scene than they had experienced in a while. But the pleasant atmosphere was lost on Koän. Reiyalindis noticed him becoming increasingly wary, glancing around them frequently with narrow eyes and an uneasy frown. "Koän," she said quietly, "is something wrong?"

He glanced at her briefly before looking away again and then he gave a short nod.

Reiyalindis felt a nervous quickening in her pulse. "Vaelon," she said, "Koän says there's something wrong."

Vaelon stopped and looked back at her. "Wrong?" he asked. "What do you mean?"

Reiyalindis glanced at Koän. He hesitated, looking around again. "We are being watched," he said tersely.

Vaelon put his hand on his sword hilt. "You're sure? By whom?"

Koän shrugged a little with a shake of his head.

Vaelon looked up the trail they were following. The terrain was becoming more and more rugged. "All right. Let's keep moving. Head to the top of that hill; we might be able to see better from up there."

They went quickly, Vaelon leading and Koän bringing up the rear.

They made it to the hill without challenge and climbed to the top. It was dotted with tough brush and grasses, but had relatively few trees to block their view. Reiyalindis stopped next to Baden, who dropped his pack, drew a telescope from it, and began sweeping the forest below.

It wasn't long before he let out a low exclamation. "What on earth . . . ?" he muttered, staring through the telescope. "What are those doing here?"

"What?" Vaelon asked. "What are they?"

"Well, I could be wrong, but . . ." Baden stopped as Koän took the telescope from him and looked through it himself in the direction Baden had been looking.

It took him only a moment to see what Baden had, and he scowled deeply. "Thræll," he said.

All of them recognized the name. Thræll were servants of the Sanretsu; beyond that, though, little was known about them. They were fierce fighters, but more alarming than that was the fact that they were always commanded by warlocks. "How is that possible?" Vaelon said, mostly to himself. "We're not even close to Sanretsu territory yet! They've never sent out a foraging party this far!"

"Not that we know of," said Baden grimly. "But people don't usually frequent this part of the forest."

"All right, everyone stay down. Baden, keep an eye on them and see what they do. Ciroy, Safaya, keep watch on the other side of the hill. Reiyalindis, get among those rocks there and stay hidden."

They all moved to obey him. From her position Reiyalindis could see Baden lying flat beside a large boulder and watching the Thræll through his telescope. Koän remained crouched near Reiyalindis's hiding place, and Vaelon stayed with Baden, keeping watch on their more immediate surroundings.

✕ ✳ ✕

"They're heading right for us," Baden said finally.

"Can you tell how many there are?" asked Vaelon.

"It's hard to say with all the trees; I can only catch glimpses of them now and then. But at least a dozen, probably more. No signs of any warlocks so far."

"They're here, all right. Thræll aren't intelligent enough to act on their own."

Safaya appeared, running in a low crouch. "Vaelon!" she hissed. "There are more on the other side of the hill—they're spreading out around the base."

"Great," muttered Vaelon. "They're surrounding us."

"Should we make a break for it while we still can?" asked Baden.

Vaelon shook his head. "No. Running would just be an invitation for the warlocks to hit us from behind."

The little group on the hill waited tensely as the Thræll continued to surround them. Soon the hill was completely ringed, a full two dozen of the ugly beasts standing evenly spaced around it. Thræll were unpleasant-looking creatures. They looked vaguely Elven but also appeared to be made out of something closer to clay and gnarled sticks than flesh and bone. Vaelon knew from personal experience that they bled and died like any other creature, but there was still something disturbingly unnatural about them.

Though there were no warlocks to be seen, Vaelon didn't doubt they were out there. Warlocks were necessary keys in holding the Thræll together. He didn't know exactly how it worked, but it was plain that the Thræll were somehow connected to their commanding warlocks' minds. If the warlocks died, the Thræll seemed to forget their purpose, striking out at any enemies near them or simply wandering away if left alone.

Vaelon gathered his friends close to him to discuss their options. "What are they waiting for?" muttered Safaya.

"Night," replied Vaelon.

"But that's hours and hours away!"

"Psychological warfare," Baden remarked drily. "We'll sit up here all tense and worried for hours on end—by the time they attack we'll be tired and on edge."

"Well, we're not going to let them get us all worked up," Vaelon said. "We're going to stay calm, and we're going to get plenty of rest. When they attack, we'll be fresh and ready for it." A plan had been formulating in his mind, and he quickly explained it to the others. "See that gully that cuts down the south side of the hill? The Thræll probably won't climb it, because it's much rougher going than just climbing the hill. Once the attack comes, I want Ciroy and Safaya to take Reiyalindis out of here down that gully."

"What?" asked Ciroy. "And leave just three of you to hold off all of those monsters?"

"Yes," Vaelon said. "And once the confusion atop the hill sets in, I want

Baden to follow. Once you're well away, Koän and I will try to lead them a different direction."

"Vaelon, that's suicide!" Ciroy exploded. At the same time, both Safaya and Reiyalindis also began to protest.

"Look," Vaelon said in a firm voice, cutting them off, "this isn't about making some heroic last stand, all right? This is about getting as many of us through this alive as possible, and that means leaving behind those who will be best able to hold off the Sanretsu—me and Koän—long enough for the rest of you to get away. I need Baden to stay and help add to the confusion, and then he'll be gone too. That's it. No arguments."

"Vaelon, you can't!" Reiyalindis said, tears standing in her eyes.

"Reiyalindis," he said gently, "you said I was the leader. I'm leading, and I need you to obey. You have to trust me. Losing two of us is better than losing all of us."

Her mouth worked up and down a few times in helpless silence, and she looked anxiously at Koän. He simply nodded, and she seemed to wilt, her eyes looking hopelessly lost. "You'll be okay," she said, her voice a little numb. "You'll both be okay. You have to be."

"And in case they don't wait for darkness to attack?" asked Baden.

Vaelon sighed. "Then there will be no chance to escape undetected, and splitting up will only make us easier to pick off. If it's still light when they attack, the only thing we can do is meet them and do our best."

"And the warlocks?"

"It's hard to say. Let's hope they're too interested in the battle to notice anyone escaping. With a group of Thrǽll this small there's probably only one warlock controlling them, but you never know."

✘ ✳ ✘

The waiting was the worst part, as the Sanretsu were probably assuming it would be. It was strange, Reiyalindis reflected; she was dreading the impending battle, but at the same time, the minutes seemed to be passing painfully slowly. She tried not to think about what was coming, but it was useless—she couldn't keep her mind on anything else. It seemed somehow unreal. Their quest had really only begun, and yet here they were, faced with destruction at the hands of a foe their mission hadn't even been concerned with. It just didn't seem like it was supposed to happen this way.

When the light finally began fading, she, Ciroy, and Safaya surreptitiously positioned themselves as close to the mouth of the ravine as they could. It looked like a spring had once flowed from the top of the hill, but if indeed that was what had created the ravine, it had long since dried up.

The darkness continued to deepen until finally the sky was pitch black. The moon cast some light over the landscape, but the ravine was filled with deep shadow that would hopefully hide them from the Thræll. Ciroy, Safaya, and Reiyalindis quietly crept into the gorge, hugging the shadows to avoid detection. Once inside they began to slowly descend, going as far as they dared before settling down to wait for the attack to commence.

They didn't have long to wait. Barely five minutes later they heard the rumbling sound of running feet, and they knew the Thræll were on their way up the hill. Reiyalindis pressed herself close into Safaya's reassuring arms as the pounding drew closer and closer. She held her breath as several Thræll passed by them on both sides of the ravine.

"Go," Ciroy said softly once the Thræll were safely past. Already they could hear the sounds of fighting from farther up the hill.

Reiyalindis's fear was the only thing that kept her from crying as they descended the ravine, moving as quickly as they could safely manage. Behind them, the shrill cries of wounded and dying Thræll filled the air.

The ravine opened up into a dry streambed that led into the trees, and three of them ran into the cloaking shadows of the forest. "All right," Ciroy said, "let's wait a few minutes for Baden."

"What if he doesn't come?" Reiyalindis asked quietly.

"Then we go on without him." Ciroy gripped her arm. "Be brave, little one. We're going to keep you safe."

"It's not me I'm worried about," she said softly.

Suddenly there was a crashing noise in the trees nearby, and the next instant everything was thrown into confusion. There were several shouts and a piercing shriek of pain, and then Reiyalindis was struck to the ground by something she did not see. The shouting continued, and something grabbed her and pulled her to her feet. "Run!" snapped Safaya's voice in her ear.

She ran. Safaya followed her for a ways, but then suddenly Safaya wasn't there anymore, and there were more cries somewhere off in the trees. Sobbing with terror, Reiyalindis kept running, stumbling over rocks and brush and trying not to imagine what was going on behind her.

The Thræll charge was beginning to lose momentum. Already eleven lay dead on the ground around Vaelon and Koän, who stood back to back near the ravine. Even as he fought, Vaelon was trying to keep an eye out for warlocks, but what he found charging at him instead was a nightmarish black knight.

Knight may not have been the right word, but it was the first term to pop into Vaelon's head as the moonlight revealed the figure that was coming for him. It was a good six inches taller than him and was dressed in pitch-black plate armor, though Vaelon didn't see how anything wearing full plate could move that fast.

It was upon him in a heartbeat, and the furious swordplay that followed would have awed even the most seasoned swordmasters of the Elven army. The Thrǽll were suddenly gone, rushing around Vaelon to keep Koän busy.

Vaelon wasn't sure what he was fighting, but it was no warlock, and it was certainly no Thrǽll. He found himself giving ground as the strange warrior hammered him relentlessly. He was hard-pressed to defend himself. The night air was filled with the sharp sounds of metal clashing against metal, accompanied now and then by brief showers of sparks.

✗ ✳ ✗

Koän was beset by far more Thrǽll than they had anticipated would attack. He had lost sight of Vaelon and his black-armored adversary some time ago, and was now fighting with his back to a boulder near the peak of the hill, snarling as he hacked at the Thrǽll surrounding him. There were too many for him to defeat alone, and he knew it.

But then he was no longer alone. New shapes appeared in the darkness, sweeping into the Thrǽll surrounding him. Koän barely had time to recognize one of his rescuers as a Dark Elf before a Thrǽll dropped onto him from the top of the boulder, throwing him to the ground.

Koän rolled sharply, throwing the Thrǽll off of him, but from out of the melee around him, a boot struck his head, kicking it forcefully into the boulder. Koän nearly lost consciousness and he barely noticed the Dark Elves destroying the Thrǽll surrounding him, nor could he feel it when they picked him up and bore him away from the scene of the battle.

The pain in his head was so intense that he could barely think, but before he passed out entirely, he noticed something strange happening to the Thrǽll. They paused in their fighting, blinking stupidly for several moments and looking around as if confused. Those near the attacking Dark

Elves began to fight back, but they did so with far less tenacity than before. Those on the outskirts of the battle began wandering aimlessly away, their expressions dull, and their movements listless.

✘ ✳ ✘

How long Vaelon's battle with the black knight had lasted, he did not know. He wasn't even entirely certain how he had managed to win. But he found himself kneeling beside the body of his opponent and had a vague memory of his sword slicing the black knight completely in half in a desperate blow that had been both masterly and lucky.

Vaelon blinked, looking around. He was in the trees. Somehow the fight had carried him completely away from the hill. He shook his head, trying to understand why he was having such a hard time thinking and then pressed his hands against his temples. His fingers touched something wet and sticky on the right side of his head, and he drew his right hand back, staring at it.

"Oh," he said with dim comprehension. His fingers were covered with blood; he had been injured.

Carefully he tried to stand, but when he did, he lost all balance and collapsed onto his back. The old wound in his shoulder flared, and the sudden pain, combined with the blow to his head, was too much for him. The world went dark.

✘ ✳ ✘

Reiyalindis fled through the trees for what seemed like hours. Finally, though, her trembling legs could carry her no farther, and she collapsed to the ground. She lay still for a moment, breathing heavily and trying to hold back tears, before crawling to a nearby boulder and huddling against it.

She had no idea what to do now. She didn't know where her friends were or what had happened to them; she didn't even know which direction she had been running. The darkness seemed suffocating, and the normal night sounds of the forest she knew so well sounded more menacing than they ever had before. Finally she could no longer hold back the tears and she began to cry, holding her hands over her mouth in an effort to stifle the sounds.

She lay there for a long time, trying to think of what to do. Should she keep moving? Should she wait? If she did keep moving, where should she go? She desperately wished Koän were there. They had been together for so long now that she had almost managed to forget what it was like to be alone. Now, though, all of the old feelings came flooding back—the sadness, the terrible loneliness, the despair. Overwhelming fear clutched at her heart, threatening to crush it.

Abruptly she heard something coming toward her and she froze, not daring to even breath. A dark shape was passing nearby, picking its way through the darkness. She could barely see it, but it was definitely not a forest animal—it was walking upright.

Either it was one of her friends, or it was a Thræll—or a Sanretsu warlock. If she called to the shape and it was an enemy, she would die. But what if it wasn't an enemy? What if she just lay there and let a friend pass right by her, never knowing she was there?

A loud thump interrupted her quandary, and the figure paused, leaning over. "Dang!" she heard it exclaim softly.

Her heart leaped, and she stood up. "Ciroy!" she said, forcing herself not to shout it.

The figure straightened and turned toward her. "Reiyalindis?"

"Oh, Ciroy!" she sobbed, making her way blindly toward him. Soon she felt his hands grasp her, drawing her into a tight hug.

For a long moment nothing was said, but finally Ciroy released her. "Thank heaven I found you," he said. "Where's Safaya?"

"I don't know," she replied. Even though he'd loosened his grip on her, she did not follow suit, but continued to hold herself close against his chest. "She was with me, and then . . . then she was gone."

Ciroy let out a great breath of air. "Dang," he muttered, his voice betraying his fear.

"What happened?" she asked.

"There were Thræll still in the forest," Ciroy replied. "Not all of them charged up the hill. I think they were expecting us to try to get away."

"Are you all right?"

"I'm fine—just a couple of scratches is all. What about you?"

"I'm not hurt. Ciroy, we've got to find out what happened to the others! Did you ever see Baden?"

"No." Ciroy's voice was tight with worry. "Come on. We've got to find a place to hide for a while."

"But we need to find them!"

"If we go running around in the dark, all we're likely to find are Thræll."

Ciroy gently picked her up and started walking, and Reiyalindis put her arm around his neck, pressing her face against his chest again.

"I'm so afraid," she whispered after a moment.

He was silent for a second and then he said, "So am I, kid. So am I."

✗ ✳ ✗

Ciroy found a defendable jumble of boulders against a low cliff of rock, and he settled down among them, holding the little High Elven girl in his lap. She refused to let go of him, and he held her close, trying to lend her what comfort he could. He was on short supply of that, though. His wife was out there somewhere, and he had no way of knowing whether she was dead or alive. He felt his gut clenching up and he forced himself to stay calm, taking several deep breaths.

Reiyalindis reached up and softly touched his cheek. "I'm sure she's all right," she whispered, sounding like she was trying to convince herself of that as well. "She's smart. She'll be okay."

"Yeah," Ciroy said, his voice thick. "Yeah. She . . . she can take care of herself."

"I'm sorry I did this to you," she whispered, the agony in her voice so palpable that Ciroy felt his own throat choking up.

He held her a little closer, gently stroking her hair. "Don't you talk like that," he said, embarrassed at how his voice trembled. "She's gonna be okay."

"But . . . what if she's not okay? You love her, Ciroy; I know that she's the most important thing in the world to you. If you lose her . . . it will be because of me."

Ciroy squeezed his eyes shut. He and Safaya had been in danger before, but not like this. He'd always been with her before. He'd never had to sit and wait, knowing that she was in mortal danger but helpless to do anything about it. He wanted to scream, but he put an iron grip on his emotions.

"For the last time, Reiyalindis," he said in a controlled voice, "stop that talk. No matter what happens to her, or to me, or anyone else, I'm never going to blame you for it—and I don't want you to either. Understand?"

The little girl was silent for a long time, struggling with herself. Finally she mumbled, "If I were you, I would hate me. I wish you hated me."

"You wish I . . . Reiyalindis, how could you ever wish something like that?"

"I think I would feel better if you hated me. Then I wouldn't be hurting someone who loved me."

Ciroy slowly shook his head. "Well, kid, I'm afraid you're stuck. Sorry."

After a long, heavy silence, she whispered, "Thank you."

Ciroy let out a long sigh. "You're welcome, kid. Now try to sleep."

What a strange little girl she was, he reflected. So innocent and vulnerable, and at the same time so mysterious! Sooner or later the truth was going to come out, and he had a feeling that he wasn't going to like it.

✗ ✳ ✗

When Vaelon awoke, it was to a throbbing headache. He winced, touching his head, and immediately felt someone touch his shoulder. "Vaelon?" a familiar voice said.

He opened his eyes a crack. "Safaya? What . . . what happened?" He slowly sat up. Safaya moved as if to help him, but she stopped with a gasp. Vaelon noticed that her right leg was in a splint, and both of her arms and part of her midriff were wrapped with bandages. "Safaya! Are you all right?"

"I'm fine," she said, "just a little beat up. You're a little worse for wear too."

He looked down at himself, noticing for the first time the bandages wrapped around various parts of his body. Looking around, he saw that they were in some sort of camp. He was lying on a stretcher, and there were Dark Elves all around them. He noticed Koän nearby on another stretcher, apparently unconscious. "What happened? Where are the others?"

Safaya's voice was tight with worry when she answered. "Baden's around somewhere—he had a bit of a scuffle too but wasn't hurt much. Ciroy and Reiyalindis are missing."

"Missing!" he exclaimed. "How were you separated?"

"I think the Sanretsu figured we might try to slip off—we ran into an ambush. I'm not sure what happened after that. Ciroy was fighting them, and I made Reiyalindis run. The next thing I knew, I was surrounded. These Dark Elves showed up in time to save me, but there hasn't been any sign of Ciroy or Reiyalindis. They have trackers out looking for them, but . . ." She stopped, her voice faltering, and then she put her face in her hands and took a deep breath. "Vaelon, I'm scared. What if . . . what if he's dead? Or captured, being dragged off to be a sacrifice?"

Vaelon reached over and gently gripped her shoulder. "Don't you worry," he said. "Ciroy's resourceful. I'm sure he's fine, and Reiyalindis too."

"I hope so. Oh, I hope so."

"What happened to Koän?"

She finally lowered her hands. "He took a blow to the head—pretty bad. It looks like his skull's cracked. The Dark Elves said they're taking us to where there are some healers. I just hope we get there in time. What was that thing you killed, anyway? The Dark Elves said they found you lying unconscious near some kind of creature in black armor, but they had no idea what it was."

"I don't know," he admitted. "But whatever it was, it was good with a sword. I've never been so hard-pressed in my life. I thought I was dead for sure." He looked around again. "Where did these Dark Elves come from?"

She shrugged. "They don't talk much. I've gathered that they patrol this part of the forest regularly, though, and that they happened to hear the fight from where they were camped for the night."

Just then Baden appeared, smiling when he saw Vaelon. "Ah, you're awake! Good!" He sat cross-legged nearby. "We may be in a bit of a spot here."

"You think?" Safaya said a little bitterly.

"The leader of these men is on his way here to talk to you, Vaelon," continued Baden. "He wants to know what we're doing out here. I didn't tell him anything, just said he'd have to talk to you. What are we going to say?"

Vaelon shook his head. "I have no idea. There's no reasonable explanation for it, except the truth—well, and that may not be entirely reasonable, either."

"Is there really a good reason to keep all this a secret?" Safaya asked. "What could it hurt for people to know what we're doing?"

"For one," said Baden, "if they find out Alhalon the Black is still alive and that we're on our way to see him, that could raise some concerns. Second, we could risk allowing word of our mission to reach unfriendly ears."

"Like who?" she asked. "The Ghost People? Who's going to tell them?"

"If we're right about the Ghost People being created," said Baden, "then there's almost certainly someone or something doing the creating. Better safe than sorry."

Safaya blinked. "Oh. I hadn't thought about that, I guess."

There was no more time for deliberation. A hard-faced Dark Elf approached, stopping at the foot of Vaelon's litter. "I am Captain Landfic Odorei, the commander of this company," he said, folding his arms across his chest. "I was told you were the leader of your little expedition."

"That's right," Vaelon replied.

"Good. Then maybe you could tell me what such a strange group is doing so deep in the Gray Forest."

"Is there a law against being this deep in the forest?" Vaelon asked mildly. He was drawing a complete blank on a story to tell, so he decided to simply refuse to give any explanation at all.

A hint of irritation appeared in the Dark Elf's eyes. "No," he said after a moment. "But it is certainly not wise, as you have discovered."

"I must admit," said Vaelon, "that we did not expect to run into a Sanretsu foraging party this far from their territory."

"This was no foraging party," said Landfic. "There were too many for that, and there were no warlocks."

Vaelon blinked uncertainly. "There had to be warlocks—if there weren't, what was controlling the Thræll? How many were there, exactly?"

"We've counted over a hundred dead Thræll. Others may have escaped."

"There had to have been at least two warlocks, then. And what do you mean by escaped? Thræll never leave a battle unless . . ." He paused, realizing something.

Landfic was thinking the same thing. "If you ask me," he said, "their leader was that thing you killed, and once it was dead, the Thræll lost interest. We cannot find the bodies of any warlocks—it had to have been that black thing. Which makes me doubly certain that this wasn't a foraging party."

"But . . . what was it?"

"I was hoping you knew. You seem to know a lot about the Sanretsu—have you fought them before?"

"I used to be in the military," Vaelon replied, his mind still on the strange black knight. "My company patrolled the forest near Sanretsu territory up in the north."

"I see. I'm afraid I need to take all of you into custody."

Vaelon gave a start. "What? You can't do that!"

"I can. Military prerogative."

"Military prerogative to take civilians into custody only applies if there is reasonable evidence the civilians are involved in a criminal endeavor or pose a threat to the security of the kingdom," Baden said. "I hardly think a small company of travelers being set upon by Sanretsu in the Gray Forest qualifies as any such evidence."

"It does because I say it does," said Landfic. "You're all up to something, and somehow it involves the Sanretsu."

"Look, we don't have anything to do with the Sanretsu!" Vaelon protested. "I don't know why they were here! We were just in the wrong place at the wrong time!"

"Perhaps," said Landfic. "But my instincts tell me that the Sanretsu finding you here was not a coincidence. You must excuse me now. I have other matters to attend to. Do not attempt to escape."

"Wait!" exclaimed Safaya, her voice a little anxious. "Has there been any word about my husband or the little girl?"

"No," the captain replied. "We will notify you as soon as we find anything." He turned and walked away.

"Great," said Baden. "Now what? If we tell him the truth, he'll lock us up for sure."

"Maybe we should just leave out the bit about Alhalon," said Vaelon. "It may be crazy to be hunting Ghost People, but it's not likely to be viewed as a threat to the kingdom's security."

"I still doubt it would satisfy our new friend Landfic," muttered Baden. "Blasted Dark Elves! No Common or High Elven military commander would take us into custody like this!"

Vaelon sighed. "The Dark Elven military plays by its own rules, I'm afraid. They technically answer to the queen and the High Commander like the rest of us, but in reality they do their own thing, and usually it's not worth interfering with them unless they get too far out of line."

"And when that happens?" asked Safaya.

With a shrug Vaelon said, "There are a few heated debates at the palace, and a compromise is reached. The Dark Elves may have strange ways sometimes, but they seem to value the unity of the kingdom enough that they've never attempted to break away from it. Except for the Sanretsu."

When the Dark Elves began to march soon afterward, they headed south. Vaelon's injuries were too much for him to be able to walk far, and

Safaya's broken leg made it impossible for her, so they were both carried on stretchers by Dark Elven soldiers. Neither of them liked it one bit, but there was nothing they could about it—just as there was nothing to be done about being taken into custody.

✗ ✳ ✗

"Drat," muttered Ciroy. He was kneeling beside a stream, attempting to spear a fish with his sword, but so far he hadn't had much luck. Reiyalindis was sitting quietly nearby, smiling a little as she watched him.

Finally Ciroy managed to skewer a couple of fish, and he built a small fire and cooked them. "Not the best eating in the world," he said, "but they'll do."

"Thank you," said Reiyalindis. "I haven't eaten fish in a very long time."

Ciroy made a face. "Not long enough for me, I'll tell you. I hate fish."

It was the day after the attack. Ciroy was still debating with himself about what to do. *Should they head back toward the hill?* There wasn't much else to do, and the Sanretsu probably wouldn't still be there, but part of him was dreading a return. He could not shake the image of finding Safaya's lifeless body lying on the forest floor.

Not knowing what happened, though, would not change anything, and he knew it. After they were finished with their meal, they started heading back.

They moved slowly and cautiously, staying alert for anything. Ciroy took them in a roundabout direction, not wanting to go back the same way they had left. Eventually they spotted the hill through the trees ahead, and at almost the same time they spotted something else—a strange, black-armored creature lying on the ground, cut in half.

"Now, what the blazes is this?" wondered Ciroy. He crouched to examine the body. "Not Human or Elf, for sure."

The area around the body was full of footprints, and it looked as though the body had been moved a little—someone else had been examining it earlier.

Ciroy tried to remove the creature's helmet, but it wouldn't budge. "Dang," he muttered. "It's like it's fastened onto him or something."

"Whose footprints are these?" asked Reiyalindis.

"Don't know. Looks like there was quite a fight here, but I think most of these footprints came after the fight. Look here—it looks like someone

91

was lying here, and there's blood all over the place." He stood still, thinking furiously, his mind trying to piece together the evidence before him.

After a while he said, "This is just conjecture, but I think someone was fighting this thing, got hurt, but managed to kill it anyway, and then collapsed. Afterward other people came along and took him—whether alive or dead, who knows?"

"Ciroy," she said, looking back the way they had come, "there's someone coming."

Ciroy whirled, instinctively crouching low and pulling Reiyalindis down as well. "Quiet now," he whispered, edging both of them off into some thicker brush.

He soon saw that Reiyalindis was right—he spotted two Dark Elves a little way down the trail, obviously following their tracks. "Dark Elves," Reiyalindis said softly.

"Or Sanretsu," replied Ciroy. He eased his sword from its sheath. "Get back and hide."

Reiyalindis obeyed, and Ciroy waited tensely, watching as the two men approached. As they drew closer, though, he saw that they were wearing uniforms, the steel-studded black leather armor peculiar to the Dark Elven military. He remained hidden anyway, alert for a trick.

"Here's that black thing the captain was talking about," one of them said as they spotted the creature's body. "No idea what it is."

"Some kind of Sanretsu magic," the other said. He came to a stop, looking around. "The tracks are getting all confused; there are too many already here."

The first Dark Elf crouched, carefully examining the ground. "I think I can make it out—they're not far ahead of us, and the tracks are more fresh than these others."

"Is that Halfbreed woman really married to this Human?"

"That's what she said. Weird, but whatever makes them happy, I guess."

Ciroy felt relief wash through him. Safaya was alive! Deciding that these two were not Sanretsu, he stood up from his concealment. "Looking for something?" he asked casually.

Both Elves jumped. "Egads!" one blurted. "There you are! I knew you were close, but not that close!"

Looking around, the other one said, "Where's the girl? We've got orders to take you to Captain Odorei."

"She's here. Who are you?"

"I'm Private Wisol, and this is Private Teari, Third Company of Hawk Battalion," replied the first man. "Your friends are with the captain already."

"Are they all right?" Reiyalindis asked, appearing from her hiding place.

Both Dark Elves were startled when they saw her. "She's a High Elf!" Wisol exclaimed. "They didn't tell us that!"

"Are they all right?" Reiyalindis repeated. "There should be four of them."

"Well," said Teari, "they're fine except for the Dark Elf."

She gasped. "Koän! Oh, no—is . . . is he . . . dead?"

Wisol shook his head. "No, but he's got a cracked skull. He's in bad shape, but they're taking him to where there are some healers."

"If you don't mind me saying, you're a strange bunch," said Teari. "But come on, we'd better get going. Follow us."

"Wait," said Wisol. "I want to take a look at this creature." He crouched beside it. "Strange, isn't it?"

Teari also turned to look. "Yeah, but we don't have any time to waste, you know."

"Just give me a second." He rolled the bottom half of the creature to its other side.

It proved to be a bad mistake. The roll placed the creature's lower half right up against its torso, and the instant they touched there was a strange snapping sound as the two halves fused together in an instant. Wisol suddenly found the black knight's armored hands wrapped around his throat, and the creature stood, lifting him from his feet.

Ciroy and Teari both reacted immediately, drawing their weapons and lunging to Wisol's aid. Ciroy slammed into the beast, hooking his foot around its ankle and throwing it to the ground. It released Wisol, who fell to the ground, gasping for air. The creature rebounded with the quickness of a cat, springing at the charging Teari.

The fight that followed was short but ugly. Wisol regained his feet and joined the attack, but even despite the three-to-one odds they did not fare very well at first. Luckily for them the creature's sword had been taken by the Dark Elves, though even unarmed it was more than a match for all of them.

Another stroke of fortune was that the creature seemed slightly disoriented, like someone struggling from a deep sleep; otherwise it would have finished them all off in short order. It killed Wisol with a crushing blow of its fist, and then pounced on Teari, forcimg him to the ground. Ciroy darted in, stabbing with all his might, and the blade found the opening underneath the creature's helmet and drove up into its brain. It collapsed, twitching violently for a moment before going still.

Ciroy was about to pull his sword free when the creature suddenly had a violent spasm, and he jumped back, releasing the sword. The creature didn't move for several more seconds, and then it had another spasm, followed several seconds later by yet another. It was like clockwork.

"Bugger," muttered Teari, dragging himself into a sitting position against a tree. "It's trying to come back to life again."

Ciroy stared. "Dang. I'll bet you anything it would too, if I pulled that sword out."

"Cut off its head," said the Dark Elf. "It didn't come back to life until the two halves of its body were touching, did you notice?"

"Yeah, I did." Ciroy drew his machete, and with a few quick strokes chopped through the beast's neck. As soon as its head was off it remained still and silent. "Now, let's see something," he muttered. Leaving his sword still embedded in the black knight's head, he touched the two halves of the severed neck back together.

There was another snapping sound, and the head reattached itself to the body. The creature resumed its spasmodic twitching.

Teari stared at it thoughtfully. "The sword is obviously preventing it from healing itself," he said. "It looks like it can be killed like any normal creature, but its life force returns after only a few moments unless something prevents it—like your sword, or being chopped in half."

Ciroy again cut off the creature's head. "I think I'll take this along with us," he said. "The farther we get these two apart, the better."

"Good idea." Teari coughed, and blood dribbled from the corner of his mouth. "But I'm not sure I'm going anywhere. I'm busted up pretty bad."

Ciroy crouched next to him and started examining his injuries. "Broken rib or two, I think," he said, "but you look fine other than that."

"I don't feel fine."

"Don't worry, we'll get you back to your company." With Reiyalindis's help, Ciroy patched Teari up as best he could. The injured soldier could still walk, but not very well.

"I don't suppose there's any way we could bring Wisol's body," said Teari. "He was a good soldier. Didn't know him too well—this was our first assignment together—but he seemed like a decent fellow."

"Afraid not," said Ciroy. "It'll be hard enough getting you out of here. I'll cover his body with rocks and maybe some others can come back and get him later."

"Right."

Once Ciroy was finished covering Wisol, the three of them started off after the Dark Elven company. It was slow going. Ciroy looped Teari's arm over his shoulders, helping him walk, but they had to stop to let him rest often. It soon became obvious that the Dark Elven company was moving much faster than they were, but there was nothing to be done but follow.

EIGHT

"So how far is it to Gaeotici?" Baden asked the grim-faced leader of their captors. "We've been walking for three days. I don't know if Koän is going to last much longer."

"Only an hour or two more," Landfic replied. "The Hawk Battalion is stationed there, and we have an excellent healer in the barracks."

Vaelon glanced at Koän. The Dark Elf's condition had not seemed to change at all in the past three days, aside from the fact that his breathing and heartbeat were gradually getting slower and slower. Also worrisome was the continued absence of any word about Ciroy or Reiyalindis. The scouts Landfic had sent to find them had not returned, and their failure to report was obviously troubling the captain. Safaya was growing increasingly distressed, and the night before Vaelon had heard her crying, even though she had tried to hide it.

Finally the city of Gaeotici came into view. It was a fairly large city, though nowhere near the size of Valsana. It had a uniformly gray look to it. *The Dark Elves are excessively fond of gray and black*, thought Vaelon. The somber coloring, however, could be overlooked, considering its more redeeming qualities. The streets were clean, quiet, and well ordered, in sharp contrast to the chaotic bustle of Valsana and other large cities farther west.

There were a great many more Halfbreeds than there ever were in the western cities too. Humans, however, were few and far between, and Common Elves were even more scarce. While Dark Elves did not exactly discourage visits from the other Elven races, the Common and High Elves rarely found any compelling reasons to see the Dark Elven cities.

Landfic took them directly to the Hawk Battalion barracks, a huge, sprawling gray building not far inside the imposing city walls. They were all taken to a small room in the barracks infirmary, where they were met by a sour-faced old healer. He silently motioned to a few beds, and Koän, Safaya, and Vaelon were deposited on them. Baden sat in a nearby chair, watching as the healer went to work.

He started with Koän, never saying so much as a word as his magic mended the younger Dark Elf's broken skull and damaged brain. Koän was soon sleeping peacefully, and the healer moved on to Safaya. "So . . . how bad is it?" she asked tentatively.

The healer said nothing but simply began his work. Safaya gasped a few times as the magic flowed through her.

"Sorry," she said. "I've never been healed by magic before."

"Does it hurt?" Baden asked.

"No. It's just . . . startling."

When the healer was finished, he rose, and Safaya said, "Thank you, sir." He ignored her and moved on to Vaelon.

"Hey," said Baden, "you aren't related to Koän there, are you?"

The healer didn't even glance at him. Once he was finished with Vaelon he left the room, closing the door firmly behind him. They heard a bolt slide into place, and they all knew without looking that guards were posted right outside their door.

"Charming fellow," murmured Baden.

"So we're really prisoners, then?" Safaya said slowly. "I was almost hoping . . . well, I'm not sure."

Vaelon shook his head. "They'll hold us here until they're satisfied we're harmless."

"How long will that take?"

"There's no way to tell."

For several hours they sat in their little prison, simply waiting. A silent guard brought them some food and then left. "This not liking to talk seems to be a racial trait," remarked Safaya.

Vaelon shook his head. "No, I've met some fairly talkative Dark Elves. This is just how they treat prisoners."

They had just finished eating when Captain Odorei entered their cell. He stood in the doorway, looking them over. "Your friend should wake by tomorrow morning," he said. Looking at Vaelon, he said, "The healer tells me you have the poison of Daaku Chikara in your body. From the fight?"

Vaelon shook his head. "No. From my previous service in the military."

"I see. Well, night is coming, so I suggest you get some sleep. You will be brought before the Tribunal in the morning."

As he was about to leave, Safaya said, "Sir, has . . ."

"No," he replied shortly. "Still no word." Then he was gone, and the door was bolted again. Safaya took a deep, shuddering breath and then sat back against the wall on her bed, drawing her knees up to her chest and wrapping her arms around them.

Vaelon watched her for a moment; she was trembling, obviously trying to keep from crying. He could only imagine how she was feeling; there was a dark pit of fear in his own stomach as he wondered what had become of Ciroy and Reiyalindis, but it had to be so much worse for Safaya.

He slowly stood up, walking to Safaya's bed and sitting on the edge. He gently placed his hand on her shoulder. "Safaya, he's going to be all right," he said, trying to sound confident.

Suddenly, to his surprise, Safaya leaned over against him, throwing her arms around his neck and burying her face in his shoulder, sobbing like a child. "Oh, Vaelon, I'm so scared!" she said in a choked whisper. "I'm so scared! I don't know what to do!"

Vaelon was distinctly uncomfortable, but he gingerly patted her on the back. "Don't you worry," he said. "He's fine. Both of them are."

"You don't know that! How can you be so calm?"

Vaelon sighed. "All part of the whole 'leader' routine, I guess," he admitted. "Leaders can't let their fear show."

For a moment longer she cried on his shoulder and then she pulled back, wiping the tears from her eyes. "I'm acting like a baby, aren't I?" she said softly. "I guess I'm not as strong as I thought I was."

"He's your husband, Safaya," he said. "I'd be worried about you if you *weren't* scared."

"I'm sorry about that." She pointed at the tearstains on his shoulder. "I didn't mean to make you uncomfortable."

"Don't be sorry; I understand. I wasn't uncomfortable."

She laughed a little. "Yes, you were. You were stiff as a post."

"Well . . . yeah. Sorry."

She closed her eyes, letting her head rest back against the wall. "It's not until times like these when you realize how much you really love them," she said. "I'm not sure how much of this my nerves can take."

"Try to sleep." Vaelon returned to his own bed. "The less you're awake, the less time you'll spend worrying."

"I don't know," she said ruefully. "The past few nights what little sleep I've been able to get was full of nightmares."

Despite her worries, however, she fell asleep quickly; she had become exhausted over the past few days, and it overcame even her fear. Watching her as she slept, Baden remarked, "You know, I've been thinking that maybe marriage isn't so bad after all."

Vaelon glanced at him curiously. "What do you mean?"

"My parents argued a lot. I think they loved each other, but it seemed to me while I was growing up that they spent more time getting on each other's nerves than anything else. My aunts and uncles didn't seem too happy about each other, either, most of the time." His eyes grew a little distant. "Money. The arguments were usually about money. Amazing, isn't it?—the more money people have to spare, the more they argue about how to use it."

"Oh, marriage isn't bad at all," Vaelon said. "My parents are as different as fire and water, but they get along just fine."

"Well, watching Ciroy and Safaya together certainly casts it in a good light. They've been married five years and they still act like giddy lovestruck teenagers. They'll probably still be acting like that when they're old and gray." He paused, thinking, and then said, "Have you ever given any thought to marriage?"

Vaelon shook his head. "Not really. There was a girl once I kinda liked, way back when, but she didn't even know I existed. You?"

"No, not by a long shot. I've never been much of a socialite." He sighed, again looking at Safaya. "I hope Ciroy's okay, for her sake. I hope Reiyalindis is okay too, poor girl."

Vaelon nodded, staring up at the ceiling. "Yeah. Me too."

✗ ✳ ✗

In the early hours of the morning they all awoke to a rattling at the door. Vaelon looked quickly toward it and saw that Koän was there, shaking the door's latch in an attempt to open it. The door was, of course, locked, and Koän slammed his fist against it in frustration.

"Koän, you're finally awake," said Vaelon, sitting up. "How are you?"

Koän glanced at him, his expression dark. "Where is she?"

"Reiyalindis?" Vaelon shook his head helplessly. "I don't know. She and Ciroy are both missing. We've been taken captive by Dark Elves, and they sent scouts to find them, but so far there hasn't been any word."

Koän scowled fiercely and pounded on the door. "Quiet in there!" one of the guards outside grumbled irritably. "You're not getting out until you're fetched, so don't make a fuss!"

Koän stopped pounding and started examining the door. Before long, though, he seemed to realize that it was far too strong to break down. "Why are we prisoners?" he demanded, looking at Vaelon.

"Their commander took us captive because he thinks we're up to something that involves the Sanretsu," Vaelon replied. "We're supposed to appear before some kind of tribunal today."

Koän, in an uncharacteristic show of anger, gave the door a solid kick and snarled something unintelligible.

This isn't going to be pretty, Vaelon thought bleakly. Being trapped in here with no idea of what had become of Reiyalindis was probably driving Koän mad; no doubt he would try to escape at the first opportunity.

Several hours passed, and all the while Koän paced back and forth in their little prison like a caged animal. Finally, though, they heard keys rattling in the lock, and Koän immediately darted to the door, tensing himself.

"Koän . . ." Baden started to say.

It was too late. The door opened, and the instant it did Koän shot through it, knocking whoever was on the other side sprawling. There was a chorus of startled shouts and a quick scuffle, and then someone roared, "After him! Shoot him if you have to!"

"Oh, great," muttered Baden. "This could get interesting."

Several Dark Elven soldiers rushed into the room, swords drawn, and one with a crossbow stayed in the doorway, pointing it at Vaelon threateningly. "Nobody move!" barked one of the soldiers.

Baden, Vaelon, and Safaya obeyed, sitting still. Vaelon watched the crossbowman warily, not wanting to do anything to make him jumpy. The three of them were soon hustled from the room, their hands tied behind their backs and surrounded by guards.

None of them spoke as they went, not wanting to aggravate their captors any further. The search was in full swing around them, but by the time they were taken into a large council chamber the elusive Dark Elf had still not been found. There were a dozen stony-faced Dark Elves sitting behind a heavy table in the council room, and alert soldiers lined the walls. One chair at the table, however, was vacant—the one in the center. Landfic Odorei was there, standing to the side of the table.

As they were brought into the room, one of the men at the table rose, his unfriendly face fixed in a tight frown. "What is the meaning of this escape?" he barked. "It's not casting you in a very good light. A bad way to begin a questioning, if you ask me!"

"My apologies, sir," Vaelon said, trying to sound respectful, "but Koän has his own agenda. His foremost duty is to guard the girl, Reiyalindis, and when he discovered that she was missing, he went a little crazy."

His frown deepening, the Dark Elf shook his head. "We will proceed with the questioning. When your friend is caught, he will join us. Hopefully, for his sake, he does not force my men to kill him." He straightened a little and said, "The leader of the Third Division, General Wanship Kamas, is on his way from a meeting in another part of the city. Until he arrives, I will conduct this interrogation. I am Major General Borkna, but you will address me as 'Sir.' Understood?"

"Yes, sir," Vaelon said automatically.

"Good. Now, let's see if we can get this done the easy way. Tell me why you were so deep in the Gray Forest."

"There is no law against exploring the Forest," Vaelon replied evenly.

Borkna's face darkened. "Don't play games with me, son," he warned. "I want to know exactly what you were doing!"

"I already told you," Vaelon replied. "We were exploring."

"Do you take me for a fool?" the major general snapped. "Why would the Sanretsu go so far out of their way to attack simple explorers?"

"I have no idea why the Sanretsu attacked us," Vaelon replied honestly. "I can only assume that it was a foraging party. Maybe they just had to travel farther to find sacrifices this time."

"Captain?" the major general said shortly.

Captain Odorei cleared his throat. "Sir," he said, "it is my opinion that the Sanretsu party were not foragers. The absence of warlocks is a clear indication that something unusual was afoot, as is the strange creature that seemed to be controlling the Thrǽll."

"Where is this creature's body, Captain?"

Landfic blinked, looking unsure of himself. "Uh . . . we didn't bring it, sir," he admitted.

"You didn't *bring* it?" the major general asked in an acid tone. "Why not?"

"I . . . uh . . . didn't think about it, sir."

"Well, start thinking, Captain! Didn't it occur to you that we might want to investigate this new creature?"

"I'm sorry, sir. We were in a rush to get the wounded to—"

"Don't give me excuses, soldier! Go send a detachment to recover that creature's body, and then get back here!"

"Yes, sir!" the captain replied with a crisp salute. Then he hurried out the door.

"You see my problem here?" the major general said, looking back at Vaelon. "We're sure it wasn't a foraging party, which leaves me no choice but to believe that they were there on very specific business—with you."

Helpless, Vaelon said, "Look, I don't know what any of this is about, I swear!"

"Then why won't you tell me what you were doing in the Gray Forest?" Borkna demanded, bringing his fist down onto the table.

"Like I said," Vaelon told him, "we were just exploring."

"Don't be stupid! A Human, a Dark Elf, and a Halfbreed running around with two Common Elves and a little girl. What race is she, anyway?"

"High Elf," Vaelon replied.

The major general stared and then said, "High Elf! Now that makes this even more interesting!" He glared at them for a moment. "Fine. General Kamas should be here soon. I'll let him pry the truth out of you. And believe me, you won't be able to hide anything from him. He can listen to your thoughts as though you were speaking them out loud." Grinning, he took his seat.

Baden glanced at his two friends. "If the general is a mind-reader," he whispered, "he can still only hear the thoughts that are actively running through your mind. Try to empty it when he's looking at you. He—"

"Silence!" Borkna commanded sharply.

They waited for about ten minutes before General Kamas arrived. He was a tall, stern-looking man, and he looked at the prisoners with little expression as he entered. "General," said the major general, as he and the other men at the table rose to salute him.

"Major General," replied the general, saluting back. "As you were."

The men sat back down, and the general, rather than going to his seat, stood in front of the three captives. "Gentlemen, my lady," he said gravely, inclining his head. "I trust you have been cooperative?"

"No, sir, they have not," said Borkna from behind him. "They refuse to explain what they were doing so deep in the Gray Forest."

General Kamas nodded slowly. "I see." He took a step toward Baden, giving him a friendly smile. "Why don't you want to tell us, my good man?" he asked pleasantly. His eyes were sharp and probing.

"We have told you, sir," Baden replied. "We were just exploring."

Kamas stared intently at Baden's eyes, and Baden, his face perfectly calm, stared right back. After a few moments, Kamas frowned slightly but then he smiled again. "Astonishing," he murmured. "I have never met a man with such precise control over his own mind. You are remarkable." Kamas turned to Vaelon. "Let's see whether your friends also have such control."

Vaelon did his best to empty his mind when Kamas looked at him, but he could tell within moments he wasn't doing a very good job. Kamas' eyes bored into his mind, and the corners of the general's mouth twitched as though he were suppressing a smile.

Quite suddenly, however, his became more serious, staring hard at Vaelon for a long moment, he said, "Lieutenant, please remove these bonds from our guests."

"Yes, sir," said a soldier behind Vaelon.

Major General Borkna, looking very surprised, rose halfway out of his chair. "General?" he said.

"It's all right, Borkna," said Kamas. "I would like to speak with these people alone for a while."

"Alone? General, are you sure . . . ?"

"Quite sure," the general replied calmly.

All of the soldiers quietly filed out of the room, leaving Vaelon, Baden, and Safaya alone with General Kamas. The general drew up a chair and sat, motioning for them to do likewise, which they did.

After a moment of thought the general spoke. "Your friend Koän escaped. Knowing what you do of him, I suppose I shouldn't be surprised." He glanced at Vaelon. "Your presence honors us, Master Sahani. But I am curious as to why you did not tell us who you were."

Vaelon sighed. "I didn't want to attract attention."

"Understandable, considering your purpose. So . . . Alhalon Cui Kahathilor still lives, does he? A most surprising, and disquieting, revelation. I suppose I can understand why you wouldn't announce your real reasons for being in the forest." He paused, regarding each of them in turn. "So you really believe there may be a way to stop the Ghost People?"

Baden shrugged. "That's what we're trying to find out."

"On the word of one little girl? Even if she is a seeress, that power is not always entirely dependable. Seers in the past have been known to be wrong—they are not immune from the errors of mortality, and sometimes misinterpret their own visions."

"We're willing to take that chance," Safaya said cooly.

The general looked mildly amused. "No need to be defensive, my lady. I'm simply making sure you realize that she could be wrong. Approaching Alhalon the Black is certainly not a light undertaking." He rubbed at his chin, thinking again, and then mused, "If he has really been alive all this time, why hasn't he emerged? And what if your visit encourages him to come back? He could cause a great deal of trouble."

"We've thought about that," said Vaelon. "We've decided the risk is worth taking if we can stop the Ghost People."

"*If.* That's the key word there." He leaned back a little. "And the other question is why the Sanretsu attacked you. Captain Landfic was quite right—that was no ordinary foraging party you ran into."

"We honestly don't know," Vaelon said. "What we're doing has nothing to do with the Sanretsu. I really think they just happened across us and decided to take us for sacrifice, their actual purpose for being there aside."

"Perhaps." Kamas tapped his chin thoughtfully, and then said, "I'm afraid I must ask you all to stay here until your friend Koän returns, hopefully with this mysterious young companion of yours. If you will all give me your word that you will not try to escape, I will trust you and not lock your doors or post guards to watch you. Is that agreeable?"

Knowing they had no real choice, Vaelon and his friends agreed. "You have our word," said Vaelon.

"Good. Feel free to explore the barracks if you like, but I must ask you not to leave the building. That will be all."

"Yes, sir." Vaelon almost saluted before remembering that he was a civilian now.

Not really feeling like wandering, the three of them returned to their room and sat despondently on their beds. The rest of the day passed slowly but it did finally end, and all three of them dropped into fitful slumber.

✕ ✳ ✕

The following day, after breakfast, the three of them took to slowly wandering the barracks together. The Dark Elven soldiers they came across ignored them for the most part, and they saw no signs of anyone they knew. Just before noon, though, the heavy double doors at the barracks entrance opened just as they were passing by.

The first person to enter was Captain Odorei. As soon as he entered, he said, "All right, get him in here, quickly!" He strode up the hallway, and behind him two Dark Elven soldiers entered, bearing a third between them on a stretcher.

And then, behind those three, Ciroy entered the barracks.

"Ciroy!" Safaya cried, immediately running toward him. With a broad grin, Ciroy caught her as she flew into his arms and spun around a few times. She was trying to say something but was crying too hard to be even the least bit intelligible. She kissed him fiercely and then threw her arms around his neck and kissed him again, and then again. "Oh, Ciroy!" she finally managed to say, and then they just kept kissing over and over again.

Finally Baden called, "Hey—you're in public, remember?"

But apparently neither of them cared.

Reiyalindis came in next, giggling. She was followed closely by Koän. Vaelon may have been mistaken, but it seemed that as the Dark Elf looked at Ciroy and Safaya, the faintest hint of a smile tugged at his mouth.

Reiyalindis ran to Vaelon and Baden, hugging both of them in turn. "Oh, I'm so glad you're both safe!" she said. "I was so worried after that fight!"

"You were worried?" Baden said with a grin. "We were the worried ones, my little friend!"

Ciroy and Safaya had finally stopped kissing, and now they were simply holding each other. Safaya sighed contentedly, closing her eyes as Ciroy gently stroked her hair. Then her eyes opened, and she pulled away from Ciroy, holding her arms out to Reiyalindis. The little High Elf smiled broadly and gladly ran to the Halfbreed woman, who knelt to catch her in a tight embrace.

"You have no idea how worried I was," said Safaya. "I'm so glad you're safe, little darling."

Reiyalindis just smiled, tightening her embrace.

Someone behind them cleared his throat, and they all looked toward him. It was Captain Odorei.

"Sorry to interrupt," he said, "but General Kamas would like to see you. Follow me, please." Landfic took them to the same chamber where they had spoken with Kamas the day before.

The general was waiting for them. He waved Landfic off, and the captain saluted and left the room.

"I just had a short visit with Private Teari," he said, "and he told me everything that happened. That was a most interesting creature you met. For those of you who may not know, it can apparently come back to life if its pieces are put back together."

Vaelon gave a start. "Come back to life? That's not possible!"

"Apparently it is. Ciroy here was thoughtful enough to bring the creature's head with him, leaving the rest of the body behind, but another detachment of men is on its way to bring the body as well. We will, of course, be very careful to not allow the two pieces to touch. But anyway, on to other matters." He looked down at Reiyalindis and smiled briefly. "I've been looking forward to meeting you, my young friend."

She didn't say anything. Kamas stared into her eyes for a few moments, then frowned. "Strange," he muttered. "Your friend was able to mask his true thoughts with carefully constructed false ones, but your mind I cannot even touch. Evidently your power blocks me." He sighed and stepped back. "Well, I'm afraid I have no real legal reason to hold you here, though I am tempted to for your own good. If you really wish to seek out Alhalon Cui Kahathi-lor, I cannot stop you. But I give you my strongest advice to abandon this mad venture. Despite what the girl has seen, or thinks she has seen, going to Alhalon the Black is folly." He gave them a dismissive wave. "Fear no further hindrance from us, but remember my warning. And try not to run into any more Sanretsu—we will probably not be there to help you again if you do."

Vaelon nodded. "Thank you, sir, for your advice."

Kamas grinned a little. "Even though you firmly intend to ignore it. Well, be off then, and good luck."

"Thank you, sir."

Within the hour they were outside of Gaeotici and moving into the forest. "Well," Baden said brightly, "considering they saved our lives, I suppose going a few days out of our way wasn't too bad."

"No," Reiyalindis said softly. She was obviously troubled about something and was staring at the ground in front of her as she walked.

"Something wrong, kid?" asked Ciroy.

"We need to stop and talk for a while," she replied. "Let's get out of sight of the city first."

Once they were well into the trees, they all stopped, sitting down to face Reiyalindis. She glanced quickly at Koän and then stood up. "I . . . I think I know what that black creature was," she began. "The knowledge came to me not long ago."

Vaelon glanced around at the group. By this time they were all used to the little girl receiving sudden bursts of inspiration, so her words didn't seem to faze any of them.

She paused for a long moment, though, until Baden said, "And . . . ?"

She took a deep breath. "They are called Dokujin. They are deadly creatures that serve the Sanretsu."

"They?" asked Vaelon.

She nodded. "I think . . . I think there are more than one. Actually . . . there are seven."

"Seven of them?" muttered Ciroy. "That's great. Do you know why that one attacked us? Did it just decide to kill us because we were handy?"

"They are used as hunters and assassins by the Sanretsu only under the most extreme circumstances. A Dokujin would not have risked its mission by attacking someone it was not sent to attack."

"So . . . it really was after us?" asked Vaelon.

"Not us," she said, her voice barely above a whisper. "You."

Vaelon felt a chill run up his spine. "Me?"

"It attacked you. Not any of the rest of us. It could just as easily have gone after any one of us, but it didn't."

"It seems the Sanretsu remember you, my friend," Baden said. "Killing four of their warlocks must have put you on their bad side."

Vaelon rested his forehead against the palm of his hand. "Wonderful. The Sanretsu will be all over us—every step of the way, for all we know."

"We're going to have to be extra cautious, then," said Safaya.

Vaelon shook his head. "No. What must happen is for the rest of you to go on without me. If I'm not with you, the Sanretsu won't have a reason to go looking for you. I'm the one they want."

"Vaelon, I need you," Reiyalindis reminded him. "If you leave, our quest will fail."

"It'll fail if we get attacked again! If those Dark Elves hadn't happened to be there, we'd all be dead already!"

Her voice took on an uncharacteristic tone of command. "Vaelon, we'll deal with one thing at a time. You must stay with us."

He looked at her helplessly. "I don't want to get you all killed!"

For a moment her big soft eyes revealed a little of the depth of her pain. "Now you know how I feel," she said gently.

"Reiyalindis—"

"Forget it, Vaelon."

He sighed. "I sure hope you know what you're doing."

Smiling a little sadly, she said, "So do I."

NINE

"So do you suppose Alhalon can read minds, the way General Kamas can?" asked Safaya as she cut up a wild carrot to eat with their supper. Reiyalindis sat down next to her and reflected on the journey. They had been moving steadily after leaving Gaeotici and were making good time.

"No," replied Baden, who was cleaning his crossbow. "Mind reading is a rare and peculiar talent, and it only shows up in people who can't do any other kind of magic."

"Really?" she said curiously. "Are you sure?"

"Positive. According to the Elven Histories, which carefully document all known kinds of magic and their respective abilities, mind reading is in a class of its own, and only certain types of minds are even capable of it. Other kinds of magic seem to interfere with mind reading; there was one case where a boy grew up being able to read minds, but in his teenage years he began to develop the ability to do sorcery. From the moment the sorcery first appeared, he could no longer read minds. No one is sure why."

Safaya nodded. "Well, I'm glad. I really wouldn't like having him poking around in my thoughts."

Vaelon glanced at Baden. "I take it you've read the Elven Histories?"

"Naturally."

"That's a feat not many have accomplished. That's a lot of reading."

Baden grimaced. "Don't remind me. It was very boring, but the useful tidbits here and there were worth it."

Vaelon glanced eastward where the setting sun was only faintly illuminating the still-distant mountains of the Great Shield. Suddenly, he looked back at Baden. "I've heard that there's nothing but wasteland beyond the Great Shield."

Nodding, Baden said, "That's what the few people who have ever made it there and back said. Just a huge, empty desert as far as the eye can see."

"Has anyone ever tried to sail around the south end of the continent and explore the coasts on the other side?"

"A few. None of them ever made it back, though."

As the night deepened, they sought their beds. Baden took the first watch, walking in a slow circle around the camp, alert for danger. Since their meeting with the Sanretsu they had been more cautious than before, and the knowledge that enemies were hunting for Vaelon made them all edgy.

Reiyalindis was having a hard time falling asleep and was simply lying there awake, watching Safaya through the darkness. The Halfbreed was lying on her side with her back to Ciroy, who had his arms around her. Reiyalindis felt even more lonely than usual, and as she watched the sleeping couple her thoughts turned to her past. Certainly she must have had a mother, but try as she might she could not summon even the tiniest memory of her mother, or of her father.

She wondered if her mother had ever rocked her to sleep, holding her close and humming a soft lullaby. She tried to imagine what it must have felt like, but that only made her want to cry, so she stifled the fabricated memory.

The more she was around other people, the more she was coming to realize how much she had been missing. Koän had been her friend for two years now, but he had not stirred these kinds of feelings in her. Though selfless and unswervingly loyal, the Dark Elf did not possess many of the qualities these others had. He had no sense of humor whatsoever, and he also lacked the caring and unreserved affection that marked Safaya's nature.

Reiyalindis realized that she felt cold, even though the night air was warm. Moving slowly and carefully, she inched closer to Safaya, wanting more than anything—for reasons she did not really even understand—to just be close to someone.

She was not careful enough, though, for as she drew closer Safaya's eyes opened. She halted, mortified, and tried to think of some way to explain what she was doing—but Safaya, it seemed, already understood. Wordlessly she held her blanket up a little, extending one hand. Reiyalindis hesitated a little, but then she smiled and shed her own blanket, scooting underneath Safaya's. She settled with her back to the Halfbreed woman, and Safaya wrapped her arms around her, holding her close.

Enveloped in an unfamiliar but pleasant glow of warmth and security, Reiyalindis drifted off to sleep.

That night she slept more soundly than she ever had before and did not wake until Ciroy gently shook her and said, "All right, lazy bones, we need to get going."

Reiyalindis yawned. Safaya was still holding her, though it was apparent that she had been awake for a while, and all of the others were already prepared to go. "Oh . . . goodness, I'm sorry," she said, sitting up. "Why didn't you wake me earlier?"

Safaya smiled, fondly running her hand over Reiyalindis's hair and down across her cheek. "You seemed like you needed the sleep." Cupping the young girl's chin in her hand, she said, "You're such a pretty girl, Reiyalindis. You're going to have to let me do your hair for you sometime."

Reiyalindis self-consciously touched her hair, which she had always simply worn down or tied back with cloth. "Do you not like it?"

"Oh, no, I like it. I just want to have a little fun with it, that's all—maybe do it up for you, like you're on your way to a grand ball." Safaya let out a girlish little giggle. "We could have all sorts of fun—you have such lovely hair."

Reiyalindis blushed. "All right."

"First," Ciroy said dryly, "I think you ought to eat your breakfast. You can start playing with each other's hair once we've put a few miles behind us today."

"Yes," Vaelon agreed. "Once the hair business starts, it can go on for hours and hours. Girls are strange that way."

"Really. And I suppose you think you know a lot about girls?" Safaya teased.

"More than you might think," he replied.

"Is that so! And where did you gain this wealth of knowledge?"

Baden grinned. "He liked a girl once."

Safaya winked at him. "Was she pretty?"

Vaelon shrugged. "I think so. I can't really remember her very well anymore. I don't think I ever spoke more than two words to her."

Safaya laughed. "A secret passion, Vaelon? Is that where all your knowledge of the female mind came from?"

"No. Actually, I think it was mostly due to my five sisters."

Baden gave a start. "Five sisters? Any brothers?"

"No. Just me."

"Aww, no wonder you're such a sensitive guy!" Ciroy said in an exaggerated imitation of a girl's voice. Safaya punched his arm.

Baden shook his head at Vaelon. "The longer we're around you, the more these dark secrets pop up, my reticent friend."

Vaelon shrugged. "If no one asks, why should I bring things up?"

When they stopped to make camp that evening, Safaya did not help as she usually did. Instead she told the men they were on their own this time, and she sat Reiyalindis down and began doing the little Elf's hair. Vaelon glanced over a few times but for a long while all that went on was a great deal of giggling. After at least seven or eight different attempts, Safaya seemed to finally decide on a style.

"Well, gentlemen, what do you think?" Safaya asked, presenting a shyly blushing Reiyalindis.

Safaya had pulled some of Reiyalindis's hair up in a bun on the back of her head, wrapping it a few times with a braid before letting what was left hang loose to her shoulders.

Vaelon was impressed. Though still very young, it was obvious that Reiyalindis would become a woman of extraordinary beauty. The hairstyle Safaya had chosen suited her perfectly, accenting her already exquisite features in a subtle but elegant manner. "Reiyalindis," he said, "use your power wisely."

She blinked uncertainly, not sure what he meant. "My power? I . . . I do try, Vaelon. I hope you don't think I'm doing all this without being sure—"

"I'm not talking about your magic, Reiyalindis."

"But then . . . what power?"

"Your looks. You, my little friend, are going to become a heartbreaker."

She looked faintly troubled at that. "I don't want to be. That sounds awful."

Safaya laughed, giving her a quick hug. "Don't be so worried! What he means is that you're going to be absolutely gorgeous when you grow up. Young men are going to fall all over themselves competing for your attention."

Her blush deepened, and in a small, uncertain voice she said, "Do you really think so?"

"Of course I do."

Reiyalindis looked around at all of them, a small self-conscious smile tugging at her mouth. And then, quite suddenly, she began to cry.

Everyone hesitated, not sure what to think, and then Reiyalindis turned sharply and ran into the trees, sobbing.

All of them began to rise, and Koän was already heading after her, but Safaya held out her hand. "No," she said. "Let me go to her. She needs another woman right now." Without waiting for a response, she followed after the young High Elf.

✗ ✳ ✗

In the forest some distance from camp, Safaya found Reiyalindis sitting on a fallen log, her face streaked with tears and her shoulders shaking as she cried. Safaya silently sat down beside her, putting her arm around the little Elf.

After a moment, Reiyalindis drew a deep breath. "I'm sorry," she whispered, managing a weak smile. "I made a fool of myself, didn't I?"

"Of course not," Safaya replied. "Do you want to talk about it?"

With a helpless little shrug, Reiyalindis said, "Well . . . I don't even really know, Safaya. I was just . . . happy." She laughed a little through the tears that were still trickling down her cheeks. "That doesn't make much sense, does it?"

"It makes perfect sense, darling," Safaya said soothingly. "I doubt the men would understand, but I do."

"Thank you. I just got overwhelmed, I guess. I mean . . . I think that moment was the happiest moment I've ever had, and . . . I just didn't know how to handle it." She choked back another sob. "I've never really thought much about being beautiful. But when I looked at all of you, I could tell that you meant it. I knew then that I was beautiful. I don't know why, but . . . it was nice."

"A girl needs to be told that she's beautiful," Safaya agreed. "Otherwise she starts to doubt it."

"Surely you never doubt it. You're the most beautiful woman I've ever seen."

"Why, thank you." Safaya hugged her. "Ciroy tells me that all the time.

Maybe someday, if I hear it enough, I may even start to believe it." She began wiping at Reiyalindis's eyes with a handkerchief. "Now, let's make you presentable before we go back. You're lucky, you know; you don't really show it when you cry. When I cry my whole face gets splotchy and ugly."

Reiyalindis smiled. "You could never be ugly."

"Don't make any wagers on that."

Looking away, Reiyalindis said, "I've been meaning to talk to you about last night."

"What about it?"

"I'm sorry I barged in on you like that."

"What? Don't be silly. I'm glad you did—and if you ever want to again, don't hesitate to ask."

She shook her head. "I couldn't. I don't have the right to impose like that."

"Nonsense."

"No." Her voice was unusually intense. "I shouldn't have even done it last night. I was just feeling so lonely . . . I was weak. But I'll be good from now on."

Safaya was perplexed. "Reiyalindis, I don't have the faintest idea what you're talking about. I don't mind, really, I—"

"No." Straightening, and obviously trying to be brave, Reiyalindis stood up. "Please don't try to understand, Safaya. Someday, maybe—but not now."

Shaking her head, Safaya also rose. "You're quite the strangest little girl I've ever met. But I love you."

Reiyalindis turned her big, deep eyes toward her, and Safaya sensed in them a strange mixture of gratitude and fear. "Thank you," she said. "No one has ever told me that before. But you shouldn't."

"Why not?"

Safaya could clearly see the battle of emotions on Reiyalindis's face, and her heart ached for her. Not for the first time she wished Reiyalindis would just open up and tell them the secrets she was holding in so tightly. But she didn't. Instead she took Safaya's hand and silently began to lead her back toward the camp.

By the time they reached it Reiyalindis had composed herself fully and she smiled a little wanly at the group. "I'm sorry for running off like that," she said. "I was just . . . well, it's hard to explain."

"It was a girl thing," said Safaya, stepping in for her.

"Ah," nodded Ciroy. "In that case, I will pretend to understand that it was perfectly natural." He grinned, and Reiyalindis smiled back.

✖ ✳ ✖

After many more days of travel, they finally reached the foothills of the Great Shield. By that time the Gray Forest had become somewhat darker; the trees and brush were thicker and faint traces of mist lingered on the ground until well into the day. Even more than that, though, Vaelon knew that every step took them closer not only to their goal, but to Ruzai as well. They all stayed extra alert now, for they were well within the normal range of Sanretsu foraging parties on top of the groups that were specifically looking for them.

After crossing through a particularly thick part of the forest, they came upon a large meadow. It was about half a mile across, filled with wildflowers and long grass, and it was sunlit and cheery. Across the meadow a steep hill jutted upward, and beyond that hill were the huge slopes of the Great Shield.

"Big, aren't they?" commented Baden, squinting up at the mountain peaks as they entered the meadow. "Ever wonder how they were created?"

"Not really," Ciroy replied. "They've just always been there, haven't they?"

"Of course not."

"How do you know?"

"Because that would just be absurd. How can something have always been there? Everything has to have had a beginning."

"If that's true," said Vaelon, "wouldn't there have to have been a point in history where nothing existed? And if so, where did everything come from?"

"I haven't quite got that part figured out yet," Baden admitted.

They crossed the meadow, heading toward the edge of the hill to the south, where it looked like there might be a pass leading into the mountains. As they reached the other side of the meadow and entered the trees again, however, Vaelon glanced back the way they had come and immediately froze.

Several figures were moving across the line of trees on the opposite side of the meadow. He couldn't make out what they were from this distance but he had a fair idea. "Baden, get your telescope," he said.

The others all stopped, and Baden glanced back at him questioningly.

He reached into his pack for his telescope and handed it to Vaelon, who peered through it toward the figures.

It was as he expected. "Thræll," he muttered. "And they've just found our trail. A blind man could see it in that grass."

"Great," Ciroy muttered sourly. "Just what we need."

Vaelon looked quickly around. "We need to get up that hill."

"Not another hill!" Baden groaned.

"I'm afraid so. I've got a plan. If we can get up there without being seen, we can watch them cross the meadow, and the warlocks—or the Dokujin, whichever—will have to come out in the open to stay with the Thræll. And that's where you come in."

Baden grinned, giving his crossbow an affectionate pat. "Right. I like that plan."

They hurried up the hillside as quickly as they could, staying in the trees to avoid being spotted. The side of the hill facing the meadow was mostly devoid of trees, and once they were well above the treeline Baden and Vaelon stealthily moved into a position where they could see the approaching Thræll below. Baden selected a bolt and loaded it into the crossbow. Vaelon looked at the bolt curiously. It was not like the others he had seen so far. Rather than having a sharp point at the end, it was blunted with a circular depression on the very tip. "What kind of a bolt is that?" he asked.

Baden winked. "Just in case it's a Dokujin leading those Thræll. From what we know of the Dokujin, they won't stay dead unless there's something keeping them from coming back to life. One of my other bolts might very well pass completely though him, and he would come back to life. This bolt, however, is designed to provide maximum impact without serious penetration. It'll enter the body, and the soft metal on the tip will sort of mushroom out, preventing it from passing all the way through while doing a great deal of internal damage."

"You amaze me sometimes. Good thinking."

Baden peered down at the meadow through the telescope on the crossbow while Vaelon watched through the other telescope. Soon it became evident that there were over a hundred Thræll, and those at the head of the group were well on their way across the meadow by the time those at the rear even entered it.

Both of them spotted the leader of the Thræll at the same time when his tall, black-armored shape emerged from the trees. "Dokujin, all right," Vaelon muttered. "Can you hit him from here?"

"I'm sure I could," replied Baden, "but I'm going to wait until the Thræll are across the meadow before I try the shot, just to be sure."

"Don't wait too long."

"Don't worry. I know what I'm doing."

They waited. Vaelon kept an eye on the advancing Thræll while Baden kept his sights on the Dokujin. As the first of the Thræll began to enter the trees, Vaelon said, "They're across."

"Right," said Baden.

The next few seconds were tense, and Vaelon nearly jumped when he finally heard the sharp thrum of the crossbow string being released. He watched the unsuspecting Dokujin through the telescope, hoping with all his might that Baden's aim was true.

The Dokujin never knew what hit him. He jerked backward off his feet, landing flat on his back with the bolt sticking out of his head. "Yes!" Baden chortled.

The Thræll paused, staring blankly around them, and then began wandering off in all different directions. "Perfect," Vaelon said. "Nice shot."

"Let's go chop that thing's head off and burn it."

"My feelings exactly."

They waited until the Thræll were well away and then went to the Dokujin. Just like the one Ciroy had stuck his sword into, this one twitched every few seconds as his life-force kept trying to return. Once they severed his head, the twitching stopped.

Baden pondered that and said, "It appears that having something in the brain has quite a different effect from complete decapitation. I wonder if it's because the body is still whole, just with its necessary functions inhibited?"

"Whatever the reason," said Vaelon, "we need to make sure he never comes back to life."

As with the other one, this Dokujin's head would not come out of its helmet, as though it were somehow attached. They built a fire and tossed the severed head into it helmet and all. To their surprise, the helmet also began to burn after a while. Though the armor looked and felt like metal, it definitely wasn't.

They built a second fire and used it to burn the rest of the creature's body. Then they buried the ashes in six different holes around the meadow. Vaelon felt that their precautions were bordering on paranoia, but he conceded that it was better not to take chances. Once finished with their gruesome task, they continued on into the mountains.

✗ ✳ ✗

"So," said Ciroy several hours later, "any idea how to find Alhalon?"

Reiyalindis nodded. "I think we're going the right direction. It shouldn't be too much longer now."

Making a face, he said, "Now that we're so close I'm starting to wonder if I really want to find this guy."

"I know what you mean," Baden agreed. He looked up, where the lofty mountains rose on each side. "You know, even though this forest and these mountains are kind of dark, it doesn't seem like such a bad place."

"I think it's beautiful," Safaya said dreamily.

"Why does no one come here, then?" asked Reiyalindis.

"We're very close to Ruzai now," Vaelon told her. "Anyone living here would be in constant danger."

"Well . . . what about farther south? Why does no one go there either?"

"The Sanretsu aren't the only dangers in the world," said Safaya. "There are all sorts of monsters in the Great Shield."

"Like what?"

"Well, like trolls, goblins, and rocs, to name a few."

"What are those?"

"Trolls are huge brutes that like to lurk in caves and eat their prey alive," said Ciroy. "They're semi-intelligent, and even use primitive weapons and armor. Goblins are much smaller, but they live in groups and are very stealthy and quick. Rocs are giant birds—like vultures with thirty-foot wingspans."

"Oh, dear, do you think we'll run into any?" she asked.

"This close to Ruzai, I doubt it," replied Vaelon. "There may be a troll or two around because they're mean enough that even the Sanretsu would avoid them, but goblins and other monsters are intelligent enough to not stay around here to be sacrificed."

"And rocs live farther south," added Ciroy.

"Good," Reiyalindis said.

The pass they were following narrowed as they went, and then it took a dip into a particularly dark wood. "That doesn't look inviting," said Safaya, stopping to look at it. "Let's see if there's a way to avoid it."

"Why?" asked Vaelon.

She shrugged. "It just doesn't feel right."

Reiyalindis nodded in agreement. "There's something strange about it. It seems unfriendly."

Vaelon looked northward. "Well, if we climb partway up that mountain slope, we ought to be able to stay out of the hollow. Let's go."

The slope was not nearly as thickly forested as the pass floor. As they went, Reiyalindis kept casting nervous glances down into the hollow, and Safaya was sniffing at the air with a worried frown. "There's something down there," she said.

"What kind of something?" asked Ciroy.

"I don't know, but it smells . . . rancid."

"Rancid? Maybe it's just rotting vegetation—it looks a bit miry down there."

"No—it's animal."

"Well, look at this!" Baden said, crouching to look at the ground.

Vaelon went to see what he was looking at. To his surprise, it was a mass of tracks—people's tracks. "People? Here? That many of them?"

"They were Ghost People," said Baden. "The tracks just end suddenly, see? They weren't here very long ago."

"Well, I'm sorry we missed them," Ciroy said dryly.

"The complete randomness of their appearances doesn't tend to make one believe they're deliberately being called into existence by any intelligent being," Baden mused. "If they were trying to destroy people, why would they appear deep in the mountains like this, where they wouldn't be likely to find anyone to kill?"

Absorbed as they all were in the discovery of the tracks, they failed to notice the creature until it was almost too late. The breeze shifted a little, and they all caught a foul stink. Vaelon didn't need Safaya's keen sense of smell to detect that odor. As one they looked in the direction it was coming from, and that was when they spotted the beast creeping up the slope toward them.

Vaelon had never seen or heard of anything remotely akin to the monster. It walked on its hind legs, but it was hunched over as it climbed, its thick fingers digging into the earth. Its shape was basically manlike, but it was far bigger, at least eight feet tall. Its thickly muscular body was covered partially by gnarled gray skin and partially by dull metal plates that looked like they had been stapled or riveted onto the creature's body. Sections of its skin were crossed by what looked like stitches, giving it the appearance of having been sewn together. Its small, sunken eyes went flat when it realized they had seen it, and with a bellowing roar it charged, its fingers and toes ripping up great clots of earth as it sped up the steep slope.

Baden, who had kept his crossbow loaded since the two women had started acting nervous, fired at the oncoming creature. The bolt glanced off a thick piece of steel that was stapled to the monster's head and buried itself deep in its shoulder—but not nearly as deep as it should have. The creature's skin, Vaelon realized, was incredibly tough.

It roared in pain and stumbled a little, but then it was charging again. Safaya fired an arrow, but it merely bounced off the beast's hide. As it approached, Vaelon ran to meet it, but even his sword made barely a scratch in the creature's skin as he slashed at it. The creature was surrounded by an overpowering stench, and Vaelon nearly gagged.

The creature paused, turning around in an effort to catch Vaelon. He nimbly dodged away, though, and saw Koän attack it from behind, though his sword seemed completely ineffective. The creature turned to face the new threat, but by the time it turned around Koän was gone.

Baden fired again, and this time the bolt sank up to its feathers in a slightly softer spot in the creature's side. The creature bellowed in pain again and turned toward the source of the pain, bearing down on Baden.

Though he was strong and skilled, Baden was not nearly as quick as Vaelon or Koän, and he did not escape the creature. Its massive hands closed around him, and it lifted him easily into the air. Ciroy was coming at it from the side, and Vaelon and Koän from behind, but it whirled to face them, backing against a tree. It held Baden against its chest with one hand, and placed the other against the side of the Elf's head. "One more step and he dies!" it grated in a harsh voice.

Shocked, Ciroy, Vaelon, and Koän came to a halt, staring. This creature could speak?

"That's better," the creature went on, its oddly shaped jaws grinding and cracking each syllable. "What are you doing in my forest?"

Vaelon hesitated and then said, "We weren't aware this was your forest."

"I didn't ask if you knew it was my forest," the beast growled. "I asked what you're doing in it."

Reiyalindis walked between the creature and Vaelon. She faced it bravely, with only the slightest trembling betraying her fear. "We're looking for you, Alhalon."

Vaelon was so stunned that his mouth dropped open, and he wondered if he'd heard right. The creature's face twisted into a hideous grin, and it stared intently at Reiyalindis. "Looking for me? And why is that, little girl?"

"We need your help."

"My help? Speak plainly, High Elf. And be careful how you answer—my servant will snap your friend's neck like a toothpick if I don't like what you say."

Vaelon realized then what was going on. This beast was not Alhalon—the old sorcerer was speaking through it.

Reiyalindis took a deep breath and said, "We're trying to find a way to destroy the Ghost People."

"And just who are they?"

"They are warriors of an unknown race who appear for brief periods of time, attacking those they come across and then vanishing again. We—"

"I see. Yes, I know of them. Ghost People, eh?" There was a long pause, and the creature looked around at all of them as Alhalon thought that over. Finally he said, "And what sparked this fool's errand?"

"I received a prompting," she replied, fighting to stay calm. "I was told to gather these people, and together we are to find a way to destroy the Ghost People."

"You are a seeress? You? Surely you jest! A little girl would not be entrusted with such a mission!"

"I was," she said, her trembling more pronounced now. "But we cannot succeed alone. That man your creature is holding has ideas of how to find where the Ghost People come from, but you are the only one with the power to help him make the instruments he will need."

"Instruments?" The creature glanced down at Baden, and said, "What kind of instruments?"

"Ones like this," she replied. She pointed at Baden's fallen crossbow. "The tube on top of that crossbow allows him to see great distances. He is a brilliant scientist."

Alhalon actually sounded curious now. "Is that right?" He paused for a few moments, and then said, "All right. I'll give you a chance—one chance. My servant will bring this man to me, and if he can sufficiently catch my interest I might help him—but only for as long as I choose to. If he does not, he will die, along with your other friends. Do we have a deal, suckling seeress?"

Reiyalindis ignored the insult. After a moment of hesitation she nodded. "Yes."

"Done, then. Make camp at the west end of this hollow, and do not attempt to go any farther. My servant will come for you when I have decided—either to bring you to me or to kill you." He looked around at them and then said, "Send the Dark Elf with my servant as well. I wish to question both of them before I agree to this."

Koän hesitated, glancing quickly at Reiyalindis. She nodded, and he frowned but then nodded in return.

"Come along, then." The creature dropped Baden to the ground, and the Elf stood up, massaging his shoulder. "Bring your instrument, Elf, but do not attempt to load the crossbow."

"I have another one that's not attached to it," Baden said, going to his dropped pack and pulling his telescope from it. "Will that do?"

"Good." The creature turned and began walking away.

Reiyalindis ran to Baden and Koän and hugged them both. "Be careful," she said to them. "Please be careful. It's all up to you, now."

"Don't worry, little one," Baden said with a wink. "If he was that interested in a simple telescope, I doubt I'll have much trouble."

"Be very careful anyway. Don't trust a word he says."

"Don't worry."

"Come!" the beast snapped.

"Bye, then," said Baden, and he and Koän began to follow the creature.

The others watched until their friends were out of sight, and then Vaelon said, "Well, we might as well get camp set up. We might be here a while."

✖ ✳ ✖

It was a quiet and slightly melancholy group that sat around the campfire that night. Reiyalindis was particularly downcast and sat with her knees drawn up to her chest, staring at the fire.

"What do you suppose that creature was?" Ciroy said, more to break the silence than anything else.

Vaelon shook his head. "I don't have the faintest idea."

"It looked ghastly," said Safaya. "And that smell! It was like the stink of rotting meat and fresh sewage all mixed together."

"It is in agony," Reiyalindis said in a sad voice.

"What do you mean?" asked Vaelon.

"Alhalon built that beast by piecing together parts from different creatures. He made it next to invincible and bent it to his will, but did nothing to ease its suffering."

Ciroy blinked. "You know, now that you mention it, parts of that thing did look an awful lot like a troll."

Safaya looked faintly sick. "That's horrible!" she said. "How could he do such a thing?"

"He cares nothing for the pain and suffering of others." Reiyalindis shifted slightly with a sigh and then said, "Ciroy, I don't want to impose, but . . . would you mind singing something?"

"Sure, kid," he replied. "Anything in particular?"

She shrugged. "Something happy. Not funny, just . . . happy."

"You got it." He thought for a moment, and then started to sing.

It was a soft, gentle song, and seemed to set Reiyalindis's mind at peace, at least temporarily. Ciroy could tell she wasn't even paying much attention to the words as much as just the general sound.

When he was finished she rose, going over to where he was sitting. She settled down next to him, leaning against him and resting her head on his chest. Ciroy was startled, but after a moment his expression softened and he put his arm around her. "You okay, kid?" he asked.

"You have a very beautiful voice," Reiyalindis said.

"Thanks."

Safaya pressed closer to him as well, sliding down far enough that she could also lay her head against his chest. She gazed at Reiyalindis, and reached over, stroking the little girl's cheek with her fingers. "Is something bothering you, dear?" she asked. "Do you miss Koän?"

Reiyalindis sighed. "Yes. I hope he'll be all right. I'm sorry if I'm intruding."

"Oh no, dear, of course not." She smiled with a twinkle in her fox eyes. "Normally I don't share my husband with other women, but this time I'll let it slide."

"Thank you." She reached over, taking Safaya's hand. "I know how much you and Ciroy have wanted children," she said. "I wish I could do something for you."

Safaya's smile turned a little sad. "And we thank you for that, little one. You're very sweet. Sometimes I wish I could have you as my own."

"That would be nice," Reiyalindis said softly. "I wish it were possible.

Perhaps we could pretend—for a little while, anyway."

"Perhaps we could."

Ciroy grinned, briefly tightening his arms around both girls. "You're a sweetheart," he said to Reiyalindis. "I suppose you're still not going to tell us just why you're so determined to always be alone?"

Reiyalindis lowered her eyes sadly. "I can't, I'm sorry. Even Koän and I must be separated eventually. He fights it, but he knows it's true."

"Well, I don't know why you think that, I really don't, but for right now you're with us." Ciroy kissed the top of her head. "So you can pretend all you want."

With a long sigh, Reiyalindis closed her eyes. "It is very nice," she murmured.

Within a few moments the little Elven girl was asleep. Safaya sighed. "Poor little dear," she whispered. "I wish I could see into that mind of hers."

Ciroy glanced over at Vaelon. "I know it's my turn, but would you take first watch?" he said. "I'm a little bit pinned down here."

Vaelon smiled. "No problem."

✘ ✳ ✘

When morning dawned, they ate a cold meal, and no sooner had they finished than Alhalon's creature appeared. Vaelon saw it first, and he nervously put his hand on his sword. Was it here to bring them to Alhalon, or to kill them?

The creature paused just outside of their camp and waited a moment, looking around at all of them. Then it turned and began walking away again.

They quickly gathered their things and followed. "Looks like we're in," Ciroy said quietly.

TEN

The home of Alhalon Cui Kahathilor was not a bit less intimidating than any of them had imagined it would be. Black and forbidding, it stood in the middle of a dark basin like some ancient, brooding monster. No thought had gone into making the place pleasing to the eye; its form was strictly functional, a plain square fortress with thick, high walls and squat, graceless towers. It seemed to watch them as they approached, with a cold, unfriendly stare that made their skin crawl. The creature led them to the gates of the fortress, and then, without a backward glance, it turned and went back toward the little hollow.

The gates stood open, and waiting just inside was Alhalon himself. He was dressed in a long black robe. His clean-shaven face was lean and hard, and his black eyes cold and aloof. He did not look especially ancient, perhaps in his early sixties, and he had a full head of stark white hair that he kept cut short. "Welcome," he intoned, a hint of mocking in his deceptively mild voice. "Luckily for you, your friends have managed to arouse my curiosity. Before I allow you to enter, however, I must apprise you of a few household rules. I am master here, and in my home my power is absolute. You will do as I say. If you do not, you will be punished. Understood?"

Knowing they had no choice, Vaelon nodded. "We understand."

"Good." Alhalon glanced down at Reiyalindis, and she seemed to shrink beneath the undisguised venom in his gaze. "I am not fond of High Elves, piglet seeress. Be very careful how you behave here. Now follow me."

The interior of the fortress was as bleak as the exterior, all unrelieved black stone. No decorations were visible, and the iron torch rings were plain, almost severe. Alhalon led them to a large room, empty save for Baden and Koän, and pointed into it. "You will stay in here," he said curtly. "Meals are taken in the dining hall. It is at the end of this hall-way here." He looked at Vaelon then and an almost malicious twinkle came into his eyes. "My home is yours," he said with that same mocking tone. "Feel free to wander, but do not open any closed doors—and do not leave the fortress. And believe me, I will know it if you try." With that he turned and walked away, but before he had taken three steps, he vanished into thin air.

Vaelon looked around the room. There were no furnishings, not even so much as a mat to lie on. "Looks like we'll be sleeping on the floor."

"I see you managed to win him over," Ciroy said to Baden.

The scientist shrugged. "It wasn't difficult. After I explained a few of my ideas, he seemed really interested. He's got a naturally curious mind."

"Did you happen to pick up anything else about him?" Vaelon asked, hoping that his friend's uncanny ability to deduce things about people might yield something useful about their host.

Baden shook his head. "Not much, I'm afraid. I do know, however, that despite his attitude, he's actually hungry for talk—he hasn't seen another intelligent being for two centuries, after all. That doesn't mean he likes us, mind you. I gathered that he has a fair amount of contempt for just about everything."

"Especially me," Reiyalindis said quietly.

Baden grimaced. "Well, yes—he obviously has no liking for High Elves. I think it would be best if you just avoided him as much as possible."

✗ ✳ ✗

Alhalon, however, made it very difficult for Reiyalindis to avoid him. He seemed to take perverse pleasure in making her uncomfortable, and insisted that she, as well as her companions, keep company with him for dinner that evening.

Safaya was surprised to find that the food itself was delicious. It con-sisted of juicy and flavorful beef steaks, a light salad of crisp lettuce and ripe tomatoes, buttery mashed potatoes, and a variety of tasty appetizers.

"This is really good," Ciroy commented. "Where do you get all this food around here?"

Alhalon smiled thinly. "I don't have to 'get' anything. Everything I need, I simply make." To emphasize his point he held up his hand, and a crystal-clear goblet of some dark red liquid appeared in his hand.

Reiyalindis, who had not as yet eaten anything, slowly cut a small bite of steak. She seemed apprehensive for some reason, as though expecting the food to be poisoned, and she hesitated a long moment before putting the meat in her mouth.

Alhalon let out a dry, hollow-sounding chuckle, his eyes glinting. "What's the matter, High Elf? Not good enough for you?"

"Oh—no." Reiyalindis shook her head a little. "It's very good."

"Perhaps you would prefer a bowl of maggots. It would be more suitable for your kind."

Safaya immediately stiffened. "That was uncalled for!" she flared.

Alhalon inclined his head in mock penitence. "I apologize, my ladies." He fixed his stare on Reiyalindis and said, "You will find no unpleasant surprises in the food, I assure you. I am not so far removed from civilization that I do not know how to properly treat guests—no matter how odious they may be."

Safaya was about to say something, but Reiyalindis quickly stepped on her foot to silence her. Safaya reluctantly picked up her fork and took another bite. Alhalon watched her, chuckling again.

Koän was staring balefully at Alhalon, his scarred eyes flashing with barely controlled anger.

Alhalon noticed and stared back, a hint of challenge in his eyes. "Was there something you wanted?" he asked in an ominous voice.

Koän's lips tightened, but he said nothing and did not move. Alhalon chuckled again, and resumed eating.

The rest of the meal was carried out in silence. When Alhalon was finished, he rose and said, "Come, Master Solignis. I am most anxious to begin. Your ideas intrigue me, and I always enjoy a good challenge." Without waiting for an acknowledgment, Alhalon turned and began walking from the room. Baden, with a wry grimace, rose and followed him.

"What an awful man!" Safaya said in a hushed voice once Alhalon and Baden were gone. "Insulting her like that!"

"I imagine he wants to do much worse," said Ciroy. "Let's not provoke him, Safaya. He's likely to treat Reiyalindis very badly while we're here, but please, for everyone's sake, don't lose your temper! He could obliterate us with hardly a thought."

"How can you sit by and let him do that to her?" she demanded angrily.

"Do you think I like it?" he replied. "We've got to stay focused here! One wrong word, and we all go down!"

"He's right," Reiyalindis said. "Please, Safaya, I know you don't like it, but he's right. I'll be okay—don't worry. Let Alhalon have his fun."

"What if he hurts her?" Safaya demanded, directing the question to her husband.

"That's an entirely different matter," Ciroy said grimly. "Sorcerer or not, if he hurts her, I'll . . ."

Reiyalindis shook her head. "He won't."

"How can you be so sure?" Safaya asked.

"Just trust me, Safaya. Please. As long as we don't provoke him, he won't hurt us."

"We're talking about a cold-blooded murderer here!" she hissed. "What's to stop him? His conscience? It doesn't seem to me that he's got much of one!"

Reiyalindis took a deep breath, and then said, "He is not your typical evil sorcerer. He will kill without any remorse, but only if it serves his purpose. He doesn't take any particular pleasure in killing—so if we don't give him a reason to, he won't."

Safaya thought that over and finally nodded—reluctantly. "Fine. I'll curb my instincts."

"Thank you." Reiyalindis hugged her tightly for a moment. "Please try not to worry. I'll be fine."

✖ ✳ ✖

Alhalon's study was nearly enough to make Baden salivate. It was stuffed with hundreds of books, most of them books he had never seen before. "Where did you get all these if you've never left your fortress?" he asked.

"I brought them with me," Alhalon replied. "The pathetic fools who tried to kill me thought they destroyed my entire home, but they missed my study—or, shall I say, I persuaded them to miss it. After I slipped away from them I went back to my home and unlocked the enchantments hiding my study. Then I spirited the entire room far away here in the mountains where I would not be disturbed."

Deciding to take a risk, Baden said, "Out of curiosity, Alhalon, why did the High Elves try to kill you? I've read the histories, of course, but histories tend to be somewhat one-sided."

"That they do. They came up with all sorts of reasons—they thought I was becoming a danger, that I would end up turning against everyone, like the Sanretsu. But the fact was, they were afraid of my power. I could best any five of their most powerful, and they knew it—so they sent fourteen." He chuckled dryly. "But they underestimated me. I could not kill all of them myself, so I simply let them kill each other."

"By posing as one of them and putting your own face on others?"

Alhalon's eyes fixed on him, and he frowned. "How did you know about that?"

"Reiyalindis told me," he replied. "It was revealed to her that you were still alive just after I met her, and she was also told how you had escaped."

"Well, well," he said softly, "is that a fact?" He seemed lost in thought for a moment and then said, "I suppose you're wondering why I never went back."

Baden hesitated but then nodded. "The question has crossed my mind."

Alhalon laughed a hollow, mirthless laugh. "I suppose it gave everyone quite a turn to find out I'm still alive."

Baden thought through his reply carefully. "Well . . . to be honest," he said, "no one knows. We haven't told anyone." He judiciously decided not to mention General Kamas.

"Ah. I suppose you were afraid they would stop you for fear that your coming here would provoke me into coming out of hiding." He laughed again. "But never fear, my good man. I am here to stay—quite permanently, I'm afraid."

Baden blinked. "What do you mean?"

"I'm well aware of the decline of the High Elven magic," he said. "I can feel through the very earth how their power is slowly weakening. The High Elves have always channelled their power through the earth, through nature and the elements. That power is waning. The magic of the Dark Elves, however, comes from within and from the aid of spirits, so my power hasn't lessened in the slightest. But I made a serious mistake when I came here." He looked around at the walls in distaste. "In my haste to evade detection by the High Elves, I surrounded this fortress with powerful enchantments that I cast with the aid of certain spirits. I thought the magic would simply hide me from detection, but it went much further than that.

"Those spirits effectively entombed me in this place—as the years passed they took my own magic from me and infused it in the very stones of this fortress, so slowly that I did not realize what was happening until too late. So long as I remain here, I retain all of my power—but my power can have no effect outside these walls. If I were to step beyond them, I would become as an ordinary man, and as I am already several hundred years old, I would immediately die." He let out another of his dry chuckles. "The spirits that helped me were not the most trustworthy sort, but I have had my revenge. I have entombed them even as they entombed me."

"Oh?" Baden asked.

"I tricked them—I lured them into my grasp with promises of giving them living bodies of their own. There is nothing a spirit desires more than a body of flesh and bone—and I gave it to them."

"Your servant from the forest," Baden guessed.

"Quite right. I cannot leave my fortress, and they cannot leave that twisted wreck of a body. And because I crafted that creature they now inhabit, they are subject to my every command. It wasn't quite what they were expecting—they were so intent on getting a body that they did not realize I would then control them."

"How many of them are in that body?"

"Hundreds." He grinned. "They do not like to share—they weren't expecting that, either."

"But if your power has no effect beyond your fortress, how can you keep control of that creature when it's out there?"

"Because we are linked," he said. "The spirits allowed the link to be made in their haste to gain the bodies I promised them, and since it was forged with their consent, I can still retain it, no matter how far they go. Their freedom has become their bondage, and here we sit; they will not reverse the magic that binds me to this place, and I will not release them."

Baden wasn't sure what to say at that point, so he just gave a sort of noncommittal nod.

Alhalon turned. "But enough talk of me. I am most interested in you, my clever friend—particularly in your theory about the Ghost People's connection to the sun. Just how do you plan to explore that? Surely you will need more than just a giant telescope."

"Well, yes," Baden said. "I've got a few ideas, actually."

"Then let's get started."

The time passed quickly. They concentrated first on building the telescope, and Alhalon, guided by Baden's precise instructions, was able to construct the massive base that would hold the huge frame before either of them realized that the night was almost entirely over. Finally, just an hour or two before dawn, Baden wearily shuffled into the room where his friends were staying. Not even bothering to get out his blanket, he lay down on the floor and promptly fell asleep.

He awoke again four hours later. His friends were still in the room, whispering quietly among themselves. He considered just going back to sleep but decided against it and sat up.

"Hey, buddy," Ciroy said. "We gave up on waiting up for you."

Baden shrugged. "We sort of lost track of time."

"How'd it go?"

"Very well; very well. He's every bit as powerful as we've been led to believe. It's uncanny how he can just make things out of thin air. We built almost the entire base for the telescope last night—it's sitting out on top of the southeast tower if you want to look at it."

"Do you think all this is really going to work?" asked Safaya.

"It's certainly got a good chance, I think. Have you already eaten?"

"No," Ciroy replied. "Alhalon showed up about an hour ago and invited us to breakfast, but we told him we'd rather wait for you, and he didn't argue."

"Well, let's go, then! I'm starving."

Work on the telescope progressed remarkably quickly. The lenses were the hardest part—not because glass was any harder for Alhalon to make, but because they had be be so precisely fashioned. Once those were complete, they were assembled in the frame. The telescope was huge, and Alhalon constructed a great many sturdy supports to hold it up. It looked incredibly complicated, for aside from simply holding it up, the supports also had to allow for the telescope to move so it could be pointed to various locations in the sky.

It took a little over a week to complete the telescope but finally Alhalon placed the final piece on—a huge filter both of them had invented together that would allow the sun to be observed through the telescope without damaging the eyes.

"There!" Alhalon was sweating a little; the tasks he had performed over the past week had required staggering amounts of power, for creating things out of nothing was one of the most difficult magical abilities of all.

Baden folded up the plans for the telescope, nodding in satisfaction.

"Nice. It's too late now to take a look at the sun, but we'll give it a try first thing in the morning."

"Excellent," agreed the sorcerer.

Alhalon's behavior had not noticeably improved over the week. When he was with Baden, he sometimes lost a little bit of his haughtiness, especially when he was caught up in the tasks at hand. But once back among the others—especially Reiyalindis—his coldly superior attitude reasserted itself. He seemed to pay special attention to Reiyalindis. The others he tolerated, but her he despised, and he made no secret of that fact. He never passed an opportunity to mock or needle her, and his loathing for her was—as Ciroy put it—thick enough to trip over. It seemed that he was venting two hundred years' worth of pent-up hatred for the High Elves upon that one small girl.

Reiyalindis bore all this admirably well, at least in Alhalon's presence. Baden was often impressed with how she refused to let him see so much as a trembling lip from her. Once alone with her friends, however, she would often collapse weeping into the nearest pair of arms—usually Safaya's. After the first two days in the fortress she took to falling asleep—often while still crying—in the Halfbreed woman's embrace.

If things were hard for Reiyalindis, though, they were worse for her friends, who were forced to watch her pain without being able to put a stop to it. Koän was taking it hardest, and Baden knew he was struggling with the fact that to react violently could cost all of them their lives. Luckily, Koän kept all of his mounting rage under the surface—but only barely.

✖ ✳ ✖

The following day Baden was so excited, he was nearly trembling as he went to the huge telescope. The moment the sun showed itself over the surrounding mountains, he fixed the telescope on it. He sat there patiently as the sun continued its course, hardly taking his eye from it until it again vanished from view. No one disturbed him as he watched, but when he finally, reluctantly, left the telescope, they were all there waiting for him. "What was it like?" Safaya asked eagerly. "Could you see it well?"

Baden gave a noncommittal shrug. "Well, I know one thing, at least."

"What?" Alhalon asked.

"The sun is a lot farther away—and a lot bigger—than I ever guessed." He sat down with a sigh. "I think we may have to find some way to significantly increase the magnification. Even with this telescope's power, I couldn't see any details—just a burning ball in the sky." He looked up at the darkening horizon. "I think I'll take a bit of a peek at the moon tonight."

"Do you think it has something to do with the Ghost People?" asked Safaya.

"No, not really. But as long as we've got this telescope, we may as well look around with it."

After another day of observing the sun, Baden and Alhalon began discussing some other options. It had become clear that the telescope alone would not be enough to gather the kind of information they needed. "There's got to be some kind of connection to direct sunlight," Baden said. "When we pulled the Ghost Man into the shadows, he didn't die, but he did become extremely agitated. And they won't willingly leave sunlight. So it has to be something else."

"Something we can't see," Alhalon murmured thoughtfully.

"Exactly. So I'm thinking we've got to make some kind of device that can detect invisible energy—like heat, for instance. That can be detected just by feeling it, but there may be other types of energy that may not be so readily apparent."

"That much is true," said Alhalon. "There are a wide variety of magical energies that I can detect through my powers, but most of them exist on the spiritual plane rather than the physical."

"And it may very well be magical energies that are creating the Ghost People."

With a shake of his head Alhalon said, "Not any magic that I can feel. Ghost People have appeared here several times, and I never felt so much as a ripple of magic. Unless it is a magic wholly alien to me, it must be a natural energy."

"We'll cover all the possibilities we can think of, just to be sure. Now, to start with, I have this." He produced a paper filled with numbers, obscure symbols, and a few diagrams. "I think I know what I'll need to put this together."

✘ ✳ ✘

Over the next several weeks, Alhalon's study slowly transformed into something more closely resembling a laboratory. He and Baden worked tirelessly, and though their work was difficult, they made steady progress. They found themselves having to almost completely abandon their normal way of thinking, creating instruments that made little sense to anyone not familiar with them. For some of them, they had to first come up with entirely new ways to produce the energy necessary to make them run—some natural, others magical. Where their technology was lacking, Alhalon patched the instruments with carefully crafted magical spells, allowing the instruments to function in ways no one had ever dreamed.

Thus it was that they finally stumbled upon a source of energy that seemed to match the behavior of the Ghost People. Almost accidentally they had created a device that could detect a peculiar type of energy—neither of them even knew what the energy was, but it was undoubtedly there. Strong surges of the energy occurred every now and then, most often once a day or even less. Through careful observation of the sun, Baden came to the conclusion that these strange pulses of energy were caused by what looked like explosions on the sun.

"Explosions?" asked Vaelon as he and his friends met with Baden just before dinner.

"I've observed some of them over the past few days," said Baden. "There's a bright flash on the sun—sometimes, when they're on the outside edge, I can see them clearly. They look like jets of flame, or explosions, and every time I saw one there was a surge of this strange energy not long thereafter. These surges seem to last random amounts of time—from a few minutes to one that was half an hour long yesterday. Just like the Ghost People. And the energy is less intense in shadow, sometimes nonexistent."

"But the Ghost People don't really show up that often, do they?" asked Safaya.

"Not that we know of," replied Baden. "But it's entirely possible that many—even most—Ghost People appearances go unobserved, in places where there are no people. That's the part that has me stumped—why they only appear in a few locations instead of everywhere."

"So what are you going to do next?" asked Ciroy.

"Well, we need some way to know for sure if the Ghost People are appearing during these surges of energy. We're working on a device that we can send high into the air to watch the land around us."

"Can you really do that?"

"We're sure going to try."

That device proved to be more simple than they had anticipated. "Why not just send the telescope into the sky?" Alhalon asked. "I could use spirits to lift it high into the air, and use a tether of magic to bring the images the telescope sees back down here."

"Can you do that?" Baden asked. "I thought your magic doesn't work outside the fortress."

A faint, cold smile appeared on Alhalon's lips. "The spirits that trapped me here missed one detail. They prevented my magic from working outside the walls and under the floor, but they had not yet managed to give my prison a ceiling before I caught on to their ploy and stopped it."

Baden's eyes widened a little. "So your magic can still work upward?"

"As long as it does not leave the boundaries of the outer wall, yes, for those boundaries exist even up in the air. It can go as high as I wish."

"Well, then, let's get to it!"

Alhalon, using a summoned spirit, lifted the telescope high into the air, being careful not to allow it to go father to the sides than the walls of the fortress. He then used a magical bond attached to the telescope to transmit the images back down into a mirror in the study. After a few hours of trial and error, they found themselves in possession of a device that could quite literally spy on a great deal of the kingdom.

"All right," Baden said, "we just need to keep moving that telescope around and hope we catch sight of some Ghost People—and then hope it's at the same time that strange energy is present."

"That's a lot of hoping," murmured Alhalon.

"I know. It may take a while. We should take turns watching it, don't you think?"

"You can't control the magic connected to the telescope."

Baden nodded. "True. Well, I guess you get to watch all day, then. Let's get cracking."

Alhalon became a permanent fixture in the large stuffed chair facing the mirror. He kept his eyes on it constantly during daylight hours, not willing to even glance away for fear of missing a glimpse of the Ghost People. The energy detector was outside, but they had an indicator in the room that was attached to it, and every time that indicator went off Alhalon quickly scanned the countryside searching for Ghost People.

His diligence paid off. One morning Baden, who had fallen asleep in another chair in the study, was awakened when Alhalon cried, "Hah! Baden, come quickly!"

Baden hurriedly approached the mirror. It was looking at a desert, and there was a large group of Ghost People trudging through it. The energy detector, he noticed, was buzzing faintly, signaling that the strange energy from the sun was present.

"They appeared at the same instant the energy did," Alhalon said.

Baden nodded. "Could be coincidence, though. Let's see what happens when they disappear. Where are we looking, anyway?"

"This is the desert east of the Great Shield, some distance north."

"Ah."

The Ghost People stayed for nearly twenty minutes. The moment they vanished, the energy detector went quiet.

"Yes!" Baden exulted. "Unless that's another coincidence, that energy is definitely connected to the Ghost People! Now, to determine what that connection is!"

"We are certainly getting closer," Alhalon said. "I think . . ." He trailed off, a frown coming to his face as he stared at the mirror.

"What is it?" Baden asked, also looking at the mirror.

Alhalon moved the view up a little, and his frown deepened. "What is that?"

Baden also began to frown, his brows knitting together in thought. "Can you get any closer?"

Alhalon did so, and both men stared intently. After a moment Alhalon breathed, "It can't be."

Baden's eyes were wide by then, and in a thunderstruck voice he muttered, "This certainly might explain a few things."

ELEVEN

It began as a dull throb, and at first it didn't concern Vaelon too much; it wasn't much worse than the almost constant ache he had grown accustomed to.

As an hour passed, though, the throb steadily grew worse. He tried to ignore it, not wanting it to show; he hated it when everyone got worried about him.

Just then Baden and Alhalon entered the dining hall where the rest of them were gathered at the table. "Well," Baden announced, "we've made a remarkable discovery. This strange energy we've found is, indeed, connected to the Ghost People. As it turns out, I was right about the Ghost People being created—and now I know who's behind it."

Everyone perked up at that. "Really?" said Safaya. "Who?"

"The Sanretsu."

Vaelon stared at him, shocked. "The . . . Are you sure?" As if the mere mention of the name made his injury worse, the pain gave a sudden flare. He grimaced and rubbed at it.

"Certain," Baden said.

"Somehow," said Ciroy, "I feel like I should have suspected that."

"How are they doing it, though?" asked Vaelon. "And what does it have to do with the sun?"

"We found a very interesting little operation out in the desert beyond the Great Shield," said Baden. "There's a gigantic mountain out there, and it and the land around it are swarming with Sanretsu—we found several entire cities in the desert, and a sort of highway connecting their cities on this side of the mountains to that desert."

"They've expanded out into the desert?" Safaya asked. "But why?"

"The magic of Daaku Chikara is severely limited," Alhalon said, his voice carrying a condescending tone, as though he were talking to ignorant children. "While it has great capacity for destruction, it is nonetheless a weaker magic because it lacks the ability to create. Take Thrꜵll, for instance—the Sanretsu did not make them with the use of Daaku Chikara but rather with witchcraft."

"They use magic other than Daaku Chikara?" Ciroy asked, scratching his head. "I didn't know that."

"Of course they do. If they didn't, all they would be able to do is destroy things—and admittedly, that is an area in which Daaku Chikara is unrivaled. No, the Sanretsu also employ witchcraft—the darkest and most dangerous kind, the enslavement of lesser demons to carry out their bidding."

"That sounds bad," said Safaya.

Alhalon smirked. "You know nothing of demons, do you? They are dangerous and unreliable as slaves. Unless carefully controlled, they will certainly kill the one foolish enough to summon them. I suspect the power of Daaku Chikara is enough to keep them in line, however, for that black magic can destroy even them, a feat no other magic can accomplish."

Vaelon noticed that he was beginning to sweat, and he quickly wiped his forehead. The pain was becoming increasingly intense, and he doubted he would be able to hide it if it got much worse. "So what's this got to do with the mountain in the desert?"

"Isn't it painfully obvious? The Sanretsu are tapping into a new power source, one they will undoubtedly wield in concert with Daaku Chikara. After finding the Sanretsu on that mountain, something became very clear to me. Some of the spirits I have summoned in the past hinted at a great power within the earth, but try as I might, I was never able to discover this power. I think that I now know why—the power is not a part of the earth, but rather is contained in an object that is inside the earth. Inside that mountain. Do you follow my meaning?"

"I think so," Ciroy said. "You mean this power is locked in some object."

"The mountain," Reiyalindis breathed, her eyes widening.

Alhalon looked at her sharply, glowering. "What are you talking about, little girl?"

She ignored his glare, and Vaelon could tell from the look on her face that she was too surprised by what had just been revealed to her to even notice Alhalon's disapproval. Her breathing quickened, and she said, "The power the Sanretsu are after isn't in the mountain—it *is* the mountain! They've found it, and they've begun tapping into it. They're already learning its secrets!"

"But could that power really be connected to the Ghost People?" asked Ciroy with a frown. "They've been showing up for five years now. If the Sanretsu have been on the mountain that long, wouldn't they have already figured it out and used it against us?"

"You are an ignoramus," Alhalon said. "Magic is not so easily learned. A new power like this could not be fully utilized in a mere half decade."

"Which explains why the Ghost People attacks are so random right now," Baden said. "They can't fully control the power yet. It must combine with that energy from the sun to create the Ghost People, and if they learn how to use it well enough, they could flood the whole world with destruction every time the bursts of energy appear."

"Or even figure out how to create the Ghost People without the energy," agreed Alhalon. "They must be stopped before they succeed in fully controlling this power."

Vaelon, who was now breathing heavily, said, "Then our task is clear now. We have to stop the Sanretsu."

"You?" Alhalon asked contemptuously. "What could your sorry little band do against the Sanretsu? If I were you I would go to the Dark Elves and convince them of the danger. Their combined might may be enough to break past the Sanretsu and capture the mountain."

"No," Reiyalindis said firmly. "The task is ours and ours alone."

Alhalon's eyes blazed as he looked at her. "Stupid girl!" he growled. "You may have a seeress's power, at least a little bit, but it doesn't take any power at all to realize that what you suggest is sheer idiocy!"

Reiyalindis straightened, lifting her chin. "Nonetheless, it must be. Gathering an army to fight the Sanretsu would fail—they are already too strong for that. It would only result in a war in which the Sanretsu would emerge victorious and virtually unopposed."

Alhalon's voice was heavy with spite. "And you can do what the Dark Elves could not? You will succeed where their power would fail? You are nothing—a pathetic little urchin suffering from delusions of grandeur."

She took a deep breath. "I have seen it, Alhalon. Even as you spoke, it was shown to me. But it was also shown that our company is not yet complete—there is one member still to join us."

"Oh?" Alhalon asked in a scathing tone. "And who is it, pray tell? Some sorcerer? No sorcerer alive has the power to contend with this threat alone!"

"Not a sorcerer," she said. "A monster."

Slightly taken aback, Alhalon said, "Monster? What gibberish is this you speak, piglet seeress?"

"Your servant, Alhalon. He must come with us."

Alhalon's face grew red with anger. "My servant?" he demanded. "You think that I'll just let you take my servant with you? You insolent little guttersnipe!"

Before any more words were spoken, Vaelon finally let himself slump forward onto the table, accidentally spilling a glass of water. He was trembling badly, and his breath was coming out in weak gasps.

"Vaelon!" Safaya exclaimed, standing up so fast she knocked her chair over as she rushed to the Elven warrior's side.

Vaelon painfully straightened in his seat. His face was streaked with sweat, and his voice was strained when he answered. "I think I need . . . to lie down."

Ciroy immediately took Vaelon's arm, and Safaya took the other, helping him stand. "Reiyalindis, go get some blankets, hurry!" Safaya ordered, and the little girl ran from the room.

"Can you make it back to our room?" Ciroy asked.

In response, Vaelon simply let out a long groan and shook his head. His knees gave way, and he sagged, causing Ciroy and Safaya to stumble at the sudden extra weight. They carefully laid him out on the floor, and Safaya hovered over him anxiously.

"Oh, it's that wound again," she muttered.

Just then Reiyalindis returned, carrying several of their blankets. She and Ciroy laid them out on the floor. Then Baden and Ciroy carefully lifted Vaelon onto them, giving him a slightly softer resting place.

Through his pain, Vaelon noticed that tears were streaming from Reiyalindis's eyes and she was desperately looking up at Alhalon. "Please," she asked, "could you do something for him?"

Alhalon's smile was chilling. "I could. But I don't want to waste the effort."

"Please!" she begged. "I'm the one you hate, not him!"

"Silly girl. Pain is part of life. You must be truly feebleminded not to have learned that by now." He turned his back and left the room.

Vaelon gave another groan and finally surrendered to the pain, his eyes clouding over until only darkness remained.

✘ ✳ ✘

Safaya's teeth were clenched as she watched Alhalon walk out. "That horrid old beast!" she hissed.

"Let it go, Safaya," Ciroy said quietly. "There's nothing to be done about it."

They all watched over Vaelon anxiously. His trembling became more and more violent, and his eyes, while open, showed no sign of coherent thought. But finally, after about half an hour, it seemed the attack began to fade, and eventually Vaelon grew still again. Even then, though, it was some time before his eyes regained their focus. "Ouch," was the first thing he muttered, his voice weak. Safaya breathed a sigh of relief.

Reiyalindis gently touched Vaelon's face. "Are you all right?" she asked, trying to wipe her tears away before he saw them.

Vaelon nodded. "It's gone now," he said faintly. "I'll be fine."

"You just rest," Safaya told him. "Would you like something to drink?" Without answering Vaelon closed his eyes again, but now his breathing was more slow and regular.

Ciroy frowned. "Did he fall asleep or just pass out?"

"He's asleep," Reiyalindis said softly, again beginning her peculiar habit of tracing the outline of the wound with her finger.

Safaya glared in the direction Alhalon had gone. "I can't believe he just left like that," she growled. "If I were his mother, I'd disown him."

Baden laughed. "Now that was an odd thing to say."

"Well, I would," she said.

"Come on," said Ciroy. "Let's get him back to our room and get ready to leave. I don't want to stay here a minute longer than I have to."

✘ ✳ ✘

Vaelon was awake and able to walk again two hours later, and by that time all was ready for their departure.

"The way I see it," said Baden as he paced back and forth in their room, "we have two choices now."

Vaelon, who was doing his best to hide the shakiness he still felt, said, "And what would those be?"

"Well, the Sanretsu now have two bases of power—the well of Daaku Chikara, and the mountain in the desert. If I remember the histories correctly—"

"Why do you say things like that?" Safaya interrupted him. "Of course you remember the histories correctly. You have them memorized."

Baden hesitated and then said, "Uh . . . I don't really know. Habit, I guess."

"Just thought I'd ask."

"Anyway, as I was saying, the histories state that the source of Daaku Chikara is an ancient well somewhere in the Great Shield, roughly the same latitude as the Ruling City."

"The same what?" asked Reiyalindis, her brow wrinkling.

"Uh . . . the same distance north," he said.

"How do we know about this well and where it is if no one has ever been able to spy on the Sanretsu?"

"Well, the Sanretsu didn't actually break off from the Dark Elves until some time after the well was discovered," said Baden. "At any rate, the point is that we need to decide which base of power we should go after—the well or the mountain."

They all thought about that for a moment. Then Ciroy said, "It would make sense to me if we went after the well first. I mean, if we cut off their access to Daaku Chikara, that would sort of solve both problems, wouldn't it?"

"I don't really know," admitted Baden. "It's possible they may be able to access the mountain's magic without Daaku Chikara."

"Any hints, Reiyalindis?" Safaya asked.

The little High Elf simply shrugged with a helpless shake of her head.

Everyone looked at Vaelon. He glanced around at all of them with a frown and said, "What, I'm supposed to know what to do?"

"You're the military man," Baden said. "Which strategy do you think is most sound?"

"This isn't a war."

"Just think of it as a covert operation."

Reiyalindis looked up at him and smiled a little. "Oh, Vaelon," she murmured. "So unassuming, as always. You already know what to do, but you hesitate to tell us because you don't want to seem pretentious."

He looked at her for a moment and then said, "Actually, it's more of not wanting to get us all killed because I made the wrong choice."

"I trust you," she said simply.

"That just makes it worse." He looked around at all of them and sighed. "Fine. Baden, did you get a look at the kind of defenses they might have at the mountain?"

"There didn't really appear to be any, at least not in the open," Baden replied. "I take it that's where we're going?"

"Yes."

"Why, if you don't mind my asking? Ciroy seemed to have a good point."

"Daaku Chikara is their main source of power," Vaelon explained. "It's bound to be much more heavily guarded than the mountain, especially since the Sanretsu probably think there's no chance of anyone even finding the mountain. Right now that mountain is the primary threat—it's that place that creates the Ghost People. We can't risk getting killed trying to get to Daaku Chikara. We'll cut through the mountains to the east side and then head north to the mountain." He paused and then said, "You do realize that we're about to take on the entire Sanretsu nation by ourselves, don't you?"

"Fun, fun," Ciroy said brightly. "Just a light workout for us bold heroes, y'know?"

"Right," Vaelon grunted.

"If anyone wants to go home," Reiyalindis said quietly, "I won't blame them."

"Me, neither!" declared Baden. "Anyone with good sense, raise your hand."

No hands went up.

"That confirms it," Baden said. "We're a pack of fools. Let's go."

Alhalon was nowhere to be seen as they made their way to the entrance of the fortress, but just as they reached it the old sorcerer appeared in front of the doors. "Leaving so soon?"

Vaelon felt his heart drop a little. Did Alhalon intend to interfere with them? "As a matter of fact," he said, "we are. We thank you for your assistance, and . . ."

"Your gratitude is meaningless," Alhalon said. He looked at Baden. "If by some miracle that miserable little cretin you're all following around doesn't get you killed, feel free to visit again. Your company is interesting."

With a flat stare at the rest of them, he added, "The invitation, however, does not extend to your friends."

"I'll keep that in mind," Baden said in a neutral tone.

Alhalon then fixed his stare on Reiyalindis. "Well, little piglet, will you now wrest my servant from me?"

She stared at him, her eyes betraying none of her feelings. Finally, in a quiet voice, she said, "No."

He grinned triumphantly. "I thought not. You are good at making peremptory demands, but lack the backbone to enforce them." He stepped aside, and the doors opened. "Get out."

They silently filed past him and out of the fortress. Once safely outside, however, Reiyalindis turned back around to face him again. "Your servant will join us," she said in an unusually steely tone, "whether you willingly release him or not."

Alhalon laughed. "Stupid girl! What power of yours could take what is mine?"

"I will not have to take him," she replied. "He will come of his own will."

Alhalon's face grew enraged. "He has no will of his own! His will is mine!"

"Your control is not as great as you think."

Fuming, Alhalon shouted, "Is that so? You dare question my power?" He closed his eyes for a moment, and when they opened again they were glinting with horrible glee. "He is coming now, piglet seeress, and he will tear your friends apart one by one right before your eyes! Then we shall see who has control!"

Koän, Vaelon, and Ciroy drew their swords, but Reiyalindis turned to them and shook her head. "Put them away," she said quietly. "You will not need them."

Vaelon hesitated, every instinct he had screaming to prepare his defenses, but finally he sheathed his sword. Koän and Ciroy did the same.

Alhalon laughed, and from the east they heard the sorcerer's servant crashing rapidly through the undergrowth toward them.

"Stand firm," Reiyalindis told her friends. "It will not harm you."

"Are you sure?" Ciroy asked nervously.

"I am sure. You must trust me."

The beast was in view by then, running toward them with its eyes burning and its lips peeled back from its teeth in a hungry snarl. "Kill!"

Alhalon commanded as it came. "Kill them all—except the little girl!" He looked at Reiyalindis with a cruel smile. "Your fate, little piglet, will be much, much worse. You will live knowing that your friends' deaths were your fault!"

Reiyalindis ignored him, watching the beast draw closer. It was heading straight for Vaelon, and looked like it had every intention of ripping him to pieces.

Just as the creature reached them, though, Reiyalindis calmly raised her hand, palm toward the beast. It ground to a halt, the suddenness of the motion gouging big furrows in the hard-packed earth at its feet. For a long, tense moment it remained motionless, staring at the tiny girl, and then it slowly bowed its head to her.

Alhalon was stunned. He stared incredulously at the beast, and then at Reiyalindis, as the enormity of what had happened dawned on him. Finally, breaking free of his shock, he shrieked, "No! No, that is impossible! He is mine—his will belongs to me!"

"Not anymore," Reiyalindis said, with just a faint hint of a victorious smile. "Good-bye, Alhalon." She turned and began walking away.

"Thief!" Alhalon shouted as they left. "Deceitful witch! Give me back my slave—he is mine! Mine!" Slowly his ranting faded as they drew farther away, the hulking beast trailing a few yards behind them.

Once out of sight of the fortress, Reiyalindis could no longer conceal her delight, and her face split into a huge grin. Ciroy patted her on the back, and said, "Well done, my little friend. Well done."

Her eyes sparkled.

Glancing back at their new companion, Safaya said, "How did you do that, Reiyalindis?"

"I'm not really sure," she replied. "I just knew it would work, that's all."

"So . . . why is he coming? And does he have a name?"

"He's coming because we need him," Reiyalindis said. "I don't know why. And he doesn't really have a name—he's actually several hundred spirits in a single body."

"Really?" Ciroy asked. "So . . . is he really a 'he,' or a 'they?' "

"For simplicity's sake let's just refer to them as one," said the little girl. She looked back at the creature momentarily and then said, "He said we can call him Chrotak."

"You can talk to him?" Vaelon asked, surprised.

"Talk isn't the right word, I think. He understands us perfectly, but he can't speak our language—not without Alhalon's help, anyway, because his vocal instruments were destroyed during that body's creation—so he simply sends his thoughts to me."

"Oh. I see. I think."

"Chrotak," said Baden. "An appropriate name."

"What do you mean?" asked Safaya. "Is that another obscure Old Elvish word?"

"Actually, yes. It means 'prison,' or in another sense, 'slave pen.' It was originally used as a term for a large camp in which prisoners of war were temporarily held before being sold as slaves. Names like that weren't at all uncommon in Old Elvish. Back then, names tended to be very descriptive, not just meaningless names like most are now."

"How do you even know all this stuff?" Ciroy demanded. "Do you speak Old Elvish?"

"Well, yes," he said. "It may be a dead language, but there are still books written in it, so I learned it in order to read them." He looked down at Reiyalindis. "Alhalon told me the spirits in that body are mischievous and not to be trusted."

"That is not true. They are actually very benevolent spirits. They recognized Alhalon's evil and so they trapped him in order to contain him. He could have stopped them, but by the time he realized what they were doing it was too late for the magic to be undone. He tricked them into inhabiting this body to take revenge on them. The body is twisted and horrible, and they are all in constant pain inside of it."

Safaya wrinkled her nose. "It stinks too," she added. "Could you convince our new friend to take a bath, by any chance?"

Reiyalindis laughed. "He would be happy to. It was Alhalon who forced him to live in such squalor before."

That night they stopped near a clear little lake, and Chrotak—eagerly, it seemed—trotted into the water and gave himself a thorough washing. The very nature of his patched-together body still caused it to emit a rank odor, but it no longer made everyone within fifty paces gag.

Now that he was no longer under Alhalon's domination, Vaelon could see that Chrotak was actually quite an amiable creature. His good nature, though, belied Chrotak's power—his skin had been magically toughened, and his strength was prodigious. All in all, Vaelon began to feel a little better about taking on the Sanretsu now that Chrotak was with them.

✖ ✳ ✖

One evening as they were making camp, Koän and Reiyalindis walked a little ways from the others. They stood not far from the edge of camp. Safaya was gathering sticks for the fire and happened to overhear what Reiyalindis was saying. She doubted the little girl had any idea that she could be heard, but Safaya's ears were very sharp and she could hear her clearly even at that distance.

"We still have a long way to go," Reiyalindis was saying, a note of worry in her voice. "It's starting to look like this could take a good while longer."

Safaya looked up in time to see the Dark Elf simply nodding.

"Oh, Koän, I'm scared. It's only a matter of time, you know." She turned toward her guardian, resting her forehead against his arm. "I've been having dreams lately—terrible dreams. I see their faces, their eyes; so empty and yet so accusing, angry, betrayed . . . so full of hurt and so very, very cold. They haunt me."

After that she fell silent, and Safaya, realizing she was eavesdropping, continued with her task. Safaya was troubled as she worked, wondering what Reiyalindis was talking about, but she was sure that if she asked Reiyalindis she would get no answer, and Koän would certainly never betray what Reiyalindis wanted to be kept as a secret.

✖ ✳ ✖

The way the trembling attendant entered the dimly lit throne room told Daaku Shukun that something had gone very wrong. He flexed his fingers, his eyes narrowing as the attendant fell to his knees before him. "Oh, great master," the attendant said, "I bring news!"

"What news?" Daaku Shukun asked.

"The last two warlocks who were sent to bring word from the Dokujin have returned. Neither of them were able to locate the Dokujin they were to report on."

Daaku Shukun let his breath out in a low hiss. Five warlocks had already returned, reporting that the Dokujin had failed to locate the Paladin, but these two had been gone much longer than the others—and now it was clear why. "They found nothing?"

"One found the scene of a battle—from what he could tell, the Dokujin ran afoul of a Dark Elven patrol outside of our territory."

"What?" he demanded. "They were under strict orders not to become involved in meaningless skirmishes!" Then his eyes narrowed. "Wait—if the Dokujin attacked Dark Elves, is it not likely the Paladin was with them?"

"That is what the warlock suspects, my lord. The second Dokujin had also left our territory, though not as far. His Thræll were found, and the warlock believes the Dokujin himself was burned."

"Was there any sign of the first Dokujin?"

"No, my lord. The warlock believes his body was taken by the Dark Elves."

Daaku Shukun rose from his seat. "Two Dokujin eliminated!" he growled. "The Paladin is a more powerful force than I had anticipated. He must be stopped, at any cost!"

"At least we now know the Paladin is most likely in the south," said the attendant.

"Perhaps," Daaku Shukun said. He waved dismissively. "Increase the patrols in the south. Now leave me."

As the attendant left, Daaku Shukun sat brooding on his throne. "Why is he here?" he muttered quietly to himself. "And who is with him? Why can I not sense his location?"

The presence of the Paladin was a constant weight in his mind, gnawing at him and instilling fear in his heart. He hated that fear—hated that he could possibly have anything to fear—but he could not dispel it.

TWELVE

The desert beyond the Great Shield stretched eastward as far as the eye could see. From what they could tell, the forest on that side of the mountains degenerated into semiarid growth, consisting mostly of cedar trees, sagebrush, and tough scrub grass. Farther up the mountain slopes, the pines were still dominant, but the travel that far up was rough and uneven, so Vaelon decided to stick to the lowlands. There were still streams and even small pools there, but as they continued farther our into the desert all traces of water vanished and there was nothing but dunes and barren rock. The gigantic mountain Alhalon and Baden had found was already visible, though it was obviously a very long way off.

"Oh, look!" Baden said excitedly, crouching beside a strange plant. It was low-growing, with teardrop-shaped leaves that were covered with long, painful-looking needles. "A cactus!"

"What is it?" Reiyalindis asked curiously. "It looks dangerous."

"I've read about them before, but I've never seen one in person," Baden said. "What a fascinating little plant!"

"Hmm," Vaelon said absently, shading his eyes to look ahead. It was very hot, and he could feel himself sweating, even though the day had hardly begun. "Are we going to be able to find anything to eat out here?"

"Rabbits," said Safaya, observing some nearby tracks. "And there are deer out here too."

"And these," added Baden, indicating the cactus.

"You've got to be kidding," said Vaelon, looking down at the needle-studded plant.

"Not at all. Apparently they're very good, once you get past the needles and the outer skin."

"Well, let's hope it doesn't come to that."

Reiyalindis seemed to wilt under the oppressive heat as they traveled that day. None of them were used to such temperatures, but it was harder on her than the others. Soon she was drenched with sweat, her hair plastered to her forehead as though she'd been hit by a spray of water. Koän made her drink a lot of water as they went, fearing she would become dehydrated, and when it became obvious that she was weakening badly he carried her on his back the rest of the day. Fortunately, she seemed to get used to it as the days wore on, and soon she was able to hold her own again.

The mountain drew steadily closer, and they began to realize just how truly immense it was. It dwarfed any of the mountains in the Great Shield, reaching so high into the sky that it staggered the imagination.

They met no resistance, and finally came upon one of the cities Baden had told them about. It wasn't very big, about the size of Coebane, but it was surrounded by strong walls of brown desert stone. It was also, as far as they could tell, completely uninhabited. After observing it through his telescope from atop a nearby hill, Baden reported that he could see no signs of people there.

"But why?" Vaelon wondered aloud. "Why did the Sanretsu build it if they don't even use it?"

"Good question," replied Baden. "Maybe after dark we should go in for a closer look."

"That may not be a bad idea," Vaelon agreed. "We might find some clues as to what's going on out here."

When darkness fell they moved closer to the city, taking cover in a stand of cedars while Koän went on alone to feel things out. The Dark Elf returned less than an hour later and in a few short words reported that the city was, indeed, completely empty.

They all went in then, poking around the abandoned houses looking for anything useful. After a short while, Baden said that he was sure the city had been deserted for at least several years.

"This doesn't make any sense," Vaelon muttered. "The city seems sound enough—it's a good, solid, defendable place. Why would the Sanretsu have built it and then just left, especially when they're so close to it anyway?"

Baden touched the wall of one of the houses, his face speculative. "If you ask me . . ." he started to say, but he stopped abruptly as a thin, tremu-lous voice reached his ears.

"Pardon me," it said.

Koän was already moving, his sword out, as he darted into the shad-ows between two houses. There was a muffled exclamation, and then Koän reappeared, his arm around the throat of a frightened, ancient-looking man. Vaelon gave a start. This man, whoever he was, wasn't an Elf, but he certainly wasn't a Human, either. Even though his frame was thin to the point of looking frail, the odd shape of his bald head made him look dis-turbingly like one of the Ghost People.

"Please forgive my interruption," the old man gasped, his skinny hands clutching at Koän's arm. "I did not mean to startle you."

Vaelon stared intently at the stranger for a moment. "Who are you?" he asked.

"My name is Ko-Tun," he replied. "I am of the Tan-Sho-Ko. Please, release me and allow me to explain."

Vaelon considered it for a moment and then nodded to Koän. The Dark Elf released the old man, who rubbed at his neck with a grimace. "All right," said Vaelon, "explain. Who are the Tan-Sho-Ko?"

"My people live here in the desert," replied Ko-Tun. "Our land was taken by the Sanretsu." He cast a fearful glance behind him at Koän. "He resembles them. Is he of their kind?"

"No," Vaelon replied. "He's a Dark Elf."

"I fear I am not familiar with the other races. We have never known any other peoples save the Sanretsu, and what we know of the other races was learned from their talk. They took our lands and enslaved our people not many years ago. Now our cities lie barren and our people labor for the Sanretsu in Ji-Ge-Lon, the Great Mountain." He looked curiously at Vaelon. "Strange—it was not foretold that you would not know these things. Come, I will take you to the sanctuary. We have much to discuss, and it had best not be in the open."

"Foretold?" Vaelon demanded. "What are you talking about?"

"Your coming was prophesied long ago," Ko-Tun said. "You are all here, even the Beast—it is exactly as foretold. Please, it would be best if we did not remain here. Sanretsu guards sometimes pass through here as they patrol the land."

Vaelon hesitated, not sure if following this old man anywhere was a good idea. But it was the best they had to go on. He glanced at Reiyalindis, hoping she'd had a burst of inspiration, but the little girl just shrugged helplessly.

"All right," he said finally, looking back at Ko-Tun. "But no tricks. We'll be on our guard, I assure you."

"I understand your hesitation," Ko-Tun said. "Come with me."

They followed the little old man into a nearby house where he descended a staircase hidden beneath a trapdoor. The stairs led to an underground passage, which was lit at regular intervals by strange luminescent stones set in the walls. It was barely big enough for Chrotak to fit down. After twenty yards it opened up into a large chamber, where half a dozen more old men like Ko-Tun were seated on cushions. "Ko-Tun!" one exclaimed. "Is it true? Are they the Deliverers?"

"They are indeed," Ko-Tun replied jubilantly. "They could be no others!"

One of the old men, who appeared to be the oldest of all, hobbled toward them. "The Paladin!" he crowed, grasping Vaelon's hand warmly. "At last you have come! I am Ri-Ghy, overseer of the Tan-Sho-Ko."

"What did you call me?" Vaelon asked, a little uncomfortable.

Ri-Ghy did not appear to have heard him and was moving on to Baden. "The Wise Man," he said. Then, to Ciroy and Safaya, he said, "The Hunters."

Ciroy shook his hand. "Uh . . . sure," he said. "You must be the Old Guy."

Ri-Ghy nodded, looking pleased. He then went to Koän, and, looking happy despite the Dark Elf's resemblance to the Sanretsu, said, "The Silent Man." He glanced at Chrotak, who was behind Koän, and said, "The Beast."

Finally the old man came to Reiyalindis, and his expression turned to one of deep sadness as he took her hand. "The Empty One," he said in a quiet voice. "I did not expect you to be so young." He patted her hand in a strangely consoling manner.

"Now hold up a second," Ciroy said. "Just what do all these names mean? You're saying we're in a prophecy?"

"You are indeed," said the old Tan-Sho-Ko. "Though I'm afraid most of you are merely mentioned in passing, it seems, as the companions and helpers of the Paladin."

Everyone looked at Vaelon. He took a step back, holding up his hands. "Now wait a second—I'm not really sure you've got the right man, here!"

"It is you," Ri-Ghy said with evident conviction. "You are here to free our people from the Sanretsu." His brow wrinkled in confusion. "Do you mean to say that is not the purpose for which you have come?"

"Uh . . . actually, I'm here because we're trying to find a way to stop the Ghost People."

"Who are the Ghost People?"

"Strange people who appear out of nowhere for short periods of time. The Sanretsu are creating them and sending them to kill my people."

Ri-Ghy's eyes lit up with understanding, and he nodded sadly. "Ah. You speak of the Se-Cho-Fa. I fear that your assessment is only partially correct—the Sanretsu are indeed loosing them upon the land, but they do so unintentionally, and it was not they who created them."

Baden gave a start. "You mean . . . the Sanretsu didn't mean to turn the Ghost People loose? It was an accident?"

"Yes, Wise Man. That is correct. The Se-Cho-Fa are as much a bane to the Sanretsu as they are to other peoples."

"But . . . if the Sanretsu didn't create them, who did?"

The old man sighed deeply. "We did."

All of them stared at him. "You?" Baden asked, and then he snapped his fingers. "Of course—the Ghost People are Tan-Sho-Ko, aren't they!"

"Yes," replied Ri-Ghy. "Or, more accurately, the drifting spirits of Tan-Sho-Ko, now long dead. But perhaps I should start at the beginning."

"Please do," murmured Safaya.

"The Tan-Sho-Ko were once a mighty people," said Ri-Ghy. "We covered the whole earth for thousands of centuries. And yet we were ever a divided people. Eventually our divisions escalated into a massive war, and in this very desert our two greatest armies clashed—a full two million souls perished in the battle."

"Two million?" exclaimed Baden.

Ri-Ghy nodded gravely. "Perhaps even more. But their deaths were not the worst part. During the battle our most powerful sorcerers also fought each other, and the magics they employed were so great and terrible that eventually they created an enormous explosion—the result of which is the Great Desert. Before, this land was green and good, but the magic left the ground poisoned and barren forever. So cataclysmic was this explosion that it killed every living thing within hundreds of miles of its center, and it even crippled the source of our magic—Ji-Ge-Lon."

"The mountain," said Safaya.

"Yes. You see, there are several types of magic—some come from within the souls of those who use it, some from the aid of spirits or demons, and some from objects of great power. Ji-Ge-Lon is one such object, and the well of Daaku Chikara is another. Undoubtedly there are others as well."

"So your magic was crippled," said Baden. "What happened then?"

"The mountain is the object that contained our magic," said Ri-Ghy. "When the explosion took place, that magic fled from the mountain throughout the whole earth."

Baden's eyes widened a bit. "Wait. Does the earth have innate magic of her own?"

"No," replied Ri-Ghy.

"Of course!" Baden exclaimed excitedly. "The High Elves use the magic in the earth as their power—but that power isn't really the earth's, is it? It's Ji-Ge-Lon's! The High Elves have been using Ji-Ge-Lon all along, not knowing that it wasn't really the earth's innate magic! And that's why the High Elves' power has been weakening, isn't it? The Sanretsu are somehow drawing that power back into Ji-Ge-Lon!"

"Exactly," Ri-Ghy confirmed. "And if they are successful, they will rule the world. But I digress—I was explaining the Se-Cho-Fa, I believe."

Vaelon nodded at Ri-Ghy to continue.

"After that terrible battle, those few of us who remained alive came to the mountain and took up our dwelling here, but the souls of those warriors who were destroyed by the explosion have no home. Those spirits are infused with the power of Ji-Ge-Lon, dooming them to eternal wandering. They rove restlessly about the earth—sometimes in small bands, sometimes alone."

"The Ghost People," Baden breathed. "But . . . how are they only appearing now? And what does the sun's energy have to do with it?"

There was a collective gasp among the ancient Tan-Sho-Ko.

"The sun?" demanded Ri-Ghy. "What do you mean, the sun?"

"Well," Baden explained, "I've been doing some studying, and I've discovered that the Ghost People appear when a certain invisible energy from the sun reaches the earth. I believe the energy is caused by explosions on the surface of the sun."

Ri-Ghy nodded thoughtfully. "This explains a certain passage in the prophecy we have never clearly understood," he said. "It reads, 'And the darkness within the light will trouble Ji-Ge-Lon, and breath life into the doomed ones.' We did not understand that contradiction, but if this energy from the sun is indeed invisible that could be the explanation."

"Evidently that energy is somehow reacting with Ji-Ge-Lon now that the Sanretsu have started pulling its power back into the mountain," Baden mused. "That's what is allowing the Ghost People to appear."

"Just how powerful is Ji-Ge-Lon?" asked Vaelon. "If the Sanretsu get control of it, what could they do with it?"

Ri-Ghy shook his head gravely. "Anything. Unlike the magics in the soul or of spirits, magics bound in physical objects have power directly proportional to the size of the object that contains it. I sense, Paladin, that you are already familiar with the power of Daaku Chikara." He looked meaningfully at the spot where Vaelon had been wounded.

"Somewhat," Vaelon said.

"The well of Daaku Chikara is what contains that power—nothing more than a hundred-foot-deep hollow cylinder, no more than ten feet across."

Vaelon's eyes widened. "So . . . Daaku Chikara's power is to Ji-Ge-Lon's what that well's size is to that monster of a mountain's?"

"Correct. You can see the kind of power we are talking about here."

"I vote we don't let the Sanretsu get it," Ciroy said dryly.

Safaya was frowning. "But how do you know all this, Ri-Ghy? How did you get this prophecy?"

"It was written by one of our most revered seers before our great last war began," Ri-Ghy told her. "It told of the disaster that would befall our people. But we ignored it, and by so doing allowed it to come to pass. It also told of our enslavement, and that we would be delivered by the Paladin." He looked at Vaelon. "By you."

"I'm still not so sure about that," Vaelon said in reply.

"It is true, whether you want to believe it or not." He looked around at all of them. "There was also a warning in the prophecy. The power of Ji-Ge-Lon is too great for any person or nation to properly control, as we learned the hard way so long ago. It must never be allowed to gather into the mountain again or destruction will follow, just as before. The Great Mountain must be forever separated from its power."

"How do we do that?" asked Ciroy.

Ri-Ghy shook his head. "That, Huntsman, we do not know."

For a moment, there was silence as everyone mulled things over in their minds. Finally Baden said, "There's still something I don't understand. If the Ghost People are really Tan-Sho-Ko, why don't they have any reproductive organs? And why are there never any women or children among them? Surely a blast that big would have killed some civilians."

Ri-Ghy smiled a little. "Our people are not like yours, Wise Man. While we appear similar to the males of your species, the fact is that there are no males or females among the Tan-Sho-Ko. We simply are. We do not reproduce. We were never born, and we do not die of natural causes. We have been here since the Earth began and were reduced to a mere ten thousand from our former millions before your races ever emerged." He sighed. "We were kept ever in our prime before the war, but since Ji-Ge-Lon's power fled, our bodies have slowly begun to decay."

"Wait," Safaya said slowly. "Doesn't that mean that if we succeed in cutting the mountain off from its power, you'll all die eventually?"

He smiled. "Yes, Huntress. It does. But it must be done. Our own foolishness brought us to this state, and eventually we will all pay the price for it."

Baden let out a great breath. "Wow," he said. "There's a whole world out there that our people know nothing about. Sometime you and I need to have a nice long chat."

"I would be honored, Wise Man. But first things first. You may rest here for the remainder of the night and tomorrow, but when darkness falls again you must go on to Ji-Ge-Lon."

✘ ✳ ✘

Though they tried to sleep during the following day, none of them got much rest. Vaelon noticed that Reiyalindis in particular hardly so much as closed her eyes. She spent most of the day sitting alone, staring off into space.

An hour before dusk, Ko-Tun explained the lay of the land to them. The city they were in was called Li-Klemlar, and there were two other Tan-Sho-Ko cities—Li-Kratta and Om-Iganore. Om-Iganore was the closest city to the mountain, some distance southeast of Li-Klemlar. Li-Kratta was to the northeast, and it was to that city they would go first. There was a broad, muddy river separating Li-Klemlar from the mountain, and there was a large raft docked near Li-Kratta that they could use to cross it. From there they would strike east, where there was a large, complex system of catacombs north of the mountain. Those catacombs, he explained, were not known to the Sanretsu, and inside these catacombs was where many of the leaders of the Tan-Sho-Ko met in secret.

"But how do you keep this place a secret?" asked Ciroy. "The Sanretsu have magic—couldn't they feel you out?"

Ko-Tun tapped his head with a wink. "We may not be as powerful as our sorcerers of old, but we are not totally defenseless. If we rose up in rebellion against the Sanretsu we would be slaughtered, but we have successfully used what little power is left to us to shield our hiding places from their magic. These sanctuaries are quite safe, believe me."

Ko-Tun then went on to explain what they were to do next. The catacombs led into the mountain, which was riddled with caves and tunnels. From those tunnels they would be able to approach what he called Bura-Ji-Ge-Lon, the heart of the mountain. Ko-Tun would guide them there, and, with help from the other Tan-Sho-Ko, they would then sever the mountain from its power.

"We will most likely not come across any Sanretsu until we draw near Bura-Ji-Ge-Lon," he said. "That is the point from which they are drawing the mountain's power back into itself using their dark witchcraft."

"Using witchcraft?" Baden asked. "You mean they're using demons to draw the power back?"

Ko-Tun's expression was a mixture of anger and revulsion. "Yes," he said, "and their foul presence in Ji-Ge-Lon is an abomination."

"We're going to have to fight demons too?" asked Safaya. "But we were told nothing can kill them but Daaku Chikara."

"This is true," said Ko-Tun, "but that is why he is here." He pointed at Vaelon.

Again Vaelon had the uncomfortable feeling that this was all a big mistake. "Me?" he asked. "What am I supposed to do against demons?"

"It is written in the prophecy that demons fear you," said Ko-Tun. "They fear you because of the darkness already within you—they will sense in you the power of their masters."

His eyes narrowed. "What exactly does it say?" he asked.

Like the other Tan-Sho-Ko, Ko-Tun had the ancient writing memorized, so he quoted the book as close to verbatim as it would translate from the language of his people. "The demons of the enemy will fear the Paladin, for they shall sense in him the very power which tortures them into obedience, for the enemy will provide the Paladin with the means of their own undoing."

"Of course," Reiyalindis said softly. "Your wound, Vaelon. The demons will sense the poison of Daaku Chikara in you, just as I can, and they will fear it. They will not harm you or anyone with you."

"But that doesn't make sense!" Vaelon said. "The Dokujin weren't afraid of me, and weren't they created using demons?"

"Created with help from the demons, yes," said Ko-Tun, "but the Dokujin, like the Thrœll, are not infused with demons, but with Daaku Chikara itself."

"I don't understand all this," Vaelon said. "I thought all Daaku Chikara could do was destroy."

"That is something of an oversimplification," said Ko-Tun. "Daaku Chikara can infuse otherwise lifeless creatures. If you were told that it can only destroy, that was probably in reference to its inability to create. It cannot create Dokujin and Thrœll, but it can possess them."

"This is all very confusing," said Safaya. "But the point is, we won't have to worry about fighting the demons, right?"

"Precisely. The demons will sense the poison in Vaelon's flesh, and they will fear him above all else, for he survived magic even they would not."

Vaelon was dumbfounded. "You mean . . . You mean that blow I received would have killed . . . a demon? And I survived? But how?"

Ko-Tun shook his head. "I do not know, Paladin. That is not written."

"Okay, that takes care of the demons," said Ciroy, "but what about the Sanretsu? Vaelon may have a talent for absorbing deadly magic, but I don't think the rest of us are similarly equipped."

Vaelon looked down at his wound, absently rubbing at it as it gave a slight twinge. Was it true? Did he really have some kind of resistance against Daaku Chikara? Or—more likely—had he just been extraordinarily lucky? "Look," he said, "maybe I should go alone."

Safaya rolled her eyes. "Here we go again."

"Don't do that," he said, a little miffed.

"Vaelon, we're not helpless, so let's not start with the 'lone hero' bit," she said. "We're all going." Then she frowned, looking at Reiyalindis. "Except . . . maybe you should stay here, Reiyalindis."

"No," she said firmly. "You'll need me."

The Halfbreed let out a long sigh. "If you say so. Sometimes I wish I could just tell you you're wrong—the problem is, you never are."

Vaelon looked back at Ko-Tun. "So what happens after we cut off the magic?"

"Then we run," Ko-Tun said simply. "The tunnels leading to Bura-Ji-Ge-Lon will be awash with Sanretsu by then, but there is another route we will take—a tunnel that leads out to the plateau. Thankfully it is on the other side of the peak from the Cruat Fortress, so hopefully we will not be seen as we cross the plateau and descend the southwest side of the mountain."

"What fortress?" asked Ciroy.

"There is a fortress that was built by the Sanretsu. It guards the trail that they use to climb to the plateau. That is where the entrance to the main caverns are—they built the fortress around it. It sits slightly higher than Lesser Peak, about the same level as Bura-Ji-Ge-Lon."

"Lesser Peak?"

"Yes. Ji-Ge-Lon has two peaks—Lesser Peak and Great Spire. The top of Lesser Peak is about eleven thousand feet high."

"And Great Spire?" Baden asked with evident interest.

"Over forty thousand feet."

"Wow," said Ciroy. "That's big."

"Yes. We must ascend carefully—it is colder, and the air there is much thinner than down here. As soon as darkness falls, we'll be on our way."

It was a five-hour trek to the city of Li-Kratta, and by the time they arrived it was past midnight. They had encountered no Sanretsu patrols on the way, though they had seen torch-bearing men in the distance several times.

Li-Kratta was as deserted as Li-Klemlar. Which was to say, Vaelon reflected, that it only appeared to be deserted—there was another Tan-Sho-Ko sanctuary hidden in the city. The sanctuary of Li-Klemlar had not been sealed when Vaelon and his friends had entered it, but in Li-Kratta they saw for themselves how the Tan-Sho-Ko used magic to guard their hidden places.

The building that housed the entrance to the sanctuary appeared completely empty, but Ko-Tun muttered a few quiet incantations, and a trapdoor appeared out of nowhere in the floor. "It takes several minutes to cast the spell that hides our sanctuaries," he said, "but it can be very quickly undone. When in place, the spell hides the sanctuaries from the physical senses as well as the magical."

The Tan-Sho-Ko in Li-Kratta helped them find the raft, which was hidden by enchantments like the ones that hid their sanctuaries. It was still the middle of the night, and Ko-Tun was confident they would be able to reach the catacombs before dawn.

"So if there's this river here," said Ciroy in a hushed voice as the Tan-Sho-Ko poled the raft across the surface of the muddy water, "why doesn't anything grow here besides sagebrush?"

"It is not the lack of water that is the main problem," said Ko-Tun. "The land itself was poisoned by the great explosion so long ago, and it will never recover. Only tough desert plants have been able to take root here, and farther east nothing grows at all."

"Hush," one of the Tan-Sho-Ko breathed, pointing toward the shore they were approaching. They all looked and saw a large collection of torches gathered there, moving slowly downstream.

"A patrol," Ko-Tun whispered. "They will probably not sense us this far out in the river."

They waited in tense silence. The Tan-Sho-Ko jammed their long poles into the mud at the bottom of the shallow river to keep the raft from drifting. In spite of the covering darkness, Vaelon knew the situation was dangerous—all it would take was one warlock casting his magic over the river to expose them. But none did, and soon the patrol was far enough down the river that it was safe to continue.

Once their group was ashore, the Tan-Sho-Ko from Li-Kratta cast off again, poling the craft back toward the city. "Come," said Ko-Tun. "It is another four hours at least to the catacombs."

"Great," muttered Reiyalindis. They had been traveling hard, and Vaelon could tell the pace was wearing her out.

"Don't you worry, kid," said Ciroy. "We'll get you there, one way or another."

There was a lot more sagebrush here than there had been on the other side of the river, some of the plants growing a good four or five feet tall. They followed a well-worn deer trail through it, and though it was slower going, they still managed to reach the catacombs before sunrise.

At a glance, the entrance to the catacombs appeared to be nothing more than a large desert rock, solid and unyielding to the touch. But when Ko-Tun unbound the enchantment, part of the rock faded away to reveal an elaborately carved, doorless entrance. Behind this was a steep, dark stairway heading down. "Everyone inside," he said. "I must replace the enchantment."

When they were all gathered in the stairwell, Ko-Tun began a long, complicated incantation, holding his hands up with his palms outward toward the entrance. It took at least two minutes, but when he was finished the doorway was covered by a nearly transparent sheen that looked like smoky glass. "We can still see out of it?" Ciroy said in surprise.

"Out of it, yes," said Ko-Tun. "But those on the outside cannot see in, and it is solid as real rock."

"Handy."

The stairwell was pitch black, but Ko-Tun produced a glowing stone from a heavy leather pouch and used it to light their way. The group went down a good thirty yards, and then the stairway ended at the beginning of a carefully carved square tunnel. There Ko-Tun put his stone away, for other such stones embedded in the walls and ceiling lit the tunnel almost brightly. "The catacombs extend for miles and miles," he said. "We spent much of the twenty thousand years we have lived here building them."

"Why?" asked Baden curiously.

"It is where we have laid our dead to rest," he said with a note of sadness in his voice. "Those we could find, anyway. Nearly two hundred thousand of our dead lie in these catacombs."

"Cheery thought," muttered Safaya with a shiver.

"We have been traveling nearly ten hours," said Ko-Tun, "and I'm sure you are tired. We will sleep here and then be on our way."

"Good idea," said Reiyalindis gratefully.

Despite the discomfort involved in sleeping on the hard stone floor of the tunnel, Vaelon slept soundly as did the others—all but Koän, of course. When Vaelon awoke he could not tell what time it was, but Ko-Tun told them that it was sometime in the early afternoon. They set out after a light, cold meal.

As Ko-Tun led them through the labyrinth of tunnels, they began to come across some of the Tan-Sho-Ko tombs. They were nothing more than long boxes in which the bodies were sealed. But the boxes were glass, allowing a full view of the carefully preserved bodies within. "That's just disturbing," Safaya said, observing a corpse that had died quite violently—as evidenced by the fact that quite a bit of it was missing. "Why do you leave them out like that where you can see them?"

"It is our custom," said Ko-Tun a little apologetically. "Before our arrogance got the best of us, very few of us ever died, and the bodies were kept in this way so they would not be forgotten. Now they serve more as a reminder of what our foolishness brought upon us."

Reiyalindis walked with her eyes firmly fixed on the ground in front of her, refusing to look at the glass boxes that were stacked four high on both sides of the tunnel. Vaelon looked around at them, though, his curiosity overcoming his revulsion. The bodies appeared just as the Ghost People did, all young men—though, he reminded himself, they only looked like men, as there was no such thing as gender among the Tan-Sho-Ko. Suddenly something dawned on him, and he asked, "Ko-Tun, if there were no males or females among your people, and no way to produce children, did you even have marriage?"

Ko-Tun shrugged. "No. There was no marriage among us, or indeed even physical affection beyond simple handshakes or comradely embraces. There was no reason for such things."

"That's just weird. No offense, of course."

Ko-Tun smiled faintly. "I'm sure we seem as strange to you as you do to us. We had observed gender differences in animals, but to find it existing among intelligent species was quite a shock to us."

Ciroy grinned slyly, hooking his arm around Safaya's waist and pulling her close to him. "I kinda like it," he said.

The macabre display of corpses went on and on. Hundreds of hallways branched off in all different directions with no apparent pattern, but Ko-Tun led them confidently.

After a little silence, Ko-Tun spoke again. "So tell me," he said, directing the question at Baden, "what do you know of this energy from the sun?"

"Not much," Baden answered honestly. "It's my theory that explosions on the surface of the sun thrust powerful waves of this energy toward the earth. What it is or what it does, I just don't know. I certainly have no idea why it would trigger the Ghost People's appearances, particularly now and not before."

Ko-Tun shook his head. "There is much about the powers of magic and of nature we do not comprehend. We may never."

"The other thing I don't understand is why the Ghost People refuse to enter shade—they have always appeared in open sunlight. Yet when we dragged one into shade, nothing happened to him. It seems to me that the energy from the sun can fill whole areas, not just places exposed to direct sunlight—but I don't understand its nature enough to make a proper study of it."

"I may have some idea about that," said Ko-Tun. "I know very little about this energy, but as for the Se-Cho-Fa refusing to leave direct sunlight, that could be explained by the nature of their deaths. You see, the explosion was not one of light, but of darkness—a vast eruption of utter blackness that swept across the land and killed all it touched. I imagine the last memories of those unfortunates were of being overcome by that darkness. It may have instilled in them a deep fear of the dark, which explains why they will not leave direct sunlight."

Baden looked dubious. "It's possible, I suppose," he said. "That would imply that the Ghost People have at least a degree of control over when or where they appear, though—otherwise how could they avoid appearing in shadow, or at night?"

Baden and Ko-Tun went on and on about various possibilities, and Vaelon, not really interested in the discussion, let his mind wander to other things. To him it wasn't really important why the Ghost People did what they did—the important thing was that they now knew how to stop them.

Sort of, he thought wryly. They knew where to go now, at least—what to actually do once they were there was another story. He hated making things up as he went along, but that was all this entire expedition had been thus far.

They traveled through the catacombs for an hour before arriving at a steeply inclining tunnel that entered the mountain itself. There they met five more Tan-Sho-Ko who joined them as they went. They spoke little, staying in the back and following silently.

The tunnels grew much more twisted and uneven, soon becoming a veritable honeycomb of intersecting tunnels and caverns. In time, they began climbing steeply, and as the hours crawled by, they all began to feel the effects of the increased altitude. The air was noticeably thinner, and some of them began to find themselves running out of breath more quickly than normal. Ko-Tun led them at an almost leisurely pace to help acclimatize them to the altitude.

They climbed for quite some time, and then, as they stopped for another rest, Baden asked, "How high are we now, Ko-Tun?"

"I cannot be certain," the Tan-Sho-Ko replied. "Between nine and ten thousand feet. We must be more cautious of Sanretsu patrols from now on."

"They do a lot of patrolling, don't they?" Safaya said.

Ko-Tun nodded. "They do indeed. Those who walk in darkness are ever fearful of misstep. Before proceeding we should stay here for a while. You will need to get more used to the altitude in order to cope with the physical strains we are sure to encounter."

The group stayed there for an entire day, and despite the extra time it took, Vaelon knew they were all grateful for the chance to get more accustomed to the thinner air. Finally Ko-Tun announced that it was time to continue, and they set out once again.

For a while they did not encounter any Sanretsu, but then, when Ko-Tun said they were within a hundred yards of the mountain's heart, Safaya suddenly motioned to Vaelon to stop.

"Wait!" she said quietly, her ears perking up. They group was making its way up across a particularly large cavern, and she pointed ahead to where a tunnel entered the cave. "Someone's coming—a lot of someones!"

There was no time to go back and find a safe hiding place, for the cavern they were in ran straight back quite some distance, and was well lit by the glowing rocks. There was, however, a deep indentation in the wall nearby, one big enough to hold all of them, and Ciroy directed everyone into it. "Get in there!" he said quietly. "Move!"

"It's no use, Hunter!" Ko-Tun said even as they were crowding into the miniature cave. "If they walk past us, they will see us!"

"We'll have to fight," Vaelon said grimly.

"No," Ciroy said. "Too risky at this point—we've got to reach the mountain's heart! Ko-Tun, can you hide this little cave?"

"Yes, but the spell takes several minutes," said the Tan-Sho-Ko.

"Then I'll buy you some time." He quickly kissed Safaya. "Stay put!" he ordered and then ran toward the approaching Sanretsu.

Safaya almost cried out and started to follow him, but Koän grabbed her, covering her mouth with his hand and holding her back. "Be still!" he hissed.

Ko-Tun's lips were moving rapidly as he held his palms outward, casting the spell of concealment as quickly as he could.

✖ ✳ ✖

Ciroy ran for all he was worth, reaching the mouth of the tunnel just as the Sanretsu patrol did. He crashed into the startled soldiers in the front, sending one of them tumbling to the ground.

Ciroy pretended to be startled by the appearance of the Sanretsu, holding his hands up to show them he meant no harm—which he really didn't. Fighting, he knew, would get him killed quickly. Instead he tried simply to delay the Sanretsu.

"Who are you?" the apparent leader of the squad of Sanretsu

demanded, pushing his way forward. He was dressed in a cowled robe, and Ciroy guessed that he was probably a warlock.

"Oh, hey there!" he said. "I . . . um . . . I'm sort of lost, see?"

"Answer the question!" barked the warlock. "Who are you, and how did you get in here?"

"Have you seen my dog?" Ciroy said in reply.

As he had hoped, the question caught the warlock completely off-guard. "Your what?" he demanded.

"My dog," Ciroy replied vaguely, scratching absently at his armpit. "Yellow dog. Nice dog. Lost him somewhere."

The warlock scowled, peering at Ciroy intently. "Seize him!" he commanded sharply. Two of his soldiers obeyed, grabbing Ciroy roughly by the arms as another soldier disarmed him.

Ciroy smiled innocently at the soldiers. "Have you fellows seen my dog?" he asked.

"Shut up!" the warlock snapped. "Don't play stupid with me, Human! Now how did you get in here?"

"I followed my dog," Ciroy replied. "But I lost him in the tunnels." He glanced upward. "Drafty, isn't it?"

The warlock's scowl deepened. "Take this idiot to the Cruat Fortress," he growled. "They'll pry some answers out of him—one way or another. And search these tunnels from top to bottom!"

✖ ✳ ✖

Vaelon watched as the soldiers trotted right past the hidden recess, obviously without the faintest idea that twelve people were behind the convincingly real-looking wall. As they passed, Vaelon realized it was a good thing they hadn't fought these men—there were a full hundred of them, as well as at least six warlocks.

When the Sanretsu were gone, all was silent. Koän finally released Safaya, who slumped to the ground with tears streaming down her cheeks. "Now what?" Baden whispered.

"We wait," Vaelon said grimly. "Once the excitement has settled down, we'll go to the mountain's heart and do what we came to do."

"No!" Reiyalindis exclaimed. "If we attack the mountain's heart they'll know something's going on, and they'll kill Ciroy!"

"He sacrificed himself so we'd have a chance of succeeding," Vaelon said firmly.

"We can't let them kill him. We're going to need him later on—we have to have him!"

Vaelon stared at her steadily for a moment. "What exactly are you saying?"

Reiyalindis took a deep breath. "We have to rescue him before we cut off the mountain from its power. Every Sanretsu here with any power will sense it when Gi-Je-Lon leaves the mountain for good—they'll be all over the place, and they'll probably kill Ciroy immediately."

"Reiyalindis, how are we supposed to pull him out of a fortress? The Sanretsu are already going to be swarming around like flies!"

"It'll die down, like you said. Please, Vaelon, you have to trust me. Ciroy still has something very important to do, and if he dies here he won't be able to do it!"

"Do what?"

"I don't know. Please, Vaelon, you know I can't see everything. I only feel what I feel."

Vaelon sighed. Every soldier's instinct he had told him that this was a bad idea, but he also knew that it was sheer stupidity to ignore Reiyalindis's feelings. "All right. Ko-Tun, what's the best way to get into that fortress?" Safaya quickly stood up, hope dawning in her eyes.

Ko-Tun looked troubled. "I must advise you, Paladin, that your friend is as good as lost. It is a very secure stronghold. Rescuing a prisoner from it is practically impossible."

"We'll have to do it impractically, then," Vaelon said. "Tell me everything you know about the place."

THIRTEEN

The Cruat Fortress was, as Ko-Tun had warned, very secure. It was not especially big, but there were only two ways in or out—the front gates overlooking the trail that wound up the mountainside, and the rear gate that opened into the mountain's main tunnel. That gate was guarded by a pair of warlocks and ten soldiers. The only way to approach it was by going up the tunnel, which the guards had a clear view down for at least thirty yards.

"I can take out one of the warlocks," breathed Baden as he and the others took stock of the situation from the shadows at the other end of the tunnel. They had left Reiyalindis and the Tan-Sho-Ko at their hiding place.

"And I can get the other one," Safaya added, drawing an arrow from her quiver.

"All right," Vaelon said. "Once they're down we'll charge the soldiers, and hopefully none of them will have time to open the gate and get inside."

Koän tapped his chest. "Yes, of course!" Safaya whispered. "He looks like a Sanretsu—he can stroll up that tunnel and once he gets close Baden and I will kill the warlocks. Then Koän will be right there to keep the soldiers from raising an alarm."

Vaelon didn't bother to ask Koän if he thought he could handle all ten soldiers; he knew what the answer would be. "Right. Sounds good."

The plan went off perfectly. Koän approached the gates confidently, and the warlocks, though both of them looked strangely at his clothing, made no move to stop him until he was only a few yards away. "Hold," said one, raising his hand. "I don't recognize you. Where are . . ."

Before he could finish a crossbow bolt sliced through his head. Only an instant later the second warlock was struck in the chest with an arrow. Both were dead before they hit the ground.

Koän didn't give the soldiers time to react before he was upon them. Chrotak sprinted up the hallway with amazing speed, crashing into the remaining soldiers, and within seconds all ten lay dead.

"Nice," Baden said with a low whistle. "I'm glad Chrotak's on our side now."

Working quickly, they carried the bodies back down the tunnel and hid them in a dark recess, and then they covered up the blood with dirt. "Now we go in?" asked Safaya, her voice betraying her anxiety.

"No," Vaelon replied, holding up one of the dead warlocks' cloaks. "Now Koän goes in. I want him to feel out the situation before the rest of us go charging to the rescue."

Koän wordlessly took the cloak, and without so much as a nod he headed back to the gate. He eased it open and slipped inside, pulling it closed again behind him.

✘ ✳ ✘

"Tell the truth, Human!" The Sanretsu warlock struck Ciroy sharply across the face.

Ciroy raised his finger to his bleeding mouth, dabbing a bit of the blood on it and then staring at it in feigned surprise. "You hit me," he said.

"I'll do much worse!" the warlock barked. "Now tell me why you are here!"

"Look, I already told you," Ciroy said patiently. "I'm looking for . . ."

The warlock gestured sharply, and Ciroy was seized by a terrible burning sensation all over his body. He collapsed to the floor, writhing and crying out in pain. The warlock left him like that for several moments, and then released him, leaving him gasping on the floor. "Perhaps now you will realize that playing the fool is not the wisest course. The truth, if you please."

Ciroy took several deep, shuddering breaths, and then said, "Wow, that hurt, mister. What'd you do that for?"

Instead of explaining why he had done it, the warlock did it again, longer this time. "Do you think I'm an idiot?" the warlock snarled.

Ciroy, despite the pain, clung tenaciously to his act. "My pa always said I was an idiot. Are you an idiot too?"

"Fool!" the warlock cried, striking him across the face again.

Ciroy's brows knitted together, and then he looked around as if bewildered. With superhuman effort he forced his trembling body to be still, and he gave the warlock a calm, empty-headed smile. "Oh, hello," he said, by all appearances completely forgetting the pain. "Are you new here? Would you like to pet my dog?"

The warlock gave him a long, steady stare, and then he drew a gleaming dagger. "I'm going to give you one more chance," he said in a level tone, "before I start slicing pieces of your body off."

Ciroy blinked. "Wow," he said, "that's a big knife."

The warlock grabbed Ciroy's left little finger. "Would you like to see how sharp it is?" he asked pleasantly. Without waiting for a reply, he cut the finger off, the razor edge of the knife slicing cleanly through flesh and bone. Ciroy gasped in pain, and the warlock smiled thinly. "I'm going to let you think this over for a while, and when I come back you'll lose another finger if you don't cooperate." Tossing the severed finger to the floor next to Ciroy, the warlock turned and left the cell.

Even in pain as he was, Ciroy didn't drop his guise for an instant. He had no way of knowing if the Sanretsu could keep watch on him even when he appeared to be alone. He began rocking back and forth, babbling quietly to himself about ouchies and mean people and lost dogs, carefully wrapping a handkerchief around the bleeding stump of his finger.

✘ ✳ ✘

"Well?" asked the commander of the Cruat Fortress. "Has your demon reported?"

The warlock opened his eyes, a faintly disgusted look on his face. "The demon tells me the prisoner is clearly insane. He's talking to himself about his lost dog and has been playing with the severed finger as if it were a child's toy."

The commander grunted. "I find it difficult to believe that a madman could find his way into the mountain without being seen—more likely he is a very clever actor." He turned to a nearby soldier. "Have the tunnels been searched?"

"They are still being searched, sir, but so far nothing has been found."

"If you ask me," said the warlock, "the only way I can think of that he may have entered undetected is to have climbed the south face of the mountain."

"And then what?" the commander demanded. "Scale the fortress walls and slip through the rear gate? This fortress is the only way in or out of this mountain! We've searched it for years and have found no trace of other routes!"

The warlock shrugged helplessly. "Perhaps he is a magician of some kind?"

"He's a Human, fool! Humans have no magic." He shook his head. "No matter. A Dokujin is on the way—he should arrive any minute now. He'll pry something out of that imbecile."

The Dokujin arrived only minutes later, striding through the front gates as if he owned the place. Though they were servants of the Sanretsu, they answered only to Daaku Shukun, which meant they outranked every other Sanretsu. That rankled the commander, but he kept his opinions to himself. "The prisoner is this way," he said, indicating a hallway. "I will show you to him."

As the commander was leading the Dokujin down the hall, they passed a warlock coming the other direction. The warlock's hood was up, concealing his features, and neither the commander nor the Dokujin paid him any heed.

Stopping outside the prisoner's door, the commander said, "In here."

✖ ✳ ✖

The Dokujin opened the door and stepped inside. The human prisoner was toying with his severed finger, scooting it along the floor like a cart while humming an off-key tune. He looked up when the Dokujin entered, and to his credit not a hint of recognition showed in his eyes.

The Dokujin, however, did recognize the Human. He recognized him very well—for the Human had killed him once.

Crouching in front of the prisoner, the Dokujin spoke, its voice a dry, dusty hiss. "So, we meet again, Human."

The man blinked uncertainly. "Pardon?"

"You should have known better than to leave me in the hands of Dark Elves, Human," the Dokujin said. "Not long ago a few of their less intelligent soldiers carelessly allowed my body to recombine. I killed quite a few of them during my escape—I made sure of it."

Realizing that his act was no longer any use, the man dropped it. "And I suppose you're here for revenge?"

"You are not my target, Human. But the one who is must not be far away." His hand flashed toward the man, catching the Human by the throat. "Where is the Paladin?" he grated.

Barely able to speak, the man gasped, "Go boil your head!"

✕ ✳ ✕

The Dokujin stood, dragging Ciroy up with him. "Tell me, or you'll lose more than just a finger," he said, drawing his sword.

It hadn't even cleared the sheath when there was a loud crunching sound, and the Dokujin abruptly went limp and collapsed to the floor, a sword jammed into its head. The commander of the fortress was already dead, sprawled in the cell doorway. Koän drew another sword and hacked the beast's head off, and Ciroy, not wasting time with unnecessary chatter, quickly stripped the commander's robe and sword from him and donned them himself. Koän locked the two bodies in the cell and, tucking the Dokujin's head under his cloak, began leading Ciroy up the hallway.

Though they took every precaution, Ciroy soon realized he had been right about the warlocks' ability to spy on him even when they weren't present. Within moments a general alarm sounded, and Sanretsu began swarming everywhere. Trying to blend in, Ciroy and Koän joined the rush and made their way toward the rear gate.

They had nearly reached it when a running soldier ran right into Koän, knocking the Dark Elf to the ground and sending the Dokujin head bouncing across the floor. The soldier stared at it for a second, his eyes wide, before Koän's blade cut through his heart.

Soldiers bore down on Koän and Ciroy, blocking their path to the gate. A warlock appeared, but rather than attacking, he snatched up the Dokujin's head and raced away with it.

Koän fought for all he was worth, trying to reach the gates, but then another warlock came, and he had to use every ounce of speed he could muster to avoid the magical attacks. Ciroy was being forced farther down the hallway.

Suddenly the gate crashed open, and Chrotak appeared, bellowing fiercely as he smashed into the shocked Sanretsu. Ignoring a dark spear of magic that struck him in the chest, Chrotak grabbed the warlock and pulled the unfortunate man in half.

Vaelon and Safaya were also there, and they managed to reach Koän, providing a clear path back to the gates. Before they could get to Ciroy, though, the Dokujin was there, grabbing Ciroy from behind. It wrapped one arm around Ciroy's chest, pinning his arms. The Dokujin's other arm wrapped Ciroy's around his neck.

"Stop!" it shouted. "Cease your fighting, or I'll break his neck!"

The battle immediately came to a halt. Vaelon and his friends slowly backed away from the Sanretsu. "That's better," snarled the Dokujin. "Now . . ."

With suddenness that made everyone jump, a crossbow bolt hissed out of the darkness of the tunnel beyond the gate, striking the Dokujin directly in the head. It fell backward, and Ciroy, jerking free of its arms, made a dash for the gate. The Sanretsu were frozen with surprise for a moment, but then they advanced again, shouting, and four more warlocks appeared. Safaya, Ciroy, and Baden retreated, followed by Vaelon and Koän, and finally Chrotak. The massive creature slammed the gate shut, and then set his shoulder against it, holding it closed.

✘ ✳ ✘

"Go!" Vaelon said to his companions. "Let's get to the mountain's heart before they can get through! Chrotak, can you hold it for a while?"

The creature gave him a curt nod.

"Good." Vaelon led them down the tunnel at a run.

There were still Sanretsu in the tunnels, but they didn't meet any before arriving back where they had left Reiyalindis and the Tan-Sho-Ko. When he saw them approaching, Ko-Tun let the shield drop. "You did it!" he exclaimed incredulously.

"This isn't over yet," Vaelon said. "Chrotak is buying us some time. Let's get to the mountain's heart."

All of them raced down the final stretch of tunnel leading to their goal, Koän and Vaelon in the lead. They soon emerged in another cavern, a smaller one with a dome-shaped ceiling. In the center of the cavern was a low stone dais, over which floated a sphere of pulsing light about ten feet across. It was red, streaked with orange and black.

The cavern also contained twenty Sanretsu soldiers and two warlocks.

Without hesitating, Vaelon launched himself at one of the warlocks. The surprised Sanretsu reacted hastily, and the seething fireball he launched at Vaelon barely missed. He didn't get another chance to fire, for

Vaelon's sword cleanly separated his neck from his shoulders.

The other warlock's aim was more true. A blast of dark power slammed into Vaelon, and at the same time the warlock brushed one of Safaya's arrows out of the air as it streaked toward him. Baden raised his crossbow, but as he fired a soldier rammed him, and the bolt struck the ceiling.

"Vaelon!" cried Safaya.

But Vaelon was already up again, racing for the last warlock. Shocked, the warlock struck again, but Vaelon charged straight through the hasty spell, the point of his sword slipping effortlessly into the warlock's chest.

With the warlocks dead, the soldiers put up a poor resistance, and Koän, Ciroy, Baden, and Safaya had little trouble disposing of them. Vaelon tried to help, but he was shaking badly and collapsed soon after killing the second warlock.

✗ ✳ ✗

Once the soldiers were dead, Reiyalindis raced across the floor, falling to her knees beside Vaelon's still form. "Vaelon, Vaelon!" she cried, frantically taking his head in her hands. "Vaelon, no! Please be all right!"

Vaelon let out a long, low groan, and his eyes opened, but he didn't speak.

"We must work quickly," Ko-Tun said as he and the other Tan-Ko-Sho arranged themselves in a circle around the ball of light. "Bring the Paladin, hurry!"

"He's hurt!" Reiyalindis objected.

"There is no time!" snapped Ko-Tun. "Bring him!"

Baden and Koän each grabbed one of Vaelon's arms and hauled him toward Bura-Ji-Ge-Lon. "What does he need to do?" asked Ciroy.

Ko-Tun gave him a helpless look. "I'm not sure. I and my fellows are to contain the fury unleashed when Ji-Ge-Lon is cut off from the mountain's heart, but as for how that is to be done . . . I was hoping he would understand his mission once he was here."

Everyone looked at Vaelon, who was trying, with little success, to stand on his own. "No idea," he muttered.

But then Reiyalindis suddenly knew. Her eyes widened, and she gasped, her hand flying to her mouth. "No!"

"What?" demanded Ciroy. "What is it? Do you know?"

Reiyalindis stared in horror at the ball of light. Then, slowly, she nodded. "The poison in his body must combine with Bura-Ji-Ge-Lon," she said in a small voice.

Baden blinked. "But . . . how?"

Tears began to leak from her eyes. "He must go into the light," she whispered.

"What?!" demanded Safaya. "Are you sure? It won't hurt him, will it?"

Slowly Reiyalindis turned her head, looking directly into Vaelon's eyes. "I don't know."

Vaelon stared at her for a moment, and then nodded decisively. "Right," he said. "Baden, Koän, you'll have to throw me in; I haven't the strength to walk."

"But . . ." Safaya began to object.

"Do it!" Vaelon said firmly, looking at Koän.

The Dark Elf hesitated for a moment, but then he nodded sharply to Baden. Looking faintly sick, Baden nodded back.

And then they threw Vaelon directly into the fiery ball.

Chrotak stumbled backward as the gate was rocked by an explosion, sending splinters of it flying in a heavy shower down the hallway. The Dokujin, the bolt removed from its head, was the first one through. It tried to dart past Chrotak, but Chrotak quickly caught him by the arm. The Dokujin began hacking at Chrotak's arm fiercely, but Chrotak ignored the ineffective blows and slammed the Dokujin up against the wall of the tunnel. He let out a bone-jarring roar into his enemy's face, and then, even as the black-armored creature struggled in vain to escape, he jerked the Dokujin's head off with a quick twist.

Chrotak spun, sending the Dokujin's body crashing into the oncoming soldiers, and then he spun again, throwing the head as far as he could in the opposite direction. Without a pause he attacked the Sanretsu, shouldering a few soldiers out of the way to rip into a group of warlocks.

Before long, the Sanretsu seemed to realize that the creature they were facing was beyond any of them, and they turned tail and fled back through the demolished gates. Chrotak watched them go, and then turned and ran after his companions, scooping up the Dokujin's head as he went.

"What's going on?" Safaya cried as Bura-Ji-Ge-Lon writhed and boiled like a seething ball of molten iron.

"Get back!" Ciroy said to her, grabbing her arm and pulling her away.

The six Tan-Sho-Ko were containing the brunt of the energy being released, a shimmering shield appearing from their hands and surrounding the ball of light. They were straining, sweat running freely down their faces, but they held firm.

And then it was over. The light gave a final erratic shudder, and then it exploded with force that would have killed everyone in the room had the shield not been in place. When the explosion died down, Vaelon was lying on the stone dais. He was most definitely not dead, but from what Ciroy could surmise, he was probably wishing he was. He writhed and convulsed in sheer agony, his strangled cries of pain ringing from the walls of the cavern.

Even as Reiyalindis rushed to Vaelon's side with a choked sob, Chrotak appeared, carrying the Dokujin's head. "Quickly, now!" said Ko-Tun. "We may not have much time! We need to get out of here!"

"Chrotak, carry Vaelon," Ciroy instructed. "I'll take that head. Ko-Tun, lead the way." As he spoke, Ciroy took a sword and its sheath from one of the fallen Sanretsu.

Ko-Tun took them to the other side of the cavern from the tunnel, and there he removed an enchantment that was concealing another, smaller tunnel. "Through here," he said. "Go, quickly."

"The Sanretsu are coming!" one of the Tan-Sho-Ko cried, pointing down the larger tunnel.

"Shield the tunnel!" barked another of them. The five Tan-Sho-Ko spread out before the tunnel, raising their palms toward it, and a shimmering shield covered the tunnel mouth. Not a moment later, a warlock's fireball exploded against it.

"Fy-Reh!" called Ko-Tun. "Hold them back as long as you can!"

"We will, Ko-Tun!" said the Tan-Sho-Ko. "Go, now!"

"Wait," said Baden, "what's going to happen to them when the Sanretsu break through?"

Ko-Tun's eyes were sad. "Do you really need to ask?"

"What, we're just leaving them?" he demanded.

"There is no choice. Go, now. I must replace the enchantment so the Sanretsu do not find this tunnel."

With a last helpless glance at the five Tan-Sho-Ko, Baden turned and hurried up the tunnel after the others. Ciroy followed him, and Ko-Tun entered last and began the enchantment. "Farewell, friends," he called back into the cavern.

"Farewell, friend," Fy-Reh replied. "Be well."

Ko-Tun sadly sealed the tunnel.

By the time Ko-Tun caught up to Ciroy and the others, they were all huddled near the opposite end of the tunnel, staring through the enchanted barrier at the emptiness of the plateau. Vaelon had relaxed a little; he was still shaking, and could not see or even think coherently, but at least he was no longer screaming and convulsing. It was dark outside, probably an hour or so past midnight. "We need to keep moving," Ko-Tun said. "Let's cross the plateau and begin descending the mountainside while we still have the cover of darkness."

"Couldn't we rest here for a while?" Safaya asked. "The tunnel is sealed, anyway, and Vaelon's in no condition to be climbing down mountains."

"There is a cave not far down the mountainside we can rest in," replied Ko-Tun. "Once the Sanretsu break past my comrades, they will know something is going on, and if they look hard enough they may find the enchantment sealing the tunnel. They never found them before because there was no reason for them to suspect they were even there. I would like to get as far from the center of activity as we can before we stop."

It was a struggle, for the mountainside was steep and dangerous, but they reached the cave safely. Ko-Tun sealed the entrance and then produced his glowing rock, casting a faint light through the cave.

Chrotak gently set Vaelon on the floor, and Reiyalindis sat beside the Common Elven warrior, softly tracing the outline of his wound with her finger. "Is he going to be all right?" Ciroy asked her.

Reiyalindis nodded. "It caused him unimaginable pain, but no permanent damage, and he is strong."

"You can say that again," said Baden. "Did you see him get hit by that warlock? I thought he was a goner for sure!"

"So did I," agreed Safaya.

"Those blows would have killed or crippled a normal man," said Ko-Tun. "Had I reserved any doubts about his being the Paladin before, they would be gone now."

Safaya took Ciroy's hand, which was still tightly wrapped with his handkerchief. "Let me see this," she said. "Is it bad?"

"Uh . . . I don't think you really want to see it," he said.

"What do you mean?"

"Well . . . it's not very pretty."

"Let me see it," she repeated firmly, unwrapping the handkerchief. When it fell away she gave a loud gasp and cried, "Ciroy, your finger! They cut off your finger!"

Ciroy grimaced. "Didn't feel too good, I'll tell you that."

"Oh, my poor, poor baby," she cried, tears running from her eyes as she gently stroked his hand, staring at the bloody stump where his finger had once been.

"Baby?" he protested mildly.

She ignored that. "I need some water. This has to be cleaned. Oh, my poor, brave darling!"

Reiyalindis left Vaelon's side and went to Ciroy, staring in horror at the injury. "Oh, Ciroy," she said.

Ciroy smiled, squeezing the little girl's shoulder with his good hand. "Hey, kid, don't worry; it's just one little finger. It'll stop hurting once the pain goes away."

Reiyalindis didn't notice the joke. "The queen will fix it," she said. "We need to get you to the queen. She's the only healer with the power to restore lost body parts."

"We've still got a job to do first, little lady," Ciroy said firmly. "This was only half of it. We can't go traipsing off to the queen for every little thing."

"But . . ."

"No buts."

With a long sigh Reiyalindis began to settle down beside him, but then she hesitated, looking back at Vaelon, who had still not regained his senses. She glanced back and forth between Vaelon and Ciroy, and then she abruptly burst into tears, sitting on the floor right there and burying her face in her hands. "I can't do this any more," she sobbed brokenly. "I can't, I can't!"

"Oh, now, don't start talking like that," said Baden, going to her and putting a comforting arm around her.

She leaned against him, still crying. "I'm going to get you all killed! I can't stand this!"

"Now, now, you are not," said Baden.

Abruptly she pulled away from him and stood up. "Yes, I am," she cried, her voice almost angry. "Can't you all see? I'm—" She stopped abruptly, and then turned and walked to the back of the cave, curling up on the ground facing the wall.

"Reiyalindis?" Baden said hesitantly.

"Please just leave me alone," she said quietly.

Things were very awkward in the cave after that. They had never seen Reiyalindis like that before, and it made all of them a little somber. Safaya cleaned and bandaged Ciroy's injury in silence, and no one spoke for quite a while.

Finally, though, Reiyalindis stood back up. Wiping at her eyes, she approached them, her eyes downcast. "I'm sorry," she said to them. "I didn't mean to lose my head like that."

"Don't you worry, kid," said Ciroy. "You've been through a lot."

"Not as much as you have," she said with a grimace. "I'm acting like a baby, and I'm not even hurt."

"There are different kinds of hurt, dear one," said Safaya. "I know you worry about all of us so much. Maybe even as much as I worry about you."

"Why would you worry about me?" she asked.

"Are you serious? If it had been up to me, there's no way I would have taken you into this mountain with us!" She held out her arms. "Now come give us a hug."

Reiyalindis's shy, endearing little smile lit her face again, and she gladly obeyed. Then she went to Baden, hugging him as well. "I'm sorry I snapped at you," she said.

"It's okay," he said. "Everyone has to let out a little steam now and then. Get some sleep, little one. You look exhausted."

"I am," she admitted. Reiyalindis went to Vaelon, touching his wound one more time, and then curled up with her head resting on his shoulder. Within moments she was asleep.

Ko-Tun was watching the little girl with sadness in his eyes. "She is an affectionate child," Ko-Tun observed. "It is a melancholy thing for one so caring to bear the burden of the Empty One."

"Why does the prophecy call her that?" asked Safaya. "What does it mean?"

He shook his head. "There is little written about her—only one sentence. It reads, 'And the Empty One, she who knows not love save it be that which is lost, shall gather them, though it rend her heart.' "

"Knows not love save it be that which is lost?" Baden said. "So it's true, then—she keeps telling us she's destined to be alone."

He nodded. "So it seems."

With a dark scowl, Safaya said, "No. No, that can't be right. I won't let it be right!"

Ko-Tun shrugged. "I know only what is written, Huntress."

"Well, it's not right, that's all!" she said defiantly.

Ciroy sighed wearily. "Let's get some sleep," he said. "We'll figure all this out once we have clear heads."

"A wise suggestion," Ko-Tun agreed. "Sleep, for come next nightfall we must finish our descent."

✗ ✳ ✗

Vaelon finally came around a few hours later, waking Reiyalindis as he stirred. Everyone else was asleep except for Chrotak—even Koän was dozing as he sat near the entrance, his long sword across his knees.

Reiyalindis was relieved. "Are you all right?" she asked, her voice very quiet so as not to awaken anyone.

Vaelon sat up, wincing, and leaned back against the wall. "Better," he said, rubbing at his wound.

Her expression fell a little. "It still hurts you?"

"Like fire," he replied. "Why?"

"Well, I was sort of hoping—it's silly, I guess, but I was hoping that what happened to you in the mountain's heart would take the poison from you."

"I'm afraid not," he said ruefully. "If anything, it made it worse."

"I'm very sorry." Reaching out, she gently touched the wound.

Vaelon watched her quietly for a moment. "Reiyalindis," he said finally, "you're a very unusual little girl, you know."

"What do you mean?" she asked.

"I mean sometimes you act like you're even younger than you really are, but other times you act very much older—much more wise and mature than other girls your age."

She smiled a little. "Kind of confusing, isn't it?"

"A little."

"It confuses me too. I feel like a little girl most of the time, I think. I know things that my power has told me, but that doesn't mean I under-stand all of it. I'm quite overwhelmed most of the time, to tell you the truth."

With a wry shake of his head he said, "I know how that feels. Finding out I'm some mighty deliverer foretold in an ancient prophecy came as a bit of a surprise."

"But you did well, Vaelon. I'm proud of you—it was very brave to have Baden and Koän throw you into Bura-Ji-Ge-Lon like that. What was it like?"

He shuddered. "You don't want to know, and anyway, I couldn't even begin to describe it."

The two of them continued their idle conversation for a few minutes, but it was brought up short when both of them heard voices from outside the cave. "Careful, you idiot!" said one man.

"Careful yourself," another retorted.

"Both of you just shut up!" snarled a third. "Keep your mouths shut and your eyes open!"

Vaelon glanced at Koän, who seemed to have already been awake for some time. Koän slowly shifted into a crouch, his sword held ready. Safaya and Ko-Tun had also awakened, and they quietly nudged Baden and Ciroy awake as well.

Though Ko-Tun assured them that no sounds they made would be audible outside the magical barrier, they waited in tense silence as a San-retsu warlock and twelve soldiers appeared, climbing down the steep slope right past the front of the cave. The warlock paused in front of it, looking around for a moment, but then moved on.

The last two soldiers also paused in front of the cave mouth, and one leaned his hand right on the barrier, lifting his foot to pull off a prickly weed that had stuck to his boot. "Blast it, I don't even know why we're bothering to look here," he grumbled.

His partner nodded. "They'd be mad to try to scale the mountain in broad daylight. If it were me, I'd have found some cave someplace to hole up in. I mean, how were they even supposed to get out here?"

"Captain says the warlocks think they might have some secret tunnel that goes into the mountain. It's a bunch of crock, if you ask me. If there was a secret tunnel, the warlocks would've found it by now."

"Maybe, maybe not. I'm starting to think maybe the Tan-Sho-Ko aren't as stupid and helpless as we thought."

"I don't even care if we find these people. I don't want to take over the world and all that other garbage the muckety-mucks are always going on about. They're going to get us all killed."

"You keep talking like that, and you'll end up being the next chosen one, buddy. Come on, that warlock is glaring at us again."

As the two soldiers clumped away, everyone in the cave slowly relaxed. "Well," said Ciroy, "it's good to know that at least some of the Sanretsu aren't bloodthirsty megalomaniacs."

"No, indeed," Ko-Tun agreed. "Many of their common folk are not so different from your own. Their leaders, on the other hand, are a different story entirely." He sighed. "At least they did not discover the secret tunnel at Bura-Ji-Ge-Lon. They would surely have been more thorough in their search of this area had they known exactly where the tunnel emerges on the plateau."

They saw no more evidence of Sanretsu that day, and Vaelon spent most of it sleeping. When night came the first thing they did was burn the Dokujin's head, and then they again began to climb downward. Of necessity they could not use any light, and it was slow going, but they managed to make it to the bottom in a little over eight hours. From there it was an hour to the city of Om-Iganore, and once there Ko-Tun led them to the safety of another Tan-Sho-Ko sanctuary.

They slept there during the day, and once night had come again they left Om-Iganore for the five-hour trek that would take them back to Li-Klemlar.

"I'm starting to feel like a bat," said Ciroy as they poled across the muddy river on another secret raft. "The nocturnal life is interesting, granted, but I miss being able to see where I'm going."

"I kind of like it," Safaya said. "It's more peaceful at night."

"Yeah, well, you can see in the dark really well. I can't."

Though there were more Sanretsu patrols than before, they made it back to Li-Klemlar without incident and were ushered before Ri-Ghy. "You did it!" the old man congratulated them. "We are forever in your debt. Ji-Ge-Lon can never again be used for such large-scale destruction, and the Se-Cho-Fa plague the land no more."

"Thank you for lending us the assistance of your people," Vaelon said to him.

"Of course, of course." He eased himself down onto his seat. "Tell me, Paladin, what are your plans now? The prophecy is not yet complete, for the Sanretsu will not willingly release our people even though their designs concerning Ji-Ge-Lon have been thwarted."

"Well," said Vaelon, "we're obviously going to have to do something permanent to Daaku Chikara. I don't suppose you have any ideas of what we could do to destroy it?"

"No, I don't, I'm sorry. You plan to travel to Daaku Chikara, then?"

"Yes."

"You must go carefully, Paladin, for they will be expecting you. Our prophecy is not the only one that mentions you. The Sanretsu have one of their own that tells them you will confront Daaku Shukun—the leader of the Sanretsu, and the most powerful warlock among them."

"Great," Vaelon said, sighing.

"We managed to steal some maps from the Sanretsu that will help you find Daaku Chikara, which resides in their capital city, Shikuragari." He indicated a sheaf of papers near him. Picking one up, he held it so Vaelon could see. "The Sanretsu use a highway that they built through this canyon here. I would suggest avoiding it—they travel on it regularly, and it is very narrow. Instead, it would be better for you to circle around through this pass, here. There is a ridge at the end that will take you to the tops of these mountains here, which form a natural highway that will take you northeast almost to Shikuragari."

Vaelon took the maps. "Thank you, Ri-Ghy."

"It is the least we can do. Good luck to you, and go safely."

"That's going to be easier said than done," Baden muttered.

FOURTEEN

After a day's rest in Li-Klemlar, Vaelon led his companions back into the Great Shield. Using the maps Ri-Ghy had provided, they followed a narrow, winding trail into the mountains, climbing at a steep rate. By the time the sun rose again, they had come out onto the tops of the mountains. "Wow," said Baden, "it really is like a highway, isn't it? You'd never guess all this was up here by looking at these mountains from below."

"It's probably pretty safe to travel during the day again," said Vaelon. "It's not likely the Sanretsu would climb all the way up here looking for us."

"Hopefully," said Ciroy.

"Let's eat, and rest for a few hours here," said Vaelon, "and then walk until nightfall."

While the others were settling down in a clump of old pines, Vaelon examined the maps again. Though the mountain range was hundreds of miles across, it wasn't that far to Shikuragari. The city lay well within the mountains, inside a large bowl-shaped hollow. There was a broad gorge that cut between two steep mountains and into the hollow, coming out some miles north of a lake nestled in a small valley in the midst of the mountains. The Sanretsu highway went through that gorge, though, so they would have to go around it, probably through another, smaller gorge farther south. "We're a lot closer to it than I'd thought," he said aloud to no one in particular. "It should take less than a week to reach Shikuragari."

Sitting next to him and looking down at the map, Baden pointed. "I take it we'll be going through this small valley here?"

"That's the plan."

"Is that a lake on the other side?"

"Yes, and on the other side of that lake is a gorge that cuts through these mountains. Shikuragari is in this hollow the gorge leads to. The Sanretsu highway is farther north, here."

"I hadn't realized the city was so far into the mountains."

"Neither had I." Vaelon folded up the map. "I'm going to get some sleep."

✖ ✳ ✖

They rested until noon, and then walked until nightfall before stopping for the night. Though it hadn't been very long since they had slept last, none of them had any trouble sleeping though the night. Koän and Chrotak kept watch.

Morning came, and as they were preparing for breakfast, Baden asked, "Has anyone given any thought to why we're doing this?"

"What do you mean?" asked Vaelon.

"Well, we set out to stop the Ghost People, right? And we did. Is this extended campaign against the entire Sanretsu nation part of that deal, or are we just doing it for fun?"

"I don't know about any of you," said Ciroy, "but I'm in it for the money."

Reiyalindis looked confused. "What money?"

"It was a joke, kid."

"Seriously, though," said Baden. "Why are we doing this? Aside from that old Tan-Sho-Ko prophecy that says we will, I mean."

"Isn't that enough for you?" asked Safaya. "It seemed genuine to me."

"I'm not saying I'm not willing," Baden said. "I'm just curious. Reiyalindis brought us along for the Ghost People, but now that's over with. Couldn't we . . . well . . . send her home?" He looked at the little Elven girl. "I'm not saying I don't enjoy your company, little one, but the danger will only increase from here on out. I'd rather not risk your neck any longer if we don't have to."

She slowly shook her head. "I was in the prophecy too, Baden. I'm afraid that the Ghost People were only part of this. They were caused by the Sanretsu meddling with powerful magics, and though that threat is past, it won't be long before something else comes up. The Sanretsu are hungry for power. They will not rest until the world is theirs."

183

Baden's eyes narrowed. "Surely you must have had some idea when this all started that there was more to this mission than the Ghost People."

"No," she replied. "I really didn't, Baden. I didn't realize that our purpose was more than just the Ghost People until I heard the Tan-Sho-Ko quoting their prophecy."

"I find it quite interesting how your magic reveals information to you," he said. "It seems as though it only tells you just as much as you need to know for the moment and nothing more. Do you have any measure of control over it?"

She shook her head. "No. I sometimes wish I did."

"But there are things you know that you aren't telling us—aren't there?"

She lowered her eyes, looking almost guilty. "It's not that I don't want to tell you, Baden. I just can't."

"Are you sure?" he pressed. "Could you tell me just a little itty-bitty bit?"

Safaya looked amused. "You just hate not knowing things, don't you?"

Baden rolled his eyes. "How can you tell?"

Reiyalindis smiled a little. "You know why I can't tell you those things, Baden. It's for the same reason you can't tell the others certain things you've already discerned on your own."

"What's this?" Vaelon asked. "Are you withholding information, Baden?"

It was his turn to look guilty. "Well . . . just a little," he said with a quick glance at Reiyalindis. "But I'm not even sure I'm right on most of it."

"I'm beginning to think I'm the only one here who's still in the dark," Ciroy complained.

✕ ✳ ✕

The forest rapidly gave way to barren, rocky ground as they moved on that day. That afternoon they climbed a steep, rocky bluff. Atop it there were almost no trees at all. They came across several small pools of foul-smelling water, as well as a few fissures in the ground that were expelling sulfurous steam. They had to practically drag Baden away from these, as he immediately developed an almost childlike delight in throwing things into them. "I wonder how deep they go," he muttered, and then launched into a long, rambling theory about how he thought such fissures came about.

It was obvious to Vaelon that Baden would gladly have camped there for several months. Finally Ciroy took him by the arm and firmly steered him away. "I don't think the Tan-Sho-Ko counted on this when they sent us this way," he said wryly. "It may have been faster to circle all the way around the Great Shield."

"But . . ." Baden said, looking longingly back at the fissure.

At that very moment, the fissure exploded in a violent blast of super-heated steam that shot well over a hundred feet into the air.

"Crimeny!" Ciroy exclaimed as he and the others scrambled quickly away.

Baden's jaw dropped, and an almost reverent expression came over his face. "Well, would you look at that," he breathed.

"*Look* at it?" Ciroy questioned. "You just about got your head blown off by it!"

"Steam!" Baden exclaimed. "Why didn't I ever think of that? Steam, of course!"

"What on earth are you babbling about?" Safaya demanded.

"Just look at that power!" Baden said. "The pressure that must have built up to cause such a blast! Think of what you could do with that! If I could build some sort of machine that used steam . . . There could be a tank of water, and a fire, and the steam would . . . and then . . . and . . . wow! It's brilliant!"

"Later, Baden," Vaelon said drily. "Later. You're lucky you're still in one piece. Let's get out of here."

Reiyalindis was trembling badly and she ran to Baden, throwing her arms around him. "Oh, Baden, that was close," she said, her voice choked. "You gave me such a fright!"

He looked a little startled as he patted her on the back. "Hey, don't worry, I'm fine. But Vaelon's right—we'd better get moving."

For the rest of the day they walked through the rocky territory, and finally, just when the sun was beginning to set, they came upon a steep rocky slope that dropped at least a thousand feet down into a narrow green valley. "That's the valley that leads to the big lake," said Vaelon, looking down into it. "On the other side of the lake there's a steep gorge that leads into the big hollow where Shikuragari lies."

"How far, then?" asked Ciroy.

"A day to get down into that valley and to the lake on the other side," said Vaelon. "From there it'll probably be another two or three days at the most to Shikuragari."

Ciroy let out a great breath. "And then the fun starts. We must be plumb crazy."

"All right, mister," said Safaya to Ciroy, "come here and let me take another look at that finger."

"Oh, I'm sorry," Ciroy replied. "I'm afraid I left it back in the Cruat Fortress. It's a ways, but I'll go fetch it if you want."

Safaya stared at him and then abruptly began to cry. "Don't say things like that!" she sobbed. "It's not funny!"

"Oh, I'm sorry, sweetie," he said, hugging her. "Hey, don't worry so much about it."

"Don't worry? Don't *worry*? Some nasty warlock carved up my baby and I'm not supposed to worry?"

"Honey, please, stop calling me that," he said plaintively. "I'm a grown man, you know."

"But you're still my baby," she sniffled, burying her face against his shoulder. "Now let me see it. It needs to be cleaned. I'll get some fresh bandages."

✕ ✳ ✕

The night was an uncomfortable one, for a cold wind arose not long after dark and persisted all night long. They all moved to the lee side of a large rock to get out of the wind, but even then the drop in temperature was pronounced. Reiyalindis huddled close to Safaya for warmth, and as she did, she again felt a pang of guilt. Though she loved the feeling of falling asleep in a caring embrace, she had purposely avoided it of late—but tonight the cold, joined with her natural loneliness, completely broke down her willpower.

None of them felt very rested the following morning, and the cold persisted, creating a distinctly chilly morning. Reiyalindis saw with concern that Vaelon moved stiffly as they broke camp, the cold evidently causing his wound to ache badly. Knowing, though, that he hated being fussed over, she didn't say anything.

The temperature climbed quickly as the sun rose, though, and before they had climbed down the long slope into the small valley below, they were comfortably warm.

"What a pretty little valley," Reiyalindis remarked as they entered it.

"Yeah," Vaelon agreed vaguely. Reiyalindis could tell that something was making him feel nervous, and he wasn't the only one—Safaya was casting wary glances around, testing the air with her keen nose.

"Something wrong?" Ciroy asked Safaya.

She made a face. "Well . . . I'm not sure. I think there might be a troll around here somewhere."

"Great," he grunted. "Just what we need."

"Would a troll attack this many people?" asked Reiyalindis.

"It depends," replied Ciroy. "If he's hungry, he might."

"Just how big are they?"

"About Chrotak's size, usually, when they're full-grown."

"Don't worry so much," said Baden. "Chrotak could easily defeat a troll."

Ciroy nodded. "Yeah, you're probably right."

They walked for several more hours without seeing any sign of the troll—but Safaya assured them that there had been at least one troll in the area very recently.

Ciroy spotted the troll as they were drawing near a small pond in the valley. It was actually two ponds, Reiyalindis noticed, but the stretch of rock separating them was only a few feet wide, giving the ponds the appearance of being the same pond with a bridge across the middle. The troll was in the trees about thirty yards from the trail, and it squatted on its haunches as they passed, staring. It was easily as big as Chrotak, and it carried a heavy halberd, probably pillaged from old victims. They kept an eye on it as they passed, but it made no move toward them.

As they neared the ponds, though, it rose and ran off, moving apelike through the trees until it vanished. "What's it doing?" Reiyalindis asked, her voice quiet even though the troll was gone.

"I guess it decided we weren't worth the trouble," said Safaya.

Ciroy, though, looked uneasy. "I'm not so sure," he said. "It wasn't acting right."

"What do you mean?" asked Vaelon.

"Well, I've been around trolls that decided not to attack, and they didn't run like that—they just kind of sauntered off, not in any big hurry. This one was acting kind of urgent—almost like a scout running off to report, you know?"

"You think it's gone to get help?"

"Possibly." He turned toward the small ponds. "Let's get out of here— we'll go to the bluff on the other side of that lake. Trolls have a hard time moving uphill. It wouldn't hurt if we moved fast."

They trotted quickly across the narrow rocky bridge between the two ponds, and were barely halfway across when a chorus of bellows erupted in the trees behind them.

"Move!" Ciroy barked.

Trolls burst out of the trees just as they reached the bluff—at least twenty of them, too many for even Chrotak to deal with.

"Impossible!" Safaya blurted. "I've never even heard of that many trolls in one place!"

"Just run!" Ciroy said to her.

They scrambled up the bluff as quickly as they could, with Koän, Vaelon, and Chrotak bringing up the rear. Reiyalindis looked back and saw that the trolls were not crossing the narrow bridge, but were instead giving the small ponds a wide berth and coming around from both sides.

They would have all probably reached safety had it not been for Vaelon, who, as he was climbing suddenly cried out in pain and clutched at his chest. Evidently completely paralyzed by the attack, he lost his grip on the rock. Koän, who was climbing a few feet to Vaelon's right, made a desperate grab for him as he fell, but his fingertips barely brushed Vaelon's arm. Vaelon slid a few feet down the rock before hitting a small ledge, and he crumpled onto it and then rolled over its edge, tumbling to the ground right in front of the gleefully howling trolls.

✗ ✳ ✗

"Chrotak!" called Koän, even as he leaped from the bluff, drawing his swords in the air and landing between Vaelon and the trolls. He attacked them with such fury that they all ground to a halt, giving Chrotak enough time to leap down, scoop up Vaelon's inert form, and begin scrambling back up the bluff.

Once Chrotak was on his way back up, Koän darted toward the bluff, but just as he reached it, one of the trolls threw a hatchet at him. The rusty, but still dangerously sharp weapon slammed into Koän's leg just as he began to climb, slicing lengthwise, clear to the bone.

Atop the bluff, Reiyalindis screamed.

Koän jerked the hatchet out of his leg and spun, throwing it back toward the oncoming trolls. It slammed into the lead troll's head, splitting the thick skull and dropping the beast in its tracks. Koän knew that he would never be able to climb fast enough to get away, so he set his back to the cliff, a sword in each hand and a defiant snarl on his lips.

"Koän!" Reiyalindis screamed again. "Koän, no!"

✖ ✳ ✖

There was a deep ravine at the top of the bluff, with a stream running along the bottom, just wide enough for them to jump over. "Go!" Ciroy commanded. "Trolls can't jump very well, and they hate water—they won't follow, they'll have to find a way around. Go!"

Safaya obeyed him, taking a running leap over the ravine. Reiyalindis, however, stood rooted in her tracks, staring in horror at the fight raging below. Koän was still alive, the ground around him littered with several troll bodies, but the odds facing him were overwhelming. Chrotak was still hauling Vaelon up the bluff, and could offer Koän no help.

Ciroy grabbed the little girl and picked her up, turning back toward the ravine. With a mighty heave he tossed her across. Safaya caught her, stumbling back and falling as the weight struck her.

"Baden! Go!" Ciroy snapped. Baden cast another glance down at the fight but then turned and followed Safaya across the ravine.

Chrotak finally emerged on top of the bluff.

"Get Vaelon across the ravine," Ciroy said, and the giant obeyed, setting the incapacitated Elf down on the other side before leaping back to help Koän.

It was too late to save the Dark Elf, though. Koän was dead, impaled against the bluff by half a dozen spears and halberds. Sickened, Ciroy said, "It's too late, Chrotak. Get back across and take Vaelon. We've got to get out of here before they find a way around that ravine."

The beast nodded shortly and headed back to the ravine, but Ciroy lingered for a moment, staring in mute disbelief at the scene below. The trolls were already on their way up the bluff, climbing clumsily but steadily. Shaking himself from his shock, Ciroy dug his fingers underneath a nearby boulder and heaved, tipping it out over the edge of the bluff. It rolled and bounced down the slope, crashing into the climbing trolls and knocking three of them back to the ground. There they remained, writhing and screeching in pain. Ciroy turned and ran, leaping over the ravine to join the others.

"Let's get out of here," he said shortly. "If we can make it to the big lake on the map, they won't bother us. They're instinctively terrified of large bodies of water, and won't go near them for any reason."

Reiyalindis was staring at him, the horror in her eyes speaking louder than screams ever could. "Koän?" she whispered.

Ciroy shook his head. "I'm sorry, Reiyalindis," he said as gently as he could.

The little girl began shaking her head back and forth. "No," she whispered. "No, no, no!" Her whole body began trembling violently, and then she fell to her knees with a heart-wrenching wail of unbearable grief.

Safaya quickly went to the little Elven girl, taking her in her arms and holding her close. "There, there," she whispered, stroking Reiyalindis's hair as the girl cried. "Oh, darling, I'm so sorry."

"We've got to go," Ciroy said urgently. Safaya nodded and stood, picking Reiyalindis up.

The lake was visible at the end of the small valley, ringed by a forest of dead trees. It was fairly large for a mountain lake, at least a mile across, and on the other side was the gorge leading to Shikuragari. The stream that ran through the ravine atop the bluff ran into the lake, and they followed it as they went. The trolls soon reached the top of the bluff, and Ciroy could hear them howling in frustration when they reached the ravine, which none of them dared cross.

By the time the trolls found a way across the stream, Ciroy had guided everyone to the safety of the lake. From its shores, he turned back to see the trolls grumbling and snarling in rage and disappointment as they retreated toward their valley.

✕ ✳ ✕

Vaelon did not recover from his attack until his friends were almost finished preparing camp for the night near the lake's edge. He groaned, his senses slowly returning, and opened his eyes to see Baden and Ciroy looking down at him. "How do you feel?" Baden asked quietly.

Even through the haze still in his brain, Vaelon could see from the looks on their faces that something was terribly wrong. "What happened?" he asked, trying to sit up.

Ciroy helped him up, letting him rest against a tree. "You had another attack," said Baden. "You fell back down the bluff as you were climbing."

Vaelon looked around the campsite and immediately spotted Reiyalindis sitting in Safaya's lap. The little Elf was staring into space with a numb expression, her eyes red and swollen from recent crying. Vaelon tensed. "Where's Koän?" he asked.

Ciroy let out a long sigh. "He jumped back down to hold off the trolls while Chrotak took you up the bluff. He . . . didn't make it."

Vaelon felt a deep chill go down his spine as Ciroy's words struck him. For a moment his mind reeled, and then a deep feeling of guilt overcame him. "It's my fault," he whispered.

"No!" Baden said sharply. "I knew you'd think that, and it's not true!"

"It is true!" Vaelon said heatedly. "It was because of me!"

Hearing him, Reiyalindis looked over, her eyes regaining their focus. She rose from Safaya's lap and went to him, her eyes brimming with sorrow. "Vaelon, do not blame yourself, please," she said softly.

He shook his head. "I told you this would happen," he said despondently. "I knew you'd chosen the wrong man. I'm not whole—I told you that!"

"Vaelon," she said gently, "I wasn't wrong. Koän isn't dead because of you—he's dead because of me."

"What?" he asked. "You? Don't be silly."

"I'm serious, Vaelon. I was the one who brought all of you along with me. I dragged everyone into danger. Even knowing what I did about Koän, I brought him with me."

"Knowing *what* about him?" asked Baden.

"That he would be taken from me," she said. As she spoke, her lip began trembling again. "Vaelon, it was not your fault, please believe me. If he had not died saving you, he would still have died. It was inevitable."

Vaelon stared at her. He couldn't think of anything to say. Finally he simply said, "Reiyalindis . . . I'm sorry."

She nodded slowly but could not speak, and finally she whirled and stumbled back into Safaya's arms where she broke down into a fresh storm of tears. She cried herself to sleep, though it took until nearly midnight before she was finally too exhausted to remain awake any longer.

Vaelon also remained awake for a long time, simply thinking. Koän, while not the most gregarious fellow, had been a good and loyal friend. It was strange to think about; they had passed through so many dangers before this, and were now on their way to facing perhaps the greatest danger of all, but Koän had not died by those dangers. He had died in a meaningless skirmish with hungry trolls, a fight that had nothing to do with their mission. It didn't seem real—it didn't seem fair.

Again Vaelon wondered why he had been chosen for this mission—he, a wounded, handicapped ex-soldier. Deep inside he knew that he really shouldn't hold himself responsible for Koän's death, that he had no control over his injury, but still the guilt was there. And the fear—the dreadful fear that something like this would happen again, that at another crucial moment his pain would overcome him, placing all of his friends in harm's way. Trying not to think about it, he stared moodily at the dying embers of the fire.

✗ ✳ ✗

Reiyalindis did not awaken until the sun was well up. She slowly stirred, her grief still fresh in her eyes. She sat still for a moment, staring numbly at the fire, and then she stood. "I . . . I need to tell you all something."

Pausing what they were doing, everyone looked at her. "What is it, dear?" asked Safaya gently.

"It's about Koän. I've never told you how he and I met . . . I wouldn't because he didn't want anyone to know. But he's . . . he's gone now, and I think you deserve an explanation." She paused for a long moment as they waited and then said, "Baden, how long have you known what he really was?"

Baden hesitated for a moment, and then said, "Well . . . to be honest, Reiyalindis, I've known all along."

She nodded slowly. "When I met you, I knew you would figure it out quickly. Thank you for not saying anything."

"Of course."

"As for the rest of you," Reiyalindis went on, "I don't know if you also guessed the truth." Ciroy, Safaya, and Vaelon all just stared at her blankly, obviously having no idea what she was talking about. She took a deep breath and said, "He wasn't just a Dark Elf. Koän was a Sanretsu warlock."

Safaya gasped and utter shock filled Vaelon's and Ciroy's faces as well. Before they could say anything, Reiyalindis hurried on. "I met him in the forest near the Sanretsu lands to the north. He had been severely mutilated and was barely alive—he could not see, hear, or speak. I guided him to the Ruling City, where the queen tended his wounds. She was able to restore his senses, and he told us what had happened to him.

"He had been raised to become a warlock and possessed very powerful magic. But in their society, the details of the rituals that keep Daaku Chikara pacified are kept secret from all but those chosen to participate in them—namely the victims and the warlocks. The people were told that the victims were given to Daaku Chikara, but they were not told exactly how. Koän—or Shomérosh as he was then called—was introduced to the sacrificial ritual when he was made a full warlock. The daily sacrifices were animals, but every month a so-called 'chosen one' was selected from their Human, Elven, or

Halfbreed prisoners to be the sacrifice—and if no prisoners were available, the monthly sacrifice was chosen from among their own people.

"By the time most students became full warlocks, Daaku Chikara has such a great hold upon their hearts that it was but a small thing for them to accept, and even perform, the sacrifices. But Koän was different. Witnessing the horror of the sacrificial ritual shocked him so badly that he knew he could never accept the evil power behind it. He renounced his position as a warlock and was about to reveal to all the people exactly what went on during the sacrifices, but he was taken captive by the other warlocks before he could even get out of the temple.

"Daaku Shukun himself carried out the punishment for heresy. He stripped Koän's magic from him—though I do not believe he would have ever used it again anyway—and then, using a hot iron poker, he burned out Koän's eyes, ears, and tongue. Then his lips were sewn together with steel wire, and there were other tortures that I do not care to mention. Afterward he was cast out of the city to die in the forest. That is how I found him."

Safaya looked sick. "And the queen was able to repair that kind of damage?"

"No other healer would have been able to, but yes, she eventually restored even his eyesight, though as you saw she could not fully repair his eyes' appearance." Reiyalindis shook her head slowly. "As thanks, Koän devoted his life to me. No matter how I tried to persuade him to leave me, he would not; he became my protector, my only friend. I knew it was only a matter of time before . . . before . . ." She stopped, trembling and biting her lip in an effort to keep from crying.

"So . . . these sacrifices the Sanretsu do—they must be pretty bad," Ciroy said.

Reiyalindis nodded. "They are horrible. The victim is flayed alive and then tied upright inside a large cauldron, which is then slowly filled with molten iron. Once the iron is set, the entire cauldron is thrown into the well, the victim kept alive until that moment by demonic spells. Daaku Chikara, unlike Ji-Ge-Lon, is a living thing, and it revels in the pain of its vassals."

Safaya put her hand over her mouth. "Oh—that's just . . . that's . . ."

"Yeah," Ciroy muttered. "It is. We've got to put a stop to that."

"We will," said Vaelon grimly. "We will."

FIFTEEN

The gorge beyond the lake was deep, narrow, and choked with trees. A small stream originating from the lake ran down its center, and a path ran alongside it.

"It doesn't look like people use this gorge much," Baden commented.

"Fine by me," said Ciroy. "The fewer people we meet, the better."

As they walked, Vaelon noted that Reiyalindis was very quiet. She kept her eyes on the ground and stayed very close to Safaya, usually holding her hand. Vaelon was very worried about her. Koän's death was a serious blow, and he wasn't sure how she would hold up.

The day was uneventful, and when night came Reiyalindis curled up on her side and stared at the fire, silent and withdrawn. After a few minutes, Safaya quietly sat next to the little girl and put her arm over her. Wordlessly Reiyalindis pushed herself up and settled into the Halfbreed's lap, nestling her head against the other woman's neck.

For a while everyone was quiet until Reiyalindis broke the silence. "Vaelon," she said, "you're still blaming yourself, aren't you?"

He didn't look at her but finally said, "A bit."

"I wish you wouldn't."

"I'll make you a deal," he said in reply. "I'll stop blaming myself as soon as you stop blaming yourself."

"It's not that simple," she said softly.

"I don't see why you say that. Look, Reiyalindis—you knew something like this would happen and you warned him—but he stayed anyway. It was his choice. Not yours."

She looked steadily at him while she seemed to sort that out in her own mind. Finally she sighed. "I know, but still . . ." Her voice trailed off.

Vaelon nodded. "I know what you mean. There's still that guilt. But a deal's a deal, right?"

With a slight nod she said, "All right, Vaelon. Deal." She sighed again and then, her voice a little choked, she said, "I'm going to miss him so much."

"I know, dear. I know," Safaya said gently, rocking her back and forth and stroking her hair.

"He was my only friend for so long," she continued. "He took care of me. He watched over me day and night. He never let anything happen to me. But now . . . he's gone."

"I know it's hard, little one," said Ciroy. "And nothing we can say will make it easier. But you'll get through this—we'll help you any way we can."

She nodded. "Thank you," she whispered, and pressed herself more tightly against Safaya. "I know you all mean well, and . . . oh, this is just making it worse!" She squeezed her eyes tightly shut and started trembling from suppressed anguish.

"Making what worse?" asked Safaya.

Reiyalindis let out a little sob. "It's making it worse because I know how much comfort you're all giving me, but I know that someday that will be gone too. Someday I'll have no one; I'll be alone—so alone. . . . Oh, I don't think I can bear it!" Reiyalindis threw her arms around Safaya and held her tightly. "I can't bear to think of you leaving me too!"

"There, there, darling," Safaya said soothingly. "Don't you worry. We're not going to leave you. Not ever."

For a moment the little girl was silent and then she said, "Yes, you will. You all will. I told Koän the same thing, and he fought it. Now you're fighting it too. But I know. I know."

"But . . ."

Turning a little, Reiyalindis pressed her face into Safaya's shoulder. "I don't want to talk anymore," she whispered. "Please. Just hold me."

Safaya sighed. "All right, little one. All right." Safaya tightened her arms around the distraught child, still gently rocking.

✘ ✳ ✘

It took several days to travel through the gorge. For the first two days they saw no signs of any people apart from themselves. On the third day, however, as they were drawing within a couple of miles of the mouth of the gorge, Chrotak paused, his brutish head perking up. Almost immediately afterward, Reiyalindis also came to a stop. Her eyes widened. "Wait!" she said. "Chrotak says there are people ahead—close, and coming toward us!"

Looking around, Vaelon pointed to a thick bank of brush a few yards from the trail. "There," he said. "Hide, quickly!"

They could not risk taking time to hide their tracks, so they all simply deserted the trail and took cover behind the brush. Only moments after they did so, two Sanretsu appeared from farther down the trail, walking slowly. One was a young man and the other a young woman. They walked hand in hand, chatting amiably and smiling.

Vaelon remained as still as possible as the young couple approached, but, to his consternation, they paused right as they drew abreast of the hidden party. "Do you come up this gorge often?" the girl asked. She was a pretty thing, with silky hair and deep black eyes.

"Oh, now and then, when I need to get away," her companion answered. "It's quiet, and no one else ever comes here."

"Are you sure it's okay?" she asked a little nervously. "The warlocks don't like people to travel outside the city without permission."

With a wink the young man said, "Ah, but I do have permission. One of the city council is a friend of my father's, and he told me it was all right."

"Oh." She looked relieved. "Good. So . . . what was it you wanted to talk to me about?"

The young man cleared his throat a little nervously and then said, "Well . . . actually, I wanted to ask you a question."

"What?"

The young man went to one knee, taking one of the girl's hands in both of his. "Eterra, will you be my wife?"

A broad smile split the young girl's face, and she pulled the young man to his feet and hugged him tightly. "Oh, yes, I will!" she exclaimed. "Of course I will!"

Vaelon glanced at his companions. Safaya's eyes were shining and she mouthed a little "oh," putting one hand near the hollow of her throat. Baden rolled his eyes.

"I love you, Eterra Orynwise," the young man said.

Eterra smiled in reply. "And I love you, Tunwin Erallioch."

Reiyalindis let out a gasp, and then clapped her hand over her mouth. Immediately Tunwin whirled toward the sound, his eyes narrowing.

"Who's there?" he demanded. "Come out!"

All of them remained still as stone, and Vaelon hoped Tunwin would think he'd just been hearing things. But Tunwin took a threatening step toward the brush and said, "I know you're back there! Come out this instant! Do you have authorization to be out here?"

Vaelon motioned sharply to Ciroy and Safaya, pointing toward the two young people. Ciroy nodded, and he and Vaelon burst out from their concealment, pouncing on Tunwin. Safaya darted past them and grabbed the frightened Eterra, holding her hand across her mouth to keep her from crying out. Then the three of them dragged their captives from the trail back into the concealment of the brush.

"Well, this is a fine pickle!" Baden growled.

"Sorry," Reiyalindis said in a small voice. "I was just surprised . . . I'm sorry."

Tunwin was struggling wildly, and Chrotak took over holding him. When she saw the huge beast, Eterra's eyes went wide with terror, and tears began to stream from her eyes.

"All right, that's enough of that," Vaelon said. "We're not going to hurt you. Just calm down, please."

Tunwin continued to struggle for a moment, but he soon seemed to realize it was useless and went still.

"Now," said Vaelon, "if we let you go, I want you to promise not to scream or try to run. If you do, our big friend here will have to put a quick stop to it—is that clear?"

Eterra nodded, her eyes still wild. Tunwin's own eyes burned with anger, but finally he too gave a short nod. Safaya slowly released Eterra, and the girl remained still, hardly daring to breathe.

Chrotak loosened his hold on Tunwin, and the young man also stood still, though his eyes darted around at all of them constantly. "Who are you?" he demanded. "How did you get here?"

"Long story," Baden said in a dry tone.

"You're going to kill us, aren't you?" asked Eterra in a quavering voice.

"No, of course not," Safaya said to her.

"Well, we can't exactly just let them go, either," Baden pointed out.

Reiyalindis approached Tunwin. "Your name is Tunwin Erallioch?" she asked.

Tunwin took a step back, nearly bumping into Chrotak behind him. "Stay away from me, High Elf witch!" he hissed.

She halted and then said, "I'm not a witch, Tunwin."

"All High Elves are," he replied. "Don't think you can fool me."

"Did you know someone named Shomérosh Erallioch?"

Eterra gasped, and Tunwin's face went white. "How do you know that name?" he asked.

Reiyalindis hesitated and then said, "He was my friend."

"Friend?" Eterra blurted. "That's impossible!"

"He's dead," Tunwin said shortly. "He died a long time ago."

Shaking her head sadly, Reiyalindis said, "I assume you mean how he was tortured and cast out to die."

"How do you know about that?"

"He told me."

With another gasp, Eterra said, "You mean . . . he's alive? Shomérosh is alive?" Vaelon was fairly sure that the sudden light in her eyes was hope.

"No," Reiyalindis said softly. "I'm afraid he died several days ago. He was killed by trolls."

The hope in Eterra's eyes faded. "Oh. Oh, I see. But—he survived his punishment?"

"Don't listen to anything these people say!" Tunwin said to her. "They're lying—they're using their magic to look into our minds to make us think they're telling the truth!"

Reiyalindis ignored him. "Yes," she said to Eterra. "He did survive. I found him in the forest and took him to our queen, and she healed him."

"Eterra, she's lying!" Tunwin said again. "You know that no traitor could possibly have lived! She's just trying to trick you!"

"No I'm not," Reiyalindis said softly. Looking deep into Eterra's eyes, she said, "Eterra, how well did you know him?"

"Very well," Eterra replied. "He was a very good friend—he was Tunwin's cousin. The three of us did everything together before he was chosen to be a warlock. And then—" She stopped, biting at her lip.

"And then?" she prompted.

"And then he betrayed us," Tunwin said darkly.

"No, Tunwin!" Eterra burst out, tears coming to her eyes. "How can you say that? I can't believe it! I won't!"

"You know as well as I do that Daaku Shukun sentenced him to death for betrayal!" Tunwin said.

"I don't believe he would do that!" Eterra asserted. "Not without a good reason!"

"Good *reason?* What reason could there possibly be? He renounced his position and was going to defect to the High Elves!"

"Tunwin, you saw what they did to him," she said quietly. "You saw how horrible it was. He was our friend. Why are you suddenly just shrugging that off?"

"Eterra, just stop it," he said wearily. "I know it was awful—but that's the punishment. Just because you and I might think it's a little extreme—"

"A little?" she demanded. "Tunwin, how can you say such things? You've told me yourself that you thought—"

"Stop!" he said again. "This isn't the time or the place! Can't you see we're in the hands of our enemies here?"

Eterra pressed her lips together tightly, saying nothing more. But the glare she directed at her fiancé clearly revealed her anger.

For a moment, silence settled, and then Ciroy said, "Well, now what?"

"Good question," murmured Vaelon.

Reiyalindis looked hesitant. Finally she said, "Eterra . . . I feel you need to know this. Shomérosh renounced his position because he discovered the truth about Daaku Chikara—the truth about the terrible rituals performed to keep—"

"Don't listen to her!" Tunwin interrupted.

Reiyalindis turned to look at him and asked, "Have you ever wondered what happens to the chosen one each month?"

"We know what happens," he said. "They are taken into Daaku Chikara's bosom. They become part of it, and they watch over us."

"Would you like to know what really happens?" she pressed. "Would you like to know the truth that caused Shomérosh to turn away from everything he had ever been taught?"

"Say no more, witch!" he said stubbornly. "I'll not listen to your lies any longer!"

Turning back to Eterra, Reiyalindis said, "You knew Shomérosh, Eterra. He was as loyal as any Sanretsu until the day he was taken into the temple of Daaku Chikara. Why do you think he abandoned that loyalty?"

"Because he was weak," growled Tunwin.

Reiyalindis ignored him and continued to watch Eterra. The girl fidgeted for several moments and then said, "What . . . what did he see in there?"

"Eterra!" Tunwin barked.

"I have to understand why he did it!" she replied defiantly. "I have to know, Tunwin!"

Reiyalindis said, "The chosen ones are not taken to any higher state of being, Eterra. Daaku Chikara does not love the people who serve it. All it loves is pain. The sacrifices are skinned alive and covered with molten iron before being thrown into the well."

Eterra's hand flew to her mouth in horror. "No!" she said. "No, that can't be true!"

"It's not true!" Tunwin said to her. "Honestly, Eterra—how could such a thing be true? You know better than that!"

"Do you, though?" Baden asked mildly.

Eterra was staring at Reiyalindis, her eyes wavering between suspicion and belief. Finally, though, she said, "What do you want from us, little girl? Who are you? Why are you here?"

Before Reiyalindis could say anything, Tunwin spoke. "Look," he said, "you can kill me if you want, but please, let Eterra go."

"For the last time," said Vaelon, "we're not going to hurt you!"

"Then why are you here?" he shot back. "I'm not an idiot, you know! I know about your people—bloodthirsty savages, all!"

"My, goodness," murmured Safaya.

"Vaelon," said Ciroy, "c'mere a minute." He drew Vaelon a few yards away. "What are we going to do with them?"

"I don't know," Vaelon replied. "If we let them go, they'll trumpet our presence from one end of the city to the other. But if we tie them up here, they could starve before anyone found them."

"But we can't take them with us! They'll be fighting us every step of the way!"

"I know. Do you have any ideas?"

"No, not really. But we'd better come up with something."

Vaelon motioned for Baden to join them. Once Baden was standing beside them, Vaelon said, "Baden, tell me everything you know about those two."

"Well," said Baden, "Tunwin is a stonecutter, though if I'm not mistaken he works several other jobs as well. Eterra spends a lot of time sewing, probably to help her parents make ends meet—both of their families are poor. I think she likes cats."

"I'm not going to ask how you know all that," said Ciroy, "but do you know anything useful about them?"

"I do, actually." Baden tapped his chin and then said, "Some of it may be a bit of a leap, but . . . I want to try something. Come on."

He went back to where their captives were standing and sat down. "Have a seat, you two," Baden said with a casual wave. "There's plenty of ground. No sense standing up all day. You can sit together if you'd like."

Tunwin and Eterra glanced at each other, and then Eterra quickly went to Tunwin. They took each other by the hand and then sat down, Eterra huddling close to her betrothed.

"Now, then," Baden said easily, "I think we need to have a little chat."

"Don't waste your breath," Tunwin said shortly.

"You know," said Baden, "I get the feeling you aren't nearly as vehement about your beliefs as you're pretending."

Tunwin looked startled but said nothing, so Baden went on. "As a matter of fact, I'd be willing to bet you're a bit of a political activist—you're probably not running around in the dark making speeches at secret meetings, but you have your disagreements with your government all the same."

"Liar!" he flared. "I'm a loyal subject!"

Baden gave him a long level stare and then said, "We won't let them hurt her, Tunwin."

Tunwin's jaw went slack, and he gave an almost violent start. "How . . . I don't know what you're talking about."

"Oh, don't be shy, now," said Baden. "You were recently punished—rather painfully, it seems—for being too outspoken, correct? And whoever punished you also threatened to hurt Eterra if you didn't straighten up."

Tunwin's eyes hardened. "You're a mind-reader! You just stay out of my thoughts, you hear? Out!"

Ciroy leaned over to Vaelon and whispered, "How does he do that?" Vaelon just shrugged.

"No, Tunwin," said Baden. "I'm not a mind-reader. Simply an observer."

"How could you possibly know about that if you didn't read my thoughts?" Tunwin challenged.

"Mostly it's just by watching your actions—people always reveal more of themselves than they mean to. Also, it was obvious from the beginning that you're in pain—you masked it well but I still saw it. Especially when Eterra hugged you and when Vaelon and Ciroy grabbed you. I'll bet anything you've got a few whip wounds on your back."

Eterra gasped. "Tunwin—you were whipped? Why didn't you say anything?"

Tunwin's jaw tightened, but Baden answered the question. "He couldn't," he said, "because the person who whipped him threatened to do something equally awful to you unless he stopped speaking his mind about certain things." Baden looked back at Tunwin. "Who was it, Tunwin? Someone fairly close to you would be my guess. Your father?"

By the sudden flinch in Tunwin's eyes, Vaelon knew Baden had guessed correctly.

Eterra drew in a sharp breath and said, "Tunwin—is this true?"

Tunwin seemed to deflate, all of the fight going out of him at once. "It's true," he said quietly. "Father heard me talking to Gutrel about the punishments imposed on those who don't obey the warlocks. He got two of his friends on the City Council to come talk to me, but it didn't do any good, so they whipped me to teach me the virtue of humility. Then Father said that, unless I started accepting the authority of the Council and the warlocks without question, he'd see to it that you were selected as the next chosen one." He looked over at her. "Please, Eterra, don't think badly of him. He was trying to protect me. He knew that if I didn't stop being stubborn I'd end up being punished just like Shomérosh."

"Oh, Tunwin," she said softly, gently touching his cheek. "You should have told me."

"I couldn't."

Reiyalindis spoke next, her face grave. "Tunwin, Eterra, you need to know why we're here. Daaku Chikara is a terrible, evil power, and we are here to put an end to it."

"Put and end to it!" Eterra exclaimed. "That's not possible! Daaku Chikara is the strongest magic in the world!"

"No," Baden said, "actually, it's not. Daaku Shukun may want you to believe that, but it's a lie."

"You would need powerful magic to defeat Daaku Shukun," said Tunwin. "He's the most powerful warlock alive. At any rate, your adventure is doomed from the start—the prophecies say that only one man will ever confront him, so you all probably won't even get close . . ." He trailed off, a thoughtful look crossing his face and then his eyes widened a little. "Unless one of you is the Paladin."

Eterra gasped, alarm showing plainly in her eyes. "The Paladin?" she asked in a frightened voice. "Is one of you really . . . him?"

Vaelon raised his hand. "Guilty as charged," he said blandly.

Eterra stared at him, looking profoundly uneasy. "You?"

"That's right," said Reiyalindis. "He is. He must challenge Daaku Shukun—and you're going to help him."

"Now, hold on!" Tunwin said quickly, raising a warning finger. "Just because I might have some reservations about some of the more exotic punishments our leaders come up with, doesn't mean I trust any of you, and it certainly doesn't mean I'm going to rebel against my own people by helping the Paladin!"

"But you will," she said. "I know you will. You can fret and stew about it for a while if you like, but in the end you're going to realize that it's what you have to do."

Both Eterra and Tunwin stared at her for a long, silent moment, clearly at a loss as to what to think.

✗ ✳ ✗

They ended up making camp for the night there, giving Tunwin and Eterra the chance to think things over. They sat near the fire talking quietly, with Chrotak standing watch nearby.

As dusk was settling into darkness, Vaelon noticed that Reiyalindis was gone. He straightened and looked around, but the little girl was nowhere to be seen. "Hey," he said, "where's Reiyalindis?"

Chrotak lifted his arm, pointing past Vaelon toward the stream. Vaelon nodded and went in that direction. He found Reiyalindis sitting on a large rock at the bank of the stream, her knees drawn up to her chest and her face pressed down into them. As he quietly drew closer, Vaelon realized that she was crying.

"Hey," he said softly, sitting down by her.

She raised her tear-streaked face, staring numbly into the water. "Hey," she replied in a whisper so quiet he barely heard it.

"Want some company?" he asked. "Or would you rather be alone?"

"Some company would be nice," she said, trying to take control of herself.

"You want to talk about it?" Vaelon wished he was better at dealing with emotions. He should have sent Safaya to look for her instead of coming himself.

"I hate myself," she said. "I hate my power. I hate what it's making me do."

203

"Oh?" he asked cautiously.

"I already killed Koän. Now I'm going to kill his friends too."

"Reiyalindis, you promised you'd stop blaming yourself. And you're not going to kill his friends."

"Yes," she said, "I am. I saw it, Vaelon. Tunwin and Eterra are going to help us. They're going to help us, and they're going to die doing it. And I have to let them."

Vaelon felt himself go a little cold. "You . . . uh . . . you saw this?"

"Yes," she whispered. "Tunwin will die first, and then a little later Eterra will also be killed. I know exactly when and exactly how. And I can't do anything to stop it—because if I do, all of us will die, and our mission will fail."

Vaelon shook his head. He couldn't think of anything to say.

With a long sigh Reiyalindis leaned over, resting her head and shoulders in his lap. "I'm so tired," she murmured. "So tired of everything. Sometimes I just want to lay down and never get back up. I really don't think I have the strength for this. I have to lead those two to their doom, Vaelon. I want to die."

Vaelon patted her shoulder. He was still uncomfortable with physical contact, but he didn't want to make her move. "I know it's hard for you," he said. "I wish I could take your burdens for you."

"I know you would if you could," she said, "and I thank you for it. I just wish . . . I just wish that I didn't have to always be afraid."

"Listen, little one, that's what I'm here for—me, and Ciroy, Safaya, and Baden. We're here to help you. Don't try to take on all this by yourself. Lean on us if you have to."

"Oh, I do," she said. "I do. You have no idea how much I do." She sighed. "Safaya is probably tired of me. I think I lean on her more than anyone. I've never had another girl to talk to before, and even though she's older than me, it has been very nice."

"Of course she's not tired of you."

"I hope not, but sometimes I think she is." She sat up, taking a deep breath. "Thank you, Vaelon. I needed a little extra strength. Don't say anything about this to anyone, all right?"

"Of course not."

"Let's get back, then, I suppose." She closed her eyes. "I'm not sure I can face Eterra and Tunwin, though. How can I, knowing that they'll be killed?"

"Maybe it won't turn out that way," Vaelon said, but it sounded more like wishful thinking than real hope.

Reiyalindis didn't bother to tell him that she knew it would, in fact, turn out that way. She squared her shoulders and began walking back to camp, and with a shake of his head, Vaelon followed.

When Tunwin saw them arrive, he stood up, his face a strange mixture of uncertainty and resolution. "We've talked it over," he said. "I sure hope you're not bewitching me."

"You've decided to help us, then?" Reiyalindis asked.

"Yes. We know there's something wrong with our kingdom, and we want to set it right."

Reiyalindis took a deep breath. From the look on her face, Vaelon could tell she was trying with all her might to keep from crying. "Thank you," she said.

"We think we can get you into the city," said Eterra. "At least, we've got a plan that should work. We'll have to do it during the night."

"Good," said Vaelon. "We'll start out tomorrow night, then."

Sixteen

"Are you sure this is going to work?" Ciroy asked dubiously. He was standing next to Vaelon and peering through Baden's telescope at the walls of Shikuragari. Vaelon was worried himself. The walls of the city were tall, strong, and built so smoothly that they were impossible to climb. It was night, but the tops of the walls were lit with many torches.

Ciroy continued, "I mean, can we really trust those two? How do you know they aren't reporting us to the warlocks right now?"

"Do you trust me?" Reiyalindis asked him.

"Of course."

"Then trust them."

Ciroy sighed. "All right."

"It's almost time," Baden said, looking up at the moon. "Are we ready?"

"Ready as we'll ever be," muttered Vaelon. "This is going to take a miracle to work, Reiyalindis. You know that, right?"

"I know," she said. "But I also know that we'll at least make it into the temple of the well safely—beyond that, I can't say."

Vaelon took a deep breath. "I guess we'll find out. Let's go."

The six of them crept stealthily toward the east wall of the city. The only gate was in the west wall, and Tunwin had told them that the east wall was the least heavily patrolled. The plan was for Tunwin to drop a rope down the wall between patrols. If they moved quickly, all six would have enough time to climb the rope before the next patrol came by. From there, the Sanretsu couple would take them down into a network of underground conduits that carried water to two dozen wells positioned throughout the city.

Once they reached the wall, they waited quietly. The bottom of the wall was in deep shadow as the torchlight high above didn't reach that far down. They waited for perhaps ten minutes before a rope came whistling down through the darkness, nearly hitting Baden.

"Go!" Vaelon whispered.

Chrotak went first with Reiyalindis clinging tightly to his back. Tunwin had told them he'd be able to get a rope strong enough to bear the giant's weight and indeed he had; the rope was as big around as Ciroy's wrist. Chrotak climbed like a cat, moving swiftly up the wall. The others followed.

Tunwin was waiting for them at the top, and as they climbed over, he hustled them to a nearby stairway that led down into the city. "Hurry!" he whispered. "The next patrol is due any minute!"

Vaelon, the last one up, quickly pulled the rope back up, and he and Tunwin carried it down the stairs. The others were already waiting in the shadows by the stairs when they arrived.

Vaelon and Tunwin left the rope in a storage shed, and then Tunwin said, "Follow me, quickly, and keep to the shadows."

The young Sanretsu led them through several dark alleyways before arriving at a well. The city seemed deserted; the only people about were soldiers on patrol. Those patrols, Tunwin told them, were not to guard against enemies, but rather to enforce a strict curfew. No unauthorized citizens, he explained, were allowed to be out of doors at night.

Crouching in the alley near the well, Tunwin quickly explained what they were to do. "I've done stonework on several of these wells," he said. "They're stone cylinders that extend down into a larger pool about twelve feet down. Climb down the rope until you're in the water, and then dive down about five feet. There's an opening on one side of the cylinder to let water from the conduits in. Go through it, and you'll surface in one of the pools. There's a narrow walkway that circles the pools, so you'll be able to get out of the water. It'll be pitch black down there, but I'll go first and try to get a torch lit. Okay?"

When everyone nodded he said, "Go to the well one at a time. Give the person before you a couple of minutes to get down before you go, and watch for patrols." He ran from the alley to the well, releasing the catch and letting the bucket down, easing it into the water to avoid making a splash. Then he climbed in and slid down the rope.

"Chrotak, you go first," Vaelon instructed. "I don't think that rope's going to hold you, but you ought to be able to let yourself down by pressing against the walls. Then you go, Ciroy. Safaya, you go down with Reiyalindis. Baden will go next, and I'll go last."

"Okay, boss," said Ciroy.

"Don't call me that."

Everyone got down the well without mishap. Reiyalindis, it turned out, could swim at least as well as most fish and had no trouble diving to the opening in the cylinder. There were torches set at regular intervals along the conduit walls, and Tunwin had one lit, casting a faint glow across the small pool.

"I hate being wet," Safaya grumbled, squeezing water out of her bedraggled tail.

"This way," said Tunwin. "There's another well near the temple. Eterra's waiting there to let the rope down to us."

He led them through the conduit, choosing the path confidently. It took them the greater part of an hour to reach their destination. Once there, Tunwin set the torch in a ring on the wall. "I'll go signal her," he said. "When the rope is down, I'll come back to let you know. This well's in a very dark place. I don't think there will be much danger of discovery here. It's not the closest one to the temple, but it's the safest."

"Sounds good," said Vaelon.

Tunwin turned and eased himself into the water, taking a deep breath before diving. Several long minutes passed, and then he reappeared, shaking his head to clear the water from it as he surfaced. "All right," he said. "Let's go."

Soon they were all standing outside the well. It was tucked in the corner of a small market square, which was dark and filled with empty stalls. Eterra was waiting there for them. As Vaelon, again bringing up the rear, climbed from the well, Eterra said, "This way."

They followed her and Tunwin into yet another empty alleyway. A patrol crossed the street in front of them as they were making their way through it, but the soldiers didn't even glance into the alley as they passed. "Alert, aren't they?" murmured Baden.

"Most patrols don't really pay much attention," Tunwin said quietly. "No one ever breaks the curfew—at least, not until tonight."

"What would happen if someone were caught breaking it?"

"They'd be taken before Daaku Shukun himself, who would decide their punishment. The last time it happened was before I was even born—the man caught was impaled on a stake in the city square."

"Ouch," Safaya grimaced.

"All's clear," Eterra whispered.

As they left the alley and crossed the street, Vaelon asked, "Tunwin, have you ever seen him? Daaku Shukun, I mean?"

"No," Tunwin replied. "He never leaves the temple, and no commoners ever see him—unless they're chosen ones or they're being taken before him for punishment. No one that happens to ever lives."

"Sounds like a cheerful fellow."

"He's ancient," Tunwin said. "They say he's the same man who first discovered Daaku Chikara, and it keeps him alive." Tunwin glanced at him and said, "Are you really . . . the Paladin?"

"That's what they tell me," he replied.

"You don't look anything like I thought you would. The stories say you're ten feet tall with skin black as pitch, long fangs, and fiery horns."

"Really! That's . . . peculiar."

"They also say you're the most evil creature to ever live."

"Oh, I'm not so bad once you get to know me," Vaelon said. "The horns kinda make folks nervous, though, so I take them off when I'm with company."

Safaya looked back at him curiously. "Goodness gracious, Vaelon, was that a joke? From you?"

"I'm feeling a little reckless tonight," he admitted.

They continued to creep through the city streets until they came to a broad square surrounding the temple of Daaku Chikara. Torches ringed the square, and a force of twelve soldiers stood in the entrance of the temple. They were dressed differently than the other soldiers, with tall plumes in their helmets and red sashes crossing their uniforms.

"Temple guards," Tunwin said quietly. "A special force—our most highly trained soldiers. They're the only people besides the warlocks and chosen ones who can enter the temple."

The temple itself was an enormous building and remarkably ugly, just a gigantic, featureless square. The temple doors stood open, which Vaelon found peculiar. "Do they always leave the doors open?"

"Always," Tunwin replied. "Supposedly they're only closed in emergencies, but it's never happened that I know of."

"Is there another way in?"

"No. It's the only entrance. Even the chimneys on the roof are blocked with heavy gratings."

"Any ideas for getting past the guards?"

He took a deep breath. "We'll need a diversion. Something to attract their attention, and hopefully draw them away from the entrance."

"Such as?"

"A fire." He tapped the building they were standing beside. "This is a military supply building, and the barracks are on the other side. It's full of food, uniforms, weapons—and barrels of pitch and naphtha."

Ciroy grinned. "Beautiful."

"Eterra and I will set the fire," said Tunwin. "The rest of you sneak around to the south side of the building and hide in the shadows there. As soon as the guards leave the entrance, you can slip inside. Beyond that, you're on your own. Neither of us have ever been in the temple, so we wouldn't be much help."

"Sounds good," agreed Vaelon. "You've been a great help."

Tunwin shook his head wryly. "I don't even know why I'm doing this. I must be crazy."

"It's for Shomérosh," Eterra said softly. "Things like that have to stop. It's not right."

Tunwin sighed. "I hope you're right. Okay, get going."

Leaving the two Sanretsu beside the supply building, Vaelon led his friends in a broad circle around the square. The south side wasn't as well lit as the west, where the entrance was, and he figured they had a pretty good chance of making a dash across to the shadows of the temple without being seen.

But then Reiyalindis grabbed his arm. "Wait," she said. There were tears shining in her eyes.

"What is it?" Vaelon whispered.

"The fire won't work, Vaelon," she said.

"It won't? What do you mean?"

She took a deep trembling breath and then pointed back toward the supply building. Vaelon and the others looked, and immediately Ciroy muttered, "Dang."

A patrol was coming up another street next to the supply building and would emerge into full view of the doorway within seconds. "Go on, get out of there!" Safaya hissed. "Get out, get out!"

It was too late, though. Tunwin was already inside the supply building, and, foolishly, he had left the door standing wide open. The patrol spotted it immediately.

They could only watch helplessly as the patrol entered the building. Eterra, who was still in the shadows outside the building, ran, following Vaelon's course around the edge of the square, probably on her way to warn them. She reached them just as the patrol emerged from the supply building, two of them dragging Tunwin between them.

Tears were streaming down Eterra's face when she joined them. "Wait, don't go!" she said as she approached. "They've caught Tunwin!"

"We know," Safaya said, giving the distraught girl a quick embrace. "We saw."

Just then Vaelon saw their chance. Noticing the commotion outside the supply building, the Temple Guards were walking quickly toward it. "Go!" he whispered. "Go, now!"

"Stay here, dear," Safaya said to Eterra just before she left. "Don't you worry—Tunwin will be fine. You'll see. Get yourself somewhere safe!"

Vaelon and his friends ran across to the temple, and when they reached it they crouched in the shadows.

Only an instant later, Vaelon heard Safaya whisper, "Eterra, what are you doing?"

"I'm coming with you," she whispered back. "I'm not going to just sit back and hope Tunwin will be all right—I've got to help!"

There was no time to argue. The Temple Guards were with the patrol now, and Vaelon knew that at any moment they would turn around to bring Tunwin before Daaku Shukun. "Inside!" he hissed. "Move!"

Vaelon was a little surprised that they got inside the temple unseen, but no one so much as glanced in the direction of the entrance as he and his friends slipped around the corner of the building, raced across the front, and darted inside. So many years of nothing unusual ever happening must have dulled the guards' wariness; they had not left even a single man to watch the entrance.

Once inside, Vaelon looked back out the entrance. The Temple Guards were returning, two of them holding Tunwin by the arms. "Hide," Vaelon said.

The hall they were in now was dimly lit and lined on both sides by stone pillars. They hid behind several of the pillars, holding still and quiet as the Temple Guards entered. Eterra bit her finger to keep from crying out as Tunwin was dragged past, vanishing deeper into the temple.

"Don't you worry," Safaya whispered to Eterra. "We'll get him back safe and sound. You'll see."

Eterra nodded with a forced smile, but Vaelon, looking down at the misery on Reiyalindis's face, guessed that Safaya was wrong. "This is it for him, isn't it?" he said, bending down to whisper to the little girl.

She closed her eyes and gave a short nod. "We will never see him alive again—but at least Eterra will never find out he was killed."

Once the hall was again empty, the intruders gathered together. "All right, let's do this," said Vaelon. "Any ideas where we're supposed to go, Reiyalindis?"

She shook her head helplessly. "I'm sorry, Vaelon. I don't know."

"I don't imagine it will be too hard to find," said Baden. "Most likely the well will be in the center of the building—things like that usually are, for some reason. Probably in a big room."

"And once we get there, then what?" asked Ciroy.

Reiyalindis shook her head. "I don't know. I only know that once we reach it, the way to destroy it will be made clear."

"Good," said Vaelon. "I suppose I'm going to meet Daaku Shukun sometime?"

"Of course," she replied. "But let's hope it's after we destroy Daaku Chikara."

"That would make me feel a whole lot better," he admitted. "Let's hurry."

✘ ✳ ✘

Tunwin had never seen Daaku Shukun before, but the moment he finally came face-to-face with the leader of his people, he knew without a doubt that he had done the right thing by helping the Paladin.

It was not just the man's appearance that assured him of that—the strange orange eyes were frightening, yes, but then, so was Chrotak. Rather, it was the all-too-palpable feeling of complete evil that surrounded the man like a poisonous cloud. Tunwin had never been so terrified in his life as he was right then, when Daaku Shukun turned from what he had been doing to gaze coldly upon him.

Of course, the bloody knife Daaku Shukun was holding didn't help improve his image any—or the fact that he had been in the process of using it to carve a strange rune into the bared skin of a kneeling warlock's back.

"What is the meaning of this?" he said, his voice a low growl.

"Forgive our intrusion, Omnipotent One," said one of the palace guards holding Tunwin, "but we captured this commoner breaking curfew."

A slow smile spread over Daaku Shukun's lips. "Really? Now what pressing matter caused you to do that, boy?"

"It appeared he was trying to set fire to the military supply building across the square," the Temple Guard said.

Daaku Shukun's eyes narrowed, his pupils becoming mere slits. "Is that right," he said. "What are you up to, boy?"

Tunwin said nothing.

Taking a step forward, Daaku Shukun tapped the bloody point of the knife against Tunwin's cheek. "Why set fire to the supply building? If you were trying to make some kind of statement, some kind of protest, you would have chosen a more meaningful target than that. No . . . it has to be for something else." He set the edge of the knife against Tunwin's cheek again and then, with a quick jerk, cut the cheek open. "Tell me, boy!" he snarled.

Tunwin gasped in pain but still refused to speak.

"If you think that hurt," Daaku Shukun said mildly, "you haven't felt anything yet. Am I making myself clear?"

Tunwin just glared.

"Now, if it wasn't to make a statement," Daaku Shukun mused, almost casually drawing the knife across Tunwin's other cheek, "what possible purpose would burning the supply building serve? No armies are coming to attack us, so destroying the food and weapons would be pointless." He leaned closer and murmured, "Was it perhaps to cause a distraction? And the purpose of that? Why, to allow someone else to slip into this temple unnoticed!" He glared hard at the Temple Guards. "But my loyal soldiers, of course, would not have been fooled by such an obvious trick—would they?"

The soldiers shifted uneasily, and Daaku Shukun's scowl turned truly ugly. "You would not have been so foolish as to leave the entrance unprotected."

When the Temple Guards failed to reply, he snarled, jamming the knife into the heart of the nearest guard. As the man fell, Daaku Shukun turned his baleful gaze on the others. "Don't you fools realize what this means?" he grated. "Who would try to sneak into the Temple? Who, I ask you, but the Paladin himself, the same man who not so many days ago crept into Ji-Ge-Lon and destroyed our long labor there? Idiots! You have allowed our greatest enemy to enter the temple of Daaku Chikara! Go, now—raise the alarm! Find him and kill him!"

As the Temple Guards rushed to obey, Daaku Shukun looked back down at Tunwin. "And you, traitor! You aided him!"

Tunwin drew himself up defiantly. "I did," he said quietly, "and he will destroy you."

"That has yet to be decided—but whatever happens, you, my friend, will not be around to see it!" Grabbing him by the front of his shirt, he jerked Tunwin toward him, directly onto the blade of the knife.

✕ ✳ ✕

When the alarm bell began ringing through the temple, Vaelon and his companions were just arriving at a large pair of double doors that Vaelon suspected housed the well of Daaku Chikara. They all froze for a brief moment, and then Vaelon barked, "Chrotak, get those doors open! We've got to move fast!"

The giant ran toward the doors, slamming his shoulder into them and shattering the latch. What lay beyond the door, though, was not the well, but some kind of horrible torture-chamber throne room. Large pots of molten iron bubbled along one wall, and along the other was a row of shackles, cages, and various instruments of torture. An iron bar bent in a half-circle was placed in the center of the room, about eight feet high and with shackles dangling from the top. Beside the iron ring there was a table, also equipped with shackles. The table was covered with blood, some fairly fresh and some old and dry. Blood also stained the floor beneath the iron half-circle. Placed in front of the table and iron ring was a large, ornate throne on a foot-high dais.

This was undoubtedly where the sacrifices took place—but where was the well?

There was a group of Temple Guards inside, and they stared at the intruders for a moment before charging. The fight was short, leaving all of the Temple Guards dead on the floor. "Blast!" Vaelon growled, looking around. He spotted another large pair of doors to his right and said, "Through there!"

"No!" Baden called. "Behind the throne—that big mural is a door!"

Vaelon looked at the throne. About ten yards behind it there was a large, grotesque mural of some kind. It was nothing recognizable, just a mad swirl of black and red in a somehow repulsive design. "That's a door?" he asked. "Are you sure?"

"Of course—look at the throne. It's rigged so it can face the other direction. And look at the iron railings on the top and bottom of the wall next to the mural."

Vaelon looked and saw that Baden was right. There were, indeed, iron railings that would allow the mural to slide out of the way; he had just not noticed them before. Now that he was looking closer, he also saw a similar rail in a circle underneath the throne, obviously there to allow the throne to swivel around. It all made sense now—the first part of the sacrifice, the flaying, was performed in this room, and then Daaku Shukun could turn his throne around to watch the iron-encased victims be thrown into the well of Daaku Chikara. The well had to be behind the mural.

More Palace Guards appeared from another doorway. "Baden," Vaelon snapped, "get that door open! Reiyalindis, Eterra, go help him!" He charged into the oncoming soldiers, with Ciroy and Chrotak right behind him. Safaya hung back, firing arrows as quickly as she could.

Eterra started to obey, but as she ran her foot became tangled in a chain on the floor and she fell. "Eterra!" Reiyalindis cried. From the sound of Reiyalindis's voice, Vaelon realized that Eterra was about to die.

There was nothing any of them could do to stop it. A warlock appeared amidst the swarm of Temple Guards, his hands blazing. Vaelon and Ciroy were cut off by a dozen Temple Guards, and Chrotak, with his back to the warlock and the girl, did not see what was happening until too late. All Vaelon could do was watch. Safaya fired her last arrow at the warlock, but just before the long shaft struck him a shimmering dart shot from his hand. The dart struck Eterra full in the chest as the girl struggled to rise.

"No!" Safaya cried, dropping her bow and running to the Sanretsu girl. In between blows, Vaelon glanced over as Safaya dragged Eterra toward Baden.

Eterra was only barely alive, and Reiyalindis, tears streaming from her eyes, dropped to her knees next to her. "Oh, Eterra, I'm sorry," she sobbed.

Over the sounds of battle, Vaelon could barely make out Eterra's reply.

"It's not . . . your fault," she said. "Please . . . just try to save Tunwin. Please. I . . ."

Eterra didn't say anything more and Reiyalindis's grief-stricken wail was enough to tell Vaelon what had happened.

"Please forgive me!" Reiyalindis cried out. "I had no choice . . . I'm so sorry!"

"What are you talking about?" Safaya asked sharply.

But there was no time to get an answer. More warlocks were appearing, and Vaelon let out a gasp as one of them sent a blast of dark energy toward Safaya and Reiyalindis. Safaya grabbed the little High Elf and threw her aside just in time, but the energy struck the Halfbreed squarely on the hip. She was flung across the room, striking the far wall forcefully and then collapsing to the floor.

"No!" Reiyalindis shrieked.

Temple guards were suddenly everywhere. Vaelon was separated from Ciroy and Chrotak, and with dismay he realized he was being forced back out the big double doors. Though he felled many of his enemies, their sheer weight of numbers pressed him back like a strong tide.

Once out in the large hallway, some of the Temple Guards began to run around the edge of the fight. Knowing that to let himself become surrounded would mean certain defeat, Vaelon broke away, racing into a smaller hallway. The Temple Guards pursued, but Vaelon outran them and managed to lose them in the maze of small corridors he found himself in.

He started to head back toward the main hallway, but as he came around a corner he saw someone just rounding another corner not five yards ahead. The man coming toward him was tall, shrouded in black robes, and his eyes were a sinister blazing orange.

Both men came to a halt, and instinctively Vaelon realized who this was.

"You!" snarled Daaku Shukun.

Vaelon felt oddly calm as he faced his enemy. This was his purpose, the single greatest reason for his existence. He still didn't know why he could resist Daaku Chikara so much better than others, but the reason was unimportant—he knew what he had to do.

He didn't give Daaku Shukun time to plan an attack. He launched himself down the corridor toward the most powerful Sanretsu in the world, knowing that speed would be his only chance of survival in this fight.

Daaku Shukun blocked Vaelon's blow with a hasty spell, and Vaelon was thrown backward, landing on his back on the floor. "Die, Paladin!" cried Daaku Shukun, directing a powerful bolt of dark energy at him.

Vaelon twisted sharply out of the way, coming to his feet, but the bolt of power turned in midair, striking him not far from his old injury. Blinding pain shot through him, but he forced it away, snatching a dagger from his belt and throwing it at his adversary.

Daaku Shukun blocked that attack as well and struck back again, but missed. Ignoring his pain, Vaelon charged, forcing Daaku Shukun farther back down the hall. The warlock had to bend all of his energy toward deflecting Vaelon's attacks, for Vaelon gave him no time to launch an attack of his own.

Finally Daaku Shukun struck Vaelon with a blazing ball of light. It felt like white-hot fire as it passed through his body. Vaelon knew it should have killed him, but somehow it didn't, though the pain it caused was excruciating.

Their battle was taking them out of the smaller corridors and back into the main hallway. Daaku Shukun backed toward the temple entrance as he continued to hammer at Vaelon. No matter how Daaku Shukun pummeled him, though, Vaelon's body somehow refused to die. Powerful, deadly spells seemed to simply be absorbed by him as he pressed the attack, and though he was bleeding from a dozen places, he continued his relentless assault—never pausing, never even slowing.

And then Vaelon's opportunity came. Daaku Shukun stumbled backward, losing his focus and nearly falling. As he tried to right himself, Vaelon struck.

Startled by his swiftness, Daaku Shukun didn't have time to react—but the three Dokujin coming from the darkness outside the temple entrance were much faster than their master.

Vaelon's sword struck the first Dokujin's weapon only inches from Daaku Shukun's face. The warlock took several hasty steps backward, and the second Dokujin darted past him, his sword seeking Vaelon's heart. Vaelon barely had time to bring his sword down, deflecting the blow.

One Dokujin had been bad enough, Vaelon thought as he was forced back down the hallway. Now he was facing three. He had known there were more Dokujin—he should have expected this.

But where were the remaining two? Hopefully still out searching for him, and not in the temple—but even if that were so, they weren't really necessary. No one without powerful magic—Elf, Human, or Halfbreed—could ever face three Dokujin at once.

✗ ✳ ✗

The fight in the throne room was not going well. Ciroy had been pressed back against a wall, and Chrotak was struggling to hold his own against half a dozen warlocks. Baden had still been trying to find a way to open the door when he was attacked by two Temple Guards and had to fall back to protect himself.

Safaya, amazingly, was not out of the fight yet. Despite being badly injured, her right leg twisted and shattered, she dragged herself toward one of the pots of molten iron. They were hung on supports so as to be able to tip over and pour their contents into smaller pots, which were being held upright by thick chains hanging from the ceiling. Safaya's right leg was totally useless, but she forced herself up on her left, grasping the lever that would release the chains and allow the pot to tip over. But in her condition, she could not budge the lever. Spying an iron prybar on the floor, she grabbed it and thrust it into the lever, jumping as high as she could with one leg and coming down on the prybar with all her weight. The latch snapped, the support chain went slack, and the huge pot of molten metal tipped over with a crash.

Molten iron splashed across the floor, flooding around the feet and ankles of a thick knot of Temple Guards. They shrieked in pain and tried to escape, but most of them fell to their deaths in the liquid metal.

All that weight coming down at once was too much for the pot's supports, and they snapped. Safaya, who had fallen after breaking the latch, was sprayed with hot coals as the massive pot crashed into the fire pit that had kept it hot. Shielding her face from the fire, she could not see the pot rolling right onto her.

✗ ✳ ✗

From across the room, Ciroy watched in horror as the huge pot rolled toward Safaya. Luckily, Reiyalindis had also noticed. A Temple Guard was lunging at her, but he missed as the little Elf darted to Safaya. Reiyalindis grabbed Safaya by the arm, and, with strength she normally would not have had, she pulled her friend clear of the rolling pot. The pursuing Temple Guard was not so lucky, and he screamed as the pot crushed him.

Momentarily distracted by the disaster, the Temple Guards fell back a little, watching in dismay as a full twenty of their comrades writhed about in the molten iron, dying with horrible screams that drowned out all other sounds. Taking advantage of the confusion, Ciroy snatched up a long spear from where it had fallen to the floor and turned it horizontally across his chest, running toward the soldiers and ramming into them with all the strength he could muster. They stumbled backward, hitting those behind them, who in turn stumbled back, directly into the spreading pool of molten iron. Ciroy rammed them again, sending five more to their dooms. He then jammed the spear into a sixth before turning and darting toward the wall, grabbing the lever of a second pot. "No!" he heard one of the Temple Guards scream as he jerked on the lever.

Another wave of the deadly liquid splashed across the floor. Ciroy flattened himself against the wall as the huge cauldron broke free of its supports, but this one did not roll. Instead it came to rest in the fire pit.

Chrotak barreled into the confused warlocks, brushing aside their ineffective attacks. Picking two of them up by the neck, he gave a tremendous roar and threw them, shrieking, into the encroaching pools of iron. Some of the Temple Guards simply lost their nerve and turned and ran.

Baden had managed to dispatch the two Temple Guards facing him, suddenly cried, "Aha!" and ran to the throne. Setting his shoulder against it, he heaved with all of his strength, his muscles bunching and straining with the effort. Slowly the throne twisted around to face the mural, and as it did, a catch was triggered. A weight was released under the floor, and as it sank down, the mural slid smoothly sideways, revealing what lay beyond.

All of the Temple Guards gave a moan of terror, shielding their faces from that which they had always been forbidden to set eyes upon. As one, they instinctively dropped—some even doing so right into the molten iron. The warlocks gave a collective gasp of horror as the focus of their power was exposed to the profane eyes of outsiders.

The well of Daaku Chikara, in Ciroy's opinion, was not impressive to look upon. It was a simple stone well, though larger around than most. There was no awful display, no brooding evil cloud hanging over it, nothing to indicate that the well was, in fact, the home of such an evil and powerful magic.

"Chrotak!" Reiyalindis cried. "Now you are free, Chrotak! Now you are free!"

With a bellow that was almost longing, Chrotak plowed through the shocked crowd of warlocks and Temple Guards. Before any of them could lift a hand to stop him, he threw himself into the well.

For a moment the room fell silent save for the agonized moans of the injured. Then, from far below, there came a dull, sullen booming sound. The floor shook violently, and a spray of fire shot up from the well, blowing a gaping hole in the ceiling right through to the night sky.

Ciroy, stumbling from the explosion, reached Safaya and dropped to his knees beside her, gathering her in his arms. "Safaya, how bad is it?" he asked anxiously, his stomach churning as he looked at the mangled ruins of her leg. She was obviously in agony and could not reply; she simply clung to him, crying in pain.

Abruptly the shaking of the ground ceased, and the room again became still. Ciroy looked over as Reiyalindis rose from where the earthquake had knocked her to the ground, her young face shining.

"It is done!" she cried.

A nearby warlock, his face twisting with rage, leveled his hands at the young High Elf. But nothing happened; no magic blazed forth. He stared dumbly down at his hands, and Reiyalindis laughed. "Your power is no more!" she cried exultantly. "Daaku Chikara is destroyed!"

The warlocks, terror-stricken, all turned and fled from the room. Those Temple Guards who could still run were not far behind.

Vaelon's strength finally gave out as the three Dokujin struck him. He fell heavily, feeling a blade slashing across his arm and another plunging into his leg. He had done his best but he knew he was finished.

The Dokujin, sure of their victory now, surrounded their helpless prey, dry laughs echoing out of their hideous masks. Vaelon tensed himself as the three beasts raised their swords, reversing their grips in preparation to jam them down into his body. Vaelon automatically began calculating the best direction to dodge, but he knew he would not be fast enough to evade all three blades. Daaku Shukun, circling around his three servants for a better view, was laughing triumphantly.

But his laugh died on his lips as the entire temple began to shake. He and the Dokujin stumbled back, the three black-armored creatures dropping their swords and collapsing to the floor like rag dolls. The orange fire in Daaku Shukun's eyes died, and he looked in disbelief in the direction of the well of Daaku Chikara. "No!" he cried. "No, that's impossible!" He began running toward his throne room, and Vaelon forced himself to his feet to pursue.

As they ran, the shaking subsided. Daaku Shukun and Vaelon passed dozens of warlocks and Temple Guards fleeing the other direction. Finally they burst into the throne room.

Daaku Shukun slowed to a walk, staring in helpless horror at the well. The stones of the well had been broken apart and lay scattered about. Vaelon came up behind him and slowed a little, waiting to see what he would do.

Daaku Shukun's eyes slowly turned to Reiyalindis, who was standing near the ruins of the well. The little girl gazed calmly back.

"You," Daaku Shukun said slowly. "It was you, wasn't it? A High Elf— of course. It was you who blocked my magic, who prevented me from being able to locate the Paladin."

"Yes, Daaku Shukun," she replied. "It was me."

Rage flared in his eyes. "And for that you will die, wretched girl!" He picked up a spear and drew his arm back, preparing to throw.

But Vaelon was right behind him. He grabbed the spear and wrenched Daaku Shukun sharply around, kicking the warlock in the stomach. Daaku Shukun released the spear and stumbled backward, but then, with a shriek of insane rage, he grabbed a fallen sword and threw himself at Vaelon.

Vaelon almost felt sorry for Daaku Shukun as he easily sidestepped the blow, thrusting his own sword completely through Daaku Shukun's chest. Daaku Shukun gasped and then coughed up a spray of blood. Vaelon kicked him off the blade, and the dying warlock fell backward into the pool of molten iron. He tried to scream, but his lungs were full of blood, and all that came out was a thick gurgle.

"There," said Vaelon as the molten iron, which had claimed so many innocent lives, now claimed Daaku Shukun's. "Now you know what it feels like."

Suddenly all of Vaelon's own pain seemed to catch up to him at once. The injury in his chest gave a fiery surge, everything went blurry, and then he collapsed.

SEVENTEEN

"Well, now," Baden murmured, staring out at the still-dark city through his telescope. He'd climbed to the temple roof through the jagged hole Daaku Chikara had blasted through the ceiling, and now he was on the lookout for retaliation.

There seemed to be little fear of that, though. Alerted by the fleeing warlocks and Temple Guards, the whole city was in an uproar. Citizens were running pell-mell through the streets, panic-stricken, and a steady stream of them were fleeing through the city gates.

"Hey, you know, folks, that really isn't necessary," he said, though obviously none of the Sanretsu could hear him. "We're not going to eat you or anything. Seriously. Go back home, stay up late, play games . . . whatever. Just don't trample people in the streets."

He watched for a moment longer and then, with a sigh, climbed back down. The others were not in the throne room any longer. They had taken Vaelon and Safaya to another, cleaner room, where they were tending everyone's injuries.

The Halfbreed woman was in bad shape. Her right leg was ruined, the bones in her hip and thigh shattered to fragments and the whole leg twisted grotesquely out of shape. The spray of the fire had burned her face and hands pretty badly as well, and sometime during the chaos she'd also broken her right wrist. The pain had been too much for her to bear, and she had passed out not long after Daaku Chikara had been destroyed. Fortunately she was not bleeding badly, and it appeared that none of her injuries, awful as they looked, were immediately life-threatening.

When Baden entered the room, Ciroy looked up at him. "Is someone coming?"

"I wouldn't worry too much," Baden replied. "The whole city is too busy with a mass exodus to send people to hunt us down."

"What, they're running? The whole city?"

"Like deer."

"Wow. That's not what I expected."

"You can never tell, really. There seems to be a fine line between what it takes to send people fleeing in panic and what it takes to get them thirsting for vengeance." He paused for a moment and then added, "Of course, if I were a Sanretsu citizen, and I saw a bunch of powerful warlocks running for their lives, I'd probably be inclined to run too."

"True."

Baden looked at Safaya. "How is she?"

Ciroy sighed. "She's busted up real bad, but I think we've still got time to get her to a healer."

"So what exactly happened back there?" Baden asked, looking at Reiyalindis, who was sitting against the wall near Safaya. "I'm assuming the spirits trapped in Chrotak's body are the ones that actually destroyed Daaku Chikara."

The little girl was drooping with exhaustion, both physical and emotional, and she raised her head wearily to look at him. "What? Oh—yes, it was them."

"If that's all it took, why didn't they just swoop down there earlier, before they were trapped?"

"It's not that simple. Alhalon unwittingly created the perfect key to Daaku Chikara's downfall. As spirits, Chrotak could do nothing against Daaku Chikara, but as a physical being, they gained tremendous power over it. When a sacrifice is thrown to Daaku Chikara, its life-force is absorbed by the well. Chrotak was simply too much for the well to handle all at once, and it was torn apart when the spirits were released."

"Isn't that kind of a strange coincidence, though?" asked Baden. "What if Alhalon had never created Chrotak?"

"Then we would have found another way."

"But . . ."

"Hey," Ciroy interrupted, "Baden, let's save the questions for later. She's tired."

"Oh," said Baden. "Of course. Sorry, Reiyalindis."

With a feeble little smile she said, "It's all right, Baden." Closing her eyes, she slid down to the floor and curled up to sleep.

Baden went to check on Vaelon, who was still unconscious. "Quite the little row, wasn't it?" he murmured. "I'm amazed we're still alive."

"Yeah," Ciroy agreed, gently stroking his wife's hair. "All but Chrotak, and he's better off now anyway. I sure feel bad about Eterra, though. I wonder what became of Tunwin."

"He's dead," Baden said sadly.

"How do you know?"

"I've known all along they were going to die. Didn't you ever watch Reiyalindis around them? She saw their deaths. I think Safaya probably figured it out too."

"Are you sure you aren't a mind-reader?"

Baden laughed a little. "Quite sure."

Ciroy and Baden took turns standing guard, but no one bothered them as they rested there. Reiyalindis slept for several hours before waking up again, and not long afterward Safaya also woke back up. The pain was still intense, but as there was little they could do for her, she simply bore it as well as she could.

Another hour passed before Vaelon finally woke up. He was obviously still in intense pain, and it took several moments for him to be able to see clearly. He groaned a little, pressing his hands against his eyes.

Reiyalindis knelt beside Vaelon. "Vaelon, how do you feel?" she asked.

"Awful," he muttered. Moving his hands from his eyes, he blinked a few times, looking up at her. "Why does my chest still hurt?" he asked. "I thought Daaku Chikara was gone."

Reiyalindis gave a long sigh. "I was afraid of that," she said. "Not all magical effects vanish when their source is destroyed, Vaelon. I guess your wound is like that."

"Wonderful," he grunted. "And all this time I was thinking it would go away. Stupid of me, I guess."

"I'm sorry, Vaelon."

With no little effort and some help from Reiyalindis, he sat up. Seeing Safaya, he grimaced. "I guess I don't have to ask how you feel. Suddenly I don't seem to hurt so much anymore."

Safaya gave him a strained smile. "Hey, Vaelon," she said weakly.

Looking at Baden and Ciroy, Vaelon asked, "How are you two?"

"Fine," Ciroy replied. "Just scratched up a bit, is all."

"Good. Where's Chrotak?"

"Gone," said Reiyalindis. "He destroyed Daaku Chikara, and the process released the spirits."

"I see. Well, that's good, I guess. At least they're not all trapped in that body anymore." He winced, pressing his hand against his shoulder. "I'll tell you, when those three Dokujin showed up, I thought I was a goner for sure."

"Three?" Baden exclaimed. "How did you beat them?"

"I didn't. They almost had me on a spit when Daaku Chikara died and they went along with it."

"I wonder where the last two were."

"Who knows? Who cares? If they'd been there, I really would be dead." Vaelon groaned and struggled to his feet. "All right, as much as I'm sure we'd all like to rest, we need to get moving. We've got to get Safaya to a healer as fast as we can. Baden, let's go try to find something we can use to make a litter for her."

"Right," said Baden, also standing.

The two men returned a few minutes later with a makeshift stretcher composed of two spear shafts and a stout tapestry. Ciroy helped them transfer Safaya to it as gently as they could manage. Baden and Ciroy carried the stretcher, and as they headed out, Reiyalindis walked beside Vaelon, taking his hand. "It's all over now, isn't it?" she said, a trace of sadness in her voice.

Vaelon glanced down at her. "Well, don't look so happy about it."

"I'm sorry, Vaelon. I am glad it's over, I guess . . . I'm glad we succeeded. It's just that I've been getting used to having friends, and . . . it's going to be hard to say good-bye."

"We don't have to say good-bye, Reiyalindis."

"I wish that were so," she said. "But we do, and soon. As soon as possible."

Ciroy looked at her, concerned. "Why?" he asked.

She ignored the question. "I'll miss all of you," she said, her voice very soft and full of such aching that Ciroy felt his eyes beginning to burn.

"We'll talk about this later," Vaelon said firmly. "In the meantime, you're staying with us until we can get things figured out."

"But . . ."

"That's an order, little one."

Reiyalindis looked down at the ground, obviously struggling with herself. "Vaelon, I . . . I don't want to hurt anyone anymore."

Vaelon frowned as he looked at her. "Reiyalindis, the danger is past," he reminded her. "You're not dragging us into peril anymore."

The young High Elf remained silent for a long time, but finally one part of herself seemed to overcome the other part, and she said, "Safaya will have to go to the Ruling City to be healed. The only healers skilled enough to repair that kind of damage are there. And the queen will be able to replace Ciroy's finger. I know the way. Maybe . . . maybe I could guide you at least that much farther before I go."

"All right," Vaelon agreed. "At least that far."

✗ ✳ ✗

From her litter Safaya had a clear view of the city of Shikuragari as they left. The entire city was empty, its inhabitants scattered into the forest like a flock of sheep before a lion. The ragged little group traveled slowly but steadily through the forest, finally emerging from the Great Shield several days later.

Not long after leaving the mountains, Reiyalindis asked to stop for the night. Seeing that it was still at least a couple of hours until dark, Safaya said, "But, dear, there's still at least a couple of hours of daylight left."

"I know," Reiyalindis replied, her expression a little more subdued than usual. "But I want to stop here. Please."

"Sure," said Vaelon. "Fine by me."

As the men were preparing camp, Reiyalindis slowly wandered to a nearby fallen tree. She sat next to it, gently touching the ground near it. Watching from where she lay on the stretcher, Safaya could see a deep sadness shadowing the little girl's face. "Reiyalindis?" she asked. "What's the matter?"

The High Elven girl took a deep breath, and the men also looked at her, pausing in their work. For a moment, Reiyalindis couldn't seem to speak, and then she said, "This is where I found Koän. He was lying right here, on this very spot. The warlocks had left him in the forest a day's travel back in the mountains, and he'd found his way here and collapsed. That's when I found him." She patted the ground, a faraway look in her eyes. "Right here."

"What were you doing this deep into Ruzai?" asked Baden.

"I don't know," she replied. "I just knew I had to come here."

Ciroy went to her and enfolded her in a hug. He didn't say anything, and he didn't need to. Reiyalindis sighed, resting her head against his chest and staring out at nothing.

✘ ✳ ✘

It took a week, a long, grueling week, to get out of Ruzai and back into Rimurea. It was still another week at least to the Ruling City, but they found a small village that had a healer. He was an ancient, bent old High Elf, and when he saw Safaya, he looked troubled.

He did as much as he could, but while he was able to alleviate most of the pain and repair some of the minor damage, he could not get the leg back into its proper shape. That, he said, would take a much more powerful healer.

They thanked him for his help and set out toward the Ruling City. Travel was a little easier now that Safaya wasn't constantly in such terrible pain, but she still had to be carried.

Finally they arrived at the gates of the city. To Vaelon's surprise, their coming was not entirely unexpected. They found an old, white-haired High Elven sorcerer waiting for them at the gates of the city.

"Vaelon Sahani," he said, startling all of them as he appeared from behind a heavily burdened handcart. "I might have known you'd have something to do with this."

Vaelon's face lit up with recognition. "Zeruin!" he exclaimed. "How have you been?"

"Well, very well," replied the old man. "Who are your friends?"

"Oh—this is Ciroy and Safaya Xagalliack, Baden Solignis, and Reiyalindis Amarainein. Everyone, this is Zeruin Argenith, a sorcerer in the queen's court. He's a friend of my father's."

Zeruin looked closely at Reiyalindis. "Your name seems familiar, little girl. Do I know you?"

"I don't think so," she replied. "But the queen does. We're on our way to see her, actually."

"Ah, yes!" he said. "You're that little girl who brought that very terribly injured Dark Elf to us some years ago. My, you've grown." He looked at Safaya. "What happened, if you don't mind my asking?"

"Sanretsu warlock," Safaya replied. "We had a bit of a scuffle with them."

"More than a bit, if my intuition serves me correctly," said the old man. Looking back at Vaelon, he said, "Strange things have been happening, Vaelon, and somehow you're involved. Several weeks ago I felt a profound shift in the earth's magic, and then only days later I heard something else while I dreamed—a terrible cry of despair that made my blood run cold. Something momentous happened, but I could make little sense of it. And then just this morning I had a deep feeling that I needed to meet someone at the gates today. Tell me, Vaelon, what has been going on?"

Vaelon looked at Reiyalindis. "Zeruin has a bit of the same gift as you," he said.

"Mostly very vague impressions, I'm afraid," the sorcerer said. "You are a seeress, child?"

"Yes," she replied, seeming a little awkward and self-conscious.

"As a matter of fact, she's the one who led us on our mission," Vaelon said. "You're right, Zeruin—something big happened. I won't go into detail here, but to make a long story short, we found a way to stop the Ghost People, and we also destroyed Daaku Chikara. The two were linked, actually."

The old man looked thunderstruck. "Daaku Chikara!" he exclaimed. "And the Ghost People? You . . . but . . . *how?*"

"It's a long story."

"Why . . . I must tell the queen immediately!"

"Yeah, do that," Vaelon said. "But keep it quiet, please, Zeruin. I don't want a huge to-do, if I can avoid it."

"No, you wouldn't, would you?" the old man said with a knowing smile. "Vaelon, you're not teasing me, are you?"

"No, Zeruin. I'm not. It's true. If you could let the queen know, we need her help—we've got some serious injuries here."

"Of course, of course! Head straight to the infirmary. I'll make sure the queen is informed at once—this is most wonderful news!" Zeruin turned and ran toward the palace.

The infirmary was a large complex attached to the palace, and they carried Safaya through the front doors, where they were met by a young High Elven attendant. "Can I help you?" she asked pleasantly as they entered.

"Yes, please," said Reiyalindis. "We're here to see the queen."

"I'm afraid the queen is very busy right now," the girl replied. She looked at Safaya and said, "I could fetch Eiyara, though. She ought to be able to help you with that leg."

"All right," said Reiyalindis. "Thank you very much."

"Please have a seat in that waiting room. Eiyara should be here shortly."

As the attendant left, they all went into the waiting room. "Fancy place," Ciroy observed as he and Baden laid the stretcher on the floor. He carefully picked up his wife, holding her like a child as he sat in a chair. Her bad leg couldn't bend very well, so Baden propped it up with another chair.

"Thank you, Baden," murmured Safaya.

"Of course," he replied, taking a seat next to Vaelon.

Vaelon looked around at the opulent waiting room, feeling distinctly out of place in the luxurious surroundings. The walls were decorated with fine tapestries, and a small table with a flower-filled vase rested in the center of the room. The chairs, chandelier, and table were all inlaid with gold and were of very fine workmanship.

They waited silently for several minutes and then Vaelon said, "So . . . who exactly is this person we're waiting for?"

"The queen's handmaid," Reiyalindis replied. "She is one of the best healers in the world, short of the queen herself. She's a very nice girl too; she looked after me while Koän was here being healed." Then she tugged at his sleeve with an impish grin, beckoning him to lean closer to her. When he did so, she whispered in his ear, "You're going to marry her someday."

Vaelon quickly straightened, shocked. "What the . . . Reiyalindis, that's not funny. Don't joke like that."

"I wasn't joking," she said.

"Joking about what?" Ciroy asked curiously.

"Nothing," Vaelon said. "Forget it."

Just then someone appeared in the doorway, and Vaelon found himself looking at the most incredibly beautiful young woman he had ever seen. She was High Elven, slim, and entirely flawless. She had clear blue eyes and long, rich golden hair. Her skin was smooth and pale. Vaelon could only stare as she entered the room.

"Oh, Reiyalindis!" she said in a gentle, sweet voice. "It's so good to see you again." Even as she spoke, she noticed Safaya's injury, and her warm smile was replaced by a look of concern. "Oh, my goodness, that looks bad. Please, bring her this way. The rest of you should wait here—you'll be summoned after she's healed." Eiyara led the way back out of the room, with Ciroy carrying Safaya close behind her.

Vaelon stared mutely at the doorway for a long moment and then looked down at Reiyalindis. "So . . . that was her?"

Reiyalindis's smile was teasing. "Yes."

"And . . . and I'm going to marry her?"

Reiyalindis nodded. "Oh, yes, you certainly are."

"You're sure."

"Positive."

"What's this?" Baden asked incredulously.

Vaelon looked back at the doorway and found himself grinning like a fool. "I might be able to come to terms with that."

Baden also stared at the doorway. "Wow. Hey, Reiyalindis, you, uh, don't happen to know any of her friends, do you?"

"Sorry, Baden," said Reiyalindis. "None of them are your type."

"Oh. Darn."

"And don't either of you say anything about this to her or to anyone else, not even Ciroy or Safaya. This is just between us. If you tell anyone else, it might not happen the way it's supposed to."

Vaelon looked over at Baden. "Not a word, or I'll gut you!" he said firmly.

Baden grinned. "You really don't want this messed up, do you?"

"Didn't you *see* her?"

"That's enough," said Reiyalindis. "No more talk of it." She did, however, give Vaelon a sly wink.

230

EIGHTEEN

They waited there for a good hour, and then a different High Elven girl entered. "Your companion is healed," she said, "but she still needs rest. You can see her now, if you wish."

They followed the girl into the main infirmary, and she led them up a long hallway lined with doors. Finally stopping at one, she opened the door to let them in. "Where is Eiyara?" Reiyalindis asked as the others went into the room.

"She was summoned by the queen after healing your friend," the girl replied. "But I'm sure she'll be back soon."

"Good. Thank you."

Inside the room, Safaya was lying on a soft bed, with Ciroy sitting in a chair beside it. Her leg was again facing the proper direction. "How are you?" Baden asked as he pulled up another chair. Vaelon also sat down, but Reiyalindis stood beside the bed and took Safaya's hand.

Safaya smiled. "I feel fine, thanks. The healer told me I needed to stay in bed until tomorrow, but I feel good as new."

Reiyalindis smiled. "I'm so glad you're all right," she said, the relief in her voice plain. "I was so afraid for you."

Safaya patted her hand. "Well, it's all done with now, isn't it?" she said.

They chatted lightly for another ten or fifteen minutes, and then there was a light knock at the door. "Come on in," called Ciroy.

When the door opened, Vaelon shot to his feet. "Your Majesty!" he exclaimed. He, Baden, and Ciroy all went to one knee, bowing their heads, as the queen of Rimurea entered the room. Safaya started to rise, but the queen held out her hand, beckoning her to remain lying down.

The queen was a tall, regal woman, aging but lacking neither grace nor beauty. She beckoned the three men to rise, and they obeyed. Behind the queen, her handmaid entered the room, closing the door behind her. "Vaelon, it's so good to see you again," said the queen, going to him and kissing his cheek. "Oh, dear boy, wasn't your last encounter with the Sanretsu enough for you? And yet here you are, again risking everything for your kingdom. I could hardly believe my ears when Zeruin told me the news, but then, I suppose I shouldn't be surprised. I always knew you were a remarkable young man."

"I didn't really have much choice in the matter," Vaelon said. "Reiyalindis can be very convincing."

"Oh, yes, I know!" the queen said, smiling as she winked at Reiyalindis. The little girl came to her, and the queen bent down, kissing the top of her head. "It's been too long, child. You've grown so much since I last saw you." She looked around and then said, "Where is Koän, my dear?"

Reiyalindis looked sadly at the floor. "He was killed, Your Majesty."

The queen's face softened. "Oh, I'm so sorry, child. So sorry." She hugged Reiyalindis, but, oddly, did not appear surprised.

After a moment they parted, and Reiyalindis said, "Your Majesty, these are my friends. Vaelon you know already. This is Baden Solignis, a scientist; without his help we would have been lost. And this is Ciroy Xagalliack and his wife Safaya, who provided invaluable service as well."

"I am very glad to meet you," said the queen. "I cannot even begin to express the gratitude the entire kingdom owes all of you."

A sly grin crossed Baden's face. "Well, you know, with a great war hero like Vaelon Sahani leading us, how could we fail?"

Vaelon gave him a warning glare, but Baden just grinned wider.

The queen laughed a little. "Still so very modest, Vaelon?" She turned to her handmaid, and said, "Eiyara, I want you to meet Vaelon Sahani. Vaelon, this is Eiyara Colsidakren, my handmaid."

Eiyara stepped forward, smiling shyly, and dropped into a graceful curtsy. "I am honored, sir."

Vaelon found that his brain had deserted him. "Um . . . uh . . . wow. I mean—no, please, you don't need to curtsy . . . uh . . . I'm just me, you know. Just plain old me."

Eiyara's eyes sparkled a little, her smile growing. "I'm glad of that, sir."

"Vaelon. Please."

"As you wish, Vaelon. I realize you don't know me, but I remember you from the first time you came here. I watched over you the first night as you were recovering from your injury."

Vaelon could tell that Baden was about to say something, so he spoke quickly to cut him off. "Really? You did? I . . . uh . . . I would have thought I'd remember someone as . . . someone like you, I mean."

A faint blush appeared on Eiyara's cheeks, though she tried to hide it. "You were unconscious, and before you awoke I had to leave to tend to another infirmary in the south for a few months, so I was never able to speak with you. I'm glad to finally have that chance."

"Uh . . . me too." Vaelon realized that he was starting to feel a little light-headed, and he had to consciously keep from staring at her.

"Dearest," said the queen to Eiyara, "would you please take young Reiyalindis for a walk in the garden?"

Eiyara smiled. "Certainly, Your Majesty." She took Reiyalindis by the hand. "Come, little one."

Reiyalindis cast a quick, confused glance at the queen but didn't argue as Eiyara led her from the room. The queen watched them leave, and when the door closed after them she said, "Eiyara is such a dear girl. She is kind and wise, and will undoubtedly surpass my own skill at healing very soon. And she has a remarkable grasp of politics as well."

Vaelon stared blankly. "Politics?"

The queen nodded. "As you all know, I have never married, and so must choose someone as my heir to the throne. I have chosen Eiyara to take my place when I am gone."

Baden made a strangled choking sound, as though he'd swallowed something too big. "What . . . You mean she'll be the new queen?" he gasped.

The queen looked puzzled. "Does that shock you?"

Baden cast a quick glance at the utterly stunned Vaelon and then said, "Uh . . . no, of course not." He pointed at his throat. "Sorry, just swallowed a bit of spit down the wrong tube, begging your pardon, Your Majesty. Didn't mean to look surprised. Nice girl."

"Yes, indeed." The queen sighed. "But I'm afraid I must discuss something unpleasant. I need to talk to you all about Reiyalindis."

Vaelon's shock vanished, replaced by apprehension. The queen looked grave, even sad, and that made him nervous. "What about her?"

The queen sat, and, once she was settled, the men did too. "I must warn you. I can clearly tell how much you have all come to love that little girl, but now that your quest is done, you cannot stay near her any longer."

Safaya gasped, swinging her legs over the bed and sitting up in spite of the fact that she was supposed to be resting. "No!" she exclaimed. "No, I'm not going to leave that poor girl all alone again, and destiny be hanged!"

The queen looked grave. "I see she has told you that it is her destiny to always be alone. But you don't know all of it. I know she wouldn't want me to tell you this, but I feel that you need to understand."

"I'm not leaving her alone!" Safaya said heatedly.

"You must," the queen said, "or you will die."

For a moment they all just stared at her, and then Vaelon said, "Die?"

The queen nodded sadly. "Just like Koän. He knew it would happen, but despite the counsel of both Reiyalindis and myself, he refused to leave her. He was lucky to have lived as long as he did."

Safaya looked horrified and couldn't speak.

Baden, his voice carefully controlled, said, "Your Majesty, what's going on here? Tell us plainly."

"She told you it was her destiny," said the queen, "but that's not precisely true. She carries with her a curse."

"A curse!" exclaimed Vaelon.

The queen looked very sad. "Yes. She herself did not know that she was cursed, but when we first met, I sensed something amiss with her. She allowed me to explore her soul with my magic, and that's when I discovered it. It is a very powerful curse, too powerful for me to break."

"She's cursed to always be alone?" Safaya asked weakly.

"Not exactly. She doesn't have to stay alone, but being with her is dangerous. The curse will eventually kill everyone close to her. Someone might stay with her for a month, a year, or even two in Koän's case, but before long, that person will die." She looked into Vaelon's eyes. "The only reason she allowed all of you to be with her for even a single minute was because she knew you had to. I can only imagine the terrible fear she has carried in her heart, knowing that at any moment her curse might kill you. It may have even been the curse that killed her parents."

Safaya looked devastated. "No," she whispered. "No, that can't be!"

"Who would do this?" Vaelon demanded. "Who would put a curse like that on her? She was just a baby when her parents died. She doesn't even remember them!"

"Isn't it obvious?" Baden growled. "Think a little, Vaelon."

Ciroy straightened, understanding dawning in his eyes. "Alhalon," he said in a grim voice. "Alhalon Cui Kahathilor."

Vaelon stared at the floor, his mind spinning. "Alhalon," he muttered. "Of course. He's the only one with the power to cast a curse like that."

The queen looked shocked. "Alhalon!" she exclaimed. "You mean to say he's still alive?"

"Oh, yes," Ciroy said darkly. "Alive and kicking. We met him."

Troubled, the queen said, "That is an unexpected revelation." Her eyes went a little distant. "Of course—that explains everything perfectly. His power was . . . is . . . greater than any other sorcerer to ever live."

"But why?" Vaelon burst out. "What possible reason would he have to curse a little baby like that?"

Baden shook his head. "It's perfectly obvious to me why he cursed her," he said. "Revenge."

"But she couldn't possibly have done anything to him!" said Safaya. "Not even her parents could have!"

"He wasn't taking revenge on her specifically. He was taking revenge on the whole High Elven race. It makes sense. Those fourteen sorcerers tried to kill him, but instead they doomed him to a life of solitude. He had to remain hidden because he knew the High Elves would try to kill him again if they discovered he had escaped, and then he became trapped in his fortress for two centuries. I can only imagine the kind of rage one could build up over that time. Her family must have somehow stumbled across his fortress, and so he was provided with a target upon which to vent his rage—a tiny, innocent High Elven baby, a representation of the hopes of the High Elven future. He cursed her to go through what he had been subjected to—a life of loneliness."

"Trapped, you say?" the queen asked curiously.

"Yes. Some spirits he employed sealed his power in the fortress he lives in, and he cannot leave it without dying."

"So that's why he remained hidden for so long," she murmured. "That was a stroke of luck for all of us. If he was free, he would undoubtedly have returned and sought revenge."

Safaya struck her fist on the bed. "That evil monster!" she cried. "Doing such a terrible thing to that sweet little girl!"

The queen let out a long sigh. "No one alive today has the power to confront Alhalon, and it is most fortunate for all of us that he cannot leave his home. Only he can lift Reiyalindis's curse, and I'm sure you realize he would never do that. So there is nothing we can do for the poor girl."

Ciroy came to his feet, his face a dark mask of anger. Vaelon was surprised; it was the first time he had ever seen Ciroy angry. "I don't care how much power that old fiend has. I'm not going to let this continue!"

"Neither am I!" declared Safaya.

"Don't be foolish!" said the queen quickly. "If you challenge Alhalon, he'll kill you!"

"So be it," said Ciroy.

Safaya nodded emphatically. "We're either going to die trying to break that curse or die when that curse kills us, because we're not going to leave Reiyalindis alone so long as we live!"

"This is exactly why Reiyalindis wouldn't tell anyone about her curse," said the queen. "For her sake, don't be rash! You realize that if you die, she will still be alone, but with the added guilt of knowing your deaths were caused by her!"

"So you expect us to just sit back and watch her go?" Baden asked. "You expect us to live the rest of our lives knowing that she's out there somewhere, miserable and alone? Knowing that she'll die miserable and alone? Sorry, Your Majesty. That's not going to happen."

The queen shook her head. "I should not have told you—but I had to. I felt that you needed to know."

"I'm glad you did," said Vaelon quietly. "If Alhalon is killed, will the curse be broken?"

"Vaelon, what you are contemplating is suicide."

"Will the curse be broken if Alhalon dies?" Vaelon repeated firmly.

The queen hesitated and then said, "Some curses continue even after the caster's death, Vaelon. A curse of this magnitude will certainly live on without him. Even if you could kill him, his death will only seal Reiyalindis's fate."

"I've heard," said Baden, "that curses as powerful as this one can still be broken after the caster's death if someone with enough magic—like you—has a certain part of the caster's body."

The queen looked almost annoyed. "You know far too much for your own good, Baden Solignis."

"So I've been told."

"Is there any way I can dissuade all of you from this?"

"No," Vaelon said. "There isn't. What do we need?"

She let out a long sigh. "Baden is right. If Alhalon will not willingly lift his curse, I could break it myself—but I would need his heart."

"Fine," said Baden. "We'll get it."

"Does he have a heart?" asked Ciroy with a snort.

"You know you don't have a chance," said the queen. "Kill Alhalon Cui Kahathilor? The very notion is madness. How could you hope to accomplish what fourteen powerful High Elven sorcerers failed to do? And how are you going to tell Reiyalindis? She will be heartbroken—she may even try to prevent it."

"How?" asked Vaelon.

The queen looked grave. "She might take her own life if she thinks it could save yours."

Vaelon hesitated, but then an idea came to him. "Perhaps it would be best if we don't tell her at all," he said. "If we just leave and don't tell her what we're planning, she'll have no reason to think we even know about the curse. And if we do die, she won't have to know that, either."

Safaya nodded. "I think you're right, Vaelon. It would be easier on her that way."

"As you wish," said the queen. "I will not tell her of your plan. I will simply tell her that I explained to you the danger of remaining with her. Tomorrow you can take your leave, and she will assume you are simply returning home."

✘ ✳ ✘

Out in the garden, Reiyalindis and Eiyara stopped to sit near a large rosebush. "I can hardly believe you and your friends were able to put a stop to the Ghost People," said the queen's handmaid.

Reiyalindis nodded, a distant look in her eyes. "Yes," she said simply, her tone suggesting she hadn't really been paying attention.

"Is something troubling you, Reiyalindis?"

The little girl sighed. "It's just . . . Tomorrow my friends will have to go back home, and I'll have to go back to the forest. It was so nice to . . ." She trailed off, a look of consternation suddenly crossing her face.

"Reiyalindis?" asked Eiyara uncertainly. "Are you all right? Reiyalindis?"

Reiyalindis did not answer, and her small body began trembling. Worried, Eiyara went to touch her arm, but Reiyalindis came to her feet. "No," she whispered.

Alarmed now, Eiyara grasped her by the shoulders. "Reiyalindis, what's wrong?" she asked. "Tell me, please!"

"She told them," said Reiyalindis. "No . . . no, she should have known not to do that . . . She told them!"

"Who told who what?" demanded Eiyara.

Reiyalindis tore free of Eiyara's grasp. "No, no, no!" she sobbed, running pell-mell back toward the palace.

Eiyara followed, pulling up her skirts so she could run, but she could not catch up to the little girl.

x ✳ x

Reiyalindis burst into the room, running straight to Vaelon, who was the closest one to her. "Vaelon, no, you can't go!" she cried hysterically, throwing herself into his arms. "He'll kill you! He'll kill all of you! Please don't go!"

Vaelon was shocked. "Reiyalindis, what do you mean?"

"Don't play ignorant!" Reiyalindis said. She pulled away, whirling toward the queen. "You told them! I can't believe you told them! Why did you do that?" Sobbing, she ran to Safaya's bed and collapsed in her lap. "Safaya, don't go! I'm not worth it! Oh, please, don't die because of me!"

Just then Eiyara arrived, breathing heavily from exertion. But before she could say anything, the queen rose. "Come, dear. We must leave Reiyalindis alone with her friends for a while."

Eiyara looked frightened. "What's happening, Your Majesty?" she asked. Vaelon didn't hear the queen's reply as the two women left the room, closing the door behind them.

Safaya held Reiyalindis until the young Elf finally calmed down. "Now, then, Reiyalindis," she said, "I can see we need to have a little talk."

Reiyalindis sat up, wiping at her eyes. "She shouldn't have told you," she said. "I knew this would happen if you found out."

"Listen, Reiyalindis," said Ciroy, "we can't just let you—"

"Yes, you can!" she interrupted, her voice fierce. "Can't you all see? I'm just one little girl. It's not worth all of your lives just to make me happy!"

"Yes, it is," said Safaya softly. "It is, Reiyalindis. Because none of us will be happy if you aren't."

"Why can't you just forget about me?" she asked, tears leaking from her eyes again. She laid her head on Safaya's chest. "I love all of you too much to let you do this."

"We love you too, kid," said Ciroy. "And that's why we have to do it."

"You can't succeed. Why even try?"

Safaya stroked her hair. "Reiyalindis, Ciroy and I want you to stay with us. You need a family, and we want you to be part of ours."

Reiyalindis sat up straight, staring at her. "You . . . You do? Really?"

"Of course we do."

"But . . . what about your jobs? You couldn't very well take me with you."

Safaya nodded. "I know, dear. But Ciroy has been offered steady jobs before, and I'm sure he won't have any trouble finding work."

"But I thought you loved what you do."

"Oh, it wasn't bad," said Ciroy. "But I've been thinking about retiring from that soon anyway. The general of the division headquartered in Orstown asks me to take a job training new recruits every time we pass through there, and I've been thinking that I'll take it."

"Just think," said Safaya. "We'd have a nice little house in the forest outside of town. We'd be a real family. Wouldn't you like that?"

Reiyalindis was trembling. "You know I would, Safaya. But it won't happen. Alhalon will kill you."

"Not necessarily," Baden said abruptly. "Actually, I've got sort of an idea."

The others all looked at him. "You do?" asked Vaelon.

"Yes, as a matter of fact, I do," said Baden. "It's very simple. Maybe too simple, in fact, now that I think about it."

"Let's hear it."

"We'll just talk to him, and while someone holds his attention I'll pop him in the head with my crossbow from behind. I really doubt he'd be expecting something like that."

"It won't work," said Reiyalindis. "His magic is everywhere in that fortress. He'll know what you're about to do, and he'll kill you."

Baden let out a long breath. "Okay," he said finally, "what if I shoot him from outside the fortress?"

"That won't work either. The fortress is surrounded by a shield. Nothing can get in without his consent, not even insects."

Baden scowled. "Well, what about air? He lets that in, doesn't he?"

"Yes, of course."

"Then I'll rig up some sort of invisible gas that will melt his eyeballs and turn his brain into porridge!"

"Wouldn't that damage his heart?" asked Vaelon.

Baden gave him a flat glare. "I was being sarcastic."

"Oh. Sorry."

"Maybe we can get him to listen to reason," said Ciroy. "I mean, if we don't go in there with hostile intentions, I don't think he'd kill us for just asking him to lift the curse. Would he?"

Reiyalindis shook her head. "He might. Remember how angry he was when I took Chrotak from him?"

Vaelon stared at her thoughtfully. "He knew who you were, didn't he? Neither of you said anything, but he surely knew you were the one he'd cursed."

She nodded. "He knew. And I could sense his triumphant gloating every moment we were there. He relished my misery. He will not willingly give it up."

"Dang it, we killed Daaku Shukun, we can kill Alhalon too!" said Ciroy.

"Daaku Shukun was a baby next to Alhalon," said Reiyalindis. "And we had Chrotak with us then."

"Reiyalindis," said Vaelon, "for everything we come up with, you're going to have a reason it won't work. But we're going to try, no matter the danger. Can't you understand that?"

She shook her head. "I'm not worth it, Vaelon. Maybe it would be better if I just killed myself like the queen said. At least all of you wouldn't die."

"Don't you dare even talk like that!" Safaya snapped angrily. "If you go do something stupid like that, I'll go after Alhalon anyway just to get even! And don't think I won't!"

"I can't just let all of you die!" Reiyalindis said, her voice choked and barely understandable. "Please, don't . . ." She couldn't finish, but simply put her face in her hands and started crying.

Vaelon rose and went to her, laying a hand on her shoulder. "We're going, Reiyalindis. Whether you like it or not."

For a long moment, Reiyalindis tried to calm herself. Finally she was able to stop crying, and she raised her tearstained face. "All right," she said in a tired voice. "I knew I wouldn't be able to stop you, but . . . I had to try. But if you go, I have to come with you."

"Why?"

"Because I have to, Vaelon. If you expect me to accept that you're going, the least you can do is accept that I am too."

Vaelon, Baden, Ciroy, and Safaya all glanced around at each other and finally Vaelon nodded. "All right. We'll leave in the morning. And Reiyalindis—don't do anything to yourself. No suicide, no running away. Promise me."

She nodded slowly, helplessly. "I promise."

"Good girl." He kissed her forehead. "It'll turn out okay, you'll see. We defeated the Ghost People and the Sanretsu together, and we'll beat Alhalon too."

Reiyalindis drew a deep, shuddering breath. "Safaya," she said in a small voice, "I don't want to be alone tonight. May I sleep in here?"

"Of course, dear, of course," said Safaya.

Vaelon rose. "I'll go get you some blankets, Reiyalindis."

Baden jumped up quickly. "I'll go with you," he said, heading for the door. "And let's grab something to eat while we're at it. I'm starving."

The two men left the room. As they walked down the hallway, Baden glanced sideways at Vaelon, and then, trying to sound casual, he said, "So . . . what's up, Your Majesty?"

Vaelon jumped. "Oh, bugger!" he exclaimed, grabbing at his head. "What am I going to do now?"

"Well, you're stuck, my friend. I mean, my king."

"Blast it, Baden, stop saying things like that!"

"I can't help it. It's too funny."

"For you, maybe." He grunted sourly.

"So what would that make you, really? You'd be king, but Eiyara would be the one chosen to succeed the queen—so who would have the greater power, you or her?"

"Her. She's the one with the grasp of politics, not me."

"I meant legally, not logically."

"How am I supposed to know? Look, I really don't feel like talking about this just now, all right?"

"You're the boss." Baden grinned.

✗ ✳ ✗

Later that evening, after darkness had settled across the land, Vaelon found himself wandering in the palace gardens. He hadn't even tried to sleep yet, knowing it would be futile. The startling revelation about Reiyalindis's curse had shaken him, to say the least—and now they were on their way to confront Alhalon, either to persuade him to lift the curse or to kill him.

Alhalon the Black. The most powerful sorcerer to ever live. How were they to kill him? He remembered all too well Alhalon's cold superiority, his complete disdain toward what he considered lesser beings, and his rage when Reiyalindis had taken his servant. There was not a chance he would lift the curse, so they would certainly need to kill him. But how? Baden's genius would be of no use now. Nor would the fighting skills of Ciroy, Safaya, or himself. The queen was right—it was a hopeless venture. And yet they all knew they had no choice—they loved Reiyalindis too much to not try.

Lost in thought, Vaelon did not notice the girl sitting on the bench in the garden until he was almost upon her. With a start, he realized it was Eiyara. She was watching him with a grave, sad look on her face. "Hello," she said softly.

"Oh—hi," he said, feeling himself growing warm again. And yet this time the nervousness was different—it was tinged with regret. Reiyalindis had foreseen that he was to marry this gentle, beautiful girl, but there would certainly be no chance of that now. She had told him that even a wrong word in the wrong place could interrupt the flow of events that would lead to his marriage to Eiyara, and he was about to do something much more serious than a wrong word. He was about to march straight to his own death.

In a brief moment of weakness, he wondered if it would be better to simply not confront the sorcerer after all. If he went, his death was all but guaranteed, and Reiyalindis's fate would remain unchanged. But if he stayed, he would live, and he would marry this breathtaking girl. He would become king, which, although not exactly appealing, certainly sounded better than dying. Why waste his life in a hopeless cause?

The moment passed, and he crushed the thought ruthlessly. He would not abandon Reiyalindis. No matter the cost, no matter the hopelessness. He knew that if he did, he would never be truly happy. He would be haunted all his life with the knowledge that Reiyalindis was somewhere out there, wandering the lonely forest with only her own broken heart for company.

"You seem pensive," Eiyara said to him.

He shrugged a little. "I suppose I am. What are you doing out here so late?"

242

She let out a long sigh. "I couldn't sleep."

"Why?"

She looked up at him, her expression cast with a peculiar sadness. For a few moments, her eyes wandered across his face, studying his features, and then she said, "Are you really going to confront Alhalon the Black?"

"You know about that?"

"The queen told me." She patted the bench beside her. "Come sit a moment, please, if you don't mind."

Vaelon nodded and sat beside her. There was a fragrance about her that he couldn't quite identify—some sort of flower, he thought—but he couldn't tell what kind. Whatever it was, for some reason it made his knees feel weak. They were not quite touching, but all the same her closeness made his heart beat faster.

She was watching him, still looking sad, and then she turned her eyes to stare at the flowers across the walk from them. "I understand why you're going," she said, her voice quiet. "Still, I wish . . . oh, I don't know."

"You wish what?" he asked.

She just shook her head a little. "Do you think you really might have a chance?"

Vaelon took a deep breath and then let it out in a heavy sigh. "No," he said honestly. "I could lie and try to put on a cheerful face, but the truth is, I don't. We're like insects to him."

She looked pained at that and said, "I wish that you didn't have to go. You and your friends have done the kingdom such a great service, and now you're going to risk your lives again, without even a rest. It doesn't seem fair."

With a shake of his head he said, "What isn't fair is Reiyalindis having to spend the rest of her life cursed like that."

She watched him quietly and then reached over, laying her soft hand on his wrist. "You all love her so much, I can tell."

Vaelon set his jaw, trying not to become emotional. "Yes," he said shortly. "We do."

"I know I don't know her nearly as well as you do, but I love her too. I felt my heart melt the first time I ever saw her. I will be hoping with all my soul for your success, Vaelon. I want you to know that."

He looked at her, and it was a struggle not to become hopelessly enchanted by her clear blue eyes. "Thank you," he said. "That means a lot to me. To all of us."

For a few minutes they didn't say anything. Finally Vaelon took a deep breath. "I'd . . . um . . . best get going, I suppose."

She nodded and moved her hand away from his wrist. "Yes, of course. You should get some rest."

He began to rise, but searing pain erupted in his chest, and he dropped to his knees with a gasp. He felt his head swimming, and his vision blacked out. The last thing that crossed his mind before all thought was scattered was, *Oh, no, not now! Not in front of Eiyara!*

The pain was so intense that he probably would have passed out, but then something else was there, a gentle warmth that began to drive the pain away. His vision returned, and his head became still. He was still kneeling, and Eiyara was kneeling beside him, her arms around him. She was holding him close to her. The warmth that had driven away the pain was coming from her.

"Vaelon?" she was saying, her voice almost frantic. "Vaelon, are you all right? Say something, please!"

Taking a deep, shuddering breath, he said, "I'm okay. It's gone now."

She gave a small cry of relief, but instead of letting him go, she only held him closer, pressing her cheek against his hair. "Oh, Vaelon, you scared me!" she said. "What happened? I felt . . . I swear it felt like Daaku Chikara!"

"It was Daaku Chikara," he said. "It's just my old wound. It acts up now and then. I'm used to it." Even as he was speaking, he noticed something peculiar. He had never really been comfortable with physical contact, but even though Eiyara was holding him more closely than he had ever been held since his childhood, he was not the least bit uncomfortable. In fact, he found—to his own embarrassment—that he did not want it to end. He stayed there as long as he dared before finally pulling away.

Even when he moved, she still kept one arm around his shoulders as he knelt there. "Your injury?" she said. "But . . . but I thought that since you destroyed Daaku Chikara . . ." Her voice faltered.

He shook his head. "You can kill the snake, but the poison already in your veins will not die with it. It will never leave me."

"Oh . . . I'm so sorry, Vaelon."

He looked at her. "How did you do that, Eiyara?"

"Do what?" she asked uncertainly.

"Not even the queen was ever able to drive the pain away so completely during an attack—but you did."

"I ... I did?" she asked. Her cheeks may have colored a little, but it was hard to tell in the dim light of the gardens. "Oh ... well, I'm not sure how. Just . . . luck, I guess." She seemed a little nervous, and that confused Vaelon.

She helped him sit back on the bench, and then she sat beside him, her hands involuntarily lifting a little, as though she wanted to keep holding him. Vaelon watched her face for a moment, amazed that anyone could be so beautiful. "Eiyara," he said hesitantly.

"Yes?" she replied.

"I ... uh ... really don't know why I'm saying this, given the circumstances, but . . . uh . . ." He paused, fighting down a wave of nervousness.

Her eyes were questioning now. "Yes?" she prompted.

"I realize that we've only just met," he went on, his throat very dry, "but I was wondering if . . . um . . . if I do happen—somehow—to come back, could I . . . ah . . . could I perhaps . . . call on you?"

Her eyes widened briefly, and it seemed to him that they were growing moist. "Oh . . . Vaelon, this is a terribly cruel thing to do to a girl," she said.

"I'm sorry," he said quickly. *Blast, what's gotten into me?* he wondered.

Eiyara laid her hand on his. "Vaelon ... I would love for you to call on me." Blushing even more, she looked away. "I was actually hoping you would ask. It's just . . ." She shook her head. "Now you're going to leave me here with only a faint hope that you'll ever come back. It's not nice to make a girl wait like that."

Her touch filled him with warmth, but it also sent a shot of guilt through him. "I'm sorry," he said. "I didn't mean—"

"It's all right," she said, squeezing his hand slightly with a shy smile. "But please forgive me if I'm a little surprised. I wouldn't have thought a brave national hero like you would have any interest in a simple handmaid like me."

"What? No, that's all backward. I'm just . . ."

"You. Yes, I know. Plain old you." She smiled. "And as I said before, I'm very glad of that." Impulsively she leaned over and kissed his cheek.

As she pulled back, she seemed even more surprised than Vaelon and abruptly shot to her feet, clapping her hand over her mouth. "Oh!" she exclaimed from behind the hand. "Oh, Vaelon, I'm sorry, I ... I wasn't thinking; I hope you don't . . . oh . . . I have to go!" Then, inexplicably, she quickly leaned down and kissed his cheek again. "Please come back," she whispered, and then with a sob she turned and fled from the gardens.

Vaelon stared after her, slowly reaching up to his face and touching the spot she had kissed. For a moment he sat stock-still but then he leaned over, putting his elbows on his knees and burying his face in his hands. His shoulders shook a little, and he could not stop the tears that escaped from his eyes.

What am I doing? he thought. He was prepared to give his life for Reiyalindis, but nothing could have prepared him for this. The wild temptation to simply abandon the whole scheme struck him full-force. Eiyara's scent still lingered there, and it served only to remind him just how much he was giving up. He imagined the kind of life he could have with Eiyara. He could have that warm, caring embrace every day; he could have that gentle power that could ease the pain he lived with whenever he needed it; he could be a father; he could grow old with the Eiyara as his companion, watching his children grow up and find loves of their own.

But then Reiyalindis's face appeared in his mind—that sweet, innocent, completely endearing little face. His feelings for Reiyalindis were hard to describe, but he knew she had become like a daughter to him. How could he ever look his own daughters in the face without remembering how he had left Reiyalindis to her cruel fate?

"It's tough, isn't it?" said a voice.

Vaelon jerked his head up, quickly wiping at his tears. "Baden? What are you doing here?"

His friend shrugged, sitting on the bench and stretching his legs out. "Just taking a walk. So I take it you and Eiyara are getting along well already? You don't waste time, my friend."

Vaelon shook his head. "Don't remind me."

"You don't want to go, do you?"

Vaelon took a deep breath. "I have to, Baden. You know that."

"But you don't want to."

Vaelon hesitated but then he finally said, "Yes, Baden. I do. I want to free Reiyalindis from her curse."

Baden was quiet for a moment, and then he said, "You don't have to go, Vaelon."

"What do you mean?"

"You could stay. You've got a lot going for you here. The rest of us can go chat with Alhalon."

"Don't even try to convince me of that, Baden. You know I'd never be able to live with myself."

"The rest of us will probably fare just as well without you as we would with you."

"In other words, you'll all be just as dead?"

He shrugged. "If that's how you want to put it."

"Give it up, Baden. I'm going."

"Well . . ." He grinned. "It was worth a shot." Then his expression sobered and he gripped Vaelon's shoulder. "Just remember Eiyara, Vaelon. You have a good reason to come back alive, so don't forget it."

Vaelon nodded. "I won't."

"Good. Now come on; we've got a long trip ahead of us, and we may as well start it out with a good night's sleep."

As the two men headed back into the palace, someone standing in the shadows of the doorway stepped out to meet them. "Fancy meeting you two here."

Vaelon recognized the voice. "General Kamas?" he said, startled.

The Dark Elf approached them, coming into the light of a nearby torch. "I understand you've had quite the adventure since we last met."

"You know about that?" asked Vaelon.

"Yes, the queen told me."

"Why? She wasn't going to tell anyone until we left."

"I didn't say she told me directly."

Vaelon gasped. "You read the queen's thoughts?" For some reason he found that profoundly disturbing.

"I didn't have to read them," he replied. "They were screaming so loud in her mind I could hear them without even trying. That was quite a feat, my friends. And you told me you didn't have anything to do with the San-retsu. But you didn't then, did you? At least, not that you knew."

"I really don't like being around you," Vaelon said. "I thought being around Baden was bad, but you're worse."

The general chuckled. "I suppose I can understand that."

"So why are you here in the Ruling City, anyway?"

"Business. That creature—the Dokujin, I gather—was inadvertently recombined. Sheer accident, stupid and avoidable, a moment of thoughtlessness that cost us nearly thirty good men."

"Thirty!" exclaimed Baden.

"Oh, yes. It fought its way out of our barracks with fury I have never before seen. That you ever managed to kill it in the first place is nothing short of amazing. Anyway, we realized then that the Sanretsu were up to something, and that their power was growing beyond what we had ever anticipated. I came here to bring the matter to the queen's attention, and we've been involved in military plans since my arrival. Though all that is no longer necessary, thank goodness."

"You were planning to go to war with them?" asked Vaelon.

"I'm sure you realize that war was inevitable, and we decided it was better to strike first, especially with creatures such as the Dokujin on the loose. I'm glad it didn't come to that, though." His expression turned a little troubled. "This business with Alhalon concerns me, Vaelon. My advice would be to leave it alone—there's nothing you can do against him. What he did to Reiyalindis is despicable, but such a venture will only result in all of your deaths, while leaving her doom unchanged."

"We've heard all that before, General," Vaelon said firmly. "We're not changing our minds."

He shrugged. "I know. And anyway, you will remember that I advised you before not to go to him—but I turned out to be wrong, fortunately. Perhaps you can produce another miracle."

"We hope so."

Kamas nodded and then shook both men's hands. "I must be on my way. Good luck to you." Then he gave Vaelon an amused wink. "With everything."

Vaelon knew that he was referring to Eiyara, and his face reddened a little. The Dark Elf chuckled as he walked away.

NINETEEN

Before they left the palace, the queen healed Ciroy, restoring his missing finger. It was an interesting process—the queen had to form a new finger first using a different kind of sorcery. She was not nearly as proficient at it as Alhalon. It took her three hours of intense labor to form the finger before using both that sorcery and her healing power to bind it to his hand. Vaelon realized then just how much work had gone into healing Koän.

When she was finished, the finger was as good as new. Ciroy was glad, of course, but Safaya seemed far more excited about it than he did, and she thanked the queen profusely.

With a smile, the queen said, "My dear girl, it was the least I could do to repay you for the service you have rendered the kingdom. Are you sure you wouldn't like to stay for the celebration?"

The queen was planning to announce the news to the whole city that evening, but Vaelon wanted to make sure he was far away by that time. "Yes, we're sure," he answered. "And I'd appreciate it if you don't mention me."

The queen looked at him sternly. "Vaelon Sahani, I am not letting you get away with that again! I will announce your name, and if you don't like it, you're more than welcome to come to the celebration to deny the charges!"

"Ah . . . that's all right," he said. "I'll pass."

"If you were still in the military I'd give you another medal." She pursed her lips and said, "Well, I'll certainly come up with a suitable reward for you all."

"That's really not necessary," he said hastily, backing quickly away. "You can reward the others—they certainly deserve it. But I'm perfectly content, really."

With a sad look the queen said, "Vaelon, I really wish you would take some small token. I hate to think of . . . well . . . I'm sure you understand. We may never see you again if things go awry with Alhalon." Looking at Reiyalindis, she said, "Are you sure you won't take any help? The High Elves may not be as powerful as we used to be, but thanks to you, our power is beginning to return. If you wait a little while, we may be of assistance."

"Not possible," Reiyalindis said. "I'm sorry, Your Majesty. I can feel the power returning as well as you. But it could take years for Ji-Ge-Lon to return to its old strength, and even at the height of their power, the High Elves were no match for Alhalon. My friends are coming because they're stubborn and unreasonable," she shot a reproachful glance at Safaya, "but I'll not risk any more lives."

The queen sighed. "I understand. Very well. Good-bye to you all, and good luck."

As they were leaving the palace, Vaelon looked down at Reiyalindis, who was walking beside him. "Can I ask you a funny question?"

"Of course," she replied.

"You seem to know Eiyara fairly well."

"Fairly."

"Last night she saw me have an attack, and she was actually able to make the pain go away. No one has ever been able to do that, not even the queen. But afterward she seemed embarrassed by it. Do you have any idea why?"

The little girl nodded. "Because she was surprised at her feelings."

"What do you mean?"

"There are two different kinds of High Elven healing magic. The first, like the queen's, is purely sorcery, dependent on the healer's magical power alone. The second, like Eiyara's, comes not only from magic, but also from the healer's own soul. Their power is tied to their emotions—the stronger their caring and compassion, the stronger their power." She looked up at him, a sad, distant look in her eyes. "And no emotion is more powerful than love."

Vaelon felt his heart skip a beat. "Love?"

"She was nervous because she realized that she'd been able to have a more profound effect on you than anyone else, and she knew it was because she loves you."

"Really? But . . . we hardly know each other!"

"Look at Ciroy and Safaya. They fell in love the first day they met, despite their difference in race." She sighed a long, deep sigh. "You're going to break her heart, Vaelon. She's going to wait here for you to return, but you never will."

"You don't know that for certain—do you?"

"I haven't foreseen it, if that's what you mean. But you don't have to be a seer to know where this will lead. Please, Vaelon—"

"Don't even start, miss," he warned.

She sighed. "Well, you can't blame me for trying."

Travel was wonderfully uneventful as they moved steadily southward, angling back toward the Great Shield. They were no longer being hunted, and the Sanretsu and Ghost People were gone. The only danger facing them now—until they reached Alhalon's fortress, at least—was that, as they well knew, Reiyalindis's curse could claim their lives at any moment. Reiyalindis knew that better than any of them, and there was no assuaging the torture it brought to her tender young soul. Despite that, however, she dared not leave them; she knew they had to have her along, though the reason for it was hidden from her.

That was her one comfort, small as it was. If there was a reason for her to be with them, then maybe, just maybe, they had some tiny chance. Secretly she thought the reason was that Alhalon might become so enraged that he would kill her on sight, sparing her friends the need to confront him. She only hoped they would have the sense to let it lie when she was dead.

At long last they again entered the Great Shield, passed Chrotak's old haunt, and approached the fortress of Alhalon Cui Kahathilor. The fortress was just like they had left it; they could even see the giant telescope atop the tower. As they approached the doorway, however, Baden frowned, looking around as though sensing something amiss. "What is it, Baden?" asked Vaelon.

Before the other Common Elf could answer, Alhalon himself appeared in the open doorway of the fortress. They all steeled themselves, and Vaelon firmly reminded himself that Alhalon's power could not leave the fortress. But the old sorcerer's reaction was not at all what they expected.

He smiled, a broad, genuine-looking smile. "Ah, my old friends," he said. "Come back for a visit?"

They were all taken aback. They had expected Alhalon to fly into a rage upon seeing them, but he looked almost cheerful.

"Wondering how I knew you were coming?" he asked. "I've been watching your escapades for some time—as much as I could, anyway—with Baden's most remarkable telescope. I must confess, however, the reason for your being here escapes me—unless it is to apologize." With that a steely glint surfaced in his eyes. "I couldn't see what happened to my servant, but he did not leave the Sanretsu city with you."

Reiyalindis took a deep breath. "He destroyed Daaku Chikara, but his body was also destroyed in the process."

"Ah, I see. Well, no matter." He gave an indifferent shrug.

Vaelon was getting a cold feeling that something was very, very wrong.

"So why are you here?" the old man asked again.

Ciroy stepped toward him. "Look," he said, "we found out what you did to Reiyalindis. We're here to ask you to lift the curse."

With that Alhalon's old, mocking smirk returned. "Oh, poor little Reiyalindis, yes," he said. "What a shame." He stared at the little girl and with a sneer said, "Do you ever wonder how you and your parents came to be here in my fortress, little piglet?"

She straightened, trying not to let her pain show. "No," she said. "I know. Chrotak told me."

"Chrotak?"

"Your servant."

"So you gave him a name, did you? It fits him. So you know, then—you know they didn't stumble across this place by accident."

"I know, Alhalon."

"Look, please just lift the curse," said Safaya. "She's only a little girl, Alhalon! She never did anything to you!"

"She is a High Elf," Alhalon growled, as if that explained everything. "I didn't send that wreck you called Chrotak out to kidnap a High Elven family just so I could turn around and lift the curse when their friends came crying to me." Then he grinned. "However, I may be persuaded to lift the curse . . . for a price."

"What sort of price?" Vaelon asked suspiciously.

Alhalon grinned and did not take his eyes from Safaya. "For her."

Safaya drew in a sharp breath, and Ciroy practically shouted, "What do you mean by that?"

"She is a very handsome woman, even though she is a Halfbreed . . . and I do get lonely in here sometimes. If she will become my willing slave, I will lift the curse."

Ciroy and Reiyalindis both started to say something, but before they could, Baden interrupted. "We'll talk it over," he said.

"What?" Reiyalindis demanded, staring at him incredulously.

"I said we'll talk it over," Baden repeated. "Alhalon, we'll be back tomorrow with our decision."

"Fair enough," Alhalon said with a smirk.

"Baden—" Ciroy started to say.

Baden took his arm and turned him around. "Come on," he said. "Let's go."

"But—"

Baden gave him a sharp, penetrating look. "Go," he repeated, his voice deadly serious. Reiyalindis looked sharply at him, and he gave her a warning glance.

Curious, they all followed him until the fortress was well out of sight. Finally, though, unable to contain himself any longer, Ciroy said, "Baden, what the blazes is this all about?"

"You can't honestly be thinking of accepting that demand!" Reiyalindis cried.

Baden drew them all into a circle. "Sit down," he said. They obeyed. "We've got a big problem."

"What?" Vaelon asked.

Baden looked around a little nervously, and then said, "Alhalon has been outside of the fortress."

Everyone gasped at once. "What!" demanded Ciroy. "That's impossible! He can't leave it!"

"Well, he has," said Baden. "I don't know how, but he has."

"But how do you know?" asked Vaelon.

"While we were approaching the fortress I noticed strange footprints on the ground," said Baden. "And then when Alhalon appeared, I looked at his shoes—there was dirt on them, the same color as the dirt on the ground outside the fortress. And there was a little burr on the bottom of his robe. There's nothing like that inside—he had to have been outside. Plus there was the way he was acting—really pleased with himself, did you notice? And that ridiculous bit about Safaya!"

"What about it?" asked Safaya.

"He doesn't really want you, isn't it obvious?" said Baden. "He just said that for amusement, to see what we'd do! He's not all that interested in women in the first place, and especially not Halfbreed women—he considers Halfbreeds inferior, beneath his dignity."

"But how could he have left the fortress?" Ciroy demanded.

"I don't know. Maybe the spirits' power over him broke when Chrotak died. Is that possible, Reiyalindis?"

The little girl looked distinctly unhappy. "Well ... I don't know, Baden. It's possible, but I really doubt it. After all, they weren't destroyed, they were just released—if anything, they're more powerful now."

Baden was thinking furiously. He stood up, pacing back and forth as he thought. "Maybe," he said, "he just found spirits more powerful than the ones trapping him to set him free."

"That couldn't be," replied Reiyalindis. "No spirits the Dark Elves have access to could break that barrier—Alhalon's power is too great."

"What's that got to do with it?" asked Ciroy.

"It's how Dark Elves get their power," Reiyalindis explained. "They don't just ask spirits nicely for aid, the spirits have to be controlled, and the more powerful the sorcerer, the greater his control over the spirits. Alhalon can control spirits far more powerful than other sorcerers can, but even he bit off a little more than he could chew with those he summoned to protect his fortress. No sorcerer could summon spirits powerful enough to undo that spell, not even Alhalon."

Baden, staring in the direction of the fortress, asked, "What about demons? Could he have used witchcraft to escape?"

"No," replied Reiyalindis. "Alhalon has even deeper contempt for witchcraft than he does for High Elves, and even if he did stoop that low, no demons could break Chrotak's magic. Alhalon is trapped there, Baden. The dirt could have come from his courtyard, and maybe the burr blew in."

Baden shook his head. "No. No. The dirt in his courtyard is different than the dirt right outside his door. It's darker. Reiyalindis, please, you've got to trust me. I don't know how he did it, but he did."

She looked into his eyes for a moment and then gave a slow nod. "Of course I trust you, Baden. But what do we do now?"

Ciroy squared his shoulders. "Same thing we were going to do before. Whether it's in his fortress or out here, it makes no difference."

"No," Vaelon said quietly. "It does make a difference. If he's found a way to get out, we can't just let ourselves die here, no matter what. We have to find a way to warn the High Elves."

"Oh, I'm afraid it's too late for that," said a chillingly familiar voice.

They all slowly rose, turning toward the voice. Alhalon was standing not ten feet away, smiling an evil smile.

"Baden, my friend, you're very clever indeed!" the old Dark Elf said. "Even more clever than I had thought! In fact—too clever. Now that you know my secret, I'm afraid it's quite impossible for me to let any of you live." Leering down at Reiyalindis, he said, "Not even you, piglet. Now that I'm free, I have no need of you for entertainment. I'll wreak my vengeance on the High Elves to my heart's content." Looking back up at Baden, he said, "It's a pity, really. I almost liked you. Your mind intrigued me."

"Golly," said Baden with heavy sarcasm, "thanks."

Alhalon just smiled. "Would you like to know how I escaped before you die?"

"Sure, why not?" said Ciroy, deliberately acting bored.

"Unlike what your sadly mistaken little guide told you," he said, shooting a poisonous look at Reiyalindis, "my freedom was, in fact, caused by my servant's death. I really can't thank you enough for stealing him from me, by the way."

"How, though?" asked Safaya. "The spirits didn't die, just the body!"

"Ah, but that's all it takes!" said Alhalon with a tight grin. Reiyalindis groaned, dropping her head into her hands. Alhalon's grin widened. "You finally see it, little piglet? Why don't you explain it to your friends? I tire of condescending to speak to them."

Reiyalindis slowly raised her head, looking slightly dazed. "I can't believe I didn't realize it before," she said. "Chrotak's spirits couldn't linger here once they had been in a physical shell—having a body made them subject to the universal laws that govern all life. When Chrotak died, the spirits were taken to the spirit world, as all spirits of living creatures are upon death. They couldn't stay here, and their power dissipated." She looked at Vaelon, Baden, Ciroy, and Safaya, her dark green eyes pleading and full of pain. "I should have realized this . . . I'm sorry, so sorry!"

CORY POULSON

Alhalon laughed. "Regret is for the weak, piglet," he said in his most contemptuous tone. "Oh, and I'm sure you're wondering why I'm still here, eh? Why, if I had been released weeks ago, would I still be hanging around here?" He leaned closer to Reiyalindis, his eyes glinting. "Because I knew you would come here. I knew that you recognized me, and that you would not be able to resist telling your friends, begging them to free you. You are weak."

"For your information," Safaya said angrily, "she didn't tell us. She never would have. The queen told us she had a curse, and we figured the rest out on our own."

Alhalon's smirk just deepened. "Is that right. How very noble of you all to die for one pathetic little wretch. I had hoped to have some enter-tainment from your return, but alas, Baden knew what was going on from the moment he saw me. Too clever, as I said. Pity. Well, my friends, I've enjoyed our conversation, but now it must come to an end, and I bid you all a very permanent farewell. Oh, but first . . ." He looked at Reiyalindis, and with a wave of his hand said, "I've lifted your curse, little worm. Don't say I never did anything nice for you."

✕ ✳ ✕

Reiyalindis felt something profound change in her body, as though a great, heavy weight were suddenly gone. Alhalon's curse, like a terrible dark cloud, faded into nothing. She was free.

But she was also about to die. She dimly saw Alhalon raising his hand toward her, power already blazing around it, and she knew that in the next instant she would feel that power ripping through her, tearing apart flesh and bone. Alhalon had lifted the curse as a last cruel joke before he killed her.

The power did blaze forth from Alhalon's hand, but it didn't hit her. From the side Vaelon leaped between them, and the blazing energy struck him in the chest, throwing him backward into Reiyalindis. "No!" she heard herself scream as they both tumbled to the ground.

Everyone moved at once. Baden lifted his crossbow, aiming the deadly instrument at Alhalon. Ciroy and Safaya split up, running to come at the Dark Elf from different sides. And Vaelon thrust himself back to his feet, his shirt and the skin of his chest smoking and sizzling. "Get out of here, Reiyalindis," he said from between clenched teeth.

Reiyalindis stared at him incredulously. He wasn't dead—but that blast should have blown him apart! It wasn't just Daaku Chikara he was resistant to—it was all magic!

Baden never fired his crossbow; a negligent flick of Alhalon's wrist sent the weapon spinning into the brush, and Baden was lifted from his feet and slammed into a tree. Both Ciroy and Safaya were similarly thrown head-long. "Fools!" roared Alhalon, hammering Vaelon with another powerful spell as the Common Elf charged. Vaelon was picked up and thrown backward in a somersault, dazed and bleeding. "You cannot win! You cannot even fight! You are helpless against me!"

To emphasize his words, he pointed his finger at Vaelon, lifting the warrior into the air and spinning him around several times. "You're strong, Vaelon," he said, "I sensed as much when we met. But you're not strong enough!" He dropped him into a heap on the ground.

Safaya was back on her feet, but Baden was still slumped against the tree, blood trickling from the corner of his mouth, and Ciroy was nowhere to be seen. The Halfbreed woman raised her bow to fire, but Alhalon sensed it, and her bow snapped in half. The arrow, suspended in the air, turned around and shot back straight at Safaya's heart. She managed to dodge a little before it hit, so that the arrow struck her shoulder instead, shattering it and passing completely though.

"No!" Reiyalindis sobbed, watching Safaya fall. "No, Alhalon, please! Please!"

"Please?" he sneered. "Do you think your pathetic tears will sway me? You and your friends are doomed, High Elf brat—as is your entire race!" He looked down at Vaelon, who was struggling back to his feet, and pointed at him again.

Reiyalindis knew that this spell would kill Vaelon. Alhalon was much stronger than anyone he had ever faced, and he was already terribly weak. Anyone else would already be dead. As Alhalon released the spell, Reiyalindis rammed into the injured warrior as hard as she could, knock-ing him clear. The deadly spell struck her instead. She felt her bones snap-ping, blinding pain worse than any fire, and then nothing at all.

✘ ✳ ✘

Vaelon stared at the broken little body in stunned disbelief. Reiyalin-dis had been thrown against a fallen tree, and she lay still beside it, her big green eyes staring vacantly up at the sky. Her dress was covered with blood, and more blood was running freely from her mouth and nose. "Reiyalindis!" he cried, crawling weakly toward her. "No, Reiyalindis, no!" Behind him, Alhalon laughed, aiming another spell at the struggling warrior.

At that moment, however, Alhalon reeled backward as a fiery bolt of flame struck him, and from another direction an icy blast also streaked toward him, barely missing. Three Dark Elven sorcerers appeared, hammering at Alhalon. With a roar of rage, he began striking back at them.

Before Vaelon could reach Reiyalindis, someone else appeared, jumping over the fallen tree and coming to her knees next to the little girl. Vaelon stared at her in shock—it was Eiyara!

The High Elven woman was trying to heal Reiyalindis, and as Vaelon dragged himself closer he saw that the little girl was not dead, as he had feared—she still clung to some tiny spark of life, a spark that Eiyara was trying desperately to keep from going out. Vaelon laid his hand over Eiyara's. "Please," he whispered, even as the battle between Alhalon and the other sorcerers raged behind him. "Please, Eiyara. Don't let her die."

Eiyara looked at him, her deep, beautiful blue eyes frightened but determined. "I won't, Vaelon," she promised. "I won't."

Alhalon was throwing flame and lightning and worse all around him, beating back the Dark Elven sorcerers, who, though powerful, were no match for their opponent. "Idiots!" Alhalon was shouting. "Why are you defending these pathetic fools? I have no quarrel with you!"

The sorcerers' replies were three balls of fiery energy. Alhalon swept them aside and blasted the sorcerers to the ground, cursing and ranting. "Die, then!" he roared. "As will all who oppose me!"

Vaelon looked up as Alhalon prepared to strike again. But just then Ciroy stepped from behind a tree not five feet behind the enraged sorcerer. One of his arms was dangling uselessly, but the other was holding Baden's crossbow. Ciroy raised it at arm's length, the armor-piercing bolt aimed at Alhalon's head, and pulled the trigger.

Alhalon was so engrossed in his battle against the three Dark Elves that he did not sense Ciroy behind him. The bolt struck him squarely in the back of the head and emerged again from his forehead, continuing on to sink past its feathers in a nearby aspen tree.

Alhalon Cui Kahathilor stood still for a moment and then crumpled to the ground.

For a long moment Ciroy, Vaelon, and the three sorcerers stared at the body, as if half expecting the old man to leap back to his feet and renew his attacks. But he didn't. He was really dead.

Ciroy dropped the crossbow and ran to Safaya, who was limping toward him, supported by General Kamas. With a quiet cry of relief, Safaya kissed him and pressed her cheek against his. Both of them had a useless arm, but they held each other tightly for a moment anyway.

"General Kamas?" Ciroy asked. "What are you doing here?"

"I'll explain later," said the Dark Elf. "I'd like to see how the child is doing."

They all came over to where Vaelon and Eiyara were kneeling next to Reiyalindis. She was still in grave danger, but Eiyara was doing the best she could, concentrating with all her might. It was a terrible injury; the little girl had been within seconds of death when Eiyara had arrived. Safaya sat beside her, tears in her eyes as she gently stroked Reiyalindis's hair.

A few yards away, two of the Dark Elven sorcerers revived Baden, who had been knocked unconscious but was not seriously injured. The third crouched beside Vaelon. "How badly are you hurt?" he asked.

Vaelon shook his head. "I'm fine. I'm fine."

"Fine? If you haven't noticed, most of the skin on your chest has been burned away."

Vaelon blinked and then looked down at himself, as if suddenly realizing that he was hurt. When he saw the blackened ruins of his chest, the pain hit him all at once. "Ugly," he muttered faintly.

"I'm afraid we can't help you," said the sorcerer. "We're not healers. I can put you to sleep to help the pain until Eiyara can see to you, though."

"No!" he said. "No, I need to see if Reiyalindis is all right."

"As you wish."

There was little more talk as Eiyara worked. It took a long time, but she was able to save Reiyalindis's life, repairing the terrible damage until the little girl was as good as new. "There," she said at last. "She'll need to sleep for a while, but she's all right."

Safaya sighed in relief. "Thank you, Eiyara. Thank you so much."

"Of course." She turned to Vaelon. "Now for you."

"No," said Vaelon. "See to the others first. Please."

"Hold still, Vaelon," she said firmly, gently touching his face.

The pain was gone almost immediately, and Vaelon was sure he had never felt better in his life. Eiyara's warm, gentle power filled him, and try as he might, he could not look away from her deep blue eyes, which gazed steadily back into his. The wounds Alhalon had inflicted were soon gone.

Again getting that shy blush in her cheeks, Eiyara reluctantly pulled away. "All right, now for you," she said, turning toward Safaya. Her gaze lingered for another brief moment on Vaelon, though, and a smile came to her lips as she finally looked away.

After healing Safaya, Ciroy, Baden, and the various injuries of the three sorcerers, Eiyara sat beside Vaelon, clearly very tired. "I suppose you're wondering why I'm here."

"A little," Vaelon said.

"It was Zeruin," she explained. "Not many days after you left, he burst into the throne room right in the middle of a meeting between General Kamas and the queen. He said he'd just had a strong impression that I was to follow you—he said it was one of the clearest visions he had ever experienced. The general offered to escort me, and he also took these three sorcerers who were with him at the time.

"Zeruin's instructions were strange, but clear: we were to follow you, but under no account were we to let you know we were there until we heard the sounds of battle. Now I understand why—if Alhalon had known of our presence, he would have been more prepared for us. I'm only grateful we were able to help."

"Strange doings," said Kamas. "I would never have imagined I'd be a witness to the death of Alhalon the Black—at the hands of a human, no less."

Ciroy shrugged. "That's what he gets for not paying attention."

Safaya, who was holding Reiyalindis in her lap, was rocking back and forth with her tears running into the little girl's hair. "It's over," she murmured. "I can't believe it's finally over."

"I suppose we ought to recover Alhalon's heart," said one of the Dark Elven sorcerers. "The queen will need it to break the curse."

"That won't be necessary," said Baden. "Alhalon was kind enough to lift the curse before he tried to kill us all. I'm sure he thought it was very funny."

✗ ✳ ✗

When Reiyalindis awoke in the early hours of the morning, she could feel Safaya's arms wrapped around her. Reiyalindis blinked in confusion. She had honestly never expected to wake up again.

She looked around, feeling a wild hope spring into her heart. Ciroy was stirring the ashes of the night's fire nearby, preparing to build it up again. Baden was also nearby, cleaning his crossbow. Vaelon, still asleep, was on his back a few yards away. To her surprise she also saw a few other people—General Kamas was talking in low tones to three other Dark Elves, and Eiyara was brushing her long blonde hair as she sat near Vaelon.

Unable to believe what she was seeing, she slowly sat up. The action woke Safaya, and she also rose, putting her hand on Reiyalindis's shoulder. "Good morning, sweetie," she said softly. "How do you feel?"

Reiyalindis stared at her blankly. "What . . . what happened?" she asked. "I thought I was dead."

Safaya smiled, affectionately cupping the girl's face with her hand. "Not dead, dear," she said, "but you came close."

"But . . . Alhalon?"

"He's gone. Eiyara showed up with some Dark Elven sorcerers, and they distracted him long enough for Ciroy to kill him. He's gone—you're free."

Ciroy noticed them talking and came over to sit next to Safaya. "Hey, kid," he said with a broad grin. "About time you woke up."

Reiyalindis was trembling, not daring to believe what she was hearing. Was it really possible?

"Don't worry," Ciroy reassured her, "you're not dead, and you're not insane. We did it, Reiyalindis. The curse is gone and so is Alhalon. You never have to be alone again."

"You can stay with us," said Safaya. "We three can be a family—if you want, of course."

Reiyalindis was beginning to overcome her shock, but she still wasn't sure what to do with herself. "If I want?" she whispered. "If I want? Oh, Safaya, Ciroy, you know I want that, more than anything—if you'll have me."

"You have no idea how much we'd like that," said Ciroy.

Staring at him, Reiyalindis said, "Can . . . can I call you . . . Daddy?"

"Hon, you can call me anything you want," he replied. "But Daddy sounds real nice, don't you think? C'mere." He held his arms out to her.

So overcome with emotion that she could barely think, Reiyalindis flew into his arms, sobbing uncontrollably and squeezing him as tightly as she could.

EPILOGUE

"Reiyalindis, can I ask you something?" said Vaelon. They were all on their way back to the Ruling City, and were just stopping for the night.

"Of course, my brave Paladin," she replied, unable to resist teasing him a bit as she allowed him to lead her a little away from the others.

"Stop calling me that," he said in a pained voice.

"But you are brave, Vaelon. You're one of the bravest men I've ever known."

"You don't have to rub it in. Look, I need to talk to you."

"All right," she said. "What is it?"

Vaelon cleared his throat. "Well . . . it's about . . . um . . . Eiyara."

"Oh?" She smiled.

"I, uh . . . well . . . I love her."

"I know. She loves you too."

"Well, yeah—I hope so, anyway."

"Of course she does."

"Yeah. But anyway, I . . . well, I've got sort of a problem."

"What's the problem? She loves you, and you love her, so go ask her to marry you. You already know she's going to. Then you can give me lots of nieces and nephews to spoil."

His cheeks turned bright red. "Well . . . yeah, but it's kind of strange, you know? The queen chose her to take her place after she's gone."

"I know," she said simply. "So?"

"Well, I don't want her to think I'm just an opportunist with my eye on the throne, you know."

"Oh, Vaelon!" she said, rolling her eyes. "She knows you better than that."

"Well, there's more than that too. I'm not cut out to be a king, Reiyalindis!"

"Don't worry, Vaelon. I'm sure the queen will live for a good many years yet. You'll have plenty of time to get used to the idea."

He took a deep breath and then exhaled explosively. "All right," he said. "All right."

Excited now, Reiyalindis said, "Can I watch you propose to her?"

"Um . . . I'd rather you didn't."

"Oh, Vaelon, please?"

"No."

"Pretty please?" she begged, clasping her hands together and giving him her cutest look.

"No," he repeated firmly.

Pouting a little, she said, "Oh, all right. I'll just have to make her tell me all about it afterward."

With a sigh he said, "I'm sure you won't have to make her. Women usually trumpet that kind of thing to anyone who'll listen."

"I know," she said with a giggle. "Isn't it fun? Now get going!"

He stared down at her. "What, now?"

"Of course now! Look at her, Vaelon, sitting there all gorgeous just waiting for you to ask her to marry you!"

"I'm sure that's not what she's thinking about."

She gave him a pointed stare. "Care to place a bet on that?"

Vaelon swallowed hard. "Ah . . . no. Not really. All right, I'm going."

"Good."

Reiyalindis watched as Vaelon nervously approached Eiyara, who was looking up at him with thinly veiled anticipation. Clearing his throat again, Vaelon said, "Eiyara?"

"Yes, Vaelon?"

"Um . . . I was wondering if you'd mind taking a walk with me for a few minutes."

"Why, of course I don't mind, Vaelon," she said, rising. "I'd love to." As she took his arm and started walking away, Eiyara looked back at Reiyalindis and gave her a wink.

Baden came up beside Reiyalindis and murmured, "You told her, didn't you?"

"Told her what?" she asked innocently.

"About the vision you had that they'd get married."

"Oh . . . maybe." She grinned at him.

Vaelon and Eiyara were back about fifteen minutes later. Vaelon looked a little dazed, but he was smiling anyway, and Eiyara's smile was radiant. "Um . . . everyone?" Vaelon said. "Uh . . . we . . . uh . . . kind of have an announcement to make."

"Well, go on!" Safaya said eagerly, her fox ears perking up.

"We've . . . uh . . . well . . ." He paused, blushing, and Eiyara nudged him. "We've decided to get married," he said quickly. "At least I think we have. I still can't entirely believe she said 'yes,' to be honest."

"Of course I said yes!" Eiyara cried.

"Congratulations!" Safaya said, clapping her hands together delightedly.

"Who'd'a thunk it," Ciroy murmured. "Well, Vaelon, go on, kiss her!"

As Vaelon self-consciously complied, Reiyalindis tugged on Baden's sleeve. He looked down at her, and she whispered, "Can you keep a secret?"

"Sure," he whispered back with a wink.

She was having trouble suppressing giggles. "I didn't really foresee they'd get married," she said.

Baden stared at her, shocked.

She put on an expression of wide-eyed innocence. "But they go so well together, don't you think?"

For a moment Baden simply continued to stare, and then he rocked backward, roaring with laugher.

THE END

DISCUSSION QUESTIONS
✳ ✗ ✳ ✗ ✳ ✗ ✳ ✗ ✳

1. Why do you think Ciroy and Safaya love each other so much despite the distrust between their peoples?
2. Most Common and High Elves don't trust Halfbreeds because of how they were created. Why do some people in the real world hate or distrust other people who are different? And why do some people, like Gumber, the innkeeper, not have those biases?
3. If you could meet General Kamas, do you think you would be comfortable with him being able to read your thoughts?
4. Why didn't Vaelon want everyone to know about the heroic things he did? If you did something great, would you want everyone to know? If you knew no one would ever find out about it, would you still do it?
5. The Tan-Sho-Ko were once the most powerful people in the world, but they let their differences and pride destroy almost their entire race. Could that happen in the real world, too?
6. Baden knew all along that Koän was a Sanretsu. Why do you think he never said anything?
7. Reiyalindis could have blamed Vaelon for Koän's death. Why do you think she didn't?
8. Even though Koän saw the same things as the other warlocks, why do you think he did the right thing when none of the others did? How could the warlocks accept such a terrible practice?
9. Many of the Sanretsu were good people. What made them go along with what Daaku Shukun and the warlocks told them?
10. Alhalon hated High Elves because they tried to kill him. Does this justify what he did to Reiyalindis? Why do people sometimes take out their anger on those who never did anything to hurt them?
11. Reiyalindis knew all along that her curse could kill her friends. Why do you think she stayed with them? What would have happened if she'd let her fear keep her from doing what she knew she had to?
12. If you could pick one character in the book to be your friend, who would it be? Why?

ABOUT THE AUTHOR

$*$ x $*$ x $*$ x $*$ x $*$

Cory Poulson was born in Ephraim, Utah, where he also attended Snow College. He has worked as a newspaper office assistant, life insurance salesman, loan collector, heavy machinery operator, warehouse manager, and bank teller. He has been a writer since elementary school, and it remains his favorite line of work. He now lives in Wyoming with his wife and five children.